A DRUMMING

Sachim stood with the one man who would listen to her, the one man who equalled her in passion and purpose. She stood with Black Hawk, whose fame as a warrior was matched by his fierce pride as a Sauk.

Together they watched the Sauk council depart from the white military encampment with their wagon piled high with goods the invaders had bribed them with.

"It is over," Black Hawk said, his hands clenched.

"Wait and talk to them," Sachim advised, the wind shifting her long hair, drifting across her face. "Perhaps it is not as you think."

Eyes at once forlorn and savage turned toward Sachim. "No? Have you not dreamed of this, spirit woman? Have you not seen the whites as numerous as ears of summer corn upon our land?"

"Then what . . ." Sachim's voice was little more than a whisper. "What will you do?"

"Talk," Black Hawk replied. "Talk to the council. And then—I shall make my war."

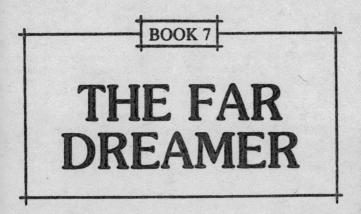

BOOK 7

THE FAR DREAMER

THE INDIAN HERITAGE SERIES

by

Paul Joseph Lederer

A SIGNET BOOK

NEW AMERICAN LIBRARY

NAL BOOKS ARE AVAILABLE AT QUANTITY DISCOUNTS
WHEN USED TO PROMOTE PRODUCTS OR SERVICES.
FOR INFORMATION PLEASE WRITE TO PREMIUM MARKETING DIVISION.
NEW AMERICAN LIBRARY. 1633 BROADWAY.
NEW YORK. NEW YORK 10019.

ACKNOWLEDGMENTS

Permission has been granted to reprint "Quen Nemia" from Frank
M. Chapman, *The Spell of the Hungry Wolf*, published by Sunstone
Press.

SIGNET TRADEMARK REG. U.S. PAT. OFF. AND FOREIGN COUNTRIES
REGISTERED TRADEMARK—MARCA REGISTRADA
HECHO EN DRESDEN. TN. USA

SIGNET, SIGNET CLASSIC, MENTOR, ONYX, PLUME, MERIDIAN
and NAL BOOKS are published by NAL PENGUIN INC.,
1633 Broadway, New York, New York 10019

First Printing, November, 1987

3   4   5   6   7   8   9   10   11

PRINTED IN THE UNITED STATES OF AMERICA

QUEN NEMIA (*Aztec*)

First I will go
But I will leave my name.
Then my name will go.
Nothing of me will remain
On this earth.
All the things that live
On this earth:
Nothing of me will be
Part of them.
At least let there be
These flowers, this song
For a time.
Then I will go.

NEZAHUALCOYOTL

You raise a song
Too huge for the sky.

*My heart has grown heavy with the loss of time
and there is no place for me upon this earth . . .*

1

WHEN she dreamed, she dreamed of the river. It was a magical thing, a life-giver, broad and gleaming in the calm of summer or murky and raging after a winter rain. It gave life to the trees, flowing past the silver birch and hickory which crowded the banks of the river and stood in a dense tangle on the midstream islands. Then with some flood-tide anger it would froth and surge destructively, tearing the earth from the mooring roots, toppling the trees it had nourished, bringing death where it once had given life. Life is magic; death is magic. The river was beyond either.

Sachim knew all of the river's names: Healer, Destroyer, Provider, Common Bond, Father, Mississippi. Sachim knew the river in its intimate forms. Sachim, the spirit woman, the agile dancer and far dreamer.

She saw the Sioux across the river and turned away.

They had camped there for the summer months, coming to the cool banks of the river, their chanting and drumming filling the summer nights like the hum of deep-throated insects. Sachim was Sauk and so she turned away.

The Sioux were a far-roaming people, but their true home was on the yellow grass plains, the flat and featureless prairie, and in the far Black Hills. The river could never be theirs as it was Sachim's, as it was the Sauk's.

Sachim moved softly through the woods. Maple leaves swirled around her leggings in a tumble of red and gold fire. Bluebirds darted among the elm and birch. Partridge flared skyward at her approach.

Beyond the trees lay the Sauk village, its bark covered,

9

sapling-poled lodges standing among the tilled fields where the Sauk grew their corn. The corn was tall now, ripening, its scent flooding the air.

The women were busy with their work, chatting together or singing as they wove mats with rushes taken from the river or scraped new hides. Often Sachim joined them although she was not required to. She was different, this Sauk woman. She had the gift of dreams.

On this, her fifteenth summer, Sachim could not recall her first dream, but she had been told it had happened when she was two years old.

"Top" was what she had called her warrior father, To-ha-hop. At a time when she, her mother and grandmother sat waiting for To-ha-hop to return from a battle with the Miami Indians, young Sachim had suddenly shrieked out, "Top is stuck with an arrow. Right here, above the belly hole."

That night To-ha-hop had been returned to the village and carried to his lodge by his brother warriors. He had died before dawn, a Miami arrow still protruding from his abdomen.

Now To-ha-hop was gone, as was Sachim's mother, who had died of the white cholera. Grandmother, who was also named Sachim, lived on. Grandmother, who also had the gift of dreams, was a small and ancient and smiling woman. Grandmother had come from the east. An Oneida Indian, she had married Sun Wolf, a far-roving Sauk, and returned to the river with her husband.

The hunters rode past Sachim as she walked through the village. White Bear pretended not to glance at Sachim, but the huge young Sauk didn't fool her. Four years older than Sachim, the gentle giant wanted to take a wife to his lodge and it was Sachim he desired.

With the warriors were two of the council chiefs, Ta-ma-kia and Keokuk, and Ma-ka-tai-me-she-kia-kiak, or Black Sparrow Hawk. The whites called him Black Hawk and this heavily muscled man with the high forehead, roached scalp lock, and hawk nose was the war leader of the Sauk, a sometimes sullen man with deep emotions and great war skills.

The hunters were gone in a storm of dust and the village was left to the women and the shrieking, scuffling naked children.

The small lodge stood among the maple trees, a dark and secluded house partly hidden by vines. The spirit mask hung above the door. A wisp of smoke rose through the hole in the roof and was lost among the maples.

Sachim stopped, frowning. There were the tracks of a horse in the soft earth before the house. Who would have come here?

Sachim ducked in through the door to the lodge without knocking. All of her remaining family lived within. The old one. Frail and as tiny as a bird, her long white hair past her waist, Grandmother sat inside the lodge on a woven mat, wearing a shapeless, fringeless buckskin dress too large for her narrow body.

Grandmother was silent and Sachim crouched beside the small fire, watching the corn soup and dumplings cook until the old one's silent time was over.

"Sachim." The voice was weak but bright. Grandmother smiled, her eyes lighting her lined face. "It is good to see you."

That was always her greeting whether she had seen Sachim hours earlier or not seen her for months.

"Your soup is very hot," Sachim said, spooning a serving from the birch-bark kettle into a wooden bowl and passing it to the old woman.

"The Sioux are not gone," Grandmother said, taking the bowl. It wasn't a question. The old woman knew without having left her lodge.

"No. But it has been a good summer. Only once did their young warriors come across the river. They took away one of White Bear's horses, but they gave it back when he went to their camp."

Grandmother Sachim chuckled softly. In her imagination she could see stripling Sioux warriors facing the mammoth White Bear, a man with shoulders like oak logs and a constant frown. The giant warrior never smiled unless he smiled at the young Sachim, but his heart was as gentle as that of any man who walked the earth.

"I was dreaming of my sister again," Grandmother said. "Of Crenna and the long-ago times. I think that means I shall soon be with her to walk the sky fields."

"You will live forever, Grandmother, and live in joy."

"No. I have lived in joy. I have lived in sorrow. That is

the magic of the world, to know pain and then to know happiness. But an old woman can endure only so much sorrow, only so much joy. Then the soul is full and it is time to walk the Sky Trail."

"You had a visitor," Sachim said. "I saw a horse's tracks."

"That one. Who was that? I do not know," Grandmother said, growing animated. "He was a white man. He said he knew I spoke their language. I gave him the last of my good cornbread with the berries and butternuts in it. He wanted me to dream. He wanted me to dream a lie."

"To dream a lie?" Sachim repeated, not understanding.

"He thought that I was you, Sachim. Your good mother gave you my name and so he thought I was you. A tall man wearing buckskins. He had a look in his eyes I did not care for." Grandmother placed her bowl aside.

"But why did he want to see me?" Sachim asked.

"Because you sing for Black Hawk. Keokuk told him it was so." The old woman made a sour face when she mentioned Keokuk's name. Keokuk was a man of vigor, but a man of too much ambition, one who had cheated at the moccasin game as a youth and had claimed another man's coup. "The white man wanted to buy our corn land."

Sachim laughed. "How can anyone buy our land? Manitou gave us the land to live upon. So long as we live upon it and cultivate it the soil is ours. Such things cannot be sold. Only things which can be carried away can be sold. Not the long land, not the sky, not the river."

Grandmother nodded, pleased. This was a woman, this Sachim. She would only grow to be more of a woman. So long as she dreamed for the Sauk the council leaders would know the will of the spirit, Manitou.

"The white man said other things. Keokuk told him you were promised to him."

"Promised to him! And who has promised him? Not you, not me," Sachim said angrily.

"He has the thought in his mind," Grandmother said.

"I am promised to no man. I will have no man."

"One day."

"Never!"

"So I thought," Grandmother said. "I was in middle years before I set eyes on a man who could lift my pulse and disturb my dreams. Then Sun Wolf came and there was only joy, a joy to flood my soul. Then one day he was gone—I should have known him sooner."

"I will not marry," Sachim insisted.

"Who knows, who can tell. I thought not too, but I did not know certain things when I was young and lost in my dreaming. When Sun Wolf came he taught me. The world is night and day, fire and water. Winter becomes summer. All of these things are circles, and without the circle life is incomplete.

"There is man, Sachim, and woman. A circle."

Perhaps, thought Sachim. Perhaps Grandmother is right; she usually was, but it was not the summer for thinking of men. Who was there to think about? The strutting Keokuk with his unearned coup feathers in his scalp lock, the hulking White Bear with his great body and child's heart? The too-handsome Tomorrow Runner with his long-lashed eyes and laughing mouth and devil's ways?

"You are sure it was Keokuk who sent him, Grandmother?"

"So the man told me." She shrugged.

"Then the council must speak to Keokuk. I will tell Black Hawk when the hunters return. What can he be thinking of? To send a white here."

"What white would dare approach Black Hawk directly? He has no love for them."

Not much at all. Black Hawk had learned to tolerate some of the Spanish men when they had built their trading posts along the Rock River and later at St. Louis. Though he trusted some whites, he found most of them useless. They traded iron pots and glass beads and steel hatchets, but Black Hawk said they needed none of these things; their fathers had not. The Sauk knew how to make good canoes of birch bark. They knew how to build tight lodges with white oak saplings and basswood strings and cover them with birch bark as their fathers had, as Manitou had instructed them. They knew how to make a bow of osage orange or of the second-year hickory and fashion arrowheads of flint or antler. They knew all they needed to know, possessed all they required. Their corn grew tall, the forests were alive with turkey and deer and moose; the lakes were wealthy with wild rice and sturgeon; the skies were bountiful— endless flocks of pigeons and ducks and geese offered themselves to Sauk hunters. Their bowls were always full; they needed nothing more.

Black Hawk had told Sachim this and she had listened without comment. That night she had dreamed.

There was an old bear in her dream, a river bear, long of claw and long of tooth. It was a prideful bear but a knowing one and it had lived long. No weapon could kill it, not a fine ash bow or a stone club, nor an oak lance. It lived on, a prowling, proud beast. But the strange hunters came and they killed it with steel and with iron and with long guns and Sachim knew that the bear was the Sauk nation.

"Our way," she had told Black Hawk, "is our way. The way of the whites is their own. When we walk through a forest we are among it; when they do so they are passing through it or hunting, seeing little. They have a god, I know, but they must not listen to his songs much. Life is in each moment, not in the faraway time which may lie ahead."

Then Black Hawk, who listened to each word his young singer of songs said, had nodded and gone out to the full council to warn against trading with the white Americans.

Grandmother had finished her meal and now she curled up in the corner, drawing her blanket over her. She was tired often now, and weak. Her soul was growing full. Sachim put the birch-bark kettle aside and left the fire burning so that the old woman would be warm.

Outside, daylight had already begun to fade. The Sioux drummers and pipers had begun again. They sang a song of bravery and of the invincibility of the Sioux nation. Sachim paid them no more mind than she paid to the frogs chorusing in the cattails along the great river, the Life-giver which was bright in the late sunlight.

She leapt a canal the Sauk had made to divert the water from the river to their cornfields, and went on, walking as she often walked—toward something which she could not name, something in the sky or deep forest or in the river itself. She was weary of this camp already and looked forward to the day when the women would begin building their temporary lodges among the vast maple forests where the trees' swelling buds indicated that the time was right for making sugar from their sweet sap.

Distantly Sachim could see women harvesting wild rice from their canoes, plucking the stalks from the murky water

of an oxbow. On the shore, other women beat the rice heads
from the stalks, their brown arms rising and falling in violent
silence. Later the men would take the stored, dried rice and
do their portion of the work. Drums would beat, and the
men, dancing in tubs with a pole or tree to hang on to,
would work the hulls off with their feet. Then each man
would fill a birch-bark basin and toss its contents high,
letting the wind carry away the chaff while the women chat-
ted and laughed or sang along, giving the children maple
candy made by using a duck's bill as a mold.

The painted warrior leapt from behind the fallen log and a
war cry rattled in Sachim's ears as she backed away from
the man with his war ax.

Sachim stood there trembling and the warrior began to
laugh.

"You . . . !" Sachim raised her small clenched fists and
shook them at Tomorrow Runner. The Sauk youth continued to laugh. He was very tall, his muscles sinewy, his face
finely chiseled. He wore his chair in a long roach with a
scalp lock behind. His chest rose and fell convulsively still.
He wiped a tear from his eye with a knuckle and stepped
suddenly to Sachim, his strong arm going around her waist
as he dragged her against him.

"So," Tomorrow Runner said, speaking down at her as
Sachim struggled to get free. "It is a good thing you were
born a woman, little dreamer. What sort of warrior would
you be?"

"What sort are you?" Sachim said, twisting free. "You are
only a boy yourself. What a childish thing to do."

"Maybe after tonight you will not think me such a child,"
Tomorrow Runner said.

"What are you talking about?"

"The Sioux who took White Bear's horse, remember?
Tonight we will take three of their horses. Myself, Antler
Tree, and Ke-ke-tai."

"You will do no such thing; that might mean trouble."

"We will do as we wish, little dreamer. Black Hawk is
gone, Keokuk is gone. Who is there to tell us what we can
do? You? I do not listen to dreams or to dreamers."

"What you are planning is incredibly foolish," Sachim
insisted. "It could even lead to blood."

The young man shrugged. "I am a warrior."

"You are a child."

"Three years older than you, Sachim. And I know a man's ways. Shall I show you?" He stepped toward her, reaching for her dress, and she whirled away, starting angrily back down the trail, her arms folded beneath her breasts. Tomorrow Runner's laughter burned in her ears.

When she looked back Tomorrow Runner had vanished into the forest. She angrily scuffed her feet against the ground as she walked. That boy would make trouble. She glanced toward the river, seeing the red sun slowly falling. There was little time to stop the youthful warriors. What could she do? She could approach one of the council members, but they might pay no attention to her. It was Black Hawk who trusted in her dreams, but few of the others did. This was no dream song anyway, but advice unasked for, interference in the council's affairs.

She hurried on as the sun sank behind the trees and the river lost its reddish flush and turned purple and somber. Fires were being lit in the camp. Smoke rose from every house. The cornfields were deserted but for a solitary hunched woman who worked on with her wooden hoe.

The lodge of Strikes the Enemy was near the river and surrounded by ash trees. Sachim could smell fish chowder cooking inside. She rapped on the wall of the house and heard indistinct muttering and movement; then a voice—Strikes the Enemy's—called, "Enter my lodge in peace."

Sachim ducked inside and let her eyes adjust for a moment. The old council chief sat cross-legged on a blanket, his deep-set eyes watching her. His wife and oldest daughter glanced at Sachim, smiled, and returned to their cooking.

"What brings you to my lodge, far-dreamer?"

"A concern for my people."

"Will you sit and speak of it?" Strikes the Enemy asked.

Sachim sat facing the chief and briefly she told him what she had learned. "If those three young men are foolish enough to raid the Sioux camp, there may be much trouble."

"They are young," the old chief said indulgently. "Let them earn their feathers."

"There may be blood."

"There is always blood. Let them count coup. Where did my first feather come from? It was a Shawnee camp. There were five of us—"

The story threatened to go on for a long while. Rudely Sachim interrupted. "We must try to stop them."

"I do not see why. What makes a warrior? Courage. The young men take a risk. Well, then, where is courage without a risk, far-dreamer? If they play now, one day the skills they learn in their games will protect the tribe. A warrior learns to fight in only one way." The old chief's hand sliced the air emphatically. "By fighting."

"You won't try to stop them?"

"No. My meal is ready, forgive me, far-dreamer. Will you eat with us?"

"No, thank you," Sachim said tightly. The disappointment in her voice was obvious.

"Look, girl," the council chief said, "I know about these things, about young warriors and their desires. I know about the Sioux. I know what a battle is. Content yourself with your dreaming. Drift away on your dream cloud and tell Black Hawk your stories when he returns."

So, that then was that. There was nothing for Sachim to do but say good-bye to Strikes the Enemy and his family and leave them to their meal. Outside, the sun was only a memory, a faint flush of color held by the sky. The first star had appeared and after looking in again on Grandmother, Sachim started toward her own small lodge.

She was troubled and as she tugged off her buckskin dress and fringed moccasins the concerns stayed with her. It was not a good night for dreaming, yet she dreamed.

The river spoke softly and she drifted on it. For a moment the stars glittered overhead and the frogs along the banks of the river grumped and croaked. Silver fish swam beneath her, brushing her naked body with their fins. A white man in buckskins came, wanting to buy the river. He carried pots made of gold and around his neck was a ribbon with many medallions. There was only Sachim to speak, Sachim and the river, and they laughed at him until he went away. But he knew many curses and when he threw his gold into the river it turned to flame and vanished, the smoke obliterating the stars until there was only Sachim and the endless night.

She rose from her dream and went out into the night to stand naked beneath the sky. It was all right—the stars still shone. Smoke rose from the Sauk lodges and the river ran on. Sachim stood there for a long while, watching the trees shift in the wind, seeing the lone hunting owl swoop low over the river.

She waited until she could no longer understand her own dream, until it had faded into the night's forgetfulness, dissipating like the smoke rising from the Sauk lodges in the evening breeze.

Tomorrow Runner lifted his hand and Ke-ke-tai put the birch-bark canoe in to the shore. Antler Tree was the first from the canoe, wading through the waist-high water to the beach which was overgrown with vines and tangled roots. They could see the dull glow of Sioux campfires against the moonless sky.

This was not Tomorrow Runner's first raid, but his first against the Sioux. He had taken a horse and a fine blanket from the Mascouten the summer before and joined in a battle against the Potawatomie, although he had counted no coup, taken no scalps. The two youths with him were younger, egged into the raid by Tomorrow Runner. Neither had entered an enemy camp before.

They moved swiftly and silently through the forest. Their practiced stealth brought them to the edge of the Sioux camp. From their bellies they watched the camp for a long while. There were over a hundred tipis in the camp. The principal chief of the Lakota Sioux was called Far Eagle. His youngest son had been one of the raiders who had taken White Bear's horse.

The dew was already on the grass beneath Tomorrow Runner's belly. The wind off the river was cool. He pointed toward the western end of the camp where the Sioux horses were kept and started that way, his friends on his heels. A Sioux brave appeared from his tipi and the three went to the ground again to wait and watch while the warrior stretched, looked at the sky, and returned to his lodge. Then they went on, approaching the horses cautiously so that the animals wouldn't be startled and whicker.

Tomorrow Hunter had his eye on a Nez Percé horse, a spotted animal captured from a faraway enemy of the Sioux. He eased toward it, congratulating himself on his luck and daring.

"Who are you!" The voice roared out of the night and Tomorrow Runner turned sharply, darting toward the woods. Antler Tree was beside him, panting deeply. The blood buzzed in Tomorrow Runner's ears. Above that sound a more deadly hum sang. The arrow buried its obsidian head in Antler Tree's back close to his spine and the young Sauk yelled out, pitching forward facefirst to sprawl against the earth.

Tomorrow Runner and Ke-ke-tai picked Antler Tree up by the arms and ran on as a second arrow narrowly missed the running Sauk. Then they were into the trees, hearts pounding furiously as they dragged Antler Tree toward the hidden birchbark. The arrow was embedded deeply in the young warrior's back and he groaned in pain as they placed him in the canoe and pushed off from shore, catching the river's current, which propelled them toward the Sauk village on the opposite shore.

Tomorrow Hunter glanced back from time to time but he saw no pursuit, just the dully glowing Sioux campfires. Now what would happen? It would do no good to deny that they had been trying to steal the Lakota's horses. Not with Antler Tree's wound. They paddled on, silently, more quickly, as if by going fast enough they could outrun the trouble that was coming.

When Sachim rose she took a minute to clear her head before dressing. There was something troubling her in a deep recess of her mind. Oh, yes, the dream, the dream of the river.

What was it Manitou was telling her? What was this a warning of? Near the council lodge there was activity. Sachim could see Strikes the Enemy and another of the old chiefs with Wabokieshiek, who was sometimes called the Prophet, although Sachim knew he did not dream, and Napope, a younger man with high rank and the gift of oration. Tope-kia, who knew medicine, was also there.

Sachim started that way, drawn by curiosity. Unless there was trouble of some kind there should be no reason for the council to meet. Not with Black Hawk and Keokuk both absent from the village.

Tope-kia, who was hunched and narrow and wore his hair uncut, gestured to Wabokieshiek, but the Prophet turned his back on the medicine man and entered the council hut where Tope-kia could not follow: for he had never taken a scalp.

"What is it, Tope-kia?"

The old man turned to look at Sachim, his worried expression giving way to a bright, brief smile. "Very much trouble. The Sioux have killed one of our young men."

"Not Tomorrow Runner!"

"No." Tope-kia's eyes narrowed. "But I think he was there. It was Tomi-me-shia's son, Antler Tree. Born the day Tomi-me-shia found the deer in the hickory tree, the deer the flood had put there."

"How was he killed?" Sachim asked, already knowing the answer.

"It is said that they went looking for Sioux horses, for adventure. Only a boyish thing."

"One which could lead to war."

"No. There must not be war over this. Young warriors do these things. But the Sioux will demand reparations. Tomi-me-shia will demand repayment for his son's life. So the council will decide."

"Antler Tree is dead?" she asked.

"I saw him just now. There is a rattle in his throat. I placed mud and jimson and powdered antler on his wound after I cut out the arrow, but it was all too late. One of the soul's tethers was cut. Just here." The medicine man touched his own back. "Next to the spine."

From the riverbank a shout went up and as Sachim turned she saw a youth sprinting toward them, waving his arm in the air.

"Sioux!"

The word struck unreasonable terror in Sachim's heart. She tried to calm herself with logic. After all, the Sauk were many and brave. The Sioux, never friends, were not exactly enemies either. They would not make war over some youthful folly.

Her logic failed to smother the flame of terror. The Sioux were coming and Black Hawk was not here. Nor was Keokuk, who, although he may have been sly and sometimes scheming, was an orator beyond compare and a peacemaker. Nor was White Bear in the camp. The giant had no civil rank, but his massive presence seemed to calm the hearts of his own people, to place caution in the minds of any would-be enemies.

There was another shout from the river and then an almost unearthly silence. During that time no human voice could be heard, nor the scraping of tools, nor the songs of the cardinals and finches, nor the hoarse calling of the crows. There was only the wind in the trees and the constant murmuring of the great river.

And then the Sioux appeared.

Sachim had seen most of them before, on the day the Sioux arrived and took up their summer camp, when the Sauk and the men from across the river had met and exchanged gifts and smoked their pipes. But now they appeared different, gaunt and stern, war bonnets trailing down their backs, beaded buckskin shirts, and fringed trousers. Far Eagle carried no buffalo pipe now. When three of his young braves had taken White Bear's horse, the Sauk had demanded an apology. The Sioux had been formal and distant, not liking to yield to any tribe's demands. A proud race, they saw themselves as the greatest warriors, the most powerful of adversaries, the strongest of allies.

They would demand an apology of their own, and perhaps more.

They brushed past Sachim, their faces set, their eyes hard. There was nothing she could do there and so she started to turn and walk away. As she did, the tall young Sioux emerged from the trees. Tall and wide at the shoulders, he wore a new elkskin shirt with much beadwork. He couldn't have been much past twenty yet he wore the bonnet of an honored warrior. His gait was a long glide, reflecting self-assurance. His nose was nearly straight, flanked by liquid, mocking eyes, and when those eyes met Sachim's she had to look away.

She stood watching until the Sioux warriors had been greeted by the council members and led inside the hut.

"Tope-kia?" She took the medicine man by the arm. He glanced at her curiously. "Who was that? The young man?"

"That one?" Tope-kia's mouth drew down. "Thunder Horse. He is Far Eagle's oldest son, an arrogant young man. Why do you ask, Sachim?"

"I thought I had seen him before." She shrugged.

"Perhaps. He rode the black horse in the race we had last year. The one Ke-ke-tai won."

"That must be it," Sachim said.

But it wasn't from the race that she knew the young warrior. She had seen him before, many times. In her dreams.

He had risen from the river naked and come to her, and always she was frightened, always she ran away, somehow making her way across the river. She had never known his name, never even known he was Sioux, but she knew his face, his stride, his eyes, in the depths of her heart.

Black Hawk frowned. He could see that something was going on in the ramshackle town of St. Louis but couldn't decide what. Flatboats tied to moorings on the river were being unloaded while along the muddy streets other whites carried goods from the stores. The house of the Spanish father, Charles Dehault Delassus, was also being emptied. What was happening? A fever or war? Why would the Spanish governor of Upper Louisiana leave if he was not being forced out?

"I don't like this," Black Hawk said.

White Bear shook his massive head. "We have to go and see what is happening. We have always been treated well here. When has Delassus not given us many presents?"

Keokuk appeared bitterly suspicious. "It is the plague. Another white plague."

"I have never seen the whites run from the plague. I have seen them burn their villages and their clothing, but never run," White Bear answered.

"Soldiers."

It was Ke-teo-mai who lifted a pointing finger. The warrior was right. There were soldiers in blue uniforms on the street, and they were not Spanish soldiers, nor were they British.

"Americans," Ke-teo-mai said. Black Hawk nodded in agreement. He had seen uniforms such as these before, far to the north, far to the east, but what were they doing here?

"What do they want? There is no battle. We saw no battle sign, heard no guns, smelled no smoke."

"We shall see," Black Hawk decided. "We have no quarrel with any of these people. No one is at war with the Sauk nation. We will go down in peace and ask."

The Sauk rode from the trees and crossed the neglected Spanish fields to the town of St. Louis. The armed, fierce-looking warriors with their roached hair and high-stepping horses drew glances from the harried-looking local citizens, and suspicious stares from the white soldiers in their faded uniforms and muddy boots.

Black Hawk paid no attention to the soldiers. He had seen
more war than any of them ever would. His father had been
war leader of the Sauk when the English fought the French
for Quebec, fought so well and for so long that the Sauk
became known as the "British Band." The English had lost,
however; and the Sauk were pushed westward and to the
south. With the Mascouten, Black Hawk had made war
against the Osage and won, once leading seven warriors
against a force of one hundred Osage. He had fought the
Cherokee and defeated them. During that war, Black Hawk's
father had died and Black Hawk had fallen heir to the war
leader's medicine bag.

Black Hawk had blackened his face in the Sauk style of
mourning and lived alone in the wilderness for five full
years, fasting and praying, living on nuts and berries and
water alone, disdaining meat and the company of his own
people. When he had returned he found the Osage again
ready to make war, and again Black Hawk had led his
people to victory. When the Chippewa had dared to raid the
Sauk camps the following year, Black Hawk defeated them
and their allies, the Kaskaskia.

He feared no army and no warrior. He was Black Hawk.

The Spanish governor's house was very busy with people
bustling in and out, carrying trunks, leading horses. Black
Hawk and his party rode past the house and into the scattered elms beyond. It wouldn't do to see Delassus as they
were, after a long ride. First they changed into their clean
buckskins and painted their faces. Black Hawk took his
ceremonial hatchet-head pipe from his parfleche and from
his war sack a bag of kinnikinnick, mixed tobacco and birch
bark. Then, after White Bear had knotted an otter tail into
Black Hawk's scalp lock, the Sauk went afoot toward the
house, Black Hawk, arms folded across his chest, pipe in
hand, leading the way.

"What do you want?" a blue-uniformed soldier called out.
He stepped onto the stairs leading into the big house, holding his musket across his chest diagonally.

"We have come to see Delassus," Black Hawk responded.

"He's busy."

The soldier's voice was firm, but Black Hawk saw his eyes
move as he met the Sauk chief's gaze. Black Hawk saw the
fear there and he nodded. "He is our friend. Tell him Black
Hawk and Keokuk are here."

The soldier looked toward the house, hesitated, and then turned, walking up the steps and into the house. The Sauk could hear pieces of a conversation in English and then the voice of Delassus.

"Yes, they are my friends. Let me at least say good-bye to them."

The soldier reappeared, inclined his head, and stepped back as Black Hawk led the way into the warm interior of the big white house. Everything had changed. The tapestries were gone, the carpets were rolled up, the ornate cedar chest had been carried away.

Delassus too had changed. The Spaniard wore a blue-gray suit and ruffled shirt. He had no wig over his iron-gray hair. His eyes appeared bleak, his narrow lips were compressed.

"Black Hawk, old friend. Keokuk." He shook hands with both men. "And White Bear—can you have grown larger!"

"We have brought no presents," Black Hawk told the Spanish governor. "This is a hunting trip and nothing else, but we did not wish the chance to see you again to go by."

"And it is the last chance, it seems," the Spaniard said.

"What is this?" Black Hawk asked. "What is happening here, Charles Delassus?"

"Come into my library and I'll tell you," the governor said. They walked across the walnut floor of the big house, passing still more movers with trunks and crates, rolled carpets and furniture.

Black Hawk had been in the library many times before, but it was totally changed. The books had been removed from the shelves and the portrait of the King of Spain which had always fascinated Black Hawk was gone. Only Delassus' walnut desk remained, and seated behind it was a man in an American officer's uniform. A smallish man with chestnut hair, he had the look of a warrior. His eyes met Black Hawk's and held his gaze until Black Hawk looked to Delassus for enlightenment.

"I have no gifts, Black Hawk," the governor said, looking around the empty room, "and very little else."

"You will smoke with us, Charles Delassus?"

"Yes." A small smile brightened the Spaniard's face briefly. "Of course. One last time."

They stood together and smoked Black Hawk's pipe, passing it from hand to hand. The unsmiling American officer watched without speaking.

"You are going away," Black Hawk said at last.

"Yes." Delassus shrugged.

"Why?" Keokuk demanded.

"The great fathers have made an agreement," Delassus said.

"What do you mean? When you came you said that the Spanish father would always hold this land and that we would always be friends," Black Hawk reminded Delassus.

"All of this has happened far away," the Spaniard said. "No one asked for my blessing, Black Hawk. No one asked for my advice. You see, I am only a minor chief, you understand? This is what has happened: Spain has grown weak, unfortunately, and a Frenchman named Napoleon has made a treaty with our king. This treaty banishes the Spanish from the Mississippi lands and gives St. Louis to the French."

"Where are the French then?" Keokuk asked, laughing. "Why do you submit to this? I see no Frenchmen."

"The man behind the desk is an American, Captain Amos Stoddard," Delassus explained patiently. "He has been chosen to accept the territory of Louisiana for France. This will be done tomorrow . . . and on the next day he will accept the territory from France on behalf of the Great Father of the Americans who has purchased this land from the French."

"There is great upheaval in Europe," Stoddard said, finally speaking as he saw the Sauk's confusion. "A man named Napoleon has come to power in France. He is too strong for the Spaniards and has demanded concessions. The Louisiana Territory is one of these. Our President, Mr. Jefferson, has offered to buy Louisiana from Napoleon, and Napoleon, wanting more money to make more war, has sold Louisiana." Stoddard, fingers steepled, remained behind the desk, half-smiling at the Indians. "Do you understand all of that?"

"No," Black Hawk answered coldly. "I do not understand. Who has sold this land? The French. Whose land is it? The Sauk's. Now I ask you, American warrior, how can these men in Europe sell land which is not theirs?"

Stoddard, returning to diplomacy, answered, "It will make little difference in your lives, Black Hawk. The American government has no intention at all in interfering with your culture, with the ownership of your fields, or of your hunting lands. Jefferson has only done this to protect America from European armies on this continent."

"The British are still here."

"Yes," Stoddard agreed. "They haven't learned their lesson yet. I have fought against the British. One day they may have to be taught again that the continent belongs to America."

"And the Sauk."

"Well, of course! That goes without saying. You have been a friend of the British, Black Hawk, and a friend of Spain. One day you will know us better and be a great friend of the United States as well."

"Yes," Black Hawk said quietly. "Let us hope it is so." He paused a moment. "A man came to our village," he said, "a white man in buckskins. You can tell me what he wanted."

"Perkins? He only wanted to talk, Black Hawk."

"Who is Perkins?"

"Bartholomew Perkins, an army guide."

"I know him," White Bear said in the Sauk tongue, "a trader."

Stoddard looked puzzled. "I'm sure he comported himself well. Perkins is a good man."

"What did he want?" Black Hawk persisted. "Whom did he wish to talk to? No one among the council saw him. He went to the old woman's lodge, the spirit dreamer, Sachim."

"Did he?" Stoddard looked surprised, but his eyes were not surprised. "I have no idea what Perkins wanted then," the American said with a fluttering gesture of his hand.

But he knew. Black Hawk could see into his eyes. He was lying, and he could guess what this Perkins had wanted at the Sauk village.

Stoddard said, "This change in administrators of the Louisiana Territory must seem puzzling, but I assure you that the United States wishes to be on good terms with you and your people."

"I hope that this is so," Black Hawk answered. But he had no confidence in this new governor. Already the man had told a lie. He had brought no gifts, no medals, nor had he bothered to send someone to the Sauk village to explain things. He had sent Perkins instead.

The Sauk changed into their traveling clothes again among

the elms. Black Hawk was deep in thought. Keokuk, untying his weasel fur from his scalp lock, asked, "What difference does any of this make to us, Black Hawk? A new white father. What is that to us?"

"I don't know," the Sauk war leader answered. "I only know it worries my heart. There is something about this I do not care for."

"We will come, we will trade with our furs, we will go away as always," Keokuk said with a dismissive shrug.

"Yes. As always," Black Hawk said, looking at the narrow, hawk-faced council chief. But if Keokuk thought nothing of it all, still Black Hawk was concerned. There was nothing his mind could grasp, but he sensed something. It was like seeing a wisp of distant smoke or feeling the earth begin to tremble before the buffalo ran.

He would ask the young Sachim. He would ask her if she had dreamed of this. She would know if anyone would.

As soon as they returned from their hunt Black Hawk would ask the girl. For now he swung up onto his gray pony's back, glanced once more at the governor's mansion, and then turned his horse's head away, riding through the elms and away from the riddle.

It was decided.

The council had met with the Sioux and decided. The Sauk would give twenty horses to the Sioux and they would surrender Tomorrow Runner and Ke-ke-tai to be punished.

"This cannot be done!" Sachim said. She looked around anxiously at the stony-faced Sauk watching the two young men being led away. "What have they done? No more than the Sioux boys did. Did we ask them for reparations when they took White Bear's horse? Speak up! Tomi-me-shia! Wolf!"

"The council has decided," Tope-kia, the medicine man said, touching her shoulder.

"The council is frightened. Frightened of the Sioux! If Black Hawk were here this would not be allowed."

"But he is not here," the small medicine man said, spreading his narrow arms.

Sachim wasn't ready to relent. "Napope! How can you allow this?"

The civil chief turned his head slowly. He was wrapped in

his striped Winnebago blanket. "It was decided," the chief said slowly. "Now go away, girl-child. It is over."

Napope turned his back and slowly walked away. Sachim glared at his bulky figure for a long moment and then tried to plead with Wabokieshiek and then with Strikes the Enemy. Neither paid any attention to her pleas.

"You would not stop this," Sachim said in frustration to Strikes the Enemy. "When I came to you, you would do nothing to prevent it. Now you will do nothing to stop the Sioux from taking the boys."

"They did what they wanted, these boys," Strikes the Enemy said somberly. "Now they must pay for what they did. They made their boys' war and failed at it. I am sorry that the tribe must lose horses, however."

Tomorrow Runner was being led to the Sioux party now. His youthful high spirits of the day before had faded. His face was a mask, hardly recognizable. Ke-ke-tai's mother wailed as he too was brought forward and turned over to Far Eagle and his people.

Sachim could only stand rigid, head thrust forward, hands clenched in anger at the Sioux, at the council, at the foolish Sauk boys.

The youths were led away to the Sioux canoes. The last Sioux to leave was Thunder Horse. The young warrior turned, looked directly into Sachim's eyes, and lifted one shoulder almost imperceptibly. Sachim saw it but made no response. It wasn't important one way or the other what the Sioux communicated with that small gesture. It might have been an apology, but an apology was going to do the Sauk boys no good.

They would be beaten by Sioux women. Humiliated in a gauntlet. Jeered and mocked and then sent home. Would they be the same young men after that?

And the Sauk dignity was going to be lessened by all of this. The Sioux had extracted too much from the council. Strikes the Enemy and Napope had done everything to pacify the Sioux, even to turning over the sons of their brothers.

Sachim watched until the party had vanished into the trees, until she could see no more, until she was alone in the council-lodge clearing. Then she turned and slowly walked away, angry, disappointed, worried.

Sachim walked toward her lodge. It was time to fast, time to dream deeply, to ask what her dream of the river meant. Would there be war with the Sioux? She walked, head down, through the fallen leaves beneath the maples, seeming to see nothing. But she knew *he* was there.

In the woods, the Prophet watched her. Wabokieshiek always watched her, ever since he had learned that like her grandmother, Sachim dreamed.

He was a big man, over six feet tall, with brooding, deep-set eyes and a constant frown. Half Winnebago, half Sauk, he wore a mustache as long and black as any dark white man's and claimed that Manitou had told him to wear it as a mark of rank. That was a lie. The Prophet did not dream and Sachim knew it.

He was a clever man and by watching nature and people closely he was able to predict many things. He had the ear of the council; Keokuk was his champion, but then Keokuk wished for power and thought that an ally like the Prophet would be useful.

Yet Black Hawk did not listen to the Prophet. It was to the young, slender, large-eyed girl dreamer that he listened, and so the Prophet had learned to hate Sachim.

First Sachim looked in on her grandmother to satisfy herself that the old woman was eating, that she had fuel for her fire and a clean blanket.

Grandmother seemed to be sleeping, but her eyes opened and the twinkle came into them, the warm smile lighting her dark, seamed face.

"You are a good granddaughter, Sachim. Look, you see to my fire. You bring me food."

"You fed me when I was a baby."

Sachim hunched over the small fire, feeding it twigs. The day was not cool, but Grandmother's blood had slowed with age and she needed more heat.

"I dream no more, Sachim," Grandmother said.

"I don't understand." Sachim, puzzled, looked at the old woman.

"I do not dream. Only of the Hanging Road, only of my sister and of her husband. I see them waving to me, calling. Did you know that my sister's husband was white? Oh, yes. A Dutchman who came from across the sea only to collect plants and make drawings of living things. A good man.

Gone long now. I see them and my good husband, Sun Wolf. That is my only dream now."

"You speak of death." Sachim moved to her grandmother and put her hand on the old woman's cheek. Grandmother took the hand between her own gnarled hands and kissed it.

"So soft, your hands, the flesh so young. You are a beautiful woman. You will find a good husband."

"One day, Grandmother," Sachim said, smiling softly.

"I would like to see his face, to know whom you have chosen."

"And you will when it happens."

"I don't know, Sachim. I have traveled far in my life— from the Eastern Sea to the Great River. Now I must make a much longer journey."

"Grandmother, please!"

"The young fear death so much. You are not near enough to it. It is good that you are uneasy with it—that is what makes life possible, I think. But the old walk near to the spirits and they grow more comfortable with it. Indeed, we anticipate it with something like joy. We know, we know that all of life is a dream, that it is a trial for the soul. All that matters is that the dream was true, that the trial was endured properly. I see you, Sachim, and I know that I have done well. I pass; new life, good life, emerged from me. So," she said wearily, closing her eyes again, "it was good and I have seen the joy in what lies ahead of me."

She fell asleep again, suddenly asleep, and Sachim knew the old woman had few reserves left. She stroked the gray head, bent and kissed her grandmother's cheek, and then left the lodge with its fire glowing softly.

It looked like rain. Bluish storm clouds hovered over the far horizon. On the beach the people would be pulling their canoes to higher ground, hoping the river did not grow angry enough to flood the low-lying cornfields.

Sachim went to her dreaming place and there she sat and she waited. She had heard of many sachems who tortured their bodies to make themselves dream. Who stayed awake for many days, placing thorns under their fingernails, flogging themselve so that they might dream.

She had never done that for she was a true dreamer, chosen by Manitou for some reason only he knew. She would sit and fast and wait and the dreams would come.

Her dreaming place was a flat rock jutting twenty feet
above the dark, flat earth surrounding it. In a crack in the
rock a gray, dead oak stood. Once an acorn had fallen into a
tiny crevice and taken root in shallow soil. In time the tree
had grown, enduring rain and wind and freezing weather. It
had flourished then, for a hundred years widening the crevice, splitting the great rock with its massive roots before time
had ended its span. The living tree had broken the great
stone. But the life of the tree was over and now the power of
time, of death, had aged the roots and rotted the massive,
twisted trunk. The tree had had its trial, and it had endured
as it should. Beneath the oak a small acorn had sprouted
roots and begun to send out a single tiny green shoot.

Sachim saw all of this and noted it without thinking about
it, just as she saw and felt the grass being fed by the rain, the
buds on the maple trees burgeoning with new life, and all of
nature being formed from seed, slowly maturing with each
new spring, swelling with sap in the summer, fading as
autumn came to the Sauk land, standing cold and barren in
the frozen winter when it seemed as if no new life could ever
emerge from beneath the snow.

A lone crow dipped toward the trees and Sachim watched
it as its greenish-black feathers caught the sunlight and its
intense yellow eyes changed to glowing coals in a sea of
black and the land around her became the river, coursing
southward toward the Spanish sea. The air was filled with
voices as the dead ones spoke, some shouting with happiness, others asking their way through the dark land or deeply
moaning, howling, or sobbing over a past wrong, a deed
neglected, or a love lost.

The voices drifted away and the sky folded around Sachim.
Then there was only the river and the rock and the twisted
oak, black against the sky.

Corn grew from the river and ripened, its tassels golden
and long, its stalks thick and green. Among the corn faceless
people moved, cutting down the good crop. Beyond them
stood many lodges, unlike the lodges of the Sauk and the
Fox, and above the houses rose smoke, and it was warfire.
Drums thundered in the sky and the faceless workers moved
on, taking the cornstalks with them in great wagons like
those the British traders used.

And then the dream was over and Sachim sat blinking in
the bright sunlight.

She had come to dream, but Manitou had told her nothing. What of the war with the Sioux? Those people in the dream had not been Sioux at all, but white. They wore wide hats and bonnets made of cloth. What could she advise Black Hawk now?

She tried to dream again, but it was no good. The visions had gone. She would fast then, and wait and pray to Manitou. The dream would become clear; it must, for the Sauk nation was threatened. In some way mysterious and amorphous, it was deeply threatened.

She would dream again.

2

ASIDE from the big walnut desk and accompanying chair, the packing crates stacked in the corners, and a gun rack, the room was empty. Captain Amos Stoddard paced the room, unbuckling his saber and tossing it clattering onto the desk. Stoddard was a veteran of the Revolution and a onetime Massachusetts legislator who had further political ambitions. President Jefferson had personally selected him to be American governor of Louisiana Territory, and by God! things would go right here.

Stoddard could be an impatient man and just now he was vastly impatient. Supplies, promised long ago, hadn't arrived. The Spanish settlers were recalcitrant and obstinate. The Sauk were unhappy and surly. Zebulon Pike, who was supposed to have taken presents upriver to the Indians, had been delayed. And Bart Perkins had botched his mission.

The door opened and Captain Stoddard turned as the lanky frontiersman, dressed in buckskins and carrying a Kentucky rifle, entered the room.

"Hello, Perkins."

"You don't sound happy," Perkins said. He looked around and then without being asked took the captain's only chair. He propped his feet up on the desk and tossed his wide-brimmed hat onto his boot toe, smiling with pleasure as he made the cast.

"Should I be happy?" Stoddard asked. His eyes went to the desk and muddy, propped-up boots.

"It was a mistake, that's all. You heard already?" the scout asked.

"From Black Hawk."

Perkins chuckled. "They got a pretty fair intelligence network, don't they? Good to remember if you ever have to fight the redskins. A runner from one camp to the next'll beat horses by days."

"I don't intend on going into battle against anyone and I don't care to hear about the techniques of the red man," Stoddard said. "What I do intend to do is carry out my assignment, and a good part of that depends on pacifying the Sauk. Now, what happened, Perkins? I thought you knew all about these Indians."

"All about them," Perkins mused, "no, sir, no one knows all about an Indian. Me, I married a Fox woman—Fox and Sauk is like cousins, you know—and I done a lot of trading up in Illinois with the Sauk. Not Black Hawk's band, but I know about him. I knew he had a spirit woman who advised him sometimes and I thought maybe this little token might have had some influence with her." Perkins reached into his stained buckskin shirt and tossed the sack of gold onto the desk.

"Yes," Stoddard said impatiently. "I know all of that." These frontiersmen who had spent years away from their own people took forever to tell a story. Was it that they needed to speak English to someone for as long as possible, or had they picked up the rambling Indian style of speaking?

"Never seen this Sachim, but I asked the way to her lodge. Found an old woman, kind of frail. She spoke English so I started to talk to her, tell her what we had in mind. She stopped me with a little laugh. Said she didn't dream no more. That I wanted her granddaughter."

"Yes?" Stoddard prompted.

"That's it, Captain. Didn't find the other woman and from the way the grandmother went on about it, she wouldn't have given Black Hawk no made-up dream advice anyway."

"So you just came back."

"Didn't seem to be much else to do," Perkins said. "Guess you'll have to go about things in a different way."

"This Black Hawk," Stoddard said with a shake of his head, "it will be difficult to deal with him at all. Do you know what he asked me? How can the French sell land which belongs to the Sauk."

"Well?" Perkins asked. Stoddard didn't answer him, and after a moment the frontiersman winked, let his feet drop to the floor, and rose. He sauntered out of the room, leaving the door open behind him. Stoddard stared at the open doorway for a long minute before he stalked to it and banged it shut.

The Sioux were gone. Black Hawk sat on his heels and stared across the river at the empty land where the Sioux tipis had been. Now and then he picked up a small stone and tossed it into the river.

"It is for the best," a soft voice behind him said. Sachim crouched beside Black Hawk and waited while the war leader sorted out his thoughts.

"It is for the best," he said at last. "What would have happened? I would have grown angry at their behavior. I would have gone to Two-Knives, my Fox brother. They would have made war with us. Many would have died.

"Now"—he shrugged—"only three of our young men have died."

"Three?"

Black Hawk nodded. "Antler Tree by the arrow. Tomorrow Runner and Ke-ke-tai by the gauntlet."

"But their wounds are healing, Black Hawk. Tope-kia has healed them."

"He has not healed their spirits." Black Hawk turned his head to study his young adviser. "Tomorrow Runner has dead eyes. He moves like a shadow around the camp, ashamed and angry. I too am ashamed and angry," Black Hawk admitted.

"I thought there might be war," Sachim said, rising to walk to the river's edge and stare across its great breadth. "I had a dream."

"A false dream, Sachim?"

"No," she said with emphasis, "only one I do not understand. There are many I do not understand. I dreamed of whites in our cornfields, Black Hawk, of whites mowing down our corn."

Black Hawk rose, his face puzzled. Was that the advice he had asked Manitou for, the dream he had hoped Sachim might have?

"Do you know what is happening in St. Louis, Sachim?"

"More whites," she answered indifferently.

"Different whites. We cannot continue to call them simply 'whites.' We must understand these people. If the British are good to us, the Americans, who speak the same tongue, are indifferent. If the Spanish were my friends, these whites may prove to be our enemies. There is as much difference among these white bands as there is between the Fox and the Sioux, the Mascouten and the Cherokee. We must understand them, Sachim. It is important that *you* learn as much as possible."

"Me? I don't care for any of them," she said sharply.

"But you must, Sachim. You carry spirits within your heart. *Our* spirits. You are important to the Sauk, more important than I am, perhaps. I can only fight, but you can dream."

"There is a time for each."

"Learn about the whites. I will tell you all I know. Know why the British give us an annuity. It is because they anticipate war with the Americans and wish us to remain allied with them as we were against the French. Know why the Spanish treated us well—because they were too few to fight the British and did not want us on the British side if there was war."

"And the Americans?"

"I do not know yet," Black Hawk said honestly, "but we must decide soon. We must understand what it is they want."

Sachim was listening, but her eyes were on a small approaching object downriver. She could see a plume of smoke against the pale sky.

"Something is coming, Black Hawk. A white boat, I think."

Black Hawk stepped up beside her and peered into the sunlight. It was a steamboat, but whose? "I must return to the village," Black Hawk said, and he started off at a trot, leaving Sachim to stare across the glittering river toward the steamboat making its way up the Mississippi.

As the boat neared the Rock River it took on size and shape. Sachim could see men on the deck. One of them wore a blue uniform. Smoke continued to puff from the black stack of the vessel. In the village, drummers announced the coming of the boat. The warriors would be painting their bodies, decorating their scalp locks, snatching up their weapons.

Sachim did not fear the boat. What could a handful of men do against the Sauk army? Yet there was apprehension in the air, a vague foreboding like that in the air before a thunderstorm, like the uncanny stillness before one of the twisting winds of summer came with its destruction.

She started back toward the village, passing the people who were rushing to the shore—painted warriors, curious, pregnant women, naked chubby children.

She saw Tope-kia, and the medicine man told her, "They are Americans. Runners from the south have come into camp. They fly a striped flag."

Sachim only nodded. Somehow, she was not surprised.

Old Strikes the Enemy, wearing his beaver coat with the feathers, carried his coup stick as he walked toward the river. Napope was in his finery, his face painted with crimson and yellow ocher. And the Prophet, wearing his wolf's head, strode past, his eyes seeing Sachim and disdaining her without focusing on her face. And then she saw the lost one.

Tomorrow Runner crouched beneath an elm tree, jabbing at something on the ground with a broken stick. When Sachim went nearer she could see what it was—a pictograph of a Sioux with holes jabbed in the eyes, hands, and heart.

"How are you, Tomorrow Runner? Did you hear a white boat is coming? Everyone is excited."

Tomorrow Runner didn't even glance up. He continued to stab at his drawing of the Sioux. Across his bare back—he could wear no shirt yet—huge welts crisscrossed his flesh. The Sioux women had done their best not just to humiliate him, but to scar him.

Sachim placed a hand on his shoulder and his wolfish eyes turned upward. For a moment his mouth split into a savage grimace and then the expression vanished, leaving only a cold stare. Sachim rose and walked away without another word.

Tomorrow Runner stared at his pictograph and after erasing it with his hand, he began to draw another.

They had beat him. He made his run through the gauntlet and the women kept striking him with their canes. Ke-ke-tai called out in pain. Tomorrow Runner would not give them that satisfaction. The Sioux women jeered, calling him a Sauk dog, and their canes fell on his back, his thighs, his abdomen, his groin. He fell and they descended on him like dogs savaging one who has gone down. He rose again and started through the gauntlet. The women beat him and tried to strike his manhood. Their eyes were alight with pleasure, and the pain was nothing compared to the anger. He wanted to kill them all, to set fire to their fat Sioux bodies, to rip them open with his war lance . . .

Tomorrow Runner finished his new pictograph and began jabbing it with his stick. He dug deeply into the breast of the woman he had sketched and ripped a deep furrow up to her throat. He turned, glanced at Sachim's back, and returned to his mad diversion.

The boat had pulled in to the shore, its boiler burbling to silence. Men leapt into the shallow water to tie lines to the big oaks and lash the boat to them. The Sauk stood and watched. After a minute, the white leader appeared, wearing a blue uniform with gold epaulets and a blue cap.

"Greetings!" he called out. "We come bringing gifts from the American father for the Sauk people."

Keokuk and Black Hawk started forward and the other chiefs followed.

"May we come ashore and visit your village?" the American asked. Beside him other Americans had appeared, holding aloft gifts for the Sauk, cloth and iron pots, steel knives and muskets.

"Come and speak in peace," Black Hawk answered, and the young American chief slipped over the rail of the steamboat to wade to the shore.

"I'm Zebulon Montgomery Pike," he said, sticking out a hand which Keokuk shook. "The American father apologizes. Our gifts were delayed. You were meant to have them before the Spanish left St. Louis."

Pike lifted an arm and his men began unloading the crates of goods from the steamboat. Napope, the supreme council chief, came forward and allowed Black Hawk to introduce him. Napope had learned English but did not like to speak it.

"I have brought medallions to you," Pike said, signaling a man who handed him a small box. "On them is the portrait of President Jefferson. He hopes you will wear them as a sign of friendship."

Napope took one eagerly and slipped the ribboned medal around his neck. The other chiefs accepted the silver medallions, some putting them on, others holding them in their hands. Pike looked toward the village and saw with surprise that a British flag flew above it.

"I will give you a new flag," Pike said, and one of his men waded to the boat to get one. "This is not British territory."

"The British have been our friends," Black Hawk said.

"But now we are your friends."

"Then," Black Hawk said, "we will fly two flags."

Pike didn't argue the point. All that mattered at this time was that the Sauk remained friendly. Zebulon Pike hadn't been sent as an ambassador, he was only delivering the presents Captain Stoddard had promised. His true mission was to find the source of the Mississippi, a months-long project which appealed to Pike's sense of adventure.

"Now let us smoke," Napope said in his gravelly voice. "Now let us give the Americans whatever supplies they wish." He fingered the profiled, wigged Jefferson on his medal and smiled. "Let us all be friends. What have we to war over? Let us eat and watch the dancers and hear the old songs."

Sachim heard the drums, the bone whistles, the cymbals sound. The dancers began a chorus of acclaim, as the Sauk and American voices mingled with the shrill screeching of celebrating children. She saw the dancers with their feathered ankles and wrists moving through the eagle dance, saw the band of whites, so pink in the face, dressed in their blue uniforms or in twill trousers and cotton shirts. The scent of fish broiling and of smoked venison, turtle, and the corncake was everywhere.

As the striped flag rose on a lodgepole next to the British flag, she turned and walked away. She did not like this. The foreboding clung to her heart. Perhaps it was the memory of the dream. But these men did not plant corn. They had no wagons; they could not be the faceless whites of her vision.

In the forest the sounds fell away; the scent and sights were of Manitou—a darting pair of butterflies, deep silver birch, a beaver waddling away toward the river.

"Hello, Sauk woman."

Sachim nearly stumbled over a tree root. She stopped and stared incredulously at the warrior leaning against the pale birch tree. He did not smile, but his eyes danced.

"You."

"Yes, it is me," Thunder Horse answered, stepping away from the tree to stand before her, bare-chested, powerful, and alien.

"But the Sioux have gone!"

"I have not. I wanted to see you one more time, Sauk woman. What is your name?"

"You should go." Sachim looked behind her. "Some of the Sauk are very angry."

The young Sioux shrugged. "What do I care? Won't you tell me your name?"

Sachim wanted to hurl a curse in the Sioux's face. She wanted to turn and stride away, she wanted to say nothing at all, but to stare scornfully at this haughty intruder. She did none of these.

"My name is Sachim," she said, feeling her mouth go dry, feeling her heart flutter annoyingly. She hated the Sioux, hated this arrogant young man.

"I will be back for you," Thunder Horse said. "I will be back with many horses one day. You will marry me, Sauk woman. Sachim."

And then he had his arm around her. Inside of Sachim's brain something screamed with protest, but she did not pull away. Her body was spellbound. The man was warm against her, strong and sure, and if he had drawn a knife from his waistband she couldn't have fled. She stared up at those mocking eyes and went limp and cold.

Her mind shouted its constant arguments: she did not want a Sioux man to touch her! She wanted no man. She hated this one more than any!

Slowly he bent his head and kissed her. His mouth was supple and warm, his lips moved demandingly over hers. He kissed her once and then released her, laughing. Sachim felt her ears burn, and her stomach knot. Her eyes flashed at him with fury.

And then he was gone, sifting through the silver birch, and when she could no longer see him her heart felt empty. She touched her lips and then turned her head and spat. But the emptiness would not go away.

She walked on three steps and then burst out in laughter herself. "Foolish woman, foolish thing," she said aloud. All the same, the day had changed, the forest had changed, the soul of the far-dreamer.

She walked on, hands behind her back, lost in thought.

As Tomorrow Runner watched her from behind a clump of bushes, the wolfish grimace returned to his face. He broke the stick in his hands violently and a splinter gouged his wrist, drawing blood. Tomorrow Runner wasn't even aware of it. He watched as Sachim was embraced by the forest and lost in it.

In the morning the steamboat was gone. When Sachim saw Black Hawk he was in high spirits.

"That American spoke well and I believe he spoke the truth. He told us of his trip and his plans. He is a warrior and not a council chief. Perhaps the Americans are like him and not so much like this new governor in St. Louis. I have sent runners ahead to the Fox villages to tell them that Pike is a good man."

"So what have we learned?" Sachim asked. Black Hawk didn't understand and told her so. "I mean, what have we learned so far about the Americans? You see, Black Hawk, I have thought about it and decided that you are right. We must learn about these people."

"We have learned nothing," Black Hawk admitted with a smile. "Except that they are here."

That was what Ke-ke-tai had learned earlier in the day. The young brave, still smarting from his beating by the Sioux women, had ridden out of the camp, wishing to be alone.

Tomorrow Runner was angry and he acted strangely now, brooding and praying with dark intent. Ke-ke-tai did not wish to become like Tomorrow Runner.

He had been caught, punished, and shamed. Now his wounds were healing and he wanted his heart to heal and so he had taken his gray pony and ridden southward with a bundle of furs. He would trade with the Spaniard, Espinoza, who had remained behind in St. Lous. Then Ke-ke-tai would buy white goods and take them back to the camp. Little Creek was there and she had promised to become his wife. He would give the white goods to her father for the wedding price.

The river ran quietly. The sky was clear and the wind ruffled the leaves of the hickory and maple trees. A bobcat turned from its kill to hiss at Ke-ke-tai before bounding away into the forest. Ke-ke-tai laughed, feeling alive for the first time in weeks.

He emerged from the forest to find the new houses along the Cuivre River. Astonished, he halted his horse and looked across the valley adjoining the river.

There were twenty white lodges there, not all of them completed. He could hear the hammering and sawing, the sound of falling axes. In the center of the town stood a larger building. Their store, perhaps, or a trading post.

Ke-ke-tai hesitated and then started his pony forward, the bundle of furs he had tied on the horse's haunches swaying and bouncing. If there was a trading post here now, it would save Ke-ke-tai from riding all the way to St. Louis. Then he could return sooner to Little Creek's father and sooner be married.

He crossed the river at a sandy ford and rode his horse up onto the flat ground. A white man with rolled-up sleeves and an ax in his hands turned sharply as the Sauk rode by. Ke-ke-tai raised a hand in a peaceful gesture, but the white simply stared in return.

Many of these men must have come from places where there were no Indians any longer; Ke-ke-tai understood that. They were as astonished to see him as he had been when as a boy he had seen his first mustached white and run away to hide under his blanket.

Ke-ke-tai's English was not good. All of his trading had been done with the Spanish, and that was his only contact with the whites. Leaders like Black Hawk and the Prophet knew the tongue well, but Ke-ke-tai had never needed to learn and so he had not. Still, he knew a few words and when he passed an ox-drawn cart loaded with freshly cut logs he asked the driver:

"Trade?" He pointed toward the large lodge.

"Trade? Trade what?" the red-faced man responded, tightening his grip on the new musket in his hand. He shook his head. "I don't want to trade."

"There. Trade?" Ke-ke-tai asked, searching for more words which might help him explain his meaning. "The big lodge."

"Carney? He might trade, I don't know," the red-faced man snapped. He was gripping his musket very tightly now. He was afraid, Ke-ke-tai decided, though why he was afraid of a lone peaceful Sauk he did not understand. He lifted his hand to this man and then rode on toward the two-story lodge.

Men were pinning more new timbers to the walls on the upper level of the store. The carpenters paused to look down at Ke-ke-tai as he rode up to the porchless front door and slid from his pony, throwing one leg over the horse's neck and dropping lightly to the ground. He hadn't expected to meet any traders here and so he hadn't painted or put on his shirt. Besides, the shirt still hurt the wounds on his back and chest where the Sioux women had struck him.

A thick man in high mule-ear boots came to the door, a corncob pipe thrust into his mouth. He had protruding ears, the neck of an ox, and a black beard. Ke-ke-tai held up his hand and this man answered the gesture.

Ke-ke-tai tried speaking in his own tongue, but the trader didn't understand him.

"Furs," he said at last in English, and he signed with his hands, indicating that he would trade.

"See what he's got, Lucas," the trader said to a lean man who had appeared from the store's interior. Ke-ke-tai grinned and motioned to the lean man, who was hollow-cheeked and clean-shaven. Ke-ke-tai's furs were good, he knew. He had brought only the best of his richly furred otter pelts, thick, unscarred beaver pelts, one fine bear robe, and a unique and valuable pelt of a white beaver.

Black Hawk had told Ke-ke-tai that in the East whites wore hats of beaver. What would a white beaver hat be worth? Enough to buy many silver and glass beads for Little Creek's father.

The narrow man looked through the furs quickly, nodding.

"They're good ones, Carney. He's got a white beaver pelt here and some fine otter."

"All right. Come on in, Injun. Bring them furs."

Carney had to gesture to make his meaning clear, but finally Ke-ke-tai understood. He untied his bundle of furs, following the two men into the dark store. Another man, much younger, sat in the corner, eating something. The only light in the room fell through narrow slits no wider than a man's hand. Ke-ke-tai looked around with curiosity and then went to a rough puncheon counter and spread out his furs, holding up an occasional fine pelt, running his fingers over the fur.

"Good stuff. See what he'll take," the big man, Carney, growled.

"They'll take most anything, won't they?"

"I don't know. Offer him some of them glass necklaces Howard brought up," the owner answered. "I don't have the time to deal with him over a few damn furs."

The beads that Ke-ke-tai saw were beautiful. Sunrise was in them, and sunset. The moon twinkled in them, and the stars. He marveled at the willingness of the whites to give up such treasures for furs when beaver were plentiful and such beads so rare.

The young man sauntered over to stand beside Ke-ke-tai. He drank something from an amber bottle and it made him smell bad. Rum, Ke-ke-tai thought, American rum. Some-times the British gave the Sauk rum, but Ke-ke-tai never drank it, not since the time it had filled his stomach with fiery sickness.

He held the beads up to the thin shaft of light that fell across the crude counter and nodded happily. These would buy Little Creek. They would make a good wedding price.

"What happened to you, boy?" the young man beside him asked. "Looks like he rode through a briar patch, don't he?" He touched the wounds on Ke-ke-tai's back and the Sauk shrugged.

"Squaw beat me," Ke-ke-tai answered with a grin.

"His squaw did this to him," the youngest man said, laughing. "Must be a hell of a squaw. And you took it, did you, Injun?"

Ke-ke-tai shrugged and turned away, not understanding, not caring for the man's breath. "Squaw beat me," he re-peated. And then his eyes fell on the silver buckle. It was ornate, inlaid with porcelain. A woman's face was carved into it somehow.

Ke-ke-tai's eyes lit up. "This," he said.

"What's he after?" Carney asked. He stopped stocking his shelves and turned around.

"The German silver buckle."

"No. That cost me two bucks. Give him his beads and get him out of here. He stinks like bear grease or something."

The lean man laughed and took the buckle from Ke-ke-tai. "Sorry, big chief."

"Beads." Ke-ke-tai pushed the beads back across the counter and pointed at the buckle. He wanted that now. He had never seen anything like it. Let them take back the beads and keep all of the furs. He wanted that buckle for Little Creek's father.

"Take the damn beads and go," the lean man growled.

"What's the matter?" Carney asked.

"He still wants the buckle, I guess."

"Listen, I've got work to do—so do you boys. Give him the beads and get him out of here! That's clear enough, isn't it?"

"Come on, big chief. Here, take the beads," the lean man said.

The younger man had a different idea of how to handle things. He picked up the necklaces and threw them in Ke-ke-tai's face. Ke-ke-tai stepped back, stunned by the rudeness of the traders. The Spanish man had never done such a thing.

"Look at him," the young yellow-haired man said with a laugh. "Scared. 'Course any big brave that lets a squaw woman beat up on him like that ain't much of a man, I guess."

Ke-ke-tai tried again. Pointing at the buckle, he said, "That."

"The big chief can't take a hint."

"What's going on!" Carney hollered in exasperation. "Can't you do anything, Willis?"

"He won't leave, Carney."

"I need help with the shelving. Dammit, Willis!"

"Throw him out then," the blond man said.

"Look, take the beads," Willis said, offering them again. "Willis!"

"This is the way you do it," the younger man said, and he took Ke-ke-tai's arm and spun him around, kicking him as he did. Then he ran him to the door and sent him somersaulting into the dust. Willis was worried, but the blond man just laughed, taking another drink of his rye whiskey. "That's the way we do it where I'm from."

Ke-ke-tai rose, shaking his head. They had closed the door behind him. Now he had nothing. No buckle, no beads, no pelts. He would have to go to St. Louis after all.

Rising, he went to the door and swung it open. He walked silently to where his furs had been spread out, stacked them again, and began bundling them with his rawhide strings.

"Dammit all, big chief," the blond man said, lifting a musket from behind his corner chair. "You just can't take a hint, can you?"

The musket ball thudded into the wall behind Ke-ke-tai and the blond man laughed as Ke-ke-tai hit the floor. *They were going to kill him*! Kill him for a bundle of furs.

Willis was next to Ke-ke-tai and as the Sauk rose he drew his knife from his belt sheath and slashed out with it. Willis fell back against the counter, blood pouring from his throat.

The blond man's eyes widened and he furiously tried to reload his musket. Ke-ke-tai leapt toward him and drove his knife into the white's belly, ripping upward.

The blond sagged against Ke-ke-tai and then fell to the floor, dead.

Behind the Sauk the big man, Carney, had snatched up a pistol from under the counter and he steadied himself to aim. Ke-ke-tai grabbed the musket; the ramrod was still protruding from the barrel as he fired.

The ramrod pierced the storekeeper's heart and he stood clutching at it for a minute before he staggered back against the wall and fell to the floor.

Ke-ke-tai looked at the smoking musket in his hands and threw it away. He went to the counter, grabbed the belt buckle with the cameo, and darted for the door. Outside, other whites were running toward the store. Ke-ke-tai leapt onto his pony's back. Bending low over the withers, he heeled his pony sharply and the little horse leapt into motion, running flat out for the forest on the verge of the new fields.

When Ke-ke-tai was in the ash woods, he slowed his horse, looking back. What a bad day it had been. But he had the buckle and that was good. Now Little Creek's father would let her marry. Now everything would be different and the bad luck which had been running a winning race against Ke-ke-tai would change.

He turned his gray pony, heading it northward toward the Sauk village on the Rock River.

"I'm Joshua Ferguson."

Captain Amos Stoddard looked up from his papers and studied the dark-eyed, dark-haired man before him. Ferguson looked to have French blood in him, and unless Stoddard was wrong there was a little Indian there as well. He was lean, broad-shouldered, and mustached.

That was all external. Ferguson had a way of projecting what was inside of him with his eyes, the set of his mouth, the stance he assumed, and Stoddard didn't like any of it. The man seemed arrogant and callous. Age twenty-five, perhaps, without a noticeable accent, Ferguson appeared determined to go places, and quickly.

"Yes?" Stoddard answered dryly.

"You don't seem to remember me, Governor. *Joshua Ferguson.*"

"No, I don't."

Ferguson grunted. "I'm the surveyor Washington sent out. Only I've got no work to do. I've discovered that the Sauk are still living on that land and have no intention of moving. Just what went wrong here?"

Stoddard didn't like the younger man's aggressive attitude. After all, what was he but a surveyor? No one had any idea of what Stoddard had been through trying to make a smooth transition from Spanish rule to American jurisdiction.

"We haven't yet worked out a treaty," Stoddard said, biting off his words.

"Or begun to negotiate."

"No," Stoddard admitted. "We had an unfortunate miscarriage early on." There was no point in explaining to this surveyor Perkins' botched mission to buy Black Hawk's "spirit woman," to induce her to persuade the Sauk to sell their rich Illinois land to the Americans.

Joshua Ferguson took a chair and drew it up next to the governor's desk, placed his elbows on the desk, and looked Stoddard in the eye.

"Maybe you had better find another way to attack this problem, Stoddard."

Stoddard! The governor grew red in the face. Who was this dusty land surveyor to burst into his office and address him, not as Your Excellency, not as Governor or even Mr. Stoddard, but simply Stoddard?

"I have several assistants working on new approaches, Mr. Ferguson. When one has been selected and results achieved," he said stiffly, "I shall see that you are informed. And now . . ." The governor rose.

"I'm not leaving yet, Stoddard. Sit down. Let me tell you this—you were sent here to govern this territory and, as a primary task, to negotiate with the Sauk and Fox Indians for land along the Mississippi and Rock rivers for settlement. You know that President Jefferson wants American settlers in here to hold the land against any Spanish or French reoccupation, to keep the damned British off this continent for good. Yet you sit here worrying about transferring papers from one hand to the other—"

"Just a minute, Mr. Ferguson!"

"No, *you* wait just a minute, Stoddard," the surveyor said. "You're not fulfilling your obligations to the American people or to the Congress or to the President. By now, one way or the other, the Sauk and Fox should have been moved off that land. I want it done. You hear me!" Ferguson said, rising sharply so that his chair scraped the floor. "I want it done."

Before Stoddard could reply, the surveyor was gone, the door banging shut behind him. The governor of Louisiana Territory stood, his teeth grinding together, his chest rising and falling rapidly with anger.

"Just who in hell do you think you are! Just who in the bloody hell . . ." Then Stoddard sagged into his chair, angry, frustrated, and just a little confused.

Outside, Joshua Ferguson swung into the saddle of his black Tennessee walking horse and nodded to the man who had been holding the reins.

"I lit a fire under him. He'll do something."

"He'd best. I've got something invested in this too," the man with the bulldog face said.

"You have, have you?" Ferguson laughed. "Sweet, I've got everything I've ever owned and everything I could borrow knotted up in this. The Sauk will go. And if the governor of this territory can't move them out, I'll figure a way to do it on my own. Believe me."

Ginger Sweet did believe him. He had hitched his wagon to Josh Ferguson's star and couldn't afford not to believe him. Ferguson had connections. More, he had determination and what Ferguson projected was usually what came about.

Ferguson envisioned a thousand white settlers in the first year that the rich Illinois lands were opened, and he envisioned making a hundred dollars from each for "surveyor's fees." If President Jefferson saw the Louisiana Purchase as a way to protect America's western border and to prevent European powers from ever again occupying North American soil, Joshua Ferguson had a simpler, less altruistic dream.

He wanted to make his fortune. Louisiana Territory was the place to do it.

Stoddard tried to get back to work, but it was impossible. Besides, his stomach was growling. His cook was a Creole with the abominable habit of putting peppers in the rice and cloves on the venison, but after two glasses of burgundy it would go down all right. Walking to the dining room, a domed white-painted room with large external doors and high windows, the governor seated himself and waited for the servants to bring his wine.

Who was Ferguson? The man annoyed and confounded

Stoddard. Joshua Ferguson seemed to think of himself as the governor and Stoddard as a mere lackey.

Stoddard moved his elbow as the servant, a French-Kiowa man as silent as the tomb and as cold, poured burgundy into Stoddard's silver-mounted crystal goblet.

He had taken a single sip of the wine before he heard the commotion in the outer hall—excited, raised voices and thumping boots. *What now*? Why had he accepted this damnable position? The appointment had seemed to be a stepping-stone to greatness, but the stone had sunk beneath his feet until Stoddard now felt as if he were wading in an endless bog.

"Sir?" The young sergeant hadn't bothered to knock and Stoddard eyed him in annoyance.

"I'm at my dinner, Sergeant Tyne."

"I realize that, sir . . ." The sergeant was nearly breathless. "But this is a matter of great importance."

"I'll decide that, Sergeant," Stoddard replied. "Just report."

"Yes, sir. There's a group of settlers out here from the Cuivre. There's been an Indian attack."

"There's *what*!"

Before the sergeant could respond, three muddy and angry settlers pushed past him and into the room. Stodddard rose in indignation. "What is this?" he managed to ask without revealing his anger.

"What this is," the leader of the settlers, a tall, bent-nosed Scandinavian, answered violently, "is a protest. Where the hell was the army? Where were you—?"

Stoddard's temper boiled to the surface. "I don't know what you are talking about, sir, and if you don't calm yourself and explain things to me, I can't see how I can do anything to help you."

The tall man took three slow breaths. "Indians. Came into the Cuivre settlement and killed three of our people. Maybe tried to rob the store. No one seems to know. It was Indians, though."

"What tribe, does anyone know?"

"Sauk. Those that saw them saw that much. Sauk, they was."

Stoddard cursed silently and momentarily turned his back. "How many Indians?" he asked quietly.

"Don't know."

"A hundred, ten, three?" Stoddard asked impatiently, walking to the settlers.

A second man spoke up. "Hank, some say there was only one of 'em."

"One? Killing three armed men?" the Scandinavian answered.

"Just tellin' you what I heard." The other man shrugged.

"It doesn't matter how many. What we want to know is what you're going to do about it, Governor."

"I will, of course, look into it. Immediately."

"Look into it . . ." the big man sputtered. "The army ought to wipe them out."

"Yes," Stoddard said with a little sarcasm. "Except, as you know, or should know, the Sauk and Fox outnumber us by ten or twenty to one. Starting a war over an isolated incident is preposterous, and you men know it. Three people are dead. Do you want to see all of your friends and family butchered? Calm down and look at things logically."

"Hard to be logical when your neighbors are killed by Indians."

"Yes," Stoddard sighed. "I know that. I assure you that we will do our best to investigate this incident and see that justice is done."

"Justice is taking the bastards that did it and hanging them!" Hank spat.

"Yes," Stoddard muttered. He went on with his assurances for a few minutes more. The settlers were hardly mollified when they finally left and Stoddard walked back to the table, seated himself, and drank his wine. Things weren't going well, not going well at all.

Black Hawk's mood was dark. He applied the last of his paint and threw his otterskin robe around his shoulders. He emerged from his pole-and-bark lodge and started toward the council hut, noticing the dark clouds to the north, the gray and white of the big river. It would storm. There may be many storms to come, he thought.

Black Hawk was not a member of the council. He had no vote, unlike Keokuk and Napope, Strikes the Enemy, and the other civil chiefs. But this was a matter that might involve war, and so Black Hawk would sit in council.

Sachim was there outside the council lodge, her own eyes concerned. "Is it as grave as I believe, Black Hawk?" she asked. The war leader nodded. It was grave.

The young man was there already. Ke-ke-tai did not appear anxious, but only a little confused. Black Hawk nodded curtly to the young warrior. Sachim touched his shoulder before following the war leader into the smoke-filled council lodge to sit on a blanket-covered mat beside Keokuk.

The whites were already there: Captain Stoddard, the American governor, a man in buckskins called Perkins, and a translator named LeClair whom Black Hawk knew well enough to trust.

When the council had seated itself, Ke-ke-tai was brought in. It was Keokuk who tossed the buckle into the center of the council circle and looked at Ke-ke-tai, waiting for an explanation.

"I traded for that. It is for Little Creek's father. A wedding price," the young man said haltingly.

"Ask him where he got it," Stoddard demanded.

"From a trading post . . . on the Quivre."

"How did he get it?" Stoddard persisted.

Ke-ke-tai shrugged and began quietly to tell his story. Sachim listened intently, believing the youth. There had been provocation, much provocation, but the fact remained: Ke-ke-tai had killed three Americans.

Napope shifted his bulk. "This is grave," he said to himself. His eyes lifted to Stoddard. "We want no trouble with you Americans, but I must ask, what is it you wish to do with Ke-ke-tai?"

"To satisfy the white settlers he must stand trial in St. Louis."

"They were trying to kill me!" Ke-ke-tai said intently.

"Does that make no difference under white law?" Napope asked Stoddard.

"Of course it does," the governor said. "In our law we have what is called justifiable homicide. Self-defense is not a crime. If this young man is telling the truth, he has nothing to fear, believe me."

Sachim said, "The whites may say that Ke-ke-tai is lying."

Napope's eyes shuttled to Sachim's, censuring her without a word. It wasn't the spirit woman's place to speak out in matters of tribal law.

Stoddard waved a hand. "I assure you that if the young warrior did nothing he will be released unharmed. If he is guilty, of course—"

"I am not guilty," Ke-ke-tai said frantically. This was all too much for him. First the beating by the Sioux women and now this. He was to have been married soon. Would Napope really let the whites take him?

Keokuk spoke up. "He has broken their law on their land. We must let them take Ke-ke-tai, as we let the Sioux take him. The American father has given his word that he has nothing to fear. Let them take Ke-ke-tai then. It will satisfy their law and we can continue to have friendship with the Americans."

Ke-ke-tai's face slowly fell and then settled into a scowl. The council was turning its back on him for the second time. He looked helplessly at Sachim and Black Hawk, but the war leader turned his eyes away.

"I assure you he will be treated fairly," Stoddard said. "You can understand how the settlers feel. They need to hear Ke-ke-tai tell his story."

"Yes," Napope said, his face suddenly relaxing—his decision had been made. "Ke-ke-tai must go. So I say."

"So I say," Strikes the Enemy agreed.

"So I say." Keokuk nodded. The other council members answered one by one: Quash-qua-me, Pa-she-pa-ho, Ou-che-qua-ka. Ke-ke-tai sat without expression, thinking of Little Creek, who waited outside for the decision. He stared at the belt buckle and silently cursed all white goods, all whites.

Black Hawk too sat silently. The American governor was smiling. Napope was smiling. The man Perkins and Quash-gua-me. A new pipe was lighted and passed around the council blanket. Sachim glanced once at Ke-ke-tai and then turned her eyes down again. The feeling was on her again. The feeling that no good could come of this, that the Sauk were standing in a great shadow they did not yet understand.

3

THE faceless men moved through the cornfields with strange long hatchets. Each stalk of corn bled as it was cut. The wagons rolled behind the mowers and were filled with bleeding cornstalks and the blood ran crimson onto the dark earth. Vultures followed the wagons and feasted on that which was left behind. The land went dry and barren and great cracks appeared in the earth. Row after row of skulls like pale pumpkins rested there. The sun went blood-red in a pale sky and then the river came. The great river at flood tide, cleansing the earth.

He was there—the young warrior, naked and proud. He was there and then he was gone as he reached out for Sachim. The river swept him past her, the water turning deep vermilion, the sky going very dark as a new storm swept across the land.

Sachim opened her eyes. It was dark in her lodge, and damp. She rose naked from her blankets and went to the door, looking out at the dewy grass, the dark trees, the faint gray of the river.

She was troubled because she did not understand her dreams. The Prophet, who did not dream, pretended to understand everything. Sachim knew nothing except that the dreams grew worse and larger and longer.

She dressed and went out into the pre-dawn. The birds were beginning to stir in the trees.

It had been two weeks since Ke-ke-tai had been taken away by the whites and nothing had yet been done. It seemed as if they had just locked him up and forgotten the trial. Keokuk had gone down to St. Louis and returned with presents and was quite satisfied with Stoddard's inaction.

"Some whites want to kill Ke-ke-tai. Stoddard did not let them," he had said, and then gone away, smoking a gift pipe, wearing a new blanket.

Sachim started toward Black Hawk's lodge, seeing the Prophet in the forest, watching as he always watched. "Pay no attention to him," Black Hawk had said. "He is jealous, that is all. He wants his sort of power as Keokuk wants to be supreme chief."

How far, Sachim wondered, was either of them ready to go to grasp that power?

"The morning is bright, Sachim," Black Hawk said in greeting, "and you make it brighter still."

"Thank you, Black Hawk." Bluntly she said, "I am worried about Ke-ke-tai. Something must be done."

"What can be done?" the war leader asked, rubbing his forehead. "We have surrendered him. There is war and there is peace."

"There must be other ways than war, Black Hawk," Sachim said, brushing back a strand of her long dark hair. "You told me to learn the white ways. I think we need a white man to tell us what might be done."

"A white?" Black Hawk frowned. "Who?"

"Name a man you trust."

"Captain Hobbs."

"The British father?" Sachim asked.

"Yes. I have fought with him. But he is far upriver now."

"Another man then," Sachim prompted.

"LeClair. He knows our tongue and the English tongue. He is a trader and values our friendship. And he was here at the council lodge when Ke-ke-tai's fate was decided."

"Then I will see him."

"Sachim," Black Hawk said with a hesitant shake of his head. "What is it you think can be done? The council has decided. Stoddard is in charge of Ke-ke-tai. You are, forgive me, only a woman-child. Who will listen to you?"

"I don't know," she admitted, "but I must try to do something. Who else is trying to help him?"

Black Hawk gestured weakly. He himself felt frustrated by Ke-ke-tai's imprisonment. Following on the heels of the trouble with the Sioux across the river it left him with a sense of futility.

"Do what you must then, Sachim, what you can. Shall I ride to LeClair's with you?"

"No. Let me do this on my own. The council may not look kindly on this."

"As you will have it. Take one of my horses."

Sachim selected a little spotted pony and waited as Black Hawk blanketed and saddled the animal. She led it then back to her lodge and tied it briefly while she walked through the dark shadows of the elms to Grandmother's lodge. Soon the band would be making the long trek to their winter hunting grounds. Could the old woman survive a long journey at her age?

"Sachim?" Grandmother turned her head and smiled. She was flat on her back, withered hands folded on her abdomen.

"It is me. I must go away for a little while, Grandmother. I will tell Sha-sak to make sure you have wood and food while I am gone."

"Sha-sak is a good woman," the old Oneida woman said. Her voice had grown scratchy and faint. She was asleep again before Sachim left the lodge.

LeClair's trading post was to the north, above the Apple River at a place called Galena. It had been a French outpost and then a British fort and later a Spanish settlement. Now, Sachim supposed, it belonged to the Americans. LeClair had outlasted all of these people. He had come before any soldier had been seen in Illinois, before the whites had made their wars in this land, so far from their home countries.

The man was small, affable, shrewd. He had been a friend to the Sauk and the Fox and the Kickapoo, giving them credit when the winters were hard and the Indians could not hunt. In return the various tribes had given their finest pelts and trade goods to LeClair when other traders might have offered more rum, more muskets.

LeClair had two sons with a Fox woman named Shining Spring, who was gone now, dead of the white cholera. The two sons ran the trading post and LeClair, no longer young, offered his services as an interpreter to the various white factions, trying to bring about understanding and maintain the tenuous peace in the long valley.

The trading post consisted of a log blockhouse, three stone buildings, and a palisade wall which would have done LeClair no good in the event of attack, since his gates were always open, day and night.

"Everyone is my friend," LeClair had said. "All men are my brothers. If my father was French, does that mean I should despise the British? Wars are made by the people in power, fought by those who have little choice. The victims are always those who wanted nothing to do with seeking power or fame."

Sachim rode the spotted horse across the narrow river and through the river oaks toward the trading post, which was quiet on this sunny afternoon. Two Fox men stood in the yard examining a horse. A bearded white watched the appraisal and chewed on a stubby pipe. Sachim lifted a hand to the Fox warriors. She did not know them, but all Fox were cousins. Once they had been one people, the old ones said, and men like Keokuk said they would be again—with Keokuk presumably as supreme chief.

Sachim swung down from her pony, loosened the woven cinch strap, and walked into the trading post.

One of LeClair's sons was sweeping the floor. He turned, his face an odd mixture of French-Belgian and Fox features. "Yes?"

"I want LeClair," Sachim said, embarrassed that her English was imperfect and silently vowing to improve it.

"He's taking a nap. This about furs or a purchase?"

"No. I need his help."

"All right." The man put his straw broom aside. "I'll see if he's awake yet."

Sachim had a long half-hour to wait, and she spent it walking up and down the aisles of the store, as always wondering how the whites could make the goods they had to sell, shiny knives and huge black iron pots, bottled medicines and shirts and trousers of cloth. Silver beads and muskets, strange and incomprehensible tools of steel. A hoe of iron or steel, when the Sauk used the shoulder blade of a deer or elk for their hoes; bowls of glazed clay smooth and delicately patterned, so many things—where did they come from? She would ask, she would learn. Black Hawk was right. The whites had come to stay; the Sauk must understand them if they were to live together.

LeClair finally emerged from the back room, looking weary and smaller than Sachim remembered him in his blue coat and checked shirt. He smiled broadly although Sachim knew he didn't remember her.

"What can I help you with, young woman?" he asked. "Something of importance?"

"Quite important to the Sauk."

"Not war, I hope," LeClair said.

"No. I need to know something of the white laws."

LeClair patted his wispy gray hair. "Into my office, then, if you will. I don't know what help I can be. I'm hardly a barrister, but what I know I am willing to share."

The office was cluttered with unpacked goods. LeClair offered Sachim a chair which she studied curiously before accepting. The little trader sat behind a desk strewn with papers and waited.

"Ke-ke-tai has been taken away," Sachim said, and she related the man's trouble and her concern. "I think they will just keep him locked away. It will break his heart. His woman does not understand. The council does not care. Stoddard does nothing."

"I see." LeClair rubbed the slack flesh of his jaw. "You know, you're right about one thing—the settlers down there want Ke-ke-tai hanged or imprisoned. Stoddard walks a fence—"

"Pardon me?" Sachim said, cocking her head.

"Sorry. Not many fences around here, are there?" LeClair answered with a soft smile. "I mean that Stoddard does not know what to do. He doesn't want to anger the whites, but doesn't want to make enemies of the Sauk."

"And so Ke-ke-tai sits in prison."

"And so he does."

"What is there to be done?" Sachim asked, folding her hands together, leaning forward.

"Go over the governor's head," LeClair said before realizing that this was another expression Sachim wouldn't understand. "Go to the Great American Father in Washington."

"The man on the medals."

"Jefferson."

"How far is Washington?" Sachim asked.

"Too far, unfortunately. What I had in mind was writing a letter. I'll be happy to draft it for you. Explain to Jefferson that the Sauk wish to be friends with the Americans now that they are here but that one of your young warriors has been incarcerated for simply defending himself. I would think," LeClair went on, "knowing President Jefferson, that he would rather see the man out of prison than risk fusing an Indian war on the frontier."

"This letter—how long will it take to reach Jefferson?" Sachim wanted to know.

"A long while, I'm afraid. Several weeks, maybe a month, and the same length of time for a response. Sorry, but I haven't any other suggestions."

"And Ke-ke-tai must sit and wait?"

"Unless Stoddard makes up his mind to do what's right instead of to please his settlers."

"I see," Sachim said with resignation. "If there is no other way, then help me with the letter."

LeClair reached for paper, pen, and inkwell, and as Sachim watched with curiosity, the little man began drafting his letter to Thomas Jefferson.

Stoddard was morose. He tried to raise fury within himself but was incapable of it. He was a beaten man. He looked at his secretary again. "Why Harrison? Tell me that, Corporal Day?"

The secretary shook his head and remained mute. He wasn't about to respond with his observations. The governor had proven ineffective in reaching Jefferson's goals. William Henry Harrison just might be able to produce results. Harrison was simply a stronger man. If Stoddard couldn't deal with the Sauk and Fox, and had no plan to move forward with after all these months, then perhaps a new negotiator was needed.

"It's that damned surveyor, Day. Joshua Ferguson. Who else would have written to the President?"

"I don't know, sir."

"Don't they know what a touchy situation I have here? I've still got that Indian under lock and key. Still have the settlers at my throat, still haven't made headway with the Sauk. What do they expect?"

"I don't know, sir," Day said, squaring a stack of memos before picking them up. "Will there be anything else this morning?"

"No, dammit all, no!" After the corporal had gone Stoddard muttered again, "Why Harrison?"

In 1800 Harrison had been appointed the first governor of Indiana. He was a solid man, and his star was obviously rising faster than Stoddard's. Didn't anyone in Washington have faith in Stoddard anymore? It really wasn't his fault if all these little problems kept cropping up. Like that murdering Sauk Indian . . . Stoddard stood at his office window, looking across the square to the jailhouse where the Indian remained under constant guard. To execute the man would set off an Indian war; to release him would infuriate the settlers, undermining Stoddard's authority. He felt more than a little like Pontius Pilate except there was no way to wash his hands of this mess.

He knew too, from secondhand sources, that Joshua Ferguson was out there stirring up the people to kill the Indian. Why, Stoddard didn't know exactly. Ferguson was too damned ambitious in a mysterious way. There was no solution that Stoddard saw, just none.

He pulled the drapes shut over the window and turned away.

Ke-ke-tai brooded. He sat on the cold floor of his cell, staring at the heavy wooden door, at the small barred window. He would die in this place. He needed sunlight to live, he needed the woods and the big river. He needed to laugh with Little Creek.

He rose and as he had done a hundred times went to the window to chip at it with the blunt knife the whites had given him on a dinner tray and forgotten to take away. The knife bent and grew jagged. The mortar holding the iron bars in the window frame fell away in the thinnest, paltriest flakes. Ke-ke-tai continued to work at it. He had to escape. He was dying in this dark and damp place and he knew now that they would never let him go. Nor could he count on the council, which had turned him over to the Americans as they had given him up to the Sioux. He chipped away, his fingers raw and split, his heart dark and angry.

Sachim had not given up. She talked to all of the council members who would listen, like the half-deaf Quash-qua-me. She shouted to be heard as she walked beside him toward the cornfields where the harvest was now under way.

"The Americans said Ke-ke-tai would have a trial, that he would be allowed to speak and tell what had happened! There was no trial. He is still in prison a month later. When will he be allowed to speak!"

"They will let him speak," the old chief said. They stopped

at the perimeter of the woods to look out at the long fields, a thousand cultivated acres where the Sauk women worked, snapping the ears of corn from the stalks, which now were fading to brown.

"We have made a bad bargain, Quash-qua-me!" Sachim said loudly. "The American father hasn't lived up to his word. Someone must go down and speak to him. The council must meet again over this."

"The council does what it must, spirit woman. We meet in council; you dream. The Prophet says that it is good. That the Americans will give us many presents for following the just path."

"The Prophet!" Sachim fell silent. It did no good to attack Wabokieshiek or Keokuk. Keokuk was more deaf to her pleas than Quash-qua-me. Keokuk saw profit in selling Ke-ke-tai, and he knew that Sachim was close to Black Hawk, advising him, dreaming for him.

"Consider it, please, Quash-qua-me, only consider it!"

"Yes, spirit woman, I will consider it." Then the old man went down into the fields. His youngest daughter was ready to have her baby and he wanted to take her out of the hot sun.

Sachim watched him go, lifted her hands and let them slap against her thighs in exasperation. Pa-she-pa-ho was on a hunt. She had spoken to Ou-che-qua-ka that morning. Strikes the Enemy would not talk to her at all. There was no point in approaching Keokuk. There was nothing more Sachim could do that day. The council seemed unconcerned with Ke-ke-tai's life. Sachim was hardly unconcerned. LeClair had told her that many of the American settlers, family and friends of the dead men, wanted to kill Ke-ke-tai. Would the council allow even that? Black Hawk would stop them, but that might lead to war. The only solution was to have Ke-ke-tai released, but only the council could do that.

She started back toward the village, agitated, angry. She would see to Grandmother's needs and then swim in the river, swim until her arms and legs were weary and her mind empty of this turmoil.

Tomorrow Runner stepped out from behind the bent ash tree and confronted her. In his hand he held his poking stick. His face was painted black and white, black to his nose, white above. He appeared like a skeleton head scorched by fire, though what his paint represented, only Tomorrow Runner knew.

"You halt," he said. He was slightly hunched, his chest rising and falling rapidly. "You halt when I approach. You halt and pray that I do not poke you."

Sachim felt fear, pity, and anger collide in her heart. What had happened to this fine young warrior, to the too-handsome, too-proud Sauk?

"I did not know you wanted me to halt, Tomorrow Runner," she said evenly.

"Yes. You must halt. Halt or die."

"Die? I am your friend, Tomorrow Runner. We grew up together. We used to play the eagle game together and run races . . ."

"I knew you then. Now I do not know you. Now you must stand still when I come or I will poke you." He had his sharp stick in both hands now. The muscles in his shoulders leapt as he clenched his fists tighter.

"Why are you angry with me?" Sachim demanded. "Am I Sioux, am I someone who has harmed you? I am not a council member, not an enemy, not anything but a friend, Tomorrow Runner."

"You are," he panted, "a female. I know what females want. To beat you and make you crawl."

"You speak of the Sioux women, Tomorrow Runner, not of me." She stepped forward, raising her hand to comfort him, but the warrior reacted with a savage thrust of his stick, that barely missed Sachim's abdomen.

"You are a woman. And the devil spirits have sent you."

"Tomorrow Runner . . . !"

But the young warrior suddenly turned and ran away, crashing through the forest, a wild yell rising from his throat, and Sachim could only shake her head in pity and walk on.

The horse was tethered outside her lodge and she looked at it in wonder. A tall, deep-chested chestnut horse, it wore a padded saddle, fringed and beaded. Its mane and tail had been braided and its coat brushed to a deep gloss.

"Where have you come from?" she asked the animal, moving to it, stroking its sleek neck. "Is someone here?" She went to the door of her lodge and called in. "Has someone come to see Sachim?" There was no answer, and looking inside, she saw no one.

The horse bent its neck to tug at some grass, and Sachim, walking around it, rested a hand on its flank, wondering. No one was in the lodge, no one in the forest.

"Where have you come from?"

She moved the horse a little way, driving its picket pin into the earth behind her lodge, where there was more grass. Then she shrugged and started toward Grandmother's house. Tope-kia was kneeling on the ground in the deep shade of the elms, searching for medicine mushrooms. As Sachim approached, the medicine man turned, grinning.

"Did you find it? The horse?"

"I found it, but where did it come from, Tope-kia? Who could have left it?"

"You don't know?" the medicine man asked, rising and dusting his knees. There was a silly grin on his crooked face and Sachim answered with annoyance.

"No, I don't know! How could I know, Tope-kia? Who left the horse at my lodge?"

"I saw him. A young man. A Sioux, Sachim. A Sioux left the horse for you."

"A Sioux . . ." She looked back toward her lodge in puzzlement.

"I see you know which Sioux warrior I mean."

"No," she snapped, "I do not."

"The son of Far Eagle, Sachim. I saw him. It was Thunder Horse who brought the pony. It is their custom, you know. A warrior always gives a gift horse to the woman he wishes to marry."

"Marry? I don't know him at all," she said sharply. "Who would marry a Sioux anyway? Take the horse away, give it to someone who has none."

"You have none, Sachim."

"No, and I have no husband either. I do well enough without either."

She walked on toward her grandmother's hidden lodge. She tried to sustain her anger, but failed. Beneath the surface pique, Sachim felt flattered, and beneath and beyond that emotion was another which she did not want to dwell on, to identify. It flooded her briefly with a warmth which she banished immediately from conscious thought. Yet it lingered at another level and caused her to smile without really knowing why as she approached her grandmother's house.

"Foolish thing," she whispered once. "There is so much to do. You are not a child, you are a dream-walker." She added, "Besides . . . a Sioux!"

Thunder Horse watched from the forest. He watched it all, seeing the surprise in Sachim's eyes as she found the horse, seeing her walk around it in wonder, lifting her eyes to the trees, where, if she had looked a little more carefully, she would have seen him.

He saw her walk up the little hill and speak to the medicine man, and he heard their conversation. Thunder Horse followed her through the trees, his moccasined feet silent as a cougar's, his lithe body quick and sure. He heard her talk to herself, her voice low and musical even in whisper. He watched her and then he smiled, knowing he was in her mind, knowing that somewhere inside that woman's heart he had touched her.

"I will have you, Sauk girl." He thought that over and then changed it. "Or you will have me."

He grinned and then turned to slip away toward the river. He was days behind his tribe, but cared not. They were on the plains, making the last great buffalo hunt of the season before winter settled. It meant nothing to Thunder Horse this year. He had found the woman he would take to his lodge and make his wife.

Thunder Horse laughed out loud and then stopped in his tracks. The Sauk warrior before him was young and strong and weirdly painted. It was a moment before Thunder Horse could see beneath the paint and recognize the man. He was one of those who had run the Sioux gauntlet. His chest and arms still showed welts. He was bent forward, breathing loudly through his mouth. In his hands was a jagged stick. Thunder Horse backed away a step or two.

"Sioux." The word rose like a curse from the Sauk's throat.

Thunder Horse put his hand on his belt knife. He had no fear of the Sauk; Thunder Horse feared nothing, no one. He had been raised to disregard fear, to scoff at it, but he would not die—not now.

"I want no battle, Sauk man."

"You are Sioux."

"Yes."

"Do you let your women do your fighting?" Tomorrow

Runner demanded. "Fight me. Do you think I am a dog to be beaten?" He made a sudden thrust with his jagged stick and Thunder Horse took another step backward.

"I fight when I must. You are a warrior as well. I see that. But there is no need for us to fight, Sauk." It wasn't the time for it. Thunder Horse could kill no Sauk, nor make an enemy of one. Not now when he meant to ask his Sauk woman to marry him. Tomorrow Runner lunged at him again with the stick and Thunder Horse turned and sprinted away through the woods, Tomorrow Runner's mad laughter burning in his ears.

He stopped at the river, anger rising up in him, but he shook his head and took a slow deep breath. He had run, but he had done the right thing. Why kill a Sauk; why fight a madman? Thunder Horse plunged into the river and began swimming toward the island where he had made his temporary camp, where he would remain until the Sauk spirit woman realized what Thunder Horse knew: that she already loved him.

Black Hawk took Strikes the Enemy by the elbow as the chief walked toward the council hut. "You know which way this must go. There is only one way to vote, Strikes the Enemy."

"And why is our war leader giving advice to a civil chief? This is not your time, Black Hawk. We are not at war." Strikes the Enemy disengaged his arm from Black Hawk's grip and halted. "I know this dream-walker of yours has been talking to the council about Ke-ke-tai. Does she have some power over you?"

"She has the power of her dreams and her wisdom," Black Hawk answered. "She is young, yet she sees much we do not."

"I do not need the advice of a young girl."

"Good advice is worthy no matter what the source. Now I, Black Hawk, am telling you: what has happened to Ke-ke-tai is a disgrace to our people. Our good faith has been trodden. Did not Stoddard make a promise? Has he kept it? If Sachim says that this is so, is she not correct? If the youngest child or our oldest woman speaks the truth, it is still the truth."

"Keokuk says—"

"*You* are no child, Strikes the Enemy, you know why

Keokuk says what he does. He thinks the Americans will make him rich. There are many of them and they wish to trade. He cannot see beyond his dreams of power and wealth."

"I cannot say how I will vote," Strikes the Enemy said, shaking his head.

"There is only one way to vote. We will not make war over this. But someone must speak to Stoddard, someone must see that Ke-ke-tai is set free. Do we wish to make another Tomorrow Runner of him? What of Little Creek, who cries in the night? What of the pride of the Sauk?"

"I must go."

"Go then," Black Hawk said angrily. "But remember that the souls of all of the Sauk nation, of all those who have walked the long Hanging Trail, hear you as you speak in council."

Black Hawk turned away in disgust and Strikes the Enemy after a moment proceeded to the council hut, angry himself. Angry and a little ashamed.

Black Hawk walked to the river to await the vote, ashamed of his council friends. No one wanted war, everyone wanted peace, but Ke-ke-tai was Sauk. All Black Hawk wished was for the council, some or all of them, to go down to St. Louis and tell Stoddard that this could no longer be tolerated, that Ke-ke-tai must have his white trial or be set free to return to his tribe.

That was all that Sachim wanted. She too was at the river, half a mile upstream from where Black Hawk sat, angrily tossing pebbles at the great river, the Provider, the Common Bond, the Destroyer.

The sun was setting beyond the trees on the western shore and the great river shone red and gold, sparkling with a thousand tribal memories, with a thousand maidens' dreams and warriors' ambitions. There was always the river; there were always the Sauk. So it must be; so it would be.

Why did her eyes go to the little island offshore where the sun lit the tips of the birch trees with golden fire and the deep shadows of the trees stained the bright water of the great river? Why did she sit and watch the island and feel the deep emotion of a coming dream in her soul? It was not time to dream; it was not time for such emotions, but still the feeling was there like the haunting wonderful implication of night wishes destined to fade to joyous daylight reality.

When the council emerged from their meeting lodge Sachim

knew it. There was a low murmuring from the village as the people moved toward the lodge, speculating. She returned to the village, meeting Black Hawk on the path.

"What have they decided?" Sachim asked. Black Hawk could only shake his head.

Emerging from the trees, they knew. Young men were dancing, women embracing. "They will ask for Ke-ke-tai's release," a boy shouted as he raced past them, and Sachim smiled with relief. Could Stoddard refuse the Sauk council? Black Hawk thought not.

"We are still powerful, are we not? Stoddard will fear our anger. He will do as the council wishes."

Quash-qua-me, Pa-she-pa-ho, and Ou-che-qua-ka were to go down to St. Louis in the morning. They would explain to Stoddard how the Sauk felt: Ke-ke-tai had not been given his promised trial and so he must be released.

Sachim said, "Now they have looked into their hearts. Now they have done what is right."

"And a part of that is due to you, Sachim," Black Hawk answered.

"To me?"

"Yes, I don't think the council chiefs could endure more of your badgering." Then Black Hawk smiled, feeling elated himself with the decision. In the back of his mind had been the idea that he would take a few selected warriors like White Bear and free Ke-ke-tai from the white prison by force. He would let no Sauk rot away in a foreign jail. Now that was unnecessary, or so he believed. Stoddard, the American governor, would certainly give in to their demands; he feared the Sauk too much, even more than he feared his white settlers.

Napope made the announcement formally to the tribe, speaking from a tree stump. Sachim watched and listened as the old man laboriously worked his way through a flowery speech which veered from the honor of the Sauk to praising the great dead warriors and promising future happiness.

She felt the great presence at her shoulder and turned her head to see White Bear there. The huge Sauk warrior glanced at her once shyly and then pretended to return his attention to Napope. He was so shy around her, this massive and brave warrior. Many times he had hinted at wanting to marry Sachim, but never once had he built up the nerve to say so. That was for the best.

White Bear was like a brother to Sachim. A friend, a strong shoulder to lean on. When a new lodge had to be built for Grandmother, it was White Bear who did most of the labor. When they needed meat, it was White Bear who brought venison and duck. He was a good friend, a strong brother, but he could never be a husband, a lover. Sachim looked up at the warrior, smiled, and briefly took his hand in hers as Napope finished his long speech.

She held his huge callused hand and watched as the civil chief of the Sauk spoke, but her mind was far away. On the island. She knew. She knew that the Sioux waited there and she could not banish him from her heart, no matter how she tried.

The barn meeting was bitter and anger-filled. Henry Greeley, who had already endured three unsatisfactory meetings with Governor Stoddard, was in a white-hot rage from the time he entered the building.

"Still hasn't hanged that Indian. Two months and he still hasn't hanged the bastard!"

Charles Simpson, who had been wagonmaster on the settlers' westward emigration and had stayed on to be acting town mayor, shook his head and tried to calm Greeley down.

"Hank, you know the bind Stoddard's in. Do you want a war with the Sauk? My God, they'd overrun us in one day! You'd have no farm, likely no family left. They can't just take the man out and lynch him."

"He killed three men. Carney was a friend of mine. So was Lucas. They were friends to all of us. Traveled west with us. Fought Comanche with us. You got a short memory, Simpson."

"Short memory? You know that's not so, Hank. Yeah, I knew Carney, liked the ornery Irishman too. Yeah, I fought beside you and Luke at Trigger Bend. That just hasn't got anything to do with *now*."

"Seems to me it does," the voice from the back of the barn said, and Simpson lifted his eyes to the land surveyor.

"What have you got to do with this, Ferguson?"

Joshua Ferguson stepped forward from the shadows to say, "I'm white, ain't I? That's what it's got to do with me. Whose land is this going to be? Ours or the Indian's? What

kind of safety have we got here for our kids, our women, if
the Indians can get away with murder!"

A murmur of support went up from the gathered farmers.
Simpson shook his head and asked for quiet. He waited
while the voices subsided, wondering about this Ferguson.
The man seemed to crave trouble. Just why, Simpson couldn't
guess; all he knew was that it was the last thing any settler in
a country where they were vastly outnumbered by the Indians needed. When the buzz of conversation had subsided,
Simpson went on.

"There's a new negotiator on his way. The Indiana governor.
Let's let Harrison have his chance at solving this before we
get ourselves excited. Use common sense. We don't need
trouble with the Sauk. It's a hard enough land as it is.
Think! Don't listen to rabble-rousers."

Joshua Ferguson folded his arms and smiled at Ginger
Sweet. Simpson could talk all he wanted. The people were
mad. Ferguson meant to see that they stayed that way,
stirred up and angry. It shouldn't be that difficult.

When the meeting finally broke up and the settlers were
making their way home by torchlight, Joshua Ferguson col-
lared Henry Greeley. "Didn't accomplish much, did it?" the
surveyor said.

"Not a damn thing," Hank huffed. "Where I'm from, that
Indian would've been lynched a month ago."

"What gives this Simpson all that power?"

"Long story," Hank Greeley said, walking with Ferguson
to his horse. "He was our wagonmaster. Folks just kind of
let him continue to take charge."

"He's not doing a hell of a good job of it, is he?" Ferguson swung aboard his horse while Sweet, his bulldog face
impassive, held the bridle.

"Not much," Greeley said, looking back at the barn,
where lanterns still glowed.

"I wouldn't worry about it, Greeley. This country's going
to change—and fast. I've got a lot of plans and I want a few
men with me who stand on the right side of the fence. I
think you're one."

With that, Ferguson was gone. Greeley, eyes narrowed,
watched the surveyor ride away. What was he talking about
exactly? Who was this Joshua Ferguson, and what made him
think he was top dog? The odd thing was that listening to
him, watching him, Greeley believed him. One thing he did

know: if there was any way for Ferguson to take the power he thought was rightfully his, the man would do it. You could see it in his eyes. Nothing was too big for him, and he would do whatever it took to get where he wanted to go.

The night birds sang in the elms. An owl cut a fleeting broad-winged silhouette against the rising moon. Ke-ke-tai stood chanting his prayers, staring out the window. In frustration he grabbed the iron bars and yanked at them until his shoulders ached and his tendons popped. Then he bowed his head and, taking a dozen slow, calming breaths, began again chipping at the mortar that held the bars of his prison window.

He would not die here. He would be free. He would take Little Creek and cross the great river, escaping into Sioux country. If the Sauk would not stand by him, then that was the way it must be. He would steal Little Creek from her father's lodge and go out onto the long plains.

He would not die here.

4

QUASH-QUA-ME looked back again at the village of the Sauk. Now he could see no one waving, wishing them a successful journey. The old chief lifted his eyes to the cloud-streaked sky and then glanced at his companions, the other council members who would speak to Stoddard about Ke-ke-tai's release. Pa-she-pa-ho, painted, his roached hair dyed red, seemed ready to fall asleep on his horse. Pa-she-pa-ho was younger than Quash-qua-me but claimed this his years as a warrior had worn his body out. He slept much, said little. Ou-che-qua-ka, called the Squirrel, was given to constant chatter and many times he had put Pa-she-pa-ho to sleep at council meetings with his involved tales. Just now the Squirrel too was silent.

The council members had been followed for a little way. Pa-she-pa-ho had pointed it out to Quash-qua-me and the old chief had just nodded. Who knew what Tomorrow Runner was thinking, what he would do? Quash-qua-me at times regretted his vote to turn the young warrior over to the Sioux for punishment. At the time it had seemed necessary to keep the peace between the two powerful tribes; but he hadn't foreseen what it would do to destroy what had been a fine, proud young man.

Keokuk drifted his pony toward the three council chiefs. He rode with his head up, mouth set arrogantly, and Quash-qua-me turned his eyes away. What did he want now? Keokuk had grown too large in his own dream. The young council chief pushed for more power, claiming that the spirits were with him: the Prophet had told him so.

"I will ride with you," Keokuk announced as he rode his red horse up beside the three older men.

"We have been delegated to speak to Stoddard," the Squirrel said.

"Yes, but I will ride with you. Can I hurt our cause?" Keokuk asked.

"We have been delegated," the Squirrel repeated. Quash-qua-me remained silent. What did Keokuk want? He had appeared to be indifferent to Ke-ke-tai's fate; now he had attached himself to the delegation. Perhaps some "dream" of the Prophet had encouraged Keokuk to come. It served no purpose to question Keokuk further or to deny him the right to ride along if he wished, so Quash-qua-me said nothing, yet he did not like it. All men do things for a reason. Keokuk was no different. Quash-qua-me again looked to the sky and then settled his gaze on the trail to St. Louis.

William Henry Harrison stood at the governor's window looking out at the prison in much the same way Stoddard had, but Harrison wasn't Stoddard. Where Stoddard saw problems, Harrison, the third son of the Declaration of Independence signer Benjamin Harrison, militiaman, states-man, gentleman farmer, saw solutions. Mistakes were made. You went past them. Nothing at all was solved by sitting and waiting for Providence to accomplish what you wished accomplished.

The President, a man Harrison had known for most of his life, wanted the Louisiana country settled as a defense against future claims by Spain or France, against incursions by the British, who were still active up and down the Mississippi Valley, wooing the Indians, planning for a second Colonial War twenty-eight years after the first.

Jefferson wanted to solidify the American claim to this new acquisition by settling the land, not by simply raising a flag. Very well then, Harrison thought, we shall do it.

The Sauk must want something. All people want something. Was it money, gifts, pacts, perhaps the release of the Indian prisoner? "There is always a way if the will is great enough," Harrison said to himself, repeating his father's words. "All that is needed is to find it."

"Is everything suitable, Mr. Harrison?"

Harrison turned at the sound of Stoddard's voice. The man looked tired. His absurd plan to convince some Indian magic woman to speak for United States interests had fallen through and he seemed to lack the imagination to proceed further.

"The accommodations? Splendid. This Indian, Stoddard . . ."

"The Sauk prisoner?"

"Yes. You have a bargaining chip there, you realize." Harrison remained standing, his military uniform precisely creased, as Stoddard sank into a chair.

"The settlers would lynch me if I released him. Is *that* what you're suggesting?"

"Under the right circumstances, yes. If people don't like it—well, they'll get over it, Governor," Harrison said confidently. Stoddard stared at him morosely. It was easy for Harrison to make the suggestion. No one would blame the Indiana governor. Stoddard watched the falling maple leaves drift past his window, thinking of his own falling career.

It was easy for Harrison to find solutions—none of the blame could be assigned to him, only the credit.

The corporal was very red-faced. A Minnesota man, he was unused to the weather in Louisiana Territory. It was late fall but the weather had turned hot and humid the last few days.

"What is it, Day?" Stoddard asked irritably.

"Sir, Sergeant Tyne reports that a delegation of Sauk Indians has come to seek an interview."

Harrison turned with interest. "Indians?"

"Tyne says they're high-ranking men, sir. Council chiefs or something."

"Show them in," Harrison said, assuming authority. The corporal looked at Stoddard questioningly.

"Show them in, Day," the governor echoed unhappily.

"Yes, sir."

The man turned sharply and went out, closing the door. Harrison's eagerness showed in his eyes, in the flush creeping across his face. "You know these people, Stoddard?"

"If they are from Black Hawk's band, council members, I've met with them before."

"You can guess what they want."

"Ke-ke-tai."

"Then they can have him. We have an opportunity here, Stoddard. A chance to forge a peace and solidify Jefferson's mandate."

Stoddard nodded dismally. All he saw in this was a fresh problem. He wondered at Harrison's constant optimism. When the door opened again, Amos Stoddard turned wearily toward it, wondering what new Gethsemane was about to be visited upon him.

Keokuk led the way into the room, confidence and pomposity radiating from his tall figure, black eyes, and broad mouth. He alone was not painted. The older chiefs followed custom and wore their colors.

Harrison's eyes fell instantly on Keokuk, sensing something in this young chief that might be useful. Ambition, greed? What it was, Harrison couldn't define, but he thought he could work with this Sauk.

Stoddard made the introductions, stumbling over the names badly. That done, he offered the Indians chairs. Only Keokuk accepted. Two of the chiefs chose to sit on the floor, while the Squirrel wandered the room picking up articles, examining them.

"We have come to find out about Ke-ke-tai," Quash-qua-me began. "What has happened to him? Why hasn't he returned home?"

"We've had to delay his trial," Stoddard said.

"Why?" Quash-qua-me asked. "You told us Ke-ke-tai would have a chance to tell his story and then he would return home. This was the promise you made, this is what we believed."

"And he will have his trial. Shortly," the governor insisted. Harrison glanced at him as Stoddard continued, blundering through a nonsensical explanation.

Quash-qua-me listened politely to Stoddard's fabricated story of the problems of selecting a jury and finding a lawyer to represent Ke-ke-tai. The old chief nodded from time to time, and then, when Stoddard was through, repeated his question: "Why hasn't Ke-ke-tai returned home as you promised?"

"I have just tried to explain, sir," Stoddard said, growing more flustered.

Harrison took a hand. "I'm sure we can see that Ke-ke-tai is released promptly so that he can return home with you to your village."

Stoddard looked stunned. Quash-qua-me nodded with satisfaction. *This* American father was a great improvement over the other.

"This afternoon or in the morning, whichever you prefer," Harrison went on, "we can go over and let you visit Ke-ke-tai, and then the day after, we can release him to you."

"Governor Harrison—" Stoddard began indignantly. But Harrison had been sent down to handle things and he had apparently already made his decision. As Stoddard watched, Harrison took a cigar from a cedar chest and lit it. Seeing the interest in Pa-she-pa-ho's eyes, the governor of Indiana offered a cigar to the Sauk, who promptly lit it with enjoyment.

Keokuk said, "Why wait two days to release Ke-ke-tai if he is to be released."

Harrison smiled at the shrewd Sauk leader. "That will allow us time to discuss other matters of importance to both the Sauk and the Americans, Keokuk."

"Matters of importance?"

"Yes, letters of peace, treaty matters." Harrison shrugged. "Perhaps a document can be drawn up so that nothing like the Ke-ke-tai matter occurs again. We can agree, for example, to allow Sauk justice to try Sauk crimes, white courts to try white criminals. Basic treaties which ensure against misunderstandings such as this one."

"Also," Harrison went on, "I would like to have a firm agreement on where whites may settle, which land they may not cross. All of these points are important to our mutual welfare."

"We are only four of the council," the Squirrel said.

"Yes, I realize that. You will of course have to have any treaty ratified in full council. My superiors will also have to sign any treaty we make, but we must have an understanding between us if we are to share this land."

Keokuk listened closely, certain that the man was after something else, something he hadn't spoken of. He was about to ask a question when Harrison rose sharply and walked to a sideboard near the huge bookcase.

"I think I will have a brandy. Will you gentlemen join me?"

Stoddard turned, gripping the arms of his chair tightly. He didn't like any of this. What was Harrison thinking?

"Brandy?" Pa-she-pa-ho asked with interest.

"It is like rum," Keokuk said knowledgeably. Rum Pa-she-pa-ho knew about. The British frequently gave them barrels of rum as gifts. Pa-she-pa-ho knew what it was and he was fond of it. He accepted a glass of brandy from Harrison, as did the other older chiefs. Keokuk declined. He wanted his head clear.

Harrison seated himself again, sipping at his own brandy. "This matter of Ke-ke-tai should never have happened," the governor of Indiana said. "I have dealt with the Fox in Indiana and with the Miami. We've had no trouble between us because we have met and talked and signed good treaties. There are many whites there now. Everyone lives in peace."

Pa-she-pa-ho held out his glass and had it refilled. The room was growing warm and he was quite content. The American had a pleasant voice and he spoke intelligently. He took another drink of brandy, swallowing half a snifter, and sat puffing on his cigar as Harrison droned on. It was difficult for Pa-she-pa-ho to continue thinking in English so he turned his thoughts inward, hardly hearing the American at all.

The Squirrel still moved about the room. Stoddard kept an eye on him as if he had invited a burglar into his home. A pair of silver candlesticks caught the Squirrel's eye and as Harrison spoke he picked them up admiringly, running a finger over the ornate work on the candleholders.

Harrison paused and said, "Keep those if you like."

The Squirrel turned, beaming. Stoddard looked at Harrison as if the man had lost his mind—giving Stoddard's household items to the Sauk.

"There will be many gifts, many valuable gifts," Harrison went on. "As friends, we expect to give you gifts of peace."

"And what do you want us to give you?" Keokuk asked pointedly.

Harrison looked surprised, thrust out his lower lip, and shrugged. "Nothing at all, Keokuk. We ask for nothing in the way of gifts. There may be certain rights we would like to purchase from the Sauk."

"Rights?" Quash-qua-me asked dully. His glass was full for the third time, soon to be empty for the third time.

"As an example," Harrison said, leaning forward toward

Keokuk, "there is a family called Fitzgerald up along the Plum River. On one side of the river they grow corn, on the other hay for their horses and oxen. Why? Because their land is encircled by Sauk land. Fitzgerald must cross the river four or five times a day. If he were allowed to farm the land adjacent to his, his life would be much easier. The Sauk do not use that land for farming or for hunting. Why not let Fitzgerald buy the land from you?"

"We do not sell land," the Squirrel said. He was at a mahogany side table, suggestively handling a silver tray.

"No, I understand that," Harrison said easily. "By all means—take the tray if you would like it."

"The land is held in common," Keokuk said.

"Yes, I know. But certainly exceptions could be made. Some sort of lease, perhaps where the Sauk own the land but a man like Fitzgerald might use it. There are certain cases like this one where the Sauk might also make a gesture of friendship—and be paid for it as well. What use is land you are not tilling, hunting on, or dwelling on?"

Harrison smiled, spread his hands, and leaned back, having made his point. Keokuk knew now. He looked at the other council chiefs. The Squirrel was still moving acquisitively around the room. Pa-she-pa-ho was sitting cross-legged, a dead cigar in his mouth, drinking brandy. Quash-qua-me, who appeared to have no interest in things now that Harrison had promised to release Ke-ke-tai, seemed far distant.

Keokuk knew now; he asked, "How much payment might there be? How much in gold dollars for the Sauk?"

Harrison smiled thinly. He had found his man. "I am authorized to pay up to two thousand gold dollars to the Sauk for certain small land concessions." In fact he was authorized to pay up to five thousand and was willing to go even higher on his own authority.

"Two thousand gold dollars is not much for an entire people," Keokuk said softly.

"Did I not say two thousand a year?" Harrison asked absently, knowing full well he hadn't. Keokuk's eyes shifted with interest.

"What land is he talking about?" Quash-qua-me asked from out of his haze.

"The Crow Meadow," Keokuk answered.

"Oh. Crow Meadow." Quash-qua-me waved a hand. "It is nothing. Nothing is there."

"Two thousand dollars a year for the Crow Meadow for this Fitzgerald to farm?" Keokuk asked.

"You misunderstand me," Harrison answered. "I said I have two thousand gold dollars to spend. For that small piece of land I could not offer that much. Perhaps we can take out a map and I could show you other small parcels you might lease to white settlers. But first," Harrison said, rising, "let us eat. I can promise you good beef and roasted sweet corn, rice, and good wine."

"Brandy," Pa-she-pa-ho said in a slurred voice. He held out his glass as he staggered to his feet.

"Of course brandy, my good friend Pa-she-pa-ho! Stoddard, why don't you give this man a cask to take home with him? We have talked enough for now. Let us eat and drink, smoke and be friends."

"We shall be friends," Pa-she-pa-ho swore, moving to Harrison, resting his hands on his shoulders. "You treat us like the Spanish father. Before, I did not know what to make of the Americans. Now I know Harrison shall be my friend."

"And you shall be mine," Harrison promised.

"Let us eat, then, and sing songs and dance," Pa-she-pa-ho said loudly.

"Excellent idea," Harrison said, slapping the painted Sauk on the back. "I want to see you dance. Even the Shawnee say the Sauk are the finest dancers there are."

"Shawnee do not dance good . . ." Pa-she-pa-ho paused for a drink of brandy. Harrison saw that the Squirrel had appropriated Stoddard's ceremonial saber, and he nodded, smiling as the council chief strapped it on.

Keokuk had seen the Squirrel pick up the sword and several other small items. He felt only disdain for the Squirrel. Keokuk did not have that sort of petty acquisitiveness. His ambitions were much larger. Much.

Ke-ke-tai heard the singing from the governor's house and he frowned, peering out the window. Lights blazed in the mansion windows. One voice, raised in a war whoop, sounded like Pa-she-pa-ho's. If it was Pa-she-pa-ho, what was he doing at the mansion, singing? Why did no one come to take him out of this place? It was dark and cold and the floor was stone. He could see no trees, nor feel the wind on his cheek, and Little Creek was far away, perhaps by now thinking of some other warrior.

Angrily Ke-ke-tai took his stub of the knife from its hiding place and began again chipping at the mortar that held the bars on the window in place, working at his task until his hands were bloody and raw once more.

Outside the window, the night was cool, and the sky clear, dusted with silver stars which paled now before the huge and golden half-moon rising in the east.

Hank Greeley watched the moon without interest. There was no romance in the big frontiersman's heart. If something couldn't be bought or sold or utilized, he had little interest in it. Greeley turned, musket in hands, at the sound of approaching footsteps.

Joshua Ferguson appeared indistinctly, and walked to Greeley, his big bulldog-faced silent companion behind him.

"Well? You find out anything?" Greeley growled.

"From Day. The governors are in there dancing around with a bunch of Sauk Indians, getting drunk and living high."

"Bastard politicians."

"Day says he overheard them—they're going to let the killer go."

"Let him go!" Greeley was so angry he sputtered. "After murdering three white men."

"Apparently. What do we do about it?" the surveyor asked.

"What do you think we do about it?" Greeley responded.

Greeley turned then and stared at the jailhouse. If he had been watching Joshua Ferguson instead, he would have seen the beginnings of a smile lift the corners of the surveyor's mouth. Ferguson was pleased with himself and the way things were going. They could hardly have been any better.

Just now there wasn't much left for Ferguson to do but wait. To sit back and wait for the gravy. He nodded to Ginger Sweet and they walked away, leaving Greeley to his brooding.

Greeley stood silently in the woods for a long minute, not realizing he was alone. When he did look around to find

Ferguson gone, it was unimportant to him. He could still see the lights in the governor's mansion, hear Indian shrieks and whoops and chanting, and he tightened his jaw.

Making his mind up suddenly, he gripped his musket still more tightly and started for the jailhouse.

Keokuk sat behind the governor's desk. The room was nearly dark—a candle flickered dully on the opposite wall. Beyond the heavy door Quash-qua-me was singing a Thunderbird song drunkenly. Pa-she-pa-ho, wearing a plumed hat, blue coat, and the saber the Squirrel had taken as a present, was dancing in the great hall. None of that meant anything to Keokuk.

Only his dream mattered—a dream which the Prophet had agreed was a true dream. Keokuk, leader of his nation. Keokuk, vastly wealthy, vastly powerful.

"It is your fate," the mustached Prophet had told him one night over a small fire. "Who is Black Hawk, who is Tecumseh? Who is Far Eagle? War leaders, men of pride. But since they are war leaders they consider matters wrongly. Everything is seen in terms of warfare. Black Hawk seeks alliances with the British for strength of arms. If he is displeased, he speaks of war always.

"Why make war when there is power to be gained more simply?" the Prophet had asked. "Why fight the whites? Stupid. They are weak, but wealthy. They will give us anything—guns, rum, gold, goods—and if we do not want them here later, we will just tell them to go and they will go, being afraid of us. They are too few and we are like the leaves on a tree. We will take their money, Keokuk," the Prophet said, bending forward so that the low embers made a red-gold mask of his face, "we will take their guns and their horses and give them that which costs us nothing in return. They want only one thing.

"The land."

The heavy door swung inward and Keokuk lifted his eyes, knowing who it was.

"Harrison."

"We need to talk, Keokuk. We need to talk about a land treaty."

Keokuk smiled in the darkness. He had the man where he wanted him. The Prophet was right: the white Americans were fools.

It was dawn before the treaty had been hammered out, before Keokuk and the council chiefs—drunk and tired—had signed it. Harrison signed for the United States, Stoddard for the territory of Louisiana. Sergeant Tyne, Corporal Day, and a Spaniard named Delgado witnessed the signing, the formal exchange of copies of the treaty, and the payment of gold money to the Sauk chiefs.

"Articles of a treaty made at St. Louis in the district of Louisiana," the treaty began, "between William Henry Harrison, superintendent of Indian affairs for the said district and territory, and the chiefs and headmen of the Sauk and Fox tribes."

At the insistence of a weary but still-semilucid Quashqua-me, Articles Six and Seven were inserted into the treaty, which would come to be known as the Treaty of 1804:

Article 6. If any citizen of the United States or other white person should form a settlement upon lands which are the property of the Sauk or Fox tribes, upon complaint being made thereof to the superintendent or other person having charge of the affairs of the Indians, such intruder shall forthwith be removed.

Article 7. As long as the lands which are now ceded to the United States remain their property, the Indians belonging to the said tribes shall enjoy the privilege of hunting upon them.

"Well?" Harrison poured himself a glass of brandy as the rising sun stained the windows of the mansion crimson and purple. He was weary but ebullient.

Stoddard shook his head and Harrison had trouble comprehending the meaning behind the gesture—frustration, resignation, his own weariness?

"That man, Keokuk," Stoddard said at last. "He would have sold you the land between here and the Rocky Mountains for a price."

"The contract is legal."

"God!" Stoddard read the copy of the treaty he held. "From the Gasconde to the Jefferson River, to the Mississippi to the mouth of the Ouisconsing River, thence to the Fox River from Lake Sasaegan . . . do you know how much land is involved, Harrison?"

"I know precisely, Stoddard—that was what I was sent here to do. Purchase seven million acres for new settlement."

"That includes most of western Illinois," Stoddard said as if he hadn't been interrupted.

"Well, then?" Harrison said, leaning back. "The Sauk didn't like us buying their land from the French, did they? They said that it wasn't the French's to sell. Now we have purchased it from the Sauk themselves. Tell me, Stoddard, what is wrong with that? The land will be settled by Americans. I held no gun to the heads of these Indian chiefs. I assure you that Congress will ratify this treaty quickly. We have done our job. What are you worried about? What can possibly be troubling you?"

Stoddard turned slowly, placing the treaty down on the desk. "Black Hawk," he said quietly, "only Black Hawk."

It was dawn and no one had yet come to open his door, to set Ke-ke-tai free. It was dawn and the mortar at last crumbled away from the bottom of the iron bar in his window. He tugged at the bar, twisting it free. Glancing anxiously at the door to his cell, he placed the bar gently on the floor.

There was room; just enough room. Ke-ke-tai leapt up, forced one arm and his head into the gap he had made between the bars, and wriggled through. His heart was pounding, his blood whirring in his ears. He landed on the ground outside on his arm and shoulder, leapt up and began to run.

He was free—running with all of his strength, his long legs carrying him toward the forest, toward Little Creek.

And then he was no longer running. Something struck him in the back of his neck and he folded up, his mouth filling with blood, his arms and legs shaking in futile, meaningless motion as his face scraped across the hard-packed earth of the alley. He lay there utterly still, the roaring of the gun in his ears. He stared at the rising sun until it burst into a vast fireball and then went black. Then Ke-ke-tai knew nothing else.

Hank Greeley walked slowly toward the sprawled body of the Indian. The constable, still in his underwear, burst from the jailhouse, musket in hand.

"Passin' by," Greeley said. "Saw the prisoner makin' a run for it."

The constable looked at Greeley and then at the dead Sauk. He felt his mouth tighten and go dry, but he could only shrug and ask his deputies to take the body away.

Keokuk had heard the shot and he went to the window of the white bedroom where he had been sleeping. Ke-ke-tai, he thought immediately. But it did not matter. Ke-ke-tai had been no one, a crazy young man always in trouble. Keokuk shut the window and went back to sleep, to dream of gold and many horses.

With the dawn, Sachim had awoken sharply. She sat up in her bed, feeling something close to fear leaping in her breast. Her heart pounded crazily for no reason at all.

She could see the soft glow of sunrise outside her lodge door, hear the birds rustling in the elms. Everything was as it should have been; yet everything was wrong.

She couldn't rid herself of the dark feeling as she dressed, tied up her hair, and went out into the morning. A long walk, she decided, was what she needed to clear her head. A long walk and then a swim in the great river.

The village was coming to life now, the children rushing out to play, pulling their moccasins on as they ran, calling to each other, dogs yapping at their heels.

The new horse was there, standing behind her lodge. It was a tall blue roan with an odd black splotch on its flank that made Sachim think of a many-armed star.

She smiled before she remembered to frown. Was the Sioux man crazy? He had seen her only that one time. Why did he not find himself a Sioux woman if he felt the need to marry? The roan lifted its muzzle to Sachim and she stroked its velvety nose absently.

"Crazy man," she said aloud. "Crazy Sioux man."

She walked on. The muscles in her long calves and thighs stretched out and her blood began pumping freely. It did nothing at all to clear her mind, to erase the foreboding she felt—or to chase the Sioux man from her thoughts.

The river was quick and cold. Sachim slipped from her buckskin dress and fringed moccasins and waded into the water, feeling its strength, its caress. Water endlessly flowing. Eternal river. Bright and powerful and timeless.

She emerged dripping from the river, the sunlight making jewels of the droplets on her coppery flesh. She stood naked for a minute on the beach, feeling the cool wind touch her body. She ran her hands over her breasts and watched the distant island before, shaking her head, she dressed quickly and returned to the village. Grandmother would need her breakfast.

In the afternoon the runners began to come into camp. The village was alert and anxious. The council chiefs were returning and the news was good. Four Sauk had been seen riding northward. Quash-qua-me, the Squirrel, and Pa-she-pa-ho had been successful. The fourth man would be Ke-ke-tai.

White Bear found Sachim at her grandmother's lodge. He ducked low to enter and nodded to Sachim. "They are coming. Will you walk down with me to welcome them home?"

"In one minute. Let me build up Grandmother's fire. The evenings are damp now that the corn is in."

"I heard a tale . . ." White Bear began hesitantly, and Sachim turned from her crouch to look into the big man's open face.

"Yes?" she prompted.

"It is nothing."

"Then why mention it? What is it you want to know, White Bear?"

"Something about a Sioux horse," the Sauk said, stuttering. The man was vast and brave but he could hardly bring himself to speak to women. Sachim smiled inwardly.

"You are right, White Bear. It is nothing."

"But who was it?" he said. His face reflected jealousy, perhaps anger.

"Only Thunder Horse. Far Eagle's son."

White Bear kept his thoughts to himself. Thunder Horse was a handsome man, proud and sure, a man of rank. Any woman, White Bear thought, would prefer such a warrior to a vast and ungainly brave like himself.

"I did not know," he said at last, "that you wanted horses."

"I didn't!" Sachim said with a little laugh. "Thunder Horse is amusing himself, I think."

White Bear watched Sachim as she worked, watched the line of her jaw, the full, pleasant lips, the wide liquid eyes, her long thighs. White Bear knew, if Sachim did not: Thunder Horse was not amusing himself. He had seen a rare beauty among the Sauk and wished to possess her.

"I did not know," White Bear said. Sachim walked to him and lifted her hands to hold his head between them.

"I wanted no horses, White Bear. I want no man just now. None, do you understand?"

But even as she spoke, she recalled the haughty, high-ranking Sioux with the deep compelling eyes. Her hands dropped away from White Bear's face and she looked around at the low fire, at her aged, sleeping grandmother.

"Let us go greet Ke-ke-tai, then."

"Yes," White Bear said. "Let us greet Ke-ke-tai and congratulate the council."

"White Bear." She touched his arm and smiled up at the warrior. "You are a good friend to me."

"I will always be your friend," White Bear answered, but that would never be enough for the Sauk brave. Sachim's hand fell away from his arm as the smile slipped from her lips. Together they started toward the village as the new gift horse whickered at them.

It was dusk before the party returning from St. Louis was visible riding up the riverside trail in the shadows of the oaks. The river was already deep violet, the sky golden orange. Black Hawk stood beside Sachim and White Bear, squinting into the near-darkness.

"I see Quash-qua-me," he said at last. "And there is Pa-she-pa-ho. The Squirrel looks to be asleep in his saddle."

White Bear said under his breath, "That is not Ke-ke-tai."

"What is Keokuk doing with them? Where is the prisoner?" Sachim said, and Black Hawk shook his head, a frown carving deep lines into his face.

"Look at the Squirrel," White Bear said, pointing a thick finger. "He wears a new coat—and a sword."

Sachim glanced at Black Hawk and then bit at her lip. Something was wrong. Something . . .

"It must have gone well," Strikes the Enemy said as he walked past them. "Look at the gifts they have brought back. Yes, it must have gone well."

"Then where is Ke-ke-tai?"

The gathered tribe parted to make room for the incoming horsemen. Keokuk looked pleased with himself, the others only tired as they rode straight toward the council hut.

"Come with me," Black Hawk said to Sachim. "Now."

He too knew there was something very wrong. Had Keokuk met the council members on the trail or had he gone down to St. Louis? Why would he do that?

Sachim's heart raced in her breast as she struggled to keep up with the long-legged Black Hawk. White Bear ambled along behind them. Already Quash-qua-me was down from his horse, entering the council hut. He was unsteady on his feet. In his hand he held a rolled piece of parchment such as the whites made their treaties on.

"A promise to let Ke-ke-tai free?" Sachim asked. Black Hawk shook his head. The man was intense, his jaw set. They reached the hut as Wabokisesiek did, and Sachim halted sharply as the mustached Prophet rounded the corner of the bark-and-pole lodge.

"Where are you going, woman?" the Prophet asked.

"Black Hawk has asked me to come."

"Black Hawk is not a council member."

"He has the right to sit," Sachim said angrily. She was frightened, but with White Bear still at her shoulder she had the nerve to speak up to the shaman.

The Prophet would have said something else but Napope, vast and lazy in his movements, had reached the hut, and with a last glance at Sachim, the shaman moved inside the lodge on the heels of the council chief.

"What now?" White Bear asked. "What is happening?"

Sachim had no answer for him. As the color faded from the sky and the frogs along the river began to chorus, they waited outside the council hut. A voice was suddenly raised in anger and it was Black Hawk's voice.

In another minute he emerged from the council house, shaking his head bitterly. He stood there taking deep slow breaths for a long minute.

"Come in, Sachim," he said at last. "Come in and hear this."

"But what is it . . . ?"

"Come in."

She wasn't usually allowed inside the council hut, for among the Sauk and Fox it was a male domain. If Black Hawk himself was seen as an outsider, she was no less than an intruder; nevertheless she followed the war leader inside to where the full council sat around a small fire. Keokuk's eyes flashed. Quash-qua-me noticed her entrance without expression. Pa-she-pa-ho just sat, head hanging. The Prophet rose angrily and jabbed a finger at Black Hawk.

"What is this woman doing here! What are you bringing her in for?"

Napope, morose and just now appearing older than his years, glanced at Black Hawk for an explanation.

"I have the right to be here," Black Hawk told the council chief. "Is that not so?"

"The girl—"

"The girl is here by my invitation. I have the right to have a counselor with me, a holy person even as Keokuk does."

"The Prophet is a true shaman," Keokuk said coldly. "He dreams for the people and so he is allowed."

"And so Sachim is allowed," Black Hawk said.

Napope looked from one man to the other and then raised a weary hand. "The woman may stay. This is not the time to debate this."

So Sachim sat beside Black Hawk, listening as the council took its first step toward tragedy.

"I still cannot understand this," Napope said. Before him the treaty paper was unrolled, weighted at the corners. "Where, then, is Ke-ke-tai?"

"Ke-ke-tai," Quash-qua-me said, "was killed. He tried to run from the jaail. He was killed."

"Stoddard would not release him?"

"Harrison would, the new American father, Harrison," the Squirrel said, holding his head. Gold epaulets gleamed on his shoulders. His saber was still at his waist.

"Then . . . ?" Strikes the Enemy asked.

"It was to be the next day, after we spoke. Perhaps we drank too much rum," Pa-she-pa-ho admitted. "We were pleased with Harrison's words. We believed he meant to release Ke-ke-tai. I still believe it."

"Then the warrior is dead," Napope said, and Sachim felt a chill creep through her. "Then Ke-ke-tai will not come home. We sent you to bring him home and you have returned with this." He snapped his finger against the treaty paper.

"The treaty is a good one," Keokuk insisted. "It will make our people wealthy. The Americans will pay us two thousand dollars each year and when we wish them to go, they must go."

"The treaty is a crime!" Black Hawk spat out. Napope tried to silence the war leader. It was not his place to speak; but there was no silencing him. "What have you done? Who can sell the land that our fathers gave us, that Manitou willed us?"

"We do not need the land!"

"Do you know how much land you have sold?" Black Hawk continued despite objections. There was fire in his eyes now. "Seven million acres! Do you know what that is?"

"Acres?" Strikes the Enemy inquired. "What is that, Black Hawk?"

"An acre is the amount of land a man can cultivate in a day with white plows and his oxen."

"Still . . ."

"Will we then see seven million whites?"

"Black Hawk, you are angry, but what you suggest is absurd," Napope said. "Still, I do not like this treaty."

"Harrison said no whites will come. Not for years. The land will be empty. We shall be paid," Keokuk said.

"Is that the future, Prophet?" Napope asked the shaman.

"The future is wealth," the Prophet answered after exchanging glances with Keokuk. The Prophet had spoken many times in council. His voice was deep and pleasant and his words well-thought-out. "The Sauk will only benefit. The fur trade alone will make us rich. When the whites do come, they will come bringing money. All of the Sauk and Fox will share in this wealth—"

"The Fox have not even been consulted," Black Hawk interrupted. "Ask Two-Knives what he thinks of this treaty!"

"The Sauk and Fox are one," Keokuk said smoothly, fighting to keep the irritation out of his voice. There had been enough resistance to this from the council heads without Black Hawk being allowed—against the law—to speak up like this.

"They will come," the Prophet went on, "they will grow a little corn, they will give us money. All will be well. This I dreamed."

Napope shook his head, still studying the treaty which he could not read. Suddenly he lifted his eyes to Sachim. "What do you dream, spirit woman? What do your spirits tell you?"

Sachim's mouth simply dropped open at first. Fascinated and amazed by the conversation, and feeling deep sorrow for Ke-ke-tai, who seemed to be forgotten by the council, she had not been expecting anyone to ask her her opinion.

She began to speak hesitantly, but as she progressed, it was as if another, clearer mind spoke through her lips, and she told the council of seven what she had dreamed.

"I have seen the whites come. I have seen our corn fall to them. In the winter there was hunger and in the summer hardship. The land slipped away from under us and we were wanderers on the earth. It was a time of blood and sorrow. Manitou was angry with us, for who can sell the wind, the great river, the land? Nothing can be sold except such things as can be carried away—that is the law, that is Manitou's wish. What are a people without a land?

"What shall we sell next? Our grandmothers, our babies? Our souls? Where do a people without a land go? Shall we be beggars on the earth? There is no law which allows land to be sold. If we grow wealthy from doing this evil thing, what good will that do our children and grandchildren and their children? It is an evil thing—and that is what I have dreamed."

Without realizing it, Sachim had come to her feet and moved forward to face the council chiefs one by one, her words filled with emotion as she clutched her breast and met their eyes. Keokuk was furious; the Prophet's face was dark. She did not care. All of her inhibitions and fears were gone. What she spoke now was from her dreams, and it was the truth.

"The treaty is bad, the treaty is a lie. Ke-ke-tai is gone, and our corn will be gone if we allow this to happen. We will have only white gold—and then what shall we do, buy corn from the Americans?

"It is a bad treaty, a lie, a shame on our people."

She finished speaking and felt a wave of embarrassment as she realized what she had done and how bold she had been, but Napope was nodding his head in agreement.

"The spirit woman is right. The land cannot be sold."

"Napope," Keokuk began, but the council chief silenced him.

"You have spoken. The Prophet has spoken. Black Hawk and his woman-dreamer have spoken. Now let us vote and say what is in our hearts."

Only Keokuk voted for the treaty in the end. Quash-qua-me, the Squirrel, and Pa-she-pa-ho repudiated the treaty, regretting the signing of it.

"Then it is done," Napope said at last. "The treaty must be ashes." He placed the corner of the document in the council fire and watched as it slowly burned. "That is the law. That is how it must be."

Sachim sat and observed, feeling proud, amazed at herself— and still a little frightened. Keokuk sat staring at her, and there was fire in the eyes of the Prophet. An evil and dark and angry fire.

"Someone must tell the whites," Strikes the Enemy said. "Someone must tell them that the Sauk council does not agree to this, that we are happy on our land and want none of their money."

Black Hawk said, "And what will they say? And where will this lead us? I do not like this, any of it!" Then the war leader stood and stalked from the council hut, leaving the council and a stunned Sachim behind.

After a minute she followed. Strikes the Enemy had begun to tell a story, Quash-qua-me to fill a pipe.

Outside it was clear and cold enough to cause Sachim's breath to show. Black Hawk had gone and the village had settled down for the evening. Fires glowed softly; the smell of meat cooking, of corn roasting, hung in the air.

Sachim was drawn to the river as she always was. She walked slowly to the beach, past the many canoes drawn up on the shore, and stood watching the quiet, darkly flowing, living creature which was the river.

Broad and eternal, it would never cease to flow, to grow wide at floodtime, to seek the sea. If it would not change, Sachim knew that she would, that she had come to a time of passage. This night she had become someone different, a woman. This night she had spoken to the council and if they had not accepted her, they had recognized her finally.

She would change and continue to grow; the Sauk would change and their way would alter. That she also knew on this night. The stars glowed softly in the sky above the Mississippi lands, and far to the south she imagined she could see the glow of many manmade lights against the darkness. The Americans were there; they too grew and contributed to the changes to come.

Did they sleep on this night with Ke-ke-tai dead? Or did they plan and build? Did they dream or sing songs or sit and wonder, as all men did, what time would construct, what time would tear down?

"Sir?" Corporal Day entered Stoddard's office, noticing the trunk open and nearly packed. The governor lifted bleary eyes to the soldier but said nothing as Day placed the letter at his elbow.

Stoddard waited until the man was gone to open the envelope with its presidential seal. Amos Stoddard scanned the letter and then read it again, his face assuming a twisted expression which was half smile, half agonized grimace.

He read the letter for the third time, staring at the signature beneath the line: "Thos. Jefferson, Pres. of the United States of America, done in Washington, D.C."

Then Stoddard rose and walked to his sideboard and its brandy bottle, not turning as the breeze from the open window blew Ke-ke-tai's pardon to the floor.

5

ELK RUN was fifteen summers old, limber and quick, a good hunter skilled with weapons. Just now he was using his arrows fitted with turtle-claw heads and his bow to hunt ducks among the wild rice. The turtle claw allowed the arrows to skim over the water like a skipping stone and take the ducks as they dozed or fed beneath the murky waters of the rice pond.

The teal ducks, startled by something unseen, took to wing just as Elk Run drew his hickory bow, and the Sauk youth sat down on the ground, smiling.

He would sit and wait, making a reed whistle for his younger sister, and in time the ducks would circle and settle again. The rice pond was their feeding ground.

With his small trade knife Elk Run began whittling, his mind and hands absorbed in the work. Beyond the pond he could hear the Des Moines rapids frothing and churning and the sound was pleasant. Elk Run's head came up and his eyes narrowed as there came another sound loud enough to be heard above the hiss of the rapids. Someone was calling, and the tongue was not Sauk.

Rising, Elk Run sheathed his knife, wiped his hands on his bare legs, and started toward the river, bow in hand. The ducks still circled overhead and Elk Run glanced skyward.

When he reached the river, he saw them. There were four keelboats on the river, and as they negotiated the rapids, men with long lines walked along the shore, chanting together, tugging the flat-bottomed boats through the white water.

Elk Run went to his belly and watched them for a few
minutes. Where could they be going? Far up the river like
the man Pike? When the last of the boats was past, Elk Run
got to his feet again, and moving through the sun-dappled,
leafless hickory and ash trees, he began to follow them,
leaping gray, fallen logs and mossy boulders as he scrambled
along the beach.

The ducks were forgotten, his sister's whistle abandoned.
This was more interesting, and perhaps more important.
Above the rapids the keelboats put in to shore and the Sauk
watched as the whites began unloading supplies.

They were soldiers, or at least some of them were, for
they wore uniforms. What were they doing here? For most
of the day Elk Run watched them. By evening they had
begun cutting timber with long two-man saws and axes.
Some of the logs were notched and placed on the ground.

Other men pitched tents. One began to cook. Elk Run
glanced at the sun and saw it was already dying. The trees
had long, crooked shadows stretching out from the bases of
their trunks. He lifted himself from the ground and started
homeward at a trot. What was happening here?

Tomorrow Runner was standing in the trail, his face painted,
his sharp stick in his hands, and Elk Run slowed his pace,
approaching the warrior slowly. Tomorrow Runner was a
friend, more, a man Elk Run had looked up to. Some said
he was mad now. Elk Run did not know if he was or not;
still Tomorrow Runner was his friend.

"Where are you running?"

Elk Run answered: "There are white soldiers above the
rapids. Building a lodge."

"British?"

"Americans. Black Hawk should know."

"Black Hawk is not here," Tomorrow Runner said. He
had crouched to squat, driving his stick aimlessly into the
dark earth. "There is something on the wind. He is in council
with the British chief, Hobbs."

"Well, then, the council should know," Elk Run said. His
friend didn't answer. His face with its skull paint was unread-
able. Tomorrow Runner looked up, made a scoffing noise,
and spat.

"The council," he said, shaking his head. "Will they help

us, give us good advice? Did they help me, did they help Ke-ke-tai?"

Elk Run braced himself for one of Tomorrow Runner's long polemics, but that was all he said.

Elk Run waited another minute, shrugged, and walked past Tomorrow Runner, who continued to jab at the dirt. What demons lived in the man now, Elk Run thought.

"Wait!" Tomorrow Runner called, and Elk Run turned back.

"Where are the whites?"

"Beyond the rapids on this side of the river."

"Have they women with them?"

"Women . . . ? No, Tomorrow Runner, no women."

Tomorrow Runner turned away then and walked up the path, leaving Elk Run to jog along the trail toward the village, wondering at Tomorrow Runner's mind.

It was Keokuk, of all the council members, that Elk Run found first, nearly running into him as the civil chief returned from the river with a string of fish.

"The white Americans are building something above the rapids, Keokuk. I don't know what it is, but how can they build there?"

Keokuk didn't answer the question. "The far side of the river?"

"This side."

"All right, then." Keokuk waved a hand as if shooing a fly and walked away from the young warrior, leaving an unasked question frozen in Elk Run's throat. Elk Run felt his ears burning. The man treated him like a child. Hadn't he three notched eagle feathers? Hadn't he counted coup against the Cherokee? It was no wonder Tomorrow Runner hated them all and thought them fools.

If only Black Hawk were there. Black Hawk would know what to do, what to say. He wouldn't hold a council meeting either, he would walk right up to the whites and ask them what they were doing, demand that they leave that land. Black Hawk was a man, a warrior, as was Elk Run. Keokuk was a politician.

Elk Run walked back to his family lodge. He was hungry. Besides, he had to exchange the duck arrows in his quiver for steel-headed war arrows.

Captain Lord Evin Bolingbroke Hobbs had traveled a

long way from Fort Meigs in Ontario to speak to Black
Hawk in the wooded valley north of the Pecatonica River of
Illinois. The British soldier had left his scarlet uniform behind and was traveling in buckskins, his blond hair curling
over his collar. He was tall, somewhat haughty, and given to
reckless tactics, understanding more of warfare as it had to
be conducted in the Americas than most of his compatriots.
Many British regular-army officers stubbornly refused to
adapt themselves to wilderness tactics, even the older ones
who had fought in the Colonial War—and there were a few
of these, like General Paige, returned to America after a
twenty-five-year absence.

Paige had told him, "It was numbers, really. That and
Cornwallis' damnable error."

"That, sir, plus tactics. And the Indians."

"The Indians were a negligible force," the general had
growled.

"Were they?" Parliament didn't think so. Without the
Indians' help now, the British would be hopelessly outnumbered. With them the odds changed dramatically. Tecumseh was being actively recruited. If Black Hawk could
also be brought into the fold, there was a real chance of
reclaiming the colonies.

Black Hawk was not only respected by the Sauk, but he
was the one leader capable of bringing the Fox, the Winnebago, the Mascouten, the Potawatomie, and the Kickapoo
together under a common banner. In a land of many councils, many small governments, it was the war leaders who
captured the imagination of the many divided people and
could galvanize them to action.

The horse whickered in the maple woods and Hobbs rose.
His sergeant lifted his musket but Hobbs waved him away.
When Black Hawk entered the camp, Hobbs stood there
alone, holding out his hand.

"Black Hawk."

"Hobbs." The two men shook hands. Hobbs glanced behind the Sauk leader at the huge Indian with the painted
face and roached hair decorated with eagle feathers. "That
is White Bear," Black Hawk said. "He rides with me."

"Call him forward, Black Hawk," Hobbs said. "Let us
smoke and drink rum and let me offer you gifts."

Black Hawk looked at White Bear, who came forward
without a word. Rum was brought by an uncertain sergeant

and the three men drank it, sitting on rocks around the low fire.

When they had smoked and Hobbs had given each man a medal with the image of George III on it, he spoke. "How is it with the British Band, Black Hawk, how is it with our friends the Sauk? Are we still friends?"

"We have traded, we have fought, we have smoked together, Hobbs. We are still friends."

"Great changes are occurring, Black Hawk," the blond captain said. "The Spanish are gone now."

"Yes, they are gone."

"And now the Americans have come west. Do you know what they want, Black Hawk?"

"I know what they want. Our land. Some of our council were foolish. They became drunk on rum and sold land to the Americans. That is not important. The rest of the council has now changed the vote."

Hobbs leaned back with evident relief. "Good. King George wondered what had happened, how our friends the Sauk could have sold their land to their enemies."

"To your enemies, Hobbs."

"Yes, and yours too, Black Hawk," Hobbs said, leaning forward again, his voice intense. "You will find that out. We have been friends for a long time, but you have never seen the British come to plow up your good land, to steal from you. We have traded fairly and tried to be good allies. The Americans want everything you have, every bit of land. What did they offer you?"

"Two thousand dollars a year."

"For how much land."

"Seven million acres."

Hobbs shook his head heavily. "Your council members were very drunk indeed, or else the Americans sent a shrewd bargainer."

"Harrison was his name," Black Hawk said.

"Harrison? The Indiana governor?"

"Just so," Black Hawk said, and he took a splash more of rum, offering some to White Bear, who shook his head negatively. The stars above the forest were huge and sparkling. Hobbs looked skyward for a moment before getting to his proposition.

"You know, Black Hawk, the long war is not over yet."

"Which war? So many are long wars," Black Hawk responded.

"King George is not happy," Captain Hobbs explained. "The French have stolen Spanish land and given it to the Americans. Jefferson is going to send thousands of people here to live to claim the land. This is wrong. It is bad for the Sauk—"

"And for the British," Black Hawk said, and Captain Hobbs slowly smiled.

"And for the British, yes. There will be war again, Black Hawk. War between the British and the Americans. It may even start here—who knows? King George needs to know which side the Sauk will be on if there is war. Will we still fight together; will we still be friends?"

"We shall still be friends," Black Hawk said carefully. "Will we fight?—I do not know. There is no war now, perhaps it will not come. At any rate, the council will decide."

"As they decided to sell the land, Black Hawk?"

"I do not know what will happen," the Sauk war leader reiterated. "There is no war. I do not know the council's mind."

"Where would *Black Hawk* stand?"

"I do not know that either. Perhaps the dreamer knows."

"The dreamer?" Hobbs was perplexed.

"The spirit woman. The dreamer, the far-seer. I cannot answer your questions now. She will tell me."

When Black Hawk and White Bear were gone, carrying away their presents, the sergeant said, "A woman? Is Black Hawk now under the control of a bloody woman, sir? A man like that—it's hard to believe."

"She must," Hobbs said, "be a special sort of woman."

"I know the Indians believe in spirits and all sorts of magic, but this is a new one on me. The course of the war, if war there is, depends on the dreams of a single Indian woman? Bless us all, bless us all," the sergeant said, "or we all stand damned."

"Yes." Hobbs's own thoughts were a little broader. If the king and Parliament had decided that the best American frontier policy was one which did not alienate the Indians, which left the British in possession without occupying the land, Jefferson's theory was that land occupied was land possessed, and without settlers the land belonged to no one but the Indians. Time would prove which policy was the more effective.

Which of the two, however, took the Indians' own thinking into consideration? Which admitted that the Indian himself had the right to occupy and govern his own land? The answer, Hobbs decided, was neither. In a sense he was attempting to dupe Black Hawk himself. But Hobbs didn't dwell long on that facet of his mission. There was God and King and Empire, and he was a British officer.

"Come on, Sergeant. Clear the camp. I don't want to be caught on American-occupied soil, and neither do you."

"No, sir."

"I want to get out of these leathers and into wool . . ." Hobbs was talking only to be doing something, to hear his own voice. His thoughts were with Black Hawk. Wondering.

With Black Hawk and with a woman he had only just heard of and never seen—one who seemed to hold the future of the Mississippi in her hands.

The woman walked along the river. Darkness closed around her as the moon sank, and the frogs quieted at her approach. She stood on the sandy spit and stared out at the island in midstream. He was gone, surely gone; but when the footsteps sounded behind her she knew who it was and she turned to find the Sioux warrior before her.

She uttered one broken syllable: "I . . ." and then was in his arms, feeling the heat of his body, the rising of his chest, the power of his arms, the strength in his lean thighs as he pressed against her and found her mouth with his own.

Sachim's own knees went weak. She was powerless against the compelling strength of the man, which summoned some repressed, surging joy, some want and need to the surface.

Her lips parted as he bent to kiss her, and she saw the stars dancing in his eyes.

"Thunder Horse," she managed to murmur. He put a finger to her lips.

"I know," he said, "I know."

"I don't want you," she said, burying her face in the hollow of his shoulder. "I want no husband, no Sioux lover. I don't want you." She lifted her eyes to his finely chiseled face. "But it will be. I have dreamed it."

She pushed away from him, angry with herself for showing weakness, and he laughed.

Thunder Horse put his hands on his hips and replied, "I have dreamed it too, spirit woman. It will be."

Sachim shook her head and turned away, looking at the ground as she walked from him, vectors of mind and soul and heart intersecting crazily inside her. She stopped briefly and without looking back said: "No more horses, please. No more horses."

Thunder Horse laughed again, and the sound was pleasant in her ears, so thrilling that when she walked on, Sachim was also smiling. She dared to look back once, and he was still there: proud, haughty, bold.

"It will be," she said with a mental shrug. Such things could not be avoided. The stars write destiny across the skies; dreams guide our lives. It must be; it would be.

Keokuk tugged at his narrow nose with his thumb and forefinger and looked up again at Napope, shaking his head. "You are wrong," he said.

Napope was indignant. The massive Sauk leader drew himself up and said, "No white can build on this land. How can you defend them?"

"We signed a treaty with them," Keokuk said, looking at Quash-qua-me, the Squirrel, and Pa-she-pa-ho, none of whom met his gaze.

"And repudiated the treaty," Napope reminded him.

"But the whites were not informed." Keokuk spread his hands. "Harrison is gone. Stoddard is gone. No one told the whites. They have come, taking our treaty in good faith. How can the Sauk now go and say, 'We have changed our minds, go away'?"

"What else can we say?"

"The treaty was proper," Keokuk argued. "It was Black Hawk who turned your mind. Black Hawk and the spirit girl."

"The council has spoken," Napope said more sharply. "Why do you stand by the Americans, Keokuk?"

"I stand by our treaty," Keokuk answered, bristling himself now. He waved an arm around the council lodge. "I have signed the treaty. Quash-qua-me signed it. And Pa-she-pa-ho, and the Squirrel. The Prophet has dreamed that it is a good treaty. How can we now change our minds?"

"It has been decided," Napope said stubbornly.

"We can at least talk to them," Keokuk suggested. "Let

us go above the rapids and ask what they are building. Let us see if any more whites are coming. What is one house on the river? Why antagonize the Americans by reneging on our treaty? We can at least ask them what is happening here. What else would you have us do? Like Black Hawk, would you have us start a war over nothing?"

Napope was silent, looking at the other council members. Strikes the Enemy stared down at the blanket beneath him. Quash-qua-me's eyes were distant. Perhaps Keokuk was right. What was one building? The Americans had been told that was their land.

With a deep sigh Napope said, "We will talk to them then. You and I, Keokuk, will ride up there tomorrow and see what is being done."

"Then you will let them stay?"

"Then we will have talked to them," Napope said, rising. He left the lodge then, not seeing Keokuk's expression: wolfish, dangerous. Quash-qua-me saw it, but he did nothing but rise and follow Napope from the lodge. Outside, the other one was waiting: the Prophet, his mustache framing his thin mouth like the wings of some dark bird.

"It is a good night, Quash-qua-me," the Prophet said. The words were respectful, but the tone wasn't. The Prophet spoke with a sneer, as if great secrets were drifting over the land and Quash-qua-me was too stupid to understand them.

Perhaps he was, perhaps he was. "It is a good night, Wabokieshiek," Quash-qua-me agreed, and then he walked through the silent camp toward his own lodge. His meal would be waiting for him. His meal and much rum.

The Prophet watched the council chief go and then he turned his head and spat. Drawing his feather cloak around him, he waited for Keokuk. There was much to discuss.

He saw the girl before she saw him, and the Prophet drew back into the shadows. She walked with her head down, her hands behind her back. She was a pretty young thing with those large eyes and full mouth, not quite Sauk in appearance, perhaps because her grandmother was Oneida.

The Prophet waited until she was nearly past him and then he spoke in a rasping whisper which halted Sachim in her tracks momentarily.

"Black Hawk is not here, woman. Without him you are vulnerable. When you dream, dream of *that*."

Sachim turned, but she saw no one. It was Wabokieshiek,

that she knew. A twisted man, an ambitious man, a jealous man. It would be easy to dismiss his warning, if that was what it was, except that Sachim knew—that the Prophet was correct. Without Black Hawk she was vulnerable to any dark mischief Keokuk and the Prophet might plan.

She continued on uneasily, seeing shadows moving in the trees, hearing sounds where there had been none before.

A man appeared suddenly before her on the path and Sachim put her hand to her breast to stand there trembling as he advanced on her.

"Sachim?" The warrior drew out of the shadows and Sachim let her breath go. White Bear, stolid, comforting, and massive, came to her and looked down into her face, his own eyes concerned.

"What is it, Sachim? Is it the Sioux? Did he do something to you?"

"No, White Bear, not the Sioux. Nothing is the matter."

"I saw you with him . . . I didn't mean to come upon you, but I saw you . . ." The big man fumbled for words like an uneasy child.

"I am sorry, White Bear," Sachim said, touching his arm.

"Sorry? Why be sorry, Sachim? If the man makes you happy, then I am happy. If he will provide for you, then I am content."

"You talk as if I have accepted him—it is nothing like that."

"No? Then your eyes lie, Sachim, and I have never known you to lie with words, or your eyes, or your dreams. He is the man—I know that; only be happy. That is all I want for you."

He bent low then and kissed her on the top of her head before ambling off into the woods like his namesake.

Sachim returned to her lodge and looked unhappily at her bed. She did not want to sleep, she did not want to dream. But then, she had never wanted to be a dreamer; one had no choice. The images coalesced in her mind and became revelations. For years she had kept silent about her dreams. There had been too much fuss over her when she had seen her father's death coming. Too many questions from the old council and from the Prophet and Tope-kia. She had pretended not to dream for a long while, telling no one about her visions.

That was the reason she did not want to get into her

bed—or so she told herself. Yet another reason hovered in the recesses of her mind, haunting her, a reason she did not wish to admit to herself.

The night was dark and empty and growing cold.

Her bed was empty too and there was a memory lodged in her consciousness, a memory of a single kiss which had numbed her lips and sent inexplicable tingling through her breasts and thighs, loosening her knee joints, turning her stomach to a reservoir of hollow aching.

The night was dark and empty and growing cold, and he was not there. That was it and she knew it. He was not there.

Thunder Horse slept apart from her and the time was coming when to sleep separately was wrong, a defiance of the universe's mandate. She was to be his and it did not matter if she was frightened, fearful of losing her independence, of adjusting to a new and strange life.

It was meant to be; it would be.

Sachim slipped naked into her bed and lay watching the single star she could see through the smoke hole in the roof of her lodge. Eventually she slept; eventually she dreamed.

When Keokuk leapt onto his spotted pony's back, the frost was still on the grass. The river was dull red and deep violet with dawn light. He rubbed his hands together and shifted, looking for old Napope.

Winter was coming, Keokuk reflected. Winter and the migration of the tribe to the southern hunting lands. If anything was to be accomplished it should be now.

What had the Prophet said? "It is the time for wealth, for power. This is my dream. It is the time, but time runs away like the river, Keokuk. Power rises like the moon and dies like it. It is the time for action."

Old Napope straggled toward his horse and Keokuk turned his head in disgust. It was time for the old ones to step aside. Napope was fat and tired and growing senile. He understood nothing of what was happening in the valley, of what was to come.

"It is a good morning, Napope," Keokuk said, and the council chief glanced at Keokuk, nodded, and grunted an indistinct answer.

Even mounting his horse was a struggle for Napope, Keokuk noticed. Every action was slow, every thought plodding.

Decisions were turned this way and that, stretched and minutely examined, at the last moment made on a whim or the realization that it was late and mealtime approached. Keokuk looked away again, concealing the scorn on his face.

"Are you ready?" Napope asked.

"Yes, I am ready."

Napope looked at the younger man, not understanding the tone of his words. Then, dismissing it from his mind, he heeled his horse and the two council members started upriver toward the new, mysterious white building.

The walls had gone up to a height of three feet. Men with sledges dragged more cut logs toward the unfinished structure while a man with a paper in his hand, sleeves rolled up, shouted at them.

When the whites saw Keokuk and Napope they halted their work and stood motionless, staring at the two Sauk. Napope lifted a hand and they rode across the long grass to the log building, which Keokuk now saw would be of great size when completed. He fingered the medal Harrison had given him, the image of Jefferson which hung around his neck on a striped ribbon, and held it up for the suspicious whites to see.

"Who has built this?" Napope asked a red-faced, brawny man.

"Who what? Who's in charge? Lieutenant Kingsley. Army engineers. You'll find him—there he is. Thin man with the red hair."

"It is a good day," Napope said in parting, and the sweating laborer shrugged.

Swinging down from their horses, the two Sauk Indians walked to where the army lieutenant awaited their approach, his eyes uneasy, his smile cheerful. He stuck out a hand, which Napope took cautiously.

"Kingsley?"

"Yes, sir. Alpha Kingsley. May I ask who you are?"

Napope introduced himself and Keokuk. Keokuk's eyes swept the size of the building and then went to the flatboats tied side by side at a green-wood wharf. He didn't bother to take Lieutenant Kingsley's proffered hand.

"Who has sent you? What is happening?" Napope asked, waving at the building. The men had gotten back to work now. Somewhere a mule brayed. A cold wind blew across the Mississippi.

"Me, sir?" Kingsley, something of a diplomat, asked. "Under a letter of authorization from the President, Governor Harrison has sent me to construct what will soon be a trading post for the Sauk and Fox Indians."

Kingsley might have been reading from his orders. Keokuk glanced sideways at the man.

"A trading post, this near to us? Who will operate it?" Napope asked.

Kingsley wiped his brow, paused to yell at a subordinate, and apologized. "I don't know, sir. I am an engineer, nothing more. I can tell you what I have been told: this will be a trading post for the mutual benefit of the Indians and the Americans, a place north of St. Louis where you may bring furs, and where, according to the presidential order, credits will be freely extended to the Sauk and Fox nations until such time as they can be repaid."

That was too much too quickly for Napope, and he asked for an explanation.

Kingsley, who had removed his cap to mop his brow with a folded scarf, explained, "I am told that the Sauk and Fox migrate to the south each winter. This year it will not be necessary for you to hunt for food, nor to uproot yourselves from your villages. Provisions may be gotten here and repaid with pelts and other goods in the spring and summer. And of course, you will be paid a stipend for allowing us to construct the trading post here . . . although I am told this land has been sold to the United States."

Napope slowly turned all of this over in his mind. Keokuk was more direct. "Where is the gold?"

"Sir?"

"You said you must pay us. Where is the gold?"

"It will be shipped upriver, so I am given to understand, at the time the trading post is completed."

Keokuk grunted. Napope gazed at the site and the workers and nodded thoughtfully. Things were not so bad then. The winter trek, always hard on the young and the very old, might be avoided this year. The whites would give them provisions, and when they could, the Sauk would bring furs or corn to the trading post as they had done under Delassus at St. Louis when the Spaniards were still there.

Keokuk seemed to be correct: good could come of this, and wealth. "I must talk to the council," Napope announced, and the lieutenant, readjusting his cap, nodded amiably.

"As you wish, sir. As I have said, I am only an engineer. My interest is in building this structure promptly and properly. I have enjoyed meeting you, but now I must get back to work."

Napope shook hands with the young American again, smiling as he did so. The council had let fear run away with them, he decided. What was wrong with this? What could not be beneficial in this? He had forgotten completely that the treaty had been repudiated. He said nothing of that to the young white builder.

Keokuk glanced at Napope and stood watching the logs being hoisted into place. He saw the tarpaulin-covered items half-hidden in the trees, but he was neither surprised nor curious.

Keokuk had seen cannon before.

From the underbrush, Elk Run and Tomorrow Runner watched the council members visit the white lodge. Blood Night, a younger brother of Antler Tree, was also there. Tomorrow Runner, his black and white paint masking his face, watched as intently as a hunting cat.

"And so you see," Tomorrow Runner said, rolling onto his back to look up at the other young Sauk warriors, "the council will do nothing. They are women. They let Ke-ke-tai die. Anyone can see they are old and fearful. What are the whites doing here if there is no treaty?"

"Black Hawk would not allow it," Blood Night said.

"Who knows what Black Hawk would do?" Tomorrow Runner mused, "What will *we* do?"

"We?" Elk Run didn't like the drift of this. Tomorrow Runner had always been bold, too bold at times.

"I don't mean to make a war." Tomorrow Runner propped himself up on his elbow. "Just let them know that this is our land, that the Sauk are not frightened of them. I don't wish to kill anyone."

"What could be done?" Blood Night asked cautiously.

"We will discuss it. Let us get more of our friends together." That was all Tomorrow Runner said, but in fact there were larger thoughts in his mind. The idea had been building since his humiliation. The council was weak. The old warriors were all faithful to Black Hawk, doing nothing unless he spoke. Black Hawk was away much, speaking to the British, planning war with them, fighting the Cherokee or the Osage. Who was there to protect the Sauk land when Black Hawk was gone?

Tomorrow Runner envisioned a secret clan, one beyond the Thunderbird and the Bear, embracing men from all of them. A secret society pledged to fight the Sioux, the Americans, to protect Sauk sovereignty. And at the clan's head: Tomorrow Runner.

"We will discuss it near the Great Falls," Tomorrow Runner said. "Bring friends who can be trusted." Then he sprang to his feet and walked off through the woods, slicing at the vines alongside the trail with his stick.

Black Hawk himself was not far away. After the meeting with Captain Hobbs he had sent White Bear home and gone on alone to Galena to talk to LeClair. Black Hawk needed to know more. Would there be a war? Did LeClair think the British wanted Sauk land? Had he heard if the Americans were coming in numbers?

LeClair had spent time with Black Hawk, reading to him from a newspaper. There were advertisements for settlers to the Louisiana Territory, tracts of land offered by a man called Joshua Ferguson along the Mississippi and above the Rock River.

"Then they will come," Black Hawk said heavily.

LeClair answered, "So it seems. There is mention of the treaty here. Called the Treaty of 1804. Ratified, it says by Congress and by the Sauk and Fox nations."

"Then Hobbs told me the truth. And the war, LeClair? Will it come?"

"There will be war. It is inevitable."

As Black Hawk rode southward, these two concepts played through all his thoughts. War would come. The Americans wanted Sauk land. Then which side could he choose, other than the side of the British, who, no matter what their eventual motives, proposed no threat at this moment to the Sauk?

Black Hawk knew too that this would not be a popular perspective. The council now favored the Americans, accepted them at their word, and were willing to suffer encroachment and take gifts from them. This was Keokuk's persuasion at work.

The land—he rode across it now, seeing the deep green

and silver of the wind-shifted grass, the far vistas, the red and gold of the turning maples, the long, long river.

Who lives upon the land owns it.

The Sauk must not allow the Americans to live upon it.

His horse was thirsty, so he paused to let it drink, standing to look out over the silver breadth of the Mississippi.

There, against the horizon, stood the dark citadel, the timbered outpost. Black Hawk yanked his startled horse's head up, mounted in one easy motion, and rode southward at a near-gallop.

He was alone but there was no caution in the war leader's heart as he rode up to the white lodge. The walls were head-high now and growing taller as block and tackle hoisted timbers upward. He sat his horse, watching, the wind shifting his roached, dyed hair, moving his scalp lock.

The young lieutenant came down to where he waited, lifting a hand to Black Hawk.

"Hello. Another Sauk come to visit our trading post? Come in and look around," Alpha Kingsley said.

"This is a fort," Black Hawk answered slowly, his eyes turning flinty.

"Constructed like one," the young officer admitted. "According to plan. The way things are with the British, it's necessary for us to have the capacity to defend ourselves. But in function it's a trading post."

"It is," Black Hawk repeated, "a fort, built against the terms of the treaty."

Kingsley pursed his lips and studied the Sauk. He was right, of course, and Kingsley, who had built other such outposts in the West, knew it full well. He had in fact seen an uncirculated document which designated the "trading post" as Fort Madison. But Kingsley was an engineer, a soldier, and beyond performing his duties, at which he was skilled and reliable, he didn't involve himself in army policy.

The Sauk Indian he now stood facing was obviously a different sort of soldier. High-ranking, determined, acute. He noted the blockhouse, the gunports, the rising central stone redoubt, and nodded—there may have even been a trace of a smile on his lips—and then turned and rode slowly away.

Kingsley turned back to his work, spurning speculation. He did, however, call out to his sergeant: "We can spare three or four more men for sentry duty! Select them, Hewitt."

Black Hawk rode on with a cold resentment building in
him. The Americans' treaty proposal had never been ratified
and yet they were here. They claimed to be building a
trading post and yet the structure was obviously a fort. Was
the council asleep or had Keokuk blinded them to these
facts?

Always in the back of his mind remained a single idea:
war was coming; which side were the Sauk on?

Her first thought was of Thunder Horse. She lay awake,
feeling an unusual nervousness snaking through her body, a
feeling that something unhappy was to come. She searched
her mind for any dream which might have been borne on the
night currents, but there was none. None besides the dream
of Thunder Horse.

Sachim shook her head. Was the man to dominate her so
much that even her dreams were washed away, her thoughts
turned to murky emotions and thrilling if confused sensations?

She would not allow that, she would not!

But she rose, her body feeling warm although the morning
was cool. Outside it had snowed for the first time. A glittering, light dusting of snow had spread itself across the broad
land. Now it was melting but the early light still danced
across it and the land was briefly jewellike, a million tiny
winking stars of all colors bright against the eye.

"Only a storm," she told herself. But the storm, unexpected and yet felt on a deep level by her body, had confused her soul and scattered her dreams.

At times she could believe these fables she told herself.

There was anger in the council lodge, so much anger that
people had gathered outside it to listen—the voices rose
clear and sharp in the frosty air. The snow crunched beneath
Sachim's feet as she made her way down into the village
wondering: how long did they have before the winter exo-
dus? How would Grandmother survive this year's long
journey?

Tope-kia found Sachim and gripped her arm above the
elbow, his toothless smile broad and excited. "Black Hawk
has returned," the medicine man said. "He is angry and the
council is angry. Keokuk is angry."

"What is the trouble, Tope-kia, the Americans?"

"Just so, just so. Keokuk says they have come to trade.

Black Hawk says they have come to prepare for war against
the British, to defend the many American settlers to come."

The many. Black Hawk was right, she knew. As many as
there were stalks of corn. Sachim crouched to listen, as did
fifty other Sauk. Black Hawk's voice was clear and powerful
within the lodge.

"Where do you stand on this treaty? You have bent this
way and the other, like reeds in the wind. They must go—we
have decided that."

"What we have decided," the voice of Keokuk said, "is
not your concern, Black Hawk. It is our decision. We are
the government of this nation, and not you."

There were many variations to the argument, so many
that Sachim grew weary as hours passed, but that was the
essence of it; and by law Keokuk was correct. By Sauk law;
but not by Manitou's law.

In the end, Black Hawk burst from the lodge and stood
staring at the people gathered there. His eyes were angry,
his heart obviously full of rancor. Yet he said nothing. He
walked through them as if they were all things to be pitied, a
people at the mercy of inept leaders and an unfeeling fate.

"There will be trouble," Tope-kia said, "there will be
trouble over this." But even he couldn't have imagined how
soon trouble would come.

Tomorrow Runner had his small band of young warriors
watching as the soldiers marched into the woods, muskets
over their shoulders. In their free hands they carried axes
and saws. The fort was going up with miraculous speed, the
walls now fifteen feet tall, the blockhouse nearly complete.

Tomorrow Runner burrowed deeper into the tall grass.
The soldiers walked past within a few feet of the Sauk
youths, still not seeing them. Tomorrow Runner glanced at
Blood Night. The young brave was poised like a cougar. Elk
Run's face was stony. In all, there were twenty of them,
twenty young men out for a war game, a game which would
teach the Americans something about the Sauk.

The soldiers vanished into the trees and Tomorrow Runner lifted his hand and rose to his feet, moving softly through
the forest, his young warriors behind him.

He slowed his pace deliberately. Now he could hear the
ringing of axes against the trees. The breeze rustled the
trees, covering any small sounds the Sauks might have made.

It was cool against Tomorrow Runner's cheek, shifting his roached hair and the feathers in his scalp lock.

He lifted his hand again and went down to his belly; the others followed his example. Crawling forward through the long grass, Tomorrow Runner reached a position behind a gray oak stump where he could see the soldiers at work.

Slowly he smiled. He tapped Blood Night on the shoulder, motioned to the others to stay put, and led his lieutenant to the source of his amusement.

The soldiers had stacked their muskets to one corner of the clearing while they worked, and now Tomorrow Runner edged to where they had been placed, his dark eyes flickering to the soldiers, who remained oblivious of the Sauk's presence. Silently he snatched up half the muskets; Blood Night took the rest and they disappeared into the forest again with their prizes.

"Now," Tomorrow Runner said as they returned to the others, "we will see what kind of soldiers these are."

The muskets were handed around to the smiling Sauk youths. Tomorrow Runner waited one more minute and then nodded. "Now!" he said, and he leapt forward into the clearing, a war cry rising from his throat as he fired his musket into the air.

The soldiers dived for their muskets and then retreated in panic as they found them missing. Tomorrow Runner's warriors fired their muskets into the air and waved war axes as they made their mock charge.

The soldiers, to a man, took to their heels and started running toward the fort. Tomorrow Runner laughed loudly, running behind a young yellow-haired soldier. The soldier looked back and the stark fear in his eyes caused Tomorrow Runner to laugh again. It was a strange and dangerous laugh.

Elk Run, trotting behind Tomorrow Runner as the soldiers raced toward the shelter of their fort, saw something change in Tomorrow Runner's expression, saw the man's face seem to set and go hard; the laughter broke off abruptly.

He was going to kill the soldier! Elk Run knew it. Tomorrow Runner, who had been toying with the yellow-haired soldier, stretched out his hand, grabbed the man's collar, and threw him to the ground, leaping at him with his war ax.

A volley of musket fire from the fort ended the game abruptly. Tomorrow Runner rolled aside, allowing his victim to scramble to his feet and stumble on toward his friends. One soldier had turned back to help and he took the yellow-haired soldier by the arm and ran with him to the fort.

"Tomorrow Runner!" The warrior called Moves by Night shouted a warning. Four soldiers had tugged a wheeled cannon to the open gate of the fort and were now loading it.

The Sauk darted for the woods, leaping fallen trees and ditches. The cannon was never touched off and after a quarter of a mile Tomorrow Runner stopped, sagged to the earth, and began to laugh again.

"Cowards, cowards!" he shouted, lifting his face to the sky.

Elk Run was beside him, and Blood Night. A hand slapped Tomorrow Runner on the back, congratulating him. His young warriors sat around him, laughing, retelling their roles in the fight, examining their new muskets. Tomorrow Runner watched his men, feeling their common joy, bathing in their congratulations. It was good. These men respected him; they would fight with him when the time came. It was good.

Tomorrow Runner had gotten his first taste of power and he wanted more.

6

THE corn feast had begun. The corn was in and stored in caches. On every fire, more corn roasted. It was time for the winter trek, but first there would be feasting and games before the Sauk left their home ground for the hunting grounds to the south.

Children danced and played and tried to steal ears of corn from the fires. Sachim sat with Little Creek and told the old tales to the young girls so that they might tell their children, so that no one would forget the traditions of the Sauk.

Little Creek was withering away, her eyes too large. She was a pretty girl, but the death of Ke-ke-tai had left her soul empty.

"Help me tell the story," Sachim said, nudging Little Creek. "Come on now, help me tell it. You tell it better than I."

The children watched expectantly, knowing the tale, wanting to hear it again. Little Creek sat on her mat and shrugged, saying nothing. Sachim began.

"This is the way corn came to the Sauk. In the old times before all of the stars had been set in the sky, in the days of the two-moons, two young Sauk warriors went hunting and killed a great deer. It was a long way back to the home camp and so they made a fire and began to roast some meat." Sachim looked at Little Creek, but the girl was just sitting, watching the ground.

Around Sachim, eager eyes waited. One little girl, called First Snow, tugged at Sachim's dress. Sachim put the three-year-old on her lap and started again.

"Now, as the warriors ate, a beautiful woman with yellow hair descended from the clouds and alighted on the earth between the two warriors.

"They were astonished, but not so much that they forgot their manners. They were Sauk, and generous and kind, and they offered meat to the woman, thinking that she had smelled the smoke rising into the clouds and become hungry. They presented her with meat and she ate.

" 'To thank you,' the yellow-haired woman said, 'I will bring a gift to you. You must wait one year, and when that year is over, return to this very spot and you will find a reward for your kindness and generosity.'

"And then the woman was gone," Sachim said, smiling at First Snow, whose eyes were wide with wonder. "Up into the sky again. When the two braves returned to their village and told their tale, the people laughed at them.

"But when the year was over they returned to the spot, and this is what they found: where the beautiful woman's right hand had rested, corn was growing. Where her left hand had rested were beans. And where she had been sitting was tobacco.

"And this is the way the Sauk came by their corn and why we are able to have this corn feast today and all eat maple candy."

"Candy!" First Snow shouted, standing on Sachim's lap to look into her eyes.

"Do we not eat candy on a holiday?" Sachim took the buckskin bag from behind her back and handed the maple candy to the children. "Now go and play the moccasin game, go and play—and don't steal corn," she added, waving a finger at them. First Snow gave her a sticky kiss and ran off, shouting at the older girls to wait for her.

Little Creek just sat there, still, and Sachim put her arm around her, holding her until the woman's head lowered to Sachim's breast and Sachim could feel the little shudder she gave.

The hooting at the edge of camp brought both of their heads up. Tomorrow Runner, wearing his skull-face paint, came running into the village followed by fifteen or twenty young men, many of them carrying new muskets.

"Now what?" Sachim wondered. "Now what is our young wild man up to?"

There was no time then to consider it. The Fox were

arriving—the brother Fox with their horses and winter provisions, with their children carried along on travois pole sledges behind the horses, with their dogs yapping at the Sauk dogs that rushed from the camp to engage them. With their dancers leading the way, singing songs of the Beginning and the hunt, the Fox came, their women dressed in their finest dresses, some a year in the making, white elkskin decorated with flattened porcupine quills, carrying baskets of black ash bark filled with gift corn.

People rushed out to greet their friends and relatives while Sauk drummers and flute players followed, raising a clamor of goodwill and welcome to the fall skies. The old chiefs clasped hands and long-separated cousins kissed and wept. The Fox warriors rode through the camp in a mock challenge; soon there would be horseraces and ball playing with blankets and muskets and pipes as the prizes as the men gambled on the tribal favorites with reckless abandon.

Little Creek rose, looked once at the color and motion of the two peoples coming together, and then walked away slowly, lost in the sorrow she felt for her lover who walked the Hanging Trail alone, calling for her.

Sachim, too, got to her feet, dusting herself off. This was the time of year she always had enjoyed—this and the spring, when the medicine feast began. Just now she had no taste for it at all and she walked to Grandmother's house to find the old woman on her feet, dressed, smiling.

"So, the corn feast. So we travel soon," Grandmother said.

"Do you want to travel this year, Grandmother?"

"Yes," she laughed. "Yes, do you think I want to stay with the old people? Those days are gone, so they say. When the Spanish men let the old stay at their trading post through the winter."

"You know much," Sachim said, surprised that her grandmother had kept up with the times from her small lodge. The Spanish were gone; the Americans had not offered to let the old remain with them. Perhaps they simply did not know. They did not know many things, it seemed; and that in the end would only make more trouble.

"So I have begun to pack," the old one said. "So I will travel. I have traveled all my life. Ten thousand years ago I walked from the Eastern Sea to the Shawnee land. Ten thousand years ago I met my Sun Wolf—oh, and was he proud and strong!—and he brought me to the great river. I will walk on. I will walk on, Sachim."

"Then I will help you pack," Sachim said. "And we shall walk together."

Bartholomew Perkins had his feet on the desk of Fort Madison's military commander, Captain Harold Davenport. Davenport was a career soldier, but his Western experience was limited. Lieutenant Kingsley's work was nearly done, the fort nearing completion, and it was Davenport's turn to carry the burden of concern over the fledgling outpost's fate. Davenport, short, balding, with periwinkle-blue eyes which were generally clouded with worry or alcohol, looked at the frontier scout without seeming to notice that Perkins' boots were wrinkling his dispatches.

"Well, they seem to have withdrawn," Davenport said, removing his cap to scratch at his thinning gray hair.

"Just a few young bucks making sport." The frontiersman yawned.

"You think so, do you?" Davenport said irritably.

"Sure, that's all it was."

"I don't like it. Are you a military historian, Perkins?"

"Me?" Perkins stroked his long jaw. "I got trouble with my personal history, sir. No, I'm not."

"Well, I am," Davenport said with more assurance. "I have read accounts of the incident at Fort Michilimackinac. In 1763. That started out innocently enough."

"Never heard of it."

"The Sauk were involved. They had a lacrosse game with the Chippewa Indians. Passions ran high. While the garrison there was diverted by the game, discipline relaxed, the tide of the game turned toward the fort. Five hundred Indians who had been occupied warring among themselves over a leather ball took it into their minds to give up the one game for another. They stormed the fort and most of the defenders were massacred before their chiefs could stop it. And that was a British fort!"

"Well then?"

"The British were Sauk allies, Perkins! We're hardly that." The captain found a roughly carved chair and sat on it, rubbing his forehead. "Emotions run high at these gatherings. Our scouts have reported that five hundred Fox have joined the Sauk."

"Could be a situation," Perkins agreed. "But it's unlikely. They gather now to do corn dances, to have a horserace or two, to maybe drink some rum."

"And that's just what's needed! I have seventy men here. There are several thousand Indians below the rapids and God knows what kind of mood they're in."

"You've got your treaty."

"Do we? That's what I thought," Davenport said unhappily. "Now St. Louis reports that the Sauk council has rejected the treaty."

The army captain continued to stroke his forehead above the eyebrows. His sinus headaches were always bad this time of year, but they had been nothing like this. Aggravated by the weather in the damp Mississippi Valley and by stress, they had become Mephistophelian.

Perkins merely yawned again. "Can't do much, Captain, but bar the gates and stand ready. I doubt the Indians are up to anything. They wouldn't have sent a bunch of young warriors out here to warn you of their intentions. Nobody was hurt, after all. Just a lark, sir, just a lark."

"Or a foreboding," Davenport said gloomily. "The British are building their forces upriver, we know that. Relations with England are strained to the breaking point. They still covet the interior. The Sauk and Fox are their longtime allies . . . and then there is that man."

"Sir?"

"That man. That surveyor. This Joshua Ferguson. He was here earlier with a party of twenty men. Settlers. They have deeds issued in Washington for four hundred sections of land—deeds issued before the ink was dry on the original treaty. They mean to move in, Perkins. And now.

"Whose duty is it to protect them? Mine. Mine. Are you a drinking man, Perkins?"

"I've been known to have a few," the scout answered, dropping his feet to the floor.

"Then let's have a few. I wondered why Captain Stoddard gave up a good post in St. Louis for a soft Eastern position with no opportunity for advancement. Now I think I am beginning to understand."

When the drums called, the riders came forward. Bonfires glowed garishly in the night and the fifty horsemen arranged themselves in a long line between the starting beacons. The race would be over a five-mile course and the best horses, the best riders among the Sauk and Fox would ride it at a dead run in the darkness. Hidden roots, depressions, and unseen rocks would thin their ranks quickly. Each man was painted, stripped to his breechclout; each carried a large wager with him.

The drums grew louder and as Sachim watched, a long line of musicians and medicine men emerged from the trees. The noise grew deafening. More timid horses pranced sideways, frightened by the sound. These animals would always be racers, never war horses.

Sachim withdrew a little, holding First Snow's tiny hand. At the moment the race started, flesh collided with flesh and the horses were liable to go any direction until their riders got them under control. Sachim wanted First Snow out of their path.

Napope was near the riders, standing to one side, his coup stick raised high. When it dropped, thunder filled the night. The horses charged out of the firelight and into the darkness, racing past the watching Sauk and Fox, the earth trembling under the drumming hooves.

And then they were gone and the crowd rushed madly toward the finish line across the village. Sachim hooked First Snow under the arms and swung her up onto her shoulders, following after the others.

First Snow had no mother and no father. A flood had taken them. Silent and shy, alternately hopeful and discouraged, she waited for her mother to return, still not understanding.

Little Creek was walking slowly toward the finish line, an otter-pelt cloak around her shoulders. Perhaps she too did not really understand that Ke-ke-tai would never come back.

"Hurry, hurry," First Snow shouted, slapping Sachim on the top of her head like an impatient jockey. Little Creek looked up and nearly smiled.

"You laugh," Sachim said, "but you do not have to be her horse."

"I would be," Little Creek said, and Sachim swung the little girl onto her shoulders. Perhaps the orphans belonged together.

And where do you belong, Sachim? she asked herself. She could hear the horses distantly, the drums and whistles, cymbals and flutes nearer by; the tribe was shouting, calling to each other, sending up sounds of life to the cold sky.

And where did she belong?

Almost without knowing it, she veered away from the trail and walked toward the river, the long-flowing, broad, and endless river, hoping that he would be there.

Thunder Horse found her on the beach and he wrapped his arms around her with gentle strength, kissing her throat, which pulsed beneath his lips, feeling the slight trembling as she pressed against him, wanting his love, fearful of it.

"It is time, woman," Thunder Horse said into her ear.

"Time?"

"Time you decide to come to me, to live with me."

Sachim swam through confusion. Her heart, her body, wanted only him, but her mind held her back from any rash decision. They were different, too different, and she did not yet understand him. He was hard, male, and Sioux. There were other considerations besides her own wants.

"The tribe needs me," she said, "Black Hawk needs me."

"Not so much as I do," he said, and his breath was warm and moist in her ear. He stroked her dark, sleek hair and she lifted her starlit eyes to Thunder Horse, this outlander, this warrior-thing, this man.

"I have an old grandmother. She needs care."

"Bring her with us."

"To the Sioux lands? To roam? She needs her lodge and her people around her."

"Sachim—" Thunder Horse said quietly, "soon I too must go. Winter is coming and the last great buffalo hunt will be held. To feed my people through the long winter. I must be there. I want one thing—for you to go with me. If there are problems we can solve them. There are solutions to everything . . . but not to a life without love."

"How can you love me when you don't know me—?" she began to ask, but Thunder Horse put a finger to her lips.

"Don't question my love. Question all else, but not that. I do not know what happened. I did not choose to love a Sauk woman. I chose to love no one, but it was planned for me.

"This is what happened, my Sachim; this is how I have sung it:

"Once the Great One gave a gift to the Sun, and the Sun gave the gift to the Moon Walkers. The Moon Walkers cast the gift to the Sky, and the Sky let it fall on the Earth like gentle rain; and rain made of it a shining Brook and we drank from the Brook and tasted it and called the Gift our Love.

"This I know. This do I sing."

And she clung to him, hearing his heart beneath his powerful chest, feeling the need rise in him, his arms tighten around her—before she turned sharply away and walked from Thunder Horse, shaking her head worriedly.

"Sachim . . . come back. It is time."

But she continued to walk on, her heart empty and yet full; her mind clear yet alive with swirling, confused needs and desires, with obligations and fears.

Now she halted and looked back, but he was gone. There was nothing on the empty path but the shadows of the tangled trees. There was no sound on the night wind but the constant murmur of the river rolling away, and the sound was mocking and bitter.

In the morning the Sauk prepared to travel southward. White Bear carried Grandmother to the travois behind the red horse. There Sachim covered her with a blanket and furs, for the weather had continued cold with a strong wind from the north.

It was a long way to the hunting grounds, a long and lonely way. Sachim looked back only once and then joined the procession of Indians following the river south.

Their temporary lodges were of hide, set up along Berry Creek where the hills fold together and a scattered oak forest decorates the land. After the first few days setting up camp, there was nothing but time. Sachim took long walks, wandering over the hills, gathering huckleberries and gooseberries, hickory nuts and pond lily.

It did no good. Her time was empty, her heart heavy, and she spent hours staring northward. From a broken hill she could look through the haze and see the distant plains. There, somewhere, a man hunted buffalo and perhaps thought of her a little.

It would be a long and solemn winter, a sorrowful time.

The dreams had traveled with her, some old, some new. When she sat alone on the rocky outcropping above the winter camp and stilled her breathing, Sachim could see far beyond the range of her vision. She would fold her arms beneath her breasts, feel a sudden tug at her heart, and then she would rise into the cobalt sky, the miles passing swiftly beneath her. She roamed far and dreamed long, traveling to the fire sky where the Thunderbird perched on his mountain peak and directed the Rain Maidens. Words were whispered to Sachim from out of the deep heart of the sky, but they were muted, unfathomable. She walked the long road where the dead had gone and sometimes saw misty faces peering down at her, laughing, pointing as they recognized her.

Then there was the river. Always the river flowing southward, a constant dream. She saw the boats, many boats on the river, the broken canoes lining the shore. Their lodges had been painted red and the camp filled with Sioux gift horses. Skeletons walked the forest, their heads down, their jaws gaping, their hands bloody.

Sachim lay flat on her back on the outcropping, staring at the sky where a few wispy, tattered clouds drifted. Another day gone, another dreamed away.

"It's not enough," she said to herself, and she rose shakily, deliberately not looking northward to the plains.

Tomorrow Runner was in the trees when she went down. He was without his paint, and instead of a stick he now carried a war lance.

"I know you now," the warrior said.

"You have always known me," Sachim said quietly. There was an energy in Tomorrow Runner she did not like, something nearly palpable. He was like a wolf before it lunges.

"Now I know all about you, woman," Tomorrow Runner said savagely.

"What do you want?"

"Me? Nothing, now, nothing just yet, *Sioux* woman."

"Why do you call me that?"

"You are Sioux. You have a Sioux lover. You ride a Sioux horse. You are a Sioux woman."

"Don't be stupid, Tomorrow Runner," Sachim snapped.

The warrior leaned forward, every muscle in his body poised. What he would have done, Sachim could only guess. The huge man was there suddenly, ambling toward them, and as Tomorrow Runner saw White Bear he snarled like an animal, slowly backed away, and then sprinted into the woods, giving a war cry.

"Madman," White Bear said with disgust. "What did he want to tell you, Sachim?"

"It was nothing," she answered with a little shrug.

"Maybe nothing. Don't think he shouldn't be taken seriously, Sachim." They turned back toward the camp, the Sauk warrior dwarfing the slender woman beside him.

"I do take him seriously, White Bear," she assured him.

"He is always up to something now. They have formed a secret clan. The Skull Clan. I found out from my cousin who was invited to join."

"Three Foot?"

"Yes, he refused them. He said he was born Bear Clan and needed no other." White Bear glanced up at nesting pigeons in the big oak and then looked again at Sachim—a soft and caring glance which he broke off as her large eyes met his.

"The council will put a stop to Tomorrow Runner's activities if he runs crazy," Sachim believed.

"He won't listen to the council! He despises them all. Only Black Hawk has his respect, a warrior's respect. There is no telling what Tomorrow Runner will do. The attack on the white fort was only a game, but he has made other little wars."

"What?" Sachim stopped and stared at White Bear in amazement. That was something she hadn't heard. "No one has whispered such a thing, White Bear."

"Because the Skull Clan is secretive. They have some sort of blood oath and a secret dance. I know that they set upon two Sioux hunters," White Bear said, lowering his voice. "And killed them. Three Foot saw the scalps."

"Oh, no." Sachim just shook her head. Raiding between the Sioux and the Sauk was not new. Death was not new to her. She only worried that the Sioux honor would compel them to strike back—at those who had nothing to do with Tomorrow Runner's transgressions.

Then she had another thought: there were Sioux hunters in the south. Could *he* be here, somewhere just beyond sight, across the river or in the long hills? She started on again, hands behind her back, head down, moccasined feet kicking at stones and acorns.

"They won't raid our camp, will they?"

"No. If they know Sauk did it they will strike back, though. At a lone hunter, a small gathering party." White Bear lifted his massive shoulders and spread his hands. "That is the way of things."

"You must tell Black Hawk," Sachim urged. "Tomorrow Runner must be disciplined—or he must leave."

"Yes, it must be one way or the other. He calls himself by a different name now, Sachim. He says he has entered a new life and must have a new name. Can you guess what he calls himself?"

Sachim nodded. She knew what name Tomorrow Runner would choose for himself.

"Skull."

The log house was nearly built. The well had proven sweet. Water was plentiful. The days were growing longer; the skies remained clear. The willows along the creek were putting out buds and new grass was trying to poke through the recently frosted earth.

Thaddeus McCutcheon was sweating freely despite the coolness of the day. He snapped his mule's reins once more and watched expectantly as the animal strained against the log chain, but still the stump wouldn't pull.

"Dammit all," McCutcheon grunted. He was red-haired, red-faced, blue-eyed, and strong enough to be suited for this new country. "More ax work," he muttered, unhitching the mule.

McCutcheon hefted his ax and dropped once again into the widening, deepening ditch surrounding the roots of the oak stump. He wiped his forehead with the back of his hand and glanced toward the house, seeing Hattie with her laundry basket out back and the kid tormenting a goose out front. The goose's honks of indignation reached Thaddeus McCutcheon's ears across the distance and he smiled to himself before his mouth set and he lifted his ax once more, chopping downward at the exposed roots of the dead tree.

He heard the goose's honking again and then another sound which chilled him. McCutcheon turned toward the house in time to see the Indians, their faces painted white, burst from the trees. Hattie stood stock-still for a second, then dropped her laundry basket, picked up her skirts, and ran for the boy, who was frozen with fear.

"Run, Charlie!" McCutcheon yelled, hoisting himself out of the ditch, running toward the house, ax in hand.

"God, no," he panted. The Indians had surrounded Hattie, and as McCutcheon, horrified, ran on, they began to hack her to bits with their hatchets. The boy tried to run, belatedly, and was grabbed by the collar and hurled to the ground.

"Damn you! Damn you!" McCutcheon was insane with fury. One of the Indians rose from the ground with Hattie's scalp in his bloody hand. The boy had a warrior on top of him and McCutcheon saw the knife rise and fall in the man's hand.

McCutcheon didn't count the Indians, or know how many there were. He didn't care. He leapt among them wild-eyed and frenzied, laying about him with his ax, feeling the steel head of it find flesh, hearing the Indians scream with pain.

McCutcheon's double-bitted ax severed arteries and broke bones. The Indians started to press forward but fell back as the homesteader slashed at them with his deadly tool.

Suddenly they were gone.

The farm was empty.

The two people McCutcheon had loved lay still and blood-ied against the dark earth. The Indians had taken their injured and dead with them; McCutcheon didn't notice. He didn't know or care if they still lurked around the farm. His berserk rage had faded to vast empty stillness. He sank to his knees, clasped his rough red hands together, and wept as he prayed.

The wind grew cool, the shadows long. He rose wearily and walked to his new toolshed for his shovel.

"We need you," Skull said, and Black Hawk simply stared at Tomorrow Runner. The man was bruised and dirty. Two of his warriors had not returned from Skull's war, which had changed from youthful exhibitionism to bloody earnestness.

Black Hawk shook his head. He looked to the vast Sauk warrior at his side and then to the small young woman across the blanket from him. Inside his hide lodge it was cool, the fire burning low, the ashwood smoke scenting the lodge pleasantly.

"No," Black Hawk said at last.

"We are ready to strike at the whites, to drive them away," Skull said intensely.

"*We*? Whom do you mean, Tomorrow Runner? I have already heard of your war. That was no war at all, but a slaughter. Now you are frightened. Now you would convince the Sauk that they should kill all the Americans."

"I am not frightened, Black Hawk" Skull replied sullenly.

"You are frightened," Black Hawk repeated. "You have

gone too far and know not how to proceed now, where to run, where to hide."

"Ma-ka-tai-me-she-kia-kiak!" Skull said, using Black Hawk's full name, "I told you we were attacked by a gang of white land stealers. We fought back."

"And since you knew this would happen, you went out today in your war paint, your clan paint, a clan which has no legitimacy! No, Tomorrow Runner, Skull, whatever your name might be, you did not find yourself attacked. Did all of the settlers have axes and rush upon you? Elk Run died from an ax wound. She-te-Kiske died of an ax wound. Winter Born lost fingers to an ax. Why do you lie! Why do you come here? You have taken young men and gotten them hurt, some killed. Now you would come to your war leader and ask for sanction!"

"I need no sanction," Skull shot back angrily.

"Then ask for none."

"You are growing old, Black Hawk."

"Be careful, young warrior," Black Hawk warned.

"Old"—he rose to his feet—"or under the influence of a witch, I do not know which way it is."

"Do not speak of Sachim in that way in my presence."

"Why? She is a witch. Sioux woman. Dirty thing."

Black Hawk tensed and then lowered his head, breathing slowly. "Go now—do not be here when I look up, Tomorrow Runner."

The lodge flap rustled in another moment and Skull was gone. White Bear poked at the fire, adding a few sticks.

"What now will happen?" Sachim asked.

"Now he shall be banned. I will see to that. The council must banish him. He is not Sauk, he is 'Skull,'" Black Hawk said.

"Why did he do it? Why make war?" the woman wondered. "Why kill the Sioux and then the whites?"

"Did you not hear him?" White Bear asked. "He says there will be war. Strike first. Strike first and hardest."

"So he says," Black Hawk said, "but that was to appease us, to persuade us to stand by him. He sees the council as weak; he knows I am not weak. He knows the Americans have angered me. He had grand hopes."

"But his words?"

"Lies."

"Then why?" Sachim asked.

"Why war? Skull wars because he likes blood. Since he likes blood, he will make more wars. Now he is an enemy of the Americans. Now he is the enemy of the Sioux. Now," Black Hawk said, lighting his pipe, "he is an enemy of ours."

"And now," White Bear asked, "what will happen?"

"Only Skull knows—or possibly," Black Hawk said with a faint smile, "the far-dreamer."

Sachim smiled in return. "Madness has its own mind."

The three of them sat silently for a long while, Black Hawk puffing on his pipestone tobacco pipe, handing it to White Bear, who only once accepted it. Sachim continued to look toward the tent flap, having no idea what the future of Skull would be, only knowing deep within her that it would have been better had the white settler killed him.

Or was Tomorrow Runner already dead? A young man of promise, humiliated—in his mind, at least, abandoned by his people. The name "Skull," the death symbol of his paint— perhaps they showed something. Perhaps the Sioux women had killed Tomorrow Runner. All that surprised her was the number of young warriors who had joined the Skull Clan. White Bear said they numbered fifty men.

"We can decide nothing," Sachim said, getting to her feet, "until he makes his course clear. It is good that we travel north again soon. Perhaps we can leave Skull behind."

"We cannot leave him behind," Black Hawk said, his face dully glowing in the firelight. "We can go away but not leave him behind. Skull is part of *us*."

"A dark part," White Bear said.

"One's shadow follows." Black Hawk shrugged massively as if shrugging off Skull's weight. He escorted his visitors to the entrance of his lodge. "Sachim," he said quietly, "I once knew a warrior with a Sioux wife. She lived among us for twenty years and raised three strong sons and died loved and respected among us."

Sachim looked away, then touched Black Hawk's arm and went out into the night. White Bear followed, but he sensed that she did not wish to talk and he left her there watching the stars.

The winter had been long, she thought as she watched their cold brilliance. Long and unhappy. Skull had brought a terrible climax to it. Yet, as there was warmth even in the cold stars, so there was a flickering, distantly gleaming warmth of promise in the night. Black Hawk had given her hope.

He cared enough to speak out. He cared enough to offer her a word of hope and of promise.

And who knew: where there was still a flicker of hope, there was always a chance of fulfillment.

So it had been said, so it had been dreamed. Sachim walked homeward, content despite the sorrow and anger of the night.

7

THEY sang as they walked northward. The trees were green with new leaves, the flowers bright against the spring grass. The river was calm and smooth, broad and comforting.

Sachim carried First Snow on her shoulders and the girl sang along, now and then bursting into laughter as Sachim tickled her ribs. Grandmother was well; she smiled as she listened to the old songs from her travois. Dogs raced through the trees, delighted to be free, to be moving, to be homeward bound.

They avoided St. Louis; the town had too many bad memories. They could see it, however, and see how it had grown. There were twenty new white buildings near the river and a large tower of some kind, unfinished, near the governor's house.

Sha-sak, who was very heavy and very funny, walked beside Sachim. "Even Little Creek is happy today," Sha-sak said. "Coming home. Soon the men will dance the crane dance, Sachim. Soon they will dance and then take wives," she went on with a mischievous grin.

"Yes, Sha-sak. But you already have a husband."

"Yes," Sha-sak sighed. "Cliff Arrow is a good man. But to be a maiden again and think, 'That warrior is dancing for me, soon he will come and play the love song on his flute. . .' " She sighed again and clutched her breast, rolling her eyes skyward.

First Snow asked, "Will a warrior dance for Sachim?"

"Oh, yes!" Sha-sak said, rubbing the girl's head. "They

will dance for Sachim. Many suitors will come to the lodge of Sachim, is that not so, Sachim?"

"Perhaps someone will come." Sachim shrugged.

"Perhaps a big man with shoulders like a bear," Sha-sak suggested.

"White Bear?" the little girl asked.

"Perhaps he will, yes, Sachim?"

"Perhaps."

The older woman said, "You are a funny woman, spirit woman. When I was a maiden . . . well . . . perhaps your dreams give you so much pleasure you do not need a man."

"Not just yet," Sachim answered vaguely.

"Or perhaps," Sha-sak said slyly, "the man you want does not know the crane dance!" Then she laughed again and Sachim had to join in. There were few secrets in the village. The two Sioux marriage horses hadn't gone unnoticed.

"Little Creek," Sha-sak said, lowering her voice, "is the maiden who needs a man. Her father is older."

"She carries grief still."

"Oh, yes!" Sha-sak said, flinging a hand out. "She carries grief, but who does not? Can she carry it all her life until it drives her down into the ground? She needs a new man to help her forget Ke-ke-tai. Forget him a little, anyway. She has forgotten how to smile—"

The sharp report of a musket from the woods cut through Sha-sak's conversation. Looking around, eyes startled, confused, Sachim saw Ha-te-ka, Napope's nephew, pitch forward on his face. Simultaneously she saw smoke rising from the woods.

Momentarily no one moved, then two men rushed to Ha-te-ka and a dozen warriors, led by Black Hawk, dashed toward the woods.

"What's happened? What happened to Ha-te-ka?" There were many more questions than answers in the first few minutes. "Was it Sioux?"

"He's shot. Look, the ball went right through his leg."

"Will he die? Where is Tope-kia? Bring him here with his medicine sack."

Sachim swung First Snow to the ground and stood with the rest of the people, shocked, uncertain. Other warriors had unpacked their weapons, some following after Black Hawk.

Ha-te-ka lay writhing on the grass, his face anguished,

holding his leg tightly until Tope-kia arrived and opened his herb bag, calling for river mud and a bandage.

Black Hawk had entered the woods at a run, his eyes fixed on the rising puff of white smoke which dissipated rapidly in the wind. He slowed as he drew nearer the position he guessed the sniper had taken and readied his own musket, glancing around at his companions.

Slowly they filtered through the shadowed woods, their feet soft against the earth, their bodies tense and ready. Black Hawk saw the stack of boulders, mossy and damp, and he veered that way. The low rock to one side was a perfect bench for a marksman.

Behind the rock Black Hawk found the footprint, and crouched by it.

"What is it?" White Bear asked.

Black Hawk looked up. "A white boot."

"White?" White Bear frowned. "Do we follow him?"

Black Hawk's answer was a long time coming as he rose and looked toward the river in the direction the sniper had gone. "No," he said at last, and there was anger in the single word.

There was good reason to follow the man, to follow him and kill him, but by now he could be nearly to St. Louis if he had had a horse hidden in the trees, and the Sauk couldn't descend on the white town in force without there being serious trouble, too much trouble for vengeance against one white.

"Why did he do it? Who could it have been, a soldier?" Black Hawk could only shake his head. Who knew? It could have been anyone. *Why* did he do it? That question was the one that plagued Black Hawk. The Sauk and Fox had been at peace with all the whites for a long while. They had been in their winter camp, stirring up no resentment, having no encounter with a single white for months.

There was no answer. It was madness. Black Hawk watched the trees moving in the wind and then he turned and walked back toward the tribe to see to Ha-te-ka.

One.

That was one. The big red hands of Thaddeus McCutcheon fumbled for the knife in his jacket pocket. He was amused to watch his hand tremble as he opened the knife and cut a notch in the walnut stock of his musket-rifle.

"That's one of the butchers," he muttered as he cut and then blew the wood chip away. One—and how many would it take to avenge the death of Hattie and little Charlie? A hundred, a thousand. Ten thousand. He would whittle away at the stock of the rifle until it looked like the woodpeckers had got it, until it was nothing but a splinter—and then he would throw it away and get himself a new gun.

Thaddeus got heavily to his knees, placed his musket aside, and folded his big raw hands together. Then he prayed. "Dear Lord in heaven, take good care of Hattie and little Charlie . . ." He had to pause and knuckle away the tears filling his eyes, coursing down his cheek. "I think I did a murder, Lord. I heard a preacher say they're heathens and got no souls. Maybe so, I don't know. Whichever it is, I'm going to go on killing 'em, Lord. I don't know if you forgive someone with that kind of anger in his heart." He unfolded his hands and looked skyward through the hickory trees. With passion he added suddenly, "But I'm going to kill 'em anyway," and then rose to snatch up his weapon and start through the woods, his conscience lightly salved.

With Ha-te-ka, his leg splinted and bound, on a travois, the Sauk started on. Sachim walked just behind the travois, not liking the mood that had come over the Indians and was seeping into her own heart.

The day was as bright as before, the grass as green, but now there was no singing, no laughter. No one knew what had happened or why. It was as if a dark cloud had come over them, lightning striking once violently.

And where it struck once, it could strike again. The warriors kept their weapons firmly in their hands now and Black Hawk had sent scouts out on either side. He had seen the tracks of only one man, but that didn't mean there weren't others out there.

They entered deep forest, where fern grew waist-high among the silver birch and maple trees, and emerged finally overlooking the long valley, home once more.

But it wasn't home. A warrior cursed. Black Hawk growled deep in his throat. People glanced at each other in disbelief and moved forward, not trusting their own eyes.

The Americans were there, living on their land, planting corn. Their lodges had been destroyed, burned down and dragged away.

"What is it, Sachim?" Grandmother, who could not see ahead, asked.

Sachim took the old woman's hand. "Whites. They are in our fields, they are on our land. They have built their own lodges and destroyed ours."

"How can that be!" Grandmother tried to turn around, to peer toward the valley. She could see nothing. Sachim had to try to describe what had happened.

"My lodge is gone. The council lodge has horses in it. Pak-wa's lodge is gone. The Bear Clan's field is plowed up. There is a boat in the rice marsh, a big boat with soldiers on it. The fort is much bigger now. I can see other soldiers outside the walls. Everything is gone! Everything."

The council had gathered at the head of the dazed band and Napope could be seen gesturing wildly while Keokuk, arms folded, listened and stared down at the valley. Black Hawk stood aside, blind with rage.

The Fox Indians began to separate themselves from the Sauk, not knowing what would follow when their cousins entered the valley. Black Hawk looked back and motioned to Sachim. She patted Grandmother's hand and went forward to stand by the Sauk war leader.

"What is it?" she asked.

"I will talk to them. I will tell them to go," Black Hawk said.

Sachim glanced at Keokuk and Quash-qua-me. "What has the council decided?" she asked in a whisper.

"They have decided nothing. They will decide nothing soon," Black Hawk said with obvious disgust.

"You must wait for their decision, Black Hawk!"

"Why must I? There is only one proper solution to this."

"Please be patient, Black Hawk," Sachim begged. Already his warriors had started to gather around him, to glare down at the valley, to mutter among themselves.

"My lodge is gone," Pak-wa said bitterly. "Who has burned my family's home?"

"They are in our field with iron plows. We must drive them out, Black Hawk."

The council members looked anxiously toward Black Hawk and then again to the valley, where settlers could be seen moving over the land behind oxen, etching dark furrows into the earth, where others built white houses, the sounds of

hammers echoing distantly. A decision had to be made, and
rapidly; there might be no holding the warriors back.

Napope threw his hands up in resignation. Keokuk, who
seemed to be fighting back a smile, walked to where Black
Hawk stood, his languorous stride irritating Sachim unrea-
sonably just now.

"It is decided. We shall proceed to the fort. The council
has invited you to come, Black Hawk."

"I am grateful," Black Hawk said stiffly.

"I suggest you leave your weapons."

"Yes," Black Hawk answered. "Sachim, leave yours as
well," the war leader said, and one of the warriors laughed.

"The woman is going?" Keokuk asked, turning slowly to
study Sachim as if he had never seen her before.

"She is going."

Keokuk shrugged as if Black Hawk had asked to take his
favorite hunting dog along and needed to be humored. Then
he turned and slowly strolled away, beckoning with one
finger to the Prophet, who came to stand at his side and
whisper a few words into Keokuk's ear.

"We will go after we have painted ourselves," Napope
said loudly. "We must remember the formalities, even in
such circumstances."

Black Hawk finally turned and walked to his parfleche to
remove his paint and knot his feathers into his roach. Sachim
waited, looking, only looking at the changes wrought in the
valley. In her heart fury burned like a tiny pinpoint of flame.
Wrong—this was wrong and although she wanted to see no
war with the whites, she knew that war might be what was
needed to drive them off the land. They had come far, these
Americans, and had placed their hopes on the new land.
They would not leave eagerly.

Black Hawk had told her to learn to think like a white,
and she tried that now. Wherever these people had come
from, they had decided on a new life, hoped for a better life.
When the Americans came they planted seed, and where
they planted, they stayed.

They had come to stay.

When the council members had made their preparations
they started toward the fort, Sachim walking last. No one
spoke. Once the Prophet turned around and stared at Sachim,
but she ignored him.

They crossed the little creek, seeing the rafts tied to the

trees, and walked silently past the rapids, which would have drowned out any attempt at conversation anyway. Here the river bulged and folded on itself, frothing into white water and whirling funnels. It was a sacred place where once the Serpent had caught Sky Warrior and taken him down to his watery home. There was discarded lumber caught on the rocks and rusting cans bobbing in a whirlpool.

Soldiers out collecting wood stopped their work and slipped into their tunics, picking up their weapons as the painted Sauk delegation approached the high gates of the fort.

A man with stripes on his sleeve and one eye missing came forward to talk to them.

"What do you want here?" he asked, and Napope answered. "Your leader."

"Captain Davenport? I'll see if he'll talk to you."

Black Hawk said, "He will talk. Tell him Black Hawk *will* talk to him."

Quash-qua-me seemed confused. "Where is the trading post? Is this not the trading post they promised us?" No one answered the old council member. The one-eyed sergeant adjusted his cap, nodded to another soldier, and started off unhurriedly toward the post, leaving the other armed men standing in a loose ring around the Sauk, not guarding them exactly, but watching them warily, their eyes from time to time lifting to the forest beyond as if expecting more warriors to emerge, war cries in their throats, weapons in hand.

The one-eyed soldier returned, nodded his head, and told the Sauk, "He'll see you, come on."

Sachim glanced at Black Hawk and saw the anger in his eyes. She looked to the great fort as Black Hawk did. He was studying it with a warrior's eye, she knew, examining the Americans' defenses, measuring distances, the numbers of guns.

They crossed a large parade ground and were led to a low log building with many doors. One of these was open and the sergeant beckoned them inside. Beyond the first room was another where the fort's commander waited with several other whites.

One of them was the buckskin-clad scout Bart Perkins, one a sly-looking man in a town suit. With him was a second man dressed in twill who had the face of a dog. In the corner a farmer stared at the Sauk with malice.

The captain stood behind his desk. "Good morning, friends.

You have returned then. Good. We have many gifts for you. The trading post is well-stocked and you may take whatever you like. Credit has been established."

"What are these people doing on our land?" Black Hawk asked bluntly.

"I don't understand you," Captain Davenport said, blinking his watery blue eyes rapidly. He spread his hands. "The land the settlers are living on is land your chiefs sold to us. I have a copy of the treaty in my desk . . ." He started that way, but Black Hawk said:

"The paper means nothing. These men were gotten drunk. They sold what was not theirs, but what belongs to all of the people."

"Nevertheless . . . a treaty has been signed. Among civilized peoples—"

"You've got their gold in your safe, don't you?" the sly-looking man said smoothly.

"What did you say, Ferguson? The gold . . . yes."

"We do not want gold, we want our land," Black Hawk insisted. Sachim looked the whites over again. The man in the corner was looking back in a way she didn't like. It reminded her of the way the Prophet looked at her.

"No one agreed to having a fort placed here," Sachim said, speaking up for the first time. "That is a violation of this treaty."

"Young lady . . ." Captain Davenport looked anxious and confused. "Just who is spokesman for your tribe? I'm sure this can be worked out. The Sauk, after all, have much more land, do you not? Across the Mississippi, I am told that you have miles of holdings."

"*This* is our land," Black Hawk insisted.

"It was," the surveyor said, "until you sold it." Black Hawk's glare could have cut Joshua Ferguson in two.

"I only know that I have a copy of the treaty signed by both sides," the army officer reiterated, "and for our part we are perfectly willing to abide by the terms." He stroked his nose with two fingers, glancing at the surveyor again and then at Hank Greeley in the corner of his office. "Of course I have no authority to alter the terms of the treaty. I have orders to abide by it, you must see that."

"You could, of course, petition the governor, but since the treaty has been approved by Congress they would have to take matters under consideration."

"You will do nothing," Black Hawk said.

"I *can* do nothing." Davenport again asked, "Who is the spokesman for you? Is it you?" he asked Black Hawk.

"I am the man who speaks for the tribe," Keokuk said, taking a step forward. "I speak for the council."

"Then . . ." Davenport looked at Black Hawk, his eyes narrowing.

"I am war leader," Black Hawk said. "You know my name, you know that if the whites do not leave, you will see me another time—and there will be a weapon in my hand."

He turned around and stalked out of the office, and after a moment Sachim followed. Joshua Ferguson smirked. Keokuk pursed his lips thoughtfully.

"Let us talk," Keokuk said. He turned his attention to Napope and Quash-qua-me. "Let us talk before some foolish warrior leads us into a war we do not want."

"That's right," Ferguson said, leaning back in his leather-covered chair, filling his pipe. "It's always better to talk out these matters. No one wants a little dispute leading to bloodshed." The surveyor turned half-around. "Maybe you'd better fetch that gold from your safe, Captain, just to show these men that we are sincere about fulfilling our end of the bargain."

Ferguson lit his pipe and leaned back again, hands behind his head. He really didn't care if there was a war or not—he could always pull up stakes and leave the territory—except that it would cut down on future opportunities. Ferguson had bargained hard for his contract as the government's official surveyor in the Mississippi valley, and his lobbying, though costly, had already reaped windfall profits. The fee he charged each settler for staking the boundaries of his land was exorbitant, but since the land itself was free, no one had balked at it. There was nothing to it. Send Ginger Sweet out each morning with a couple of assistants and lounge around the fort collecting fees from the newly arriving settlers.

By Ferguson's reckoning he was already very wealthy. He wanted more.

Two enlisted men arrived with four sacks of gold coins and spilled them out on the captain's desk. Keokuk moved forward a step. There was a deep light in his dark eyes. A reflection of the gold, Ferguson decided. There was a man you could work with, unlike Black Hawk.

Quash-qua-me asked, "Can we buy goods in your trading post?"

"Anytime at all," the captain said. "Hank Greeley here has been licensed as sutler and Indian-trading-post operator. But for now there is no need to spend any gold if you don't want to. Isn't that right, Hank?"

"We don't need cash," Greeley said. "Government's offered credit and we mean to stand by it. You people have wintered away; spring's here, good beaver hides can be had, huh? I'll buy all you can bring in. Beaver, otter, ermine. Beaver's the thing. They're suddenly wearing beaver hats in the East. Crazy for 'em. I'll pay you top prices. Dollar a prime hide."

"The land—" Napope began.

Keokuk said, "What do we need with this land? A little corn. A little rice. Squash. We can grow that anywhere— across the river. It is good that the fort has been built here, good that the Americans have come. The trading post will give us all we need. The beaver are many; we will grow wealthy."

"That's right," Ferguson said encouragingly. "We can all grow richer off this. The settlers have their land, you have the trading post."

"And you?" Keokuk asked.

"Me, I get by," Joshua Ferguson said, and he couldn't keep the thin smile from forming on his lips.

"And we will have peace," Captain Davenport said. "That is uppermost, is it not?"

Quash-qua-me asked, "When can we visit the trading post?"

"Why, right now. Right now, isn't that right, Greeley?"

"Sure," Greeley said, rising. He added under his breath, "And we can hope the bastards don't cut our throats." He hadn't forgotten the trouble at Carney's trading post on the Cuivre. Maybe nothing like that could happen on the army post, but you never knew—the Indians couldn't be trusted. Nobody could figure out what went on in their minds. If it wasn't for the vast profits Greeley meant to make in the fur trade . . . But that was the most important matter at the moment.

"Come on," Greeley said jovially. "I'll be happy to open up for you men. Whatever you want, take. You just have to sign the book. Make your mark. When you bring me furs, I'll scratch your name off."

They went out in a group, but Captain Davenport remained behind, still uneasy. That Black Hawk . . . A single gold-eagle coin lay on the floor behind his desk and he stooped to pick it up, examining it minutely, with a sort of wonder, thinking not a bit of the intrinsic value of the coin but of what it represented.

Sweeping out through the orderly room, the Sauk and their white escorts passed a big man with red hands. He was leaning on his musket, just watching. When they had passed, he turned his head and spat.

"Help you?" the duty corporal asked.

"Name's McCutcheon. Thaddeus McCutcheon. Came to offer my services to the army."

"To enlist, you mean?" the young corporal asked.

"No, son, not to enlist. I'm a hunter. That's it. Meat hunter. Thought the army might need someone to stock their larder."

"I'll ask the captain if he'll see you," the soldier responded, rising. He looked only once at the big man and then turned away. He didn't like what he saw in those eyes. Still, there was every chance the army might take on a good buffalo hunter. Soldiers had other duties; civilians not engaged in farming were rare. *Just a buffalo hunter,* the corporal told himself as he knocked at the captain's door.

Why, then, had the orderly room seemed just a little colder when he had entered it—the day a little darker?

Sachim waited beneath the pine trees, watching the river run as the tall evergreens swayed in the brisk wind. She could see smoke rising from white houses, see American soldiers moving about outside the fort. Once a donkey brayed and someone laughed distantly.

Black Hawk was somber, sitting on the needle-strewn slope, his arms around his knees, occasionally picking up a fascicle of dry pine needles and tearing it angrily apart.

He was in no mood to speak and so Sachim said nothing. She only stood watching the distances, the wind shifting her long hair, drifting it across her face.

"They have been gone too long," he said at last, not taking his eyes from the fort.

"All things take time, Black Hawk."

"Yes. The good as well as the bad."

It was almost another hour before the council members

emerged from the fort. Black Hawk stood, hands clenched, the tendons on his neck standing taut.

Soldiers escorted council members, and with them they had a mule-drawn wagon piled high with goods. "It is over," was all Black Hawk said.

"Wait and talk to them," Sachim advised.

"It is over." Eyes at once forlorn and savage turned toward Sachim.

"Perhaps it is not as you think."

"No? How do you think it has gone, spirit woman? Have you not dreamed of this? Have you not seen the whites as numerous as ears of summer corn upon our land?"

"Then what . . . ?" Sachim's voice was little more than a whisper. "What will you do?"

"Talk," Black Hawk replied. "Talk to the council. And then perhaps . . . I shall make my war."

Upstream it was raining. The river ran murky and brown, and the soil was washed away.

The river was red.

Keokuk talked to the rest of the tribe as campfires burned beside the river and a constantly hooting owl sat in some tree watching. Whose soul was that calling from the forest? Sachim wondered.

"There are many gifts," Keokuk said to the gathered Sauk. "Take what you want. There are many more goods in the trading post. We have made a bargain and now we will honor it."

"You have sold our souls," a voice muttered. Keokuk ignored the voice as he ignored the owl.

"We will cross the river and build lodges on new land. We will plant corn and it will grow as it always has. We will trap beaver and mink as we always have and trade them for whatever we need."

"And what will the Sioux say?" Sachim asked.

"The Sioux? It is our hunting ground as well as theirs. Let them make their summer camp somewhere else. When have we feared the Sioux?"

"When have we lived upon their land?"

"Woman," Keokuk said, "we know *you* do not fear the Sioux. Why should we?"

Pa-she-pa-ho laughed out loud, and he was not alone.

Sachim felt her jaw tighten. From the shadows which moved in the firelight the Prophet stared mockingly.

"I will not cross the Mississippi," Black Hawk said. "No! I refuse to! Those who will go, let them; those who wish to remain with me, prepare to fight."

"You are speaking outside the law," Napope cautioned.

"The law has already been broken!" Black Hawk answered passionately. "You have already sold our birthright for a few beads, for a little rum, for a blanket!"

"I warn you," Napope said, "be cautious, war leader."

"Be cautious. And be a shame to our blood," Black Hawk answered with disgust.

Keokuk said, "Why do we debate with this man? It has been decided. The council has spoken."

"The council has behaved with cowardice," Black Hawk couldn't keep himself from saying.

Keokuk hissed, "You will be silent, Black Hawk."

"Yes, I will be silent," the war leader said. "But I will not remain here, not now. I will not cross the Mississippi so that Keokuk can have his gold and Quash-qua-me his trinkets."

Then Black Hawk was gone. Sachim tried to touch his arm, to speak to him as he passed her, but he saw no one, heard nothing. His mind was so filled with anger, he was blinded to anything outside his own bleak thoughts.

"We must make peace with him," Pa-she-pa-ho said worriedly.

"Let him make peace with us." Keokuk turned to face the others. "We have made a treaty. It was our right."

"He will make war," Pa-she-pa-ho said gloomily.

"He will not! Who will follow him against the will of the council?" Keokuk asked.

"Too many," Quash-qua-me said. "Far too many." He stood watching the darkening forest and then shook his head.

Before nightfall the Sauk began crossing the river. Some used hastily constructed rafts, others canoes which had survived their winter storage. Still others rode their horses, holding children aloft.

Sachim watched as the last minutes of sunset colored the skies and the tribe seemed to be swallowed up by the dark river as they moved away from her.

White Bear appeared at her side and touched her elbow. "I am sorry. I am going."

"Going?" She turned to the massive warrior. His face glowed a dull red in the dusk.

"With Black Hawk," he explained.

"But where! Where are you going?"

"To see what can be done. To the British. I am going, and Ha-te-ka and Pak-wa."

"To make a war?"

"If it is decided." White Bear shrugged. "I go because my war leader has asked me. Sachim . . ." His huge hands fell on her shoulders. "I will not be here to dance the crane dance. You would not have chosen me for a husband anyway, would you?" She looked away and White Bear said, "Never mind—I ask for nothing but your friendship. You shall always have mine."

He touched her head curiously. He looked into her eyes briefly and then at the river, turning heavily to walk away, leaving Sachim alone.

She walked back to the top of the hill, seeing the fires glowing in the windows of the white cabins, the larger fire at the fort. Sha-sak waited with Grandmother, keeping her warm in the night.

"Well, have you finished your lovemaking?" Sha-sak asked. Sachim tried to answer her smile but failed. Grandmother was awake. She touched Sachim's hand.

"I want to see his grave once more. My husband's resting place. Take me to where Sun Wolf lies."

"Yes, Grandmother."

"He sleeps, and beside him your mother. Husband and daughter . . . both gone. I wish to join them more each day. If it were not for you, Sachim . . ."

"Hush."

"When I am gone, see that I lie there—next to them. Please. I ask you this, Sachim."

"You will live forever."

"Then I am a new species," Grandmother said with a laugh which became a dry cough. "Promise me, Sachim."

Grandmother's eyes were sincere, almost pleading. The wrinkled, dry hand of the old Indian woman closed around Sachim's wrist as she spoke.

"I promise," Sachim said quietly. "You know I will do as you wish, Grandmother."

"Good. It is good then . . ." She lay back, contented.

Sha-sak said, "Where is that lazy husband of mine? Cliff Arrow! Have you fallen to sleep or found a jar of rum?"

Sleepily Cliff Arrow rose to his feet and came to his wife. He paid no attention at all to Sha-sak's gibes. Sha-sak delighted in games and gossip and jokes. She was incapable of being serious about life for a long period of time. This, Cliff Arrow understood; for that he loved his big hardworking woman.

"I have my canoe on the beach—unless some white has stolen it." Cliff Arrow scratched his bony arm. "We should go now. It is nearly dark and the serpents come out at night on the river." Cliff Arrow spoke quietly as if all of his conversation was merely reflection, not meant to be shared. With Sachim he lifted the blanket on which Grandmother lay and they started down through the dark pines as the last rays of the dying sun bled onto the water and touched the tips of the trees with brilliant gold.

They paddled across the river, not fighting the current but letting it carry them as far as it would. Sachim let her hand dip into the cold dark face of the Life-giver and then she tasted the water. Looking back, she could see the white fires like fireflies against the dark land.

"I did not want to go with Black Hawk," Cliff Arrow said in his familiar monotone. "Perhaps I should have gone, but where are they going? Where is their war?"

"His war," Sachim answered, almost unheard, "is here. It is here."

8

CAPTAIN Hobbs, his eyes rubbed raw, put the letter from the military governor of Upper Canada aside and tugged at a loosening front tooth. He lifted his eyes to the orderly who had knocked and entered without saluting. Since they were officially in foreign territory, Illinois, Hobbs had instructed his men to wear no military garments, never to salute or carry weapons that might be identified as British military arms.

"They're here, sir," Hollingshead said to his commander. Hollingshead, whose mother was Welsh, and father a London tailor, was one of many who served Captain Hobbs out of personal loyalty, even to the point of risking his life by infiltrating American territory and attempting to raise an insurrection, which was certainly a capital crime under American law.

"All right, show them in, please."

Hobbs sucked at his loose tooth, and looked once to the inner door that led to his quarters here in this abandoned capitol building in this fur-trading center of Desiree. He stood, straightened his coat, and briefly glanced around the decaying interior of the log building, reflecting ironically on its contrast with the fifty-room country house where he had been born thirty-two years earlier to an effete and sorrowful lord and an indifferent mother.

The Sauk war leader came in, looking tired himself. Mud covered Black Hawk from his moccasined feet to his waist. The rain hadn't let up for three days. Hobbs nodded, knowing Black Hawk did not care to shake hands. His silent

141

lieutenant, the giant, was behind the Sauk chieftain, carrying a musket-rifle decorated with feathers and brass studs driven into the stock. This White Bear stood to one side of the door, as if ready to defend to the death his liege.

These were men. Hobbs couldn't have explained his fascination with wild country, from the Congo to western Illinois, but it had always been there; and he, who should have been breaking debutantes' hearts with his blond good looks, dressing in fashionable silk and scarves, needed the far places, dirty buckskins. He needed to be in the company of men who, friend or enemy, exuded strength and had been formed in the raw lands.

Black Hawk was one of these.

Hobbs seated himself in his puncheon chair behind the dilapidated desk which had been the old fur trader's and folded his hands together, resting his chin on his knuckles.

"How did you find me?" Hobbs asked.

"A white in the forest is like a buffalo herd on the plains," Black Hawk said. "Always noted."

Hobbs laughed. "That is why we lost the last war, one supposes."

Black Hawk said intently, "I have fought in a hundred wars. If one is lost it means nothing when the next must be fought."

"But the Americans grow stronger every day, Black Hawk. We hold Canada still, but if there was a strong American push into that country we would be beaten again. There would be no British presence at all left in the New World."

"The 'New World'?"

"No matter—you have come for a reason."

"Yes, a reason."

Hobbs guessed, "Only war would bring you."

"It is war, Hobbs. The Americans have taken our land. Foolish old chiefs have taken gifts for it. Greedy young men have accepted it."

"You do not."

"No, I do not accept it."

"I thought not," Hobbs said. "Nor does King George like it." Hobbs rose and wandered the room aimlessly, looking at a tattered, obsolete map on the wall.

"King George," Black Hawk said with a shadow of sarcasm, "does not like Americans at all because they have taken something he did want—much of his kingdom."

Hobbs astonished Black Hawk by laughing out loud. "You are right of course, Black Hawk. So it goes in history, in war. One people moves in, another is dispossessed. In the end it is all numbers and weapons—and will. The will to possess or survive."

"I am a warrior," Black Hawk said flatly, and for a moment Hobbs just looked at the Sauk leader.

"It is pretentious of me to explain warfare to you," Hobbs said apologetically.

"I do not understand you."

"Never mind." Hobbs returned to his desk, sat down, and slapped his paper knife against the scarred desktop. "You are ready to fight now against the Americans?"

"It must be."

"Yes."

"With a few new muskets and powder. With British allies. . ."

"There will be none," Hobbs said.

"You wish to defeat the Americans."

"Of course, but there will be no British troops in Illinois. Not now. There will be no weapons for the Sauk. Not in Illinois."

"Then I am wasting my time," Black Hawk said angrily.

"No. Listen to me, Black Hawk. There is trouble on the seas between the Americans and the British. War is coming."

"Then . . . ?"

"We are too far from our Canadian outposts here. Illinois, Louisiana, are difficult to supply, impossible to defend even with Indian allies. The war will be fought in the East."

"Tecumseh." The Shawnee chief was preparing for a major struggle.

"You know him then," Hobbs said.

"I know his dream. An Indian nation. Shawnee, Creek, Cherokee, Chickasaw against the whites. The only way to turn back numbers is with numbers, is that not so, Hobbs?" Black Hawk asked.

"And the Sauk?"

"What do you mean?"

"Shawnee, Creek, Cherokee. And what of the Fox and the Sauk?"

"It is impossible," Black Hawk said flatly. "It is like asking the Sioux to fight beside the Sauk."

"And if it isn't done?" Hobbs suggested. "Then perhaps it is the end of all the Indian people."

"Not of the Sauk!"

"Let us hope not," Hobbs said.

"You mean that, don't you?" Black Hawk said.

"Of course." Hobbs was surprised.

"Yes. I know you are King George's man. I know you do what he says, but I believe you. Tell me this, Hobbs: if you will not help us fight, what can we do then?"

"Help *us* fight."

"Whom do you mean—King George?"

Hobbs rose, walked to the inner door, and rapped twice. White Bear tensed slightly, moving deeper into the shadow of the corner. If Black Hawk trusted this soldier, it was good. White Bear himself had not yet learned to trust any white.

The man who emerged from the room wasn't British, or even white. He wore a feathered cape, a bear-claw necklace, and paint on his face. He was Shawnee.

"Tenskwatawa," Black Hawk said. He knew the Shawnee prophet, Tecumseh's brother.

"It is I, Black Hawk. The time has come. My brother has sent me. Join us on the Wabash or be prepared to lose all—land, honor, and life."

Black Hawk looked at Hobbs and smiled faintly. "I think it is not such a surprise to you that I am here, British."

Hobbs answered, "Even a Sauk makes a little noise in the woods."

"I spoke to a Fox warrior. You know him," Tenskwatawa said. "Two-Knives told us what is happening to you. Two-Knives knew, Hobbs knew. Tecumseh knows."

The Shawnee prophet went on. "Your council has betrayed you. Your council, any council, can grow weak. It can fail the people. I know—we have paid the price for our own council's foolishness. Now the time of the councils is gone, Black Hawk. Now it is the time of the war leaders. The British stand with the Shawnee. Stand beside both of us."

Then the Shawnee hobbled toward the door—he was slightly crippled—leaving Hobbs alone with White Bear and Black Hawk.

Hobbs said nothing; he only watched. White Bear was the one to ask the fateful question: "What then do we do, Ma-ka-tai-me-she-kia-kiak?"

"What can we do?" Black Hawk asked rhetorically. "The Shawnee prophet knows. He knows. It is the time of the warriors."

The young men danced and Sachim watched them. They bent low and spread their feathered arms, ducked their heads and turned sharply from one side to the other as the fire backlighted the crane dance. It was that night in spring; it was a time of renewal.

Maidens, knowing what was to come on this night, watched from the shadows, giggling or gossiping in whispers. Soon they would be maidens no more, the chosen ones—those who succumbed to the charms of the young Sauk dancers.

Sachim watched with an indulgent smile as tiny First Snow imitated the warriors' dance, her head bobbing, outspread arms jabbing at the air. Overhead it was starry; a fountain of smoke and fire rose against the night sky.

"Tonight, Sachim!" Sha-sak laughed, nudging her with an elbow. "Which warrior will come to your lodge?"

"None I hope," Sachim answered honestly. "Let them play their flutes for Tanaka or Little Creek. Not for me."

"But some will come. The spirit woman of the Sauk, our far-dreamer, is beautiful and many a warrior wants to lie down with her."

"It is not time."

"It is not time," Sha-sak said above the drums and whistles of the dancers. "And one day perhaps you will say, 'Now the time has passed.' A woman is no good alone. Neither is a man. We are night and day, summer and winter. A whole."

"You would be pleased to see all our maidens courted and married tonight, Sha-sak."

"Of course!" the big woman laughed. "Then they would all lie in their beds and laugh at night, all be happy and not lie dreaming of some man from far away who might never come."

The crane dance went on, but Sachim's thoughts turned to other things. It was time to plant corn and they hadn't yet cleared new fields; their rice fields were across the river in the sloughs, so perhaps they would have no rice; Black Hawk was gone.

He was gone to make a war, and no one, not even the council members, knew where he was now.

The dance continued; the fire burned brighter yet as the children ran to throw on twigs to feed it. Sachim rose and walked toward her lodge. They had not yet had the time to build permanent lodges on this side of the river and so their slightly dilapidated hide-and-pole lodges now had to be used. Sachim, Grandmother, Little Creek, and a woman called Ta-wa-shuk shared a common lodge.

Grandmother slept; the lodge was dark and still. Sachim lay down and watched a single star through the open smoke flap overhead. She listened to the drums and the laughter of her people and tried to sleep, but it was impossible.

The people would be up till dawn on this night of romance. Soon the others would return to the lodge and she would be awakened again. Later still the young braves would begin playing their flutes amid the constant movement of the game, the giggling of young women. Sachim yawned, rolled onto her side, and tugged her striped blanket up. She slept, but it seemed to be only five minutes or so before Ta-wa-shuk and Little Creek slipped in, trying to be quiet while First Snow laughed at something. They started a small fire and closed the tent flap.

"Comb your hair, Little Creek, here is your porcupine brush."

"No one will be coming," Little Creek whispered, but opening an eye, Sachim saw her brushing her long hair while Ta-wa-shuk changed into a new dress.

Ta-wa-shuk was seventeen and flirtatious, eager for a husband. This was the night she had waited for over the long winter. Sachim sat up; there was no point in trying to sleep.

"Sachim, get up!" First Snow said excitedly. "Soon they will be coming."

Little Creek shushed the child. "We are supposed to be asleep."

"No one is sleeping," First Snow argued.

"But you have to pretend!"

"Put your new dress on, Sachim, your white elkskin," Ta-wa-shuk said urgently.

First Snow went to take it from her woven trunk. "Here it is, Sachim. So pretty too!"

"All right," Sachim said, "thank you."

She dressed as the other women chattered excitedly. "Ha-te-ka will come, I know he will," Ta-wa-shuk said.

"His leg is wounded. Perhaps he went to his lodge to sleep," Little Creek teased.

"He will come. Or perhaps Pak-wa. He is strong, Pak-wa."

"Perhaps Skull is back and he will come."

"Ugh. Don't even tease."

"They are out there," Sachim said. "Somewhere I hear a flute. Put out the fire. Quickly!"

The women got into their blankets, First Snow giggling uncontrollably. Sachim was right. Across the camp now they could hear flutes being played. The maidens one by one would rise from their beds and creep out. If the flute kept playing the same song, they would return to their lodge. If, however, it changed to the love song, they would know the warrior was playing for them. Then it was the woman's choice whether she would return to the lodge, rejecting the man, or stay with him, consenting to be his wife.

"I hear—" First Snow began.

"Sh!" Little Creek said sharply.

Someone was outside their lodge now and in a minute a flute began to play. First Snow giggled again.

"You first, Sachim!" Ta-wa-shuk whispered. "Go out and see who it is."

Sachim crawled from her bed and went out into the starry night. The flute continued to play and after a time she ducked back into the lodge.

"Who is it?" Ta-wa-shuk asked. "Was it Ha-te-ka?"

"I couldn't see him."

"Little Creek . . ." Ta-wa-shuk pushed her friend from the bed. "Go and see if it is you he calls. See who it is!"

Little Creek too slipped out and Sachim lay in the darkness listening to the continuing melody of the flute. Ta-wa-shuk's eyes were wide in the starlight. She held her breath as she waited.

When Little Creek returned, she was in a devilish mood. "He wasn't playing for me," she said, and crawled in bed.

Ta-wa-shuk sat straight up and pushed Little Creek's shoulder hard. "Who is it? You know, don't you?"

"No," Little Creek said, but it was obvious she did.

"Tell me. I'll do something bad to you while you sleep, Little Creek, I promise!"

The flute played on. Little Creek said, "Go out and see, then, if you want to know."

"Evil woman, bad friend," Ta-wa-shuk said. She was ner-

vous. For all of her flirtatiousness she was at heart afraid of
men, uncertain of what came after marriage although the
older women had told her many times.

"Go see. See who it is."

"*Skull*," First Snow laughed, ducking under her blankets
to get away from Ta-wa-shuk.

Ta-wa-shuk went to the tent flap and peered out. "Go on
and see," Little Creek urged. Looking back once, Ta-wa-
shuk went out and they heard the flute change to the love
song. First Snow giggled under her blankets.

The tune broke off as Ta-wa-shuk reentered the lodge and
with evident disgust threw herself onto her bed. "How can
he even play the flute!"

"It was not Ha-te-ka?"

"No!" Ta-wa-shuk sat straight up. "*Nikia*. He has no
front teeth! How can he even play the flute."

She lay down, throwing an arm over her face, disappointed and still angry. It was an hour before Ha-te-ka did
come, and this time it was Ta-wa-shuk who was sent out
first. She was gone a long time and when she came back she
was smiling.

"Well, will you marry him?" First Snow asked excitedly.

"I don't know, I don't know," she answered. But she did
know and so did they.

The night passed in that way. Across the camp there
would be fluting and still more laughing; other warriors
came courting at Sachim's lodge, so many that she grew
weary of it.

"I wish dawn would come," she said at one point, "and
chase all these silly young men home." No one answered.
First Snow had long ago fallen asleep. Little Creek and
Ha-te-ka sat facing each other in the dark, gossiping in a
torrent of whispers.

"You first, Sachim."

"I don't care who it is, now that Ha-te-ka has come,"
Ta-wa-shuk insisted.

Sachim went out again, her eyes heavy. The sky was
paling slightly in the east although the stars were still bright
in the sky. Good, she thought, soon it would be dawn and
they could all sleep.

The moon was only now beginning to rise, a deep gold
half-ball behind the trees, and by that light Sachim could see
the warrior sitting cross-legged on the ground, flute to his

lips. She turned to go back into the lodge and heard the tune change, becoming the love song, becoming something which turned her slowly and lifted her heart to a frantically beating thing beneath her breast.

"Thunder Horse."

The Sioux rose and came to her and Sachim was unable to move as he dragged her to him, kissed her, and stood stroking her hair, smiling down at her, his fine strong body pressed to hers, his eyes alive with moonlight.

"Thunder Horse," she repeated, and her cheek rested against his chest as he rubbed her back with his powerful hand and bent to kiss her neck.

"I was a week learning the tune," he said with a smile. "You did not like my Sioux way of courting and so I became a Sauk for tonight at least."

"I still can't—" His kiss ended the protest. His breath was warm against her cheek, his arms a secure and love-filled place to be.

"You can, Sachim. After a winter apart you know we must have each other. You know this as well as I."

"But how can we do this? How can we love?"

"Because I am Sioux?"

She shook her head. "There is Grandmother."

"We shall take care of her. I will move here with you. I want you to come with me to my father's camp once, and then I will live here—as Sauk if you wish."

"There may even be war!"

"Sachim," Thunder Horse said seriously, quietly, "I know about war. Hunger. Sorrow. This is the way life is and no one can stop death from coming or know what tomorrow will bring. Perhaps great pain, blood.

"I only know this, woman: joy alone is our protection against the pain of life. Love is joy. One suffers; with love one does not suffer so. All things are meant to be shared. By a man and a woman."

"Thunder Horse . . ."

"I know." He put his finger to her lips. "You are uncertain, but I ask you for nothing at this moment. In the morning I will be at the old place, on the island. Come if you can love me and live as my wife. I have raised my song; do what must be done to make your heart happy."

He kissed her again, so lightly that when he withdrew it seemed only a distant memory of a promised kiss. He said,

"I have raised my song," and then Thunder Horse was gone, walking through the forest as the eerie mingling lights of the moon and coming dawn blended, forming a soft glow neither red nor gold, but magical and deep. A tall strong figure was silhouetted against this light among the straight dark motionless forms of the pines—and then was gone, like a dream of a man.

Crickets sang a constant chorus as Sachim made her way back to the lodge and lay down on her bed. "Who was it, Sachim?" Little Creek whispered. "Who was it?"

"It is no one. Someone at another lodge. No one is out there."

She lay back, watching the sky through the smoke flap, hearing the birds of morning awaken and begin to sing. She lifted a finger to her lips, touching them, and then closed her eyes. Her heart still pounded. He had returned and raised his song, this Sioux warrior, and the song he raised was too huge for the sky.

Sachim still wore her new white buckskin dress when she awoke. She was amazed that she hadn't slipped out of it before lying down. That was not like her at all.

Looking around the lodge, she saw that it was still very early. She couldn't have slept for more than an hour or two. First Snow lay sleeping soundly, knees drawn up, fists clenched, unformed mouth slightly open, tiny snores rising softly. Grandmother was asleep. Little Creek and Ta-washuk slept as well. They had had a long night and now they walked through their dreams of strong young warriors who—

Sachim sat up suddenly. *Thunder Horse*. He had been no dream. Her heart began to race. She looked at her hands and found them trembling.

Foolishness, foolishness.

And yet she rose, brushed her hair, and tied it back. She rinsed her face with the water from the ash-bark basket beside her rush bed and looked toward the lodge entrance. She waited on her knees, unable to decide, fearful and yet needing.

"Go to him."

Sachim turned her head. Grandmother lay there, smiling. She lifted a hand. "Go to him, Sachim," she repeated. "That is the way it should be."

"Go to him? To whom, Grandmother?"

"Go to him. I am not so old that I do not see, do not hear. Not so old yet that I do not dream. Be young; you are. Love; you do. Go—it is necessary."

Sachim turned slowly toward the entrance to the lodge and with measured strides slipped from the hide house. The sun was low yet, filling her eyes with brilliant spots of color, haloing the trees as the pale moon floated, seemingly balanced on the tops of the pines.

The air was cool and scented with pine. The river could be heard beyond the hills. Sachim was walking purposefully now, one part of her mind holding her back while the other echoed her Grandmother's words.

Be young. Love. Go.

She walked more swiftly now and from time to time she broke into a run. She had to force herself to slow down as she crested the hill and saw the splendor of the sun on the golden river.

Then she was walking down the hill through the pines and maple trees. She was walking and then she gave up resistance to it all, surrendered propriety to need, to urgency.

Be young. Love.

She was running down the hill slope now, slipping and weaving. She too had the right to love; she too had the right to live. And somehow, before she knew how, she was in the birchbark and paddling toward the island in midstream, feeling ashamed of her boldness. Still the wild rush of need and wanting carried her along and she paddled faster as the sun broke free of the tangle of trees on the far shore and glared in her eyes.

She was a woman of dignity and reserve; she felt distanced from this other woman, the one who raced toward the island as if only that mattered, only him, as if she might already be too late. Yet she could not slow herself, could not be the reserved Sachim.

The sunlight was brilliant on the water. The sky was white. The island was a dark, serrated form floating on the river. She guided her canoe to the shore and for a time just sat in it, looking at the trees, feeling suddenly foolish.

"Sachim."

Thunder Horse emerged from the pines to stand watching, waiting, and she leapt from the canoe into the water and ran to him, tears inexplicably flooding her eyes.

Then she was in his arms, trembling, feeling the warmth

of his body against hers. He was necessary. There had to be Thunder Horse in her life. Not *a man*, a warrior-husband, but only him, and she clung to him as he kissed her forehead, eyes, ears, and mouth hungrily before scooping her up as if she weighed nothing, carrying her with him into the forest where he had made his lodge.

It was a simple lean-to of pine boughs with a bed of pine needles over which blankets had been placed. Sachim felt herself being lowered onto the bed. Then he was standing over her, dressed only in his loincloth. Above Thunder Horse's head sunlight winked through the gaps in the lean-to's roof. Sachim lay there unmoving, only half-believing in the reality of the moment.

This had happened before, all of it. Somewhere, sometime in some dream of longing.

He was on his knees now, looking into her eyes. His own glowed softly and she could see the caring in them, the want. She stretched out her arms and drew Thunder Horse to her, feeling his arms slip beneath her shoulders.

They lay still; the only sound was the wind in the forest and the river whispering past. Sachim could not have said why, but tears had begun to flow again, brimming up in her eyes, trickling away down her cheek as Thunder Horse lay still beside her, holding her as if she were a child.

She touched his powerful chest with her fingertips, amazed at the maleness of him. Lifting her head, she kissed his shoulder and again his face turned toward her, tasting her tears, as his lips found hers and they kissed deeply.

He rose again to his knees and then stood. Sachim sat up, not knowing what to do, knowing that she had done it long ago—once in some dream.

She slipped her dress over her hips and then up over her head and lay back, wondering why she felt no shame, no embarrassment as Thunder Horse let his loincloth drop to the floor and lay down beside her, his arm behind her neck, his right hand on her thigh, tugging her to him to meet his flesh with her own, to press against him and greedily accept his needful kiss.

"I have waited forever," Thunder Horse said.

"I know."

They spoke no more. They knew it, both of them. Their love had begun long ago, before time. Sachim had fought the knowledge of it: the need of man for woman, woman for man, the certainty that Thunder Horse had once before met her soul. Now she knew it could not be resisted, that love had come once to her, that it would not end.

Love beyond time.

He lay with her, running his finger across her eyebrows, kissing the hollow at the base of her throat, his eyes still holding that deep, knowing, fascinated glow. They had found each other somehow. Among all of the world's people.

He reached toward her, and she could feel him shudder. His eyes were closed now and he murmured a single word that made no sense. Sachim stroked his dark hair and drew him nearer until he was closer yet, beside her, within her, among her.

Who she was, what she was then, she did not know. Sachim no longer thought, but only touched, felt, loved, and the day went by as she slowly and inexorably passed from need to discovery and loving knowledge.

Sachim's eyes fluttered open. She had fallen asleep without realizing it, and drifted through a warm and mysterious dream.

He lay still beside her. She placed her hand on his strong shoulder and let it travel across his muscular back to his waist. She bent her head and kissed his spine, her dark hair spilling across his back, and he slowly opened his eyes.

"Did I sleep, I'm sorry," Thunder Horse said.

"I slept too. I dreamed."

"I do not feel that I dreamed," he said, sitting up. "I feel that I have awakened, finally."

On their knees they faced each other and Thunder Horse held her so tightly that she lost her breath.

"There is much to talk about," she said at last.

"Yes."

"Everything you said . . ." she began hesitantly.

"I meant it."

"You wish to live among the Sauk?"

"I wish to live with you," he said, brushing back her hair with his fingertips.

"Then we shall have to talk to the council. I want to talk to Grandmother. My friends . . ."

"Then we shall do it all," Thunder Horse said, his lips following her collarbone to her shoulder. His words, his presence, reassured her. For a time she was able to lie back with him and think of nothing else in the world again.

It was late afternoon before they emerged, hand in hand, from the lodge and started toward the canoe. Thunder Horse had decided to wear his formal bonnet, which despite his youth had eagle feathers trailing to the middle of his back. He wore his buckskin shirt and leggings. "The bonnet," he had told Sachim, "will do no harm—it will remind them of who my father is."

"And what will your father say to this marriage?" Sachim asked.

"Far Eagle!" Thunder Horse laughed. "Just what your people will say: 'There are many beautiful Sioux women who make fine moccasins and flesh out the buffalo. Why marry a Sauk?' "

"And what will you say, Thunder Horse?"

"I will say, 'Father, it must be. So my heart speaks.' "

Sachim kissed him on the cheek and waited as Thunder Horse placed his belongings in the canoe and held it for her. They paddled in silence across the river. The sky was clear, the river empty and wide.

They beached the birchbark beyond the great rocks where the cave of the great spirit dwelled. Many of the tribe had seen the spirit. It was white, with wings like a swan's, but ten times larger.

They walked up the path which wound through the rocks and trees and went down again into the village. They passed through the heart of it, receiving looks of astonishment, indifference, anger, and pleasure.

It was to Napope's lodge that Sachim led the Sioux warrior. The council chief studied Sachim, looked over the bonneted Sioux, and asked them to sit.

"Smoke with me," Napope invited Thunder Horse. A part of his hospitality was appeasement. The Sauk had moved across the river and onto Sioux land. Although the Sauk had an equal claim to it, and the Sioux used it only as a seasonal hunting camp, still tacit agreement had acknowledged that it was Sioux soil, a fact Napope was well aware of.

With Black Hawk gone it was no time for trouble with Far Eagle's band.

"You wish to be married," Napope said, lighting his pipe.

"Yes," Sachim let Thunder Horse speak for them.

"So it has been rumored. So the far-dreamer has accepted your horses at last."

"Yes," Thunder Horse said. He took the pipe from Napope

and puffed at it without inhaling, handing it back with a slight bow.

"You will take her away or . . ."

"I wish to live among your people, Napope. So Sachim wishes it, so it will be. She is concerned for her grandmother."

"Can you be content here, Thunder Horse?" the old chief asked, rubbing his eyes.

"Where she is, I am content."

"You are very young," Napope said with a grimacing smile. "But that is for you to decide. What does your father say?"

"We will visit Far Eagle soon and tell him. He has only said that I am a crazy man with a heavy heart. Now he may say I am crazy, but my heart will no longer be heavy."

"It may be good for the Sauk to have the son of the Sioux war leader among us as a friend," Napope said. "It may save trouble. But what if it does not prevent trouble, Thunder Horse?" the council chief asked, lifting his eyes from his blanket.

"There is always a chance of trouble."

"What if there were war between our people? Could you fight with us? Could you kill a Sioux warrior, your father perhaps?"

"No more than you could kill your son, Napope," Thunder Horse replied.

"Then what would you do? If the people grew angry with all Sioux—with you among us—what would you and Sachim do then?"

Sachim finally spoke. "Then, Napope, we would have no people. We would go away into the far country, we would take Grandmother with us, we would be alone, sleep together, hunt as we must." She looked to Thunder Horse, wondering if she had spoken out of turn. Could he accept such a life? Away from his own people?

"Thunder Horse?" Napope inquired.

"My woman has spoken. That is what would happen. I will not war on the Sioux, ever. I will not war against the Sauk from this day forward. I swear this by Manitou and my woman's heart."

"Then," Napope sighed, "you may dwell among us as you wish. It has happened before. A woman. A good Sioux woman. But her life was not easy at first. The Sauk women did not care to have her here and they mocked her ways."

"I know this. Once a warrior brought a Crow woman to our camp. Crow are hated among us. She could not live there in happiness. One day she drowned herself in the river."

"And then?" Napope questioned.

"I am no Crow woman," Thunder Horse said. "I am the son of a war leader. I am Sioux. There is no one in your camp who can drive me to such an end. You know this, Napope."

"I know it. It is so. Go then. Build your lodge where you will. Live in happiness."

Outside, Sachim hugged Thunder Horse briefly. Her legs were trembling. She laughed. "I didn't realize how nervous I was."

"What could he do to us, Sachim? What can anyone do to us? As you say, we would go away. I am a hunter, I am a warrior. I will take care of you always, no matter where we must wander."

"Yes." She saw that he meant it, deeply meant it, as she looked into his eyes. "We must see Grandmother."

"If you wish. Will she wish to see a Sioux warrior?"

"She will want to see you, yes." Grandmother, Sachim explained, was not Sauk herself, but Oneida. Perhaps she had gone through much the same thing as the Crow woman. She had never spoken of it to Sachim; Grandmother spoke seldom about herself or about her life with Sun Wolf, and then, only of their love.

"That is the gift," she had said more than once. "Love is the gift. Go gather dreams, go gather furs and trade goods. Sit alone with them if you will. Foolish love is better than an empty life. True love *is* all of life. Love foolishly if you must, but love long."

Keokuk burst into Napope's lodge just as he was putting his cold pipe away. "I saw the Sioux here. What is happening, Napope?"

"He will marry our dreamer, Sachim."

"And take her away?" Keokuk asked with what seemed to be relief.

"And live among us."

"Thunder Horse!"

"And why not—will that not bind our tribe with Far Eagle's band?"

"I don't like it," Keokuk said. He sat, and in a serious breach of etiquette lit Napope's pipe without being invited. "I don't like Sioux. I don't like the spirit woman."

"They want only to marry and have babies, to sleep together and grow old together," Napope said, watching with distaste as Keokuk lit his pipe.

"So they say. This is what they may tell you, but who pretends to dream in opposition to the Prophet? Who is a wanderer from our enemy's tribe? Who is Black Hawk's confidante? Who is the son of the Sioux war leader?"

"What are you saying, Keokuk?"

"I say only that there may be something here that has not been revealed. Who are our enemies? The Sioux. Who is angry with us? Black Hawk. Perhaps others are seeking power among the Sauk—those who do not agree with the council."

"Not Black Hawk. He is too much a man. His loyalty goes beyond question, Keokuk."

"I may be wrong. I only suggest it," Keokuk said, placing the redstone pipe aside again. "But having this Sioux in our camp . . . I do not like it, Napope. I feel evil here."

Napope was left with that thought as Keokuk rose and went out into the night.

The Prophet emerged from the shadows to ask Keokuk, "Did he listen?"

Keokuk smiled. "He has been given something to think about."

"She must go, Keokuk," the Prophet said, looking toward the camp where Sachim and her Sioux lover had gone.

"Because she contests your dreams?"

The Prophet was briefly angry. "Because she lies about her dreams! She supports Black Hawk. Black Hawk would take your power."

"And Sachim yours," Keokuk pointed out. He had known the Prophet too intimately not to know what he was thinking.

"She lies for Black Hawk," the Prophet said. "The council grows uncertain when she speaks. Both of them must go. Black Hawk is away now—what better time to rid ourselves of the woman? What better excuse?"

"The council fears Far Eagle. They dare not offend the Sioux."

"So, He-who-has-been-everywhere," the Prophet said, using Keokuk's full name, "the moment has come and now you have no heart for it."

"For what?"

"You know what I am speaking of. Wealth will come. Power. The council is old. Black Hawk is gone. Who can stand in our way but this tiny woman?"

"I won't do it," Keokuk said, suddenly perceiving his meaning. "No."

"Then you too fear the Sioux."

"I fear," Keokuk told Wabokieshiek, "going one step too far when our time has ripened and we need only wait."

The Prophet shrugged. "As you will, Keokuk. I am nothing, only the one who hears the spirits. Do as you wish."

"Yes. As I wish," Keokuk said, but now his eyes too were on the path Sachim and Thunder Horse had taken to the village. "As I wish."

Grandmother was awake and sitting up when Sachim entered the lodge. Sachim went to her knees and held her grandmother's hands. "I have a surprise for you," she said.

"A surprise?" the old woman said.

"Well, then you knew. You knew how it would be."

"How it must be, Sachim. But let me see him, let me see this man who can take your heart and hold it."

Sachim nearly bounded away toward the entrance to the hide lodge. Grandmother smiled softly. So it was her time. Her time to love and perhaps bear children, to live through pain and the anxiety of trying to please another, working toward the ultimate joy of being one with another.

And my name is Sachim too, Grandmother thought. So many years ago I too was young and afraid—even more shy than my granddaughter—and I did not know what to do once the blanket was opened and a new world waited beyond it.

She had walked away from a painful past, Grandmother had. In the end her own world had turned to pain, to dreadful disillusionment, to ashes. But she had witnessed love and then found it for herself and she knew that only love could buoy one through life. Oh, people survived without it, working at their chores, doing for others, becoming older, wiser, more confident; but all of that was worthless. No task was worthwhile, no honor, no appreciation if there was not one person to give to, to receive from, to be with as life walked on toward its dark end.

Did Sachim know how it had been with Sun Wolf when he was young and wild and strong, laughing as he made love, proud as he demanded the Sauk accept his Oneida bride? No; how could she know? That was the burden and the privilege of age—a lifetime's experience. And the frustration of age was not being able to pass experience, wisdom, on to someone else who needed it.

The young, perhaps, are better off not to know what lies ahead, Grandmother reflected. Perhaps better off not to know of pain. It is, anyway, their life, and not that of the old. Why dim their fires, why scold or complain or darken their horizons? To the young all is possible and *will* be done.

That is as it should be, as Manitou willed it.

The young man entered and he was handsome and sure of himself, of his strength and masculinity. He was proud and tall and strong as a cougar and polite to an old woman, taking her hand in his own young hands to be introduced; and Sachim's young eyes shone.

That was all they needed. They were all they could be, all that they were meant to be.

"It is right," Grandmother said. "Be happy and be loved by each other."

Then the old woman slept and Thunder Horse and his bride slipped from the lodge to watch the evening sky, to hold hands in silence and wonder what they had embarked upon.

Bartholomew Perkins opened one eye. He lay on his back on his leather-strap-and-ticking bed in Fort Madison, hands behind his head, one boot propped up on the bedrail. His roommate was wiping his feet outside, stamping around on the plankwalk, trying to knock the pervasive red-clay mud off his boots.

Perkins closed his eyes. He didn't like this man. He was dirty, for one thing. Perkins, a frontiersman himself, knew how hard it could be to stay clean, especially in the winter, on a long hunt where no water could be found; but this man made no effort at all.

He stank like buffalo. A few times Perkins had almost pointed out that the Mississippi River was only a few hundred yards away and a man might do worse than get a little cold—he might stink to death.

The door opened and banged shut. Thaddeus McCutcheon walked across the room, still trying to knock the mud from his boots, his feet thudding against the floorboards with each step. Perkins groaned and sat up.

"Any luck?" he asked without any enthusiasm.

McCutcheon had sagged onto his own slovenly cot. He looked at Perkins indifferently. "Some. There's meat."

McCutcheon had his pocketknife in his hand and he took a deep notch out of the stock of his musket. "What's that for?" Perkins asked.

"Bear," McCutcheon answered. "I always notch for bear."

"I favor bear meat," Perkins said.

"Didn't bring the meat. He had rot. Gangrene, I mean. Brought buffalo. Sixteen on the wagon."

Perkins didn't answer. McCutcheon turned his head, spat, then hooked the tobacco out from his jaw with a crooked forefinger. That done, he was ready for bed, and the hunter lay back and was snoring deeply in minutes, his rifle beside him.

"Stink," Perkins said, and he swung his own feet to the floor, looking for his soft buckskin boots. He slipped them on and walked outside to watch the stars. Across the parade ground a few soldiers still hung around Hank Greeley's trading post, smoking and drinking.

"Bear," Perkins muttered. Since when did you find bear where you found buffalo? Well, that was McCutcheon's business, he supposed. The man was impenetrable, surly. Perkins didn't like bunking with him. As two of the few civilians here, they had been naturally put together, but Bart Perkins would rather bunk with the enlisted men—if they didn't bathe, then, by God, someone would bathe them!

He sauntered toward the enlisted barracks, glancing once up at the sky, which was now clouding over. He passed the cookshack, where soldiers in shirtsleeves were unloading McCutcheon's high-wheeled meat wagon, and continued on.

Perkins paused, frowning. There was something up. All the lights were on in the barracks. In the captain's office, a lantern blazed away as well.

Looking toward the massive front gate, he saw that it was now closed. There seemed to be more than the usual number of sentries on the wall. Sergeant Monk, his face set, was crossing toward the commander's office, buttoning his tunic. His single eye flickered to Perkins.

"What are you doing out, Bart?" Monk asked. He didn't stop walking, so Perkins fell in beside him.

"What's going on, Monk?"

"You didn't hear? War. War with the damned British."

Perkins halted and Monk hurried on. On the surface, things didn't seem urgent. Not out here. The British had no substantial force in the area, but Perkins knew full well why there was so much excitement.

The Indians.

The British had used them every chance they got during the Revolution. They would use them now if they could, and Fort Madison was virtually surrounded by Sauk and Fox Indians, who, if they chose to, could drive the Americans out and burn the place to the ground. It wasn't good, wasn't good at all. Perkins abandoned his idea of sleeping in the enlisted barracks—men would be coming and going all night, supporting the sentries.

The scout returned to the room he shared with McCutcheon—if worse came to worse, he could take his bedroll and his musket and sleep outside.

There was a candle burning in the room and Perkins paused outside it uncertainly. Instead of swinging the door open wide and striding in as he had every right and reason to, Perkins for some uncertain reason paused at the door, slowly slid the bar, and peered in.

McCutcheon was awake and sitting up. His face was deeply shadowed by the feeble glow of the candle, which painted dark circles beneath his eyes and down his throat. He was just sitting there, fully dressed, stroking what seemed to be a small animal or a piece of dark fur. Perkins knew suddenly what it was.

A scalp. McCutcheon's mouth moved soundlessly as he stroked the scalp. Then, as Perkins watched through the inch-wide gap of the door, the meat hunter took a buckskin sack from beneath his bed and placed the scalp inside. There was already something in the bag. Many somethings, Perkins thought. More scalps.

A notch for every bear, is it? Perkins thought. And how many notches were on that .50-caliber musket McCutcheon used? Bart Perkins eased the door shut and turned away.

In the captain's office, a meeting was in progress. Bartholomew Perkins went in and took a seat to one side beside Lieutenant Frank Higgins, who glanced at him with curiosity.

The man who was doing the talking was not Captain Davenport, but a Delaware Indian runner named Broken

Saber, who had been sent down from the barracks at Chicago with the news.

"Colonel says there is war. Ships with cannon had a war in the sea," Broken Saber said. "That is in the letter. Colonel told me to say that. Black Hawk has gone north. Many Sauk and Fox warriors with him. They say he will fight with the Shawnee, Tecumseh. Fort Meigs has been attacked."

"But the Sauk are across the river," Lieutenant Monique said. "There's no report of trouble."

"The Sauk are apparently divided," Davenport said. "The council on the side of peace, Black Hawk wanting war."

Monique said, "It's in our best interests to keep them divided."

"I suggest, sir," Lieutenant Higgins put in, "that we invite Keokuk and Napope up here, give them more presents, and ask for a treaty of peace."

"Yes, of course. Where do the Sioux stand?"

"So far as anyone knows, they're disinterested in what goes on on the eastern side of the Mississippi. They're not exactly on good terms with the Sauk anyway."

"Bart?" the captain asked.

"That's a pretty good assessment," Perkins answered. "I don't think the Sioux need to be considered."

"That's something."

"Of course there are the Mascouten, the Winnebago, the Kickapoo," Perkins pointed out. "They ought to be considered."

"Are they British-influenced?"

"Don't know, sir. All I know is Black Hawk stands high with all of them. So long as he's warring in the east, I don't think there's a problem."

"But . . . ?"

"But if Black Hawk returns and offers them leadership, if he can convince them it's in their best interests to kick the Americans out . . ." Perkins shook his head. "They've damn sure got the strength to do it, sir."

"Monique?"

"I think we'd better make every effort to counteract any British influence in the area."

"I'll get a letter off to Regiment. We need money—and a damned good negotiator."

Lieutenant Higgins asked, "Anyone sure that the British

are actively trying to recruit the Indians in the Mississippi Valley?"

"Broken Saber?" Davenport said.

"A British man was captured. A soldier. Another man with him was killed. This one was taken to the Chicago barracks. They made him give his name: Captain Hobbs, British officer. He wore no uniform so they would hang him, but he escaped. Maybe," Broken Saber said, "Kickapoo warriors helped him escape. They think maybe."

Davenport rubbed his watery blue eyes and looked at his officers and men. "That's all we know at this point. Gentlemen, we are at war and surrounded by potential enemies. We had damn well better do our best to keep the bulk of the Indian nations out of this war or we'll be backed up all the way out of Louisiana Territory. There will be, must be, no incidents to trigger the Indians off—especially the Sauk."

After the others had gone, Bart Perkins rose and walked to the captain's desk. The commanding officer seemed surprised to find the scout still there.

"What is it, Bart?"

"Something you should know about, sir," Perkins said, and he told him about McCutcheon and his "bears."

"Dammit all!" Davenport exploded, rising from behind his desk like a jack-in-the-box. "That's all we need! A madman killing Sauk. He'll be arrested. Right now. Tonight."

But he wasn't. By the time Sergeant Monk and two armed soldiers arrived at McCutcheon's quarters, the meat hunter was gone. Where or when, no one knew.

Perkins waited outside until the soldiers were gone, Monk to report the unhappy news to the captain. Then the scout entered the room, picked up his bedding, and snuffed out the candle.

He would sleep outside after all, he decided. McCutcheon was gone but there was still a stink to that room and Perkins didn't like it. It stank like death.

9

THE rolling hills gave way to endless flat prairie. The grass was new and deep green, dotted with wildflowers: daisies, black-eyed Susans, bluebells. Thunder Horse leaned low from his horse's back and plucked a perfect blue-violet lilac from the earth, presenting it to his wife.

"How far is it now?" Sachim asked.

"Woman, you ask that with each mile. Does it make you nervous—the thought of coming to my father's camp?"

"Nervous, yes. When there is something unpleasant to do I want to do it as soon as possible, Thunder Horse."

"It will not be unpleasant—or not too unpleasant," he amended.

"It is all right, isn't it?" Sachim asked, looking away.

Thunder Horse halted his pony. "Is what all right, my Sachim?"

"All of this. Me. You are sure?"

His gaze went to the empty land around them. For mile after endless mile there was only the green of the prairie grass, the colorful dotting of flowers. Overhead a lone hawk flew.

"We must rest, get down," Thunder Horse said.

"I am not tired," she protested.

"We must rest."

Thunder Horse took his blanket and spread it on the grass. Sachim walked to him, her eyes still questioning.

He gestured toward the blanket. "Lie down. We have far to ride."

Sachim shrugged and did so, closing her eyes. The scent of

the grass was sweet, the breeze cooling on her body. Larks sang distantly. She felt him lie beside her and when she reached out she found him naked, sun-warmed. She opened her eyes to see his smile. Beyond Thunder Horse two yellow butterflies tumbled through the air.

"You were very tired," she said, running her hand up and across his strongly muscled thigh to his hard abdomen.

"Very. So were you, Sachim. You just did not know it."

She let him undress her then, tugging her skirt down and off her ankles. He paused to kiss her inner thighs lightly, to take her feet between his strong hands and remove her moccasins, kneading her soles.

Thunder Horse loomed over her, blocking out the sun. He took her blouse off and sat looking at her naked body for a time, then bent his lips to her breasts and kissed her before resting his head next to her heart, listening to the pounding of it as she stroked his hair and held him tight.

"I *was* tired," she said, smiling. Thunder Horse lifted his head to look into her eyes. "Very tired."

He rolled to her, kissing her neck, his body moving against hers. He was lithe and strong and urgent. Sachim closed her eyes and lay back, feeling a trembling begin in her own thighs as Thunder Horse approached her, his hands gentle, his breathing rapid. He was the life force which surrounded them, swirling through all of the secret places on the earth, bringing forth all that existed. His need was a passion toward bringing life, the need Manitou had planted in his male heart; but his need was gentle and caring and reassuring. That too was put into his heart by Manitou—the need to love and to cling to the loved one, to bring her joy and pleasure, comfort and warm forgetfulness.

If joy can be a dream, then Sachim dreamed as life pulsed against her and flowed within her, blurring her conscious mind so that there was no room for any thought or emotion but love.

As it should be, as it all should be.

It was sundown before they saw the Sioux village spread out across the plains beside the gently flowing Wapsipinicon River. There were so many tipis that the sight overwhelmed Sachim. A hundred campfires flickered, like embers thrown off by the red, dying sun. They rode toward the fires and the camp of the Sioux, and people turned to look toward them.

Two boys came running to greet Thunder Horse and to peer uncertainly at Sachim.

Nearer the village, hands were raised in welcome. Men shouted out to Thunder Horse and he called back. They too looked at Sachim, measuring, assessing, perhaps wondering what spirit had gotten into Thunder Horse's heart to cause him to choose this slim young Sauk woman.

"That is my father's tipi," Thunder Horse said, nodding at a yellow lodge larger than the rest. The outside of the tipi was painted with totem signs, a red sun and a blue running elk.

Before they had reached the buffalo-hide lodge a man ducked out the flap and stood, hands on hips, bare-chested, watching their approach.

"Your father," Sachim said quietly. She had always been uneasy when Far Eagle's name was mentioned, perhaps because Black Hawk had once told her what a fierce adversary the Sioux could be when aroused.

Without realizing it, Sachim held her horse back a little, allowing Thunder Horse to precede her.

"Father!" he shouted and, throwing his leg over his horse's head, he leapt lightly to the ground. He walked to his father and embraced him. The old chief looked over his son's shoulder, eyeing Sachim.

"Now I know," Far Eagle said. "The spirit woman of the Sauk."

"Yes," Thunder Horse said, turning, his arm still around his father's shoulders. "I told you so."

"I had forgotten. Now I recall. Skinny one, big eyes."

Thunder Horse laughed. Far Eagle did not, nor did Sachim, who could see disappointment in the old man's tone. Old, Far Eagle was. His gray hair hung straight down his back, but his body was that of a much younger man and he held himself erect. There was a powerful grace about him. Sachim could see where Thunder Horse's strength had come from.

"Will she dismount?" Far Eagle asked.

"Sachim? Come into my father's lodge."

She slipped from her horse's back and walked toward the firelit tipi, seeing the deep red band of sunset along the western horizon, smelling the buffalo meat roasting, seeing tribal members hanging back in the shadows, peering at this woman who had taken their young war leader's heart.

"This is my wife," Thunder Horse said.

"This is my daughter-in-law," Far Eagle said with less enthusiasm. "A Sauk."

Then the chief turned and went back into his tipi. Thunder Horse smiled. "He still does not understand, Sachim. Don't worry, it will be all right. We will stay only a little while among my people and then return to your village."

"I am not uncomfortable," she lied.

"Good. Come now." He touched her hand briefly and then entered the tipi, Sachim following. A low fire burned in the center of the great buffalo lodge, smoke rising in a curlicue toward the smoke vent above.

"Sit," Thunder Horse said. This had been his home too, Sachim reflected. He was at ease here. She was not. The old chief sat cross-legged on the floor, watching her. In the corner was a younger woman, dark hair plaited into two braids, her eyes anxious and curious.

"Heart Song!" Thunder Horse said. Then to Sachim: "This is my sister."

"Hello," Heart Song said with painful shyness. Perhaps the girl had long ago been intimidated by her powerful father; perhaps that was only her way.

"I am happy to see you, to know you," Sachim said, and she smiled. Heart Song smiled in return—nervously, with a glance at her father. "We shall be sisters now, and friends," the Sauk woman added. Far Eagle made a rumbling noise in his throat.

"We shall find an older woman to guide this one," Far Eagle said. "She can scrape hides and make a lodge for you. Until then you may stay here."

"Father," Thunder Horse said, "I mean to live among the Sauk."

"Don't speak nonsense," Far Eagle snapped.

"I mean it."

"For the sake of a woman!"

Thunder Horse shrugged. "Just so."

"You will lose your rank. You will be among enemies. You will be an outcast. For a *woman*?"

"Yes."

"You are blind, blinded by a skirt! They call her a spirit woman and it seems she must be to cast this mad spell over my warrior son." He glared at Sachim and she had to turn her eyes away. She had been merely uneasy before but now with Far Eagle's angry disapproval in the open she also felt intimidated. Thunder Horse was not.

"My heart leads me, not a spell. This is how it shall be; this is what I have decided. We will stay a little while and then go."

"If you go, Thunder Horse, then stay away!"

"I will do as you wish, Father. But consider your words."

"They have been considered," Far Eagle said, hurling a stick into the fire so that it sparked and spilled embers. "Leave and you are no longer Sioux. I can tolerate a foreign woman among us, but not an ungrateful son. One with such promise."

"As it may be, so be it," Thunder Horse said.

"You will give up all for her—rank, your people?"

"If I must."

"Then there is nothing further to say. Go and do what you will, only do not return."

Sachim felt a cool breeze, heard the whisper of moccasined feet, and she turned to look up into the face of a young warrior. There was something familiar about him. He was very dark, his eyes smug, his body powerful, his face scarred. She had never seen this man, yet it seemed she had, somewhere.

"My brother, Yellow Sky," Thunder Horse said, and then it became clear. He was familiar because of his resemblance to Thunder Horse, but the face was one controlled by a dark force; the eyes were piercing, hostile, the mouth set crookedly. He wore scalps on his leggings, and weasel skin knotted into long dark hair he wore in a single heavy braid.

"This is the one?" Yellow Sky asked his father. Far Eagle just nodded, staring at the fire, brooding. Yellow Sky's lips curled. A long silence followed. Far Eagle sat unmoving, watching the fire, perhaps seeing lost dreams there. Yellow Sky stared at Sachim. Apart from them all, Heart Song worked nervously at the meal she was preparing.

"Give your talisman to Yellow Sky," Far Eagle said abruptly. "He is war leader now. You are disgraced."

Thunder Horse slipped the sun-symbol necklace he wore from around his neck and handed it to his brother, who snatched it from him. The sun symbol turned and gleamed in the firelight.

"I do not want it this way," Thunder Horse said, rising to stand over his father. "I came back only for your blessing, only to bring Sachim into our camp so that you might know her."

"Now I know her. Now you may take this Sauk witch from our camp," Far Eagle said without lifting his eyes. Yellow Sky's smirk became unendurable.

For a long minute Thunder Horse stood over his father, searching for something to say, but there was nothing. "Come," he said at last to Sachim, and she rose to find herself facing Yellow Sky, who wore the talisman.

His eyes seemed to penetrate her skull, to strip her clothing from her, to look into her heart and find nothing at all that he was not contemptuous of. Thunder Horse had to push his brother aside before they could leave the tipi and emerge outside into the cool, fresh air.

"So you see," Thunder Horse said, "I told you it would not be so bad."

"You have given up much for me," Sachim said quietly; then she felt his hands on her shoulders, as he turned her and she looked up into his eyes.

"Do you not understand yet, Sachim? I would give up even my life for you. Our love will endure. It is beyond all of the world. Beyond all."

Then he kissed her once, a kiss interrupted by Yellow Sky emerging triumphantly from the tipi. "You will leave your horses, so Far Eagle speaks," he said.

"I am taking none but those we ride," Thunder Horse answered.

"Leave those too—walk away from the camp in disgrace."

"Don't try my patience, Yellow Sky," Thunder Horse said. "Keep my horses, grow wealthy. My own war horse I keep."

Yellow Sky made a strange hissing noise and just for a moment Sachim thought he would attack his brother, but he seemed to think better of that as he studied Thunder Horse. "Do as you will then," Yellow Sky said, turning away.

"Thank you, my brother," Thunder Horse murmured. He watched Yellow Sky's back as the new war leader walked away into the camp shadows. Taking a slow deep breath he turned to Sachim with a tight smile. "Perhaps we should not stay too long in this camp, Sachim."

"As you wish, my husband."

Thunder Horse's smile deepened and he hugged her. Sachim

said, "You are leaving everything: horses, weapons, clothing, blankets."

"I am taking everything that matters."

"One day, perhaps—"

"Shush. Don't speak of one day. Let us go and love and be together. I can make new arrows, capture new horses. I cannot find another Sachim to be my wife."

"Thunder Horse . . ." a voice said.

The whispered words came from the darkness. They turned to find Heart Song. She pressed something into Sachim's hand, kissed her brother's cheek, and fled again to the darkness.

"What is it?" Sachim asked, and Thunder Horse looked at the tiny object, a ring made of woven horsehair.

"It was my mother's ring. Wear it." He placed it on her finger and then looked to the sky. "Wear it always."

Sachim's hand was trembling as she raised the ring to her eyes, a ring woven long ago on some winter night by a woman now dead, worn by her. A symbol of the past, a vow for the future.

"Come now," Thunder Horse said, taking her shoulder. "Let us ride away from this place and sleep out on the prairie. In our own world."

Still Sachim could sense the sadness in him. He was leaving his home, his people, his family. But Thunder Horse was not a man to dwell on such things or even mention them. They mounted their ponies and rode away, leaving Thunder Horse's past behind, riding together out onto the starlit plains toward their own future.

Thunder Horse sat his horse proudly. Sachim liked to watch him ride; the way his eyes searched the far horizons intrigued her. His body, lean and hard, was an amazement to her still. Her Sioux warrior was many things: hunter, friend, confidant, and protector.

His eyes were now on the distances, a hunter's eyes, searching perhaps for the great buffalo herds, but he seemed to feel Sachim watching him and his gaze returned to her. Smiling eyes met those of Sachim, and she felt her heart melt.

"I know," Thunder Horse said quietly. "My own heart is so very full, Sachim." He leaned toward her and touched her arm gently. Just a small gesture, a deep one.

Thunder Horse led her to a place of the wild roses. They grew in abundance along the river bottom. Quail sang in the brush. Blackberries rambled over rocks and wound themselves around the oak and willow trees. The sun was going down and the slanting rays through the foliage brought the little dell to magical life.

"Here I shall make us a small lodge," Thunder Horse said. "Here it shall be our time and none of the world's."

They stayed there for three days. In the mornings, Sachim would awake, stretching luxuriously. The scent of the roses was in the air—Thunder Horse had even woven some living plants into their lodge.

He was there beside her, and that was always miraculous. To awake and find him there, no dream, but a warm and giving man. She lay beside him just watching him sleep, watching his chest rise and fall.

Then his eyes would suddenly open, feeling her presence, and he would drag her down to him, laughing as he saw his Sauk woman, hair loose across her breasts and down her back.

"How did you know?" Sachim asked the first time.

"That you were there, watching? My heart knew, Sachim. Don't ask me—all of this is magic." He kissed her neck and let his hands run down her back, sending a chill through Sachim's body, quickening her pulse.

He was strong against her, his eyes filled with wonder. When they met he was gentle yet unrestrained and Sachim's body seemed to grow heavy, soft, composed of nothing but nerves and flesh as his warm breath touched her cheeks and ear, as his lips found hers and he held her there against him, her thighs against his powerful legs, his arms locked around her.

Thunder Horse whispered, "I can see it. I can see that you love me when your eyes shine like that."

She laid her head against his chest and whispered, "I too can see it, Thunder Horse. I never knew that I could live beyond dreams, that there was one more life beyond the one I lived. You lead me to the stars, my Sioux warrior. Such a place to walk!"

The days were warm briefly and Thunder Horse wore only his breechclout as he fished along the stream. It was a place he recalled from his boyhood and there was still something of the boy about him as he hoisted a flapping silver fish from the sunlit river on his line and shouted "Ah-haiee!" grinning as Sachim came to him.

They sat together, at times hardly speaking. The sun was warm on their backs. Sachim wore only a skirt as they watched the glitter of the river, the wind working magic among the trees as butterflies drifted past and cardinals fluttered through the trees.

Thunder Horse's hand was soothing against her back and she leaned her head back. Slowly he rubbed her neck, looking once at her, kissing her once lightly. There was nothing else they wanted to say, to do, to be, but be a man and a woman alone.

They walked through the forest together and Sachim was constantly amazed. Things she had seen alone, she now saw with her. Together they would lift their hands to point out a raccoon with four waddling young, the nest a thrush had made in a rotted log, the pattern of the water-polished stones along the falls. He saw and felt as she did. Some mysterious unity beyond the joining of flesh had settled over them—or perhaps it had always been there waiting for them to discover it.

"We—together—" Sachim said, "are the meaning of life."

Thunder Horse cocked his head and pondered it. Finally he just nodded, and they went on walking.

When the nights grew cooler Thunder Horse would tug her blankets up around her shoulders as if she were a child; and many nights he would sit up, watching her. "I always knew I loved you," he whispered one night, "but not like this. Manitou smiles. He looks down on our love and smiles."

It could not last forever. There came a time when they packed their few belongings and started back toward the big river. They rode silently out of the dell, the wind growing cool as they reached the crest.

"Wait," Sachim said, touching her husband's hand, and he held up his horse to look back into the tiny valley. There a long slanting ray of sunlight shone through the trees and struck their lodge. Sachim smiled at Thunder Horse and said mysteriously, "Thank you, husband."

They rode away from the dell then and back onto the long plains. They passed a small buffalo herd plodding southward, grazing as they went, and a massive shaggy bull raised his head defiantly.

"Don't worry, great one," Thunder Horse said, raising his

hand to the bull buffalo, "we need no meat and no hides. We pass as friends."

The buffalo snorted and tossed his head so that his great snarled mane shifted violently. Sachim laughed. "Should we hurry on?"

"No," Thunder Horse said quite seriously. "I have spoken to him. Now he knows."

They slept out that night near a small winding stream and started on again at dawn. By midafternoon they were into forest, pines mingled with huge oaks and many maple trees. The country began to roll gently; there were deer everywhere.

"Will they remain angry—your people?" Sachim asked.

"I hope not, but yes, I think so," Thunder Horse said as they watered their horses at a small lake among the trees. "My father always assumed that I would take his position. It has been that way, father-to-son, for a thousand years."

"At least he has Yellow Sky," Sachim said, remembering the man with a shudder.

"He has Yellow Sky," Thunder Horse said without further comment.

"And among the Sauk, will it be any better for you?"

Thunder Horse shrugged. "Napope has said I may stay. That," he added wryly, "is more than my father would allow me."

"If we—"

Sachim was interrupted by the humming sound, the sudden *thunk* of an arrowhead into flesh. Her horse reared up wildly, an arrow protruding from its flank. Thunder Horse hurled Sachim to the ground and leapt toward his own horse, snatching bow and arrows from his roll.

A second arrow, a third, and a fourth whipped through the air, two striking the earth near Sachim, one splashing into the lake.

"Stay here, stay down," Thunder Horse shouted. Then he was off at a run, weaving through the woods, and Sachim whispered a silent prayer.

"Not now, Manitou, Great Spirit, we have only just begun."

She saw Thunder Horse's coppery back for another instant and then he was gone into the trees. No more arrows came, but Sachim heard a horse being ridden away.

Thunder Horse leapt a fallen oak log, notching an arrow even as he ran on. There was a flash of color ahead of him, movement, and he instinctively veered that way, holding bow and arrow in his left hand.

The man with the skull paint leapt up in front of him—a wild-eyed young warrior with a musket in his hands. Thunder Horse flung himself to one side as the warrior touched the musket-rifle off, smoke belching from the octagonal muzzle, fiery particles of unburned powder searing Thunder Horse's flesh as the musket ball whipped past him and embedded itself in an ash tree.

The young warrior started to run, changed his mind, and turned, war ax in hand. Thunder Horse drew his bowstring and let it loose again; the ashwood bow drove the arrow deep into the abdomen of the skull-painted warrior, who flopped back against the earth, pawing at the arrow, blood flowing freely from his mouth.

Thunder Horse felt sudden searing pain and then heard the report of a second musket. He was spun around by the musket ball, which passed through his shoulder beneath his collarbone. Thunder Horse felt his knees buckle, but he was alert enough to notch a second arrow, and from his knees he fired at the oncoming attacker.

The staghorn arrowhead ripped through the throat of the second painted warrior and he crumpled up, falling to the earth to lie still atop the broken branches of a fallen pine.

Thunder Horse, still on his knees, studied the forest around him, hearing horses, movement. He had to move. The musket shots would summon other warriors.

That was easier said than done. His mind whirled, his ears rang, and when he tried to rise he stumbled. Blood flowed hotly from the wound in his shoulder, streaking his chest with crimson.

Thunder Horse cast his bow away. His left arm was useless. He took his knife from its belt sheath and staggered toward the cover of deeper woods.

He heard the whisper of moccasins against the dry leaves and he went to the ground, dragging himself on his belly into a thicket of blackthorn and raspberries.

Sachim. He had to get back to Sachim, but now there was someone between himself and the lake. His shoulder pulsed with pain but Thunder Horse made no sound, barely moved. He was as still as a serpent in the underbrush, waiting and watching.

Then he saw him. The warrior came forward a few steps

at a time, eyes watchful, searching. He too wore skull paint.
His roached hair identified him as a Sauk.

Thunder Horse watched as the man inched forward, bow
and arrow ready. Thunder Horse had to blink away the
perspiration which stung his eyes as it trickled down off his
forehead. The pain in his shoulder was nearly unendurable.
Once he felt himself starting to black out, to drift away into
that painless world beneath the level of consciousness, and
he had to fight it off with sheer willpower.

"Sachim," he said silently. He must stay alert, he must be
victorious no matter how many enemies were out there.
Sachim was many things: prophet, woman, child, sage. Many
things, but she was no warrior. How could a person like
Sachim hurt a living thing? Manitou had given her a gentle
heart.

The skull warrior came nearer. If he had turned his head
slightly to the left he would have seen Thunder Horse lying
there, still as death, but his eyes were on the forest ahead of
him, where his own fellow warriors lay twisted, dead.

Thunder Horse gathered his strength. The knife in his
hand felt cool. His flesh crawled with insects and perspiration born of pain. His shoulder was fire-filled.

Thunder Horse rose from the underbrush and lunged at
the skull warrior. The man fell back, trying to bring his
arrow around, but Thunder Horse was quicker. The knife in
his hand rose high, flashing briefly in the sunlight that filtered through the trees, and then plunged downward into
the skull warrior's throat.

The warrior made a brief gurgling sound and thrashed
about wildly, clawing at Thunder Horse's face and arm.

Then he was still, dead. Thunder Horse yanked his bloody
knife free and started toward the lake at a staggering run,
the name *Sachim* echoing in the back of his skull, which
ached and throbbed and seemed to contain a hive of humming
hornets.

He could see the glimmer of the sunlit lake through the
trees as he forced his way through the forest, fighting off
the clinging vines and low branches.

Then he saw her, still against the ground, still sound.
She rose and rushed to him, her face anguished, her arms
going around his waist, helping to support him as they went
to the water's edge and then sagged to the ground.

"There may be more," Thunder Horse panted. "Come, get on your horse."

His breathing was ragged. Blood still flowed copiously. Sachim managed to get Thunder Horse to his feet, to help him onto his horse before she mounted her own wounded pony and they rode away, northward, looking back constantly to see they were not being followed.

Thunder Horse weaved in the saddle. When it became obvious he could go on no longer, Sachim insisted they halt and led them up to a small wooded knoll clotted with maples, dominated by a huge stack of boulders more than two lodges high.

There she took Thunder Horse from the back of his pony, feeling him sag against her. He was heavier than she had thought. She had to half-carry him to a recess between two great boulders and lay him down there. She looked at his wound with apprehension.

"Sachim."

"Hush."

"Kiss me."

"Don't be foolish."

But his arm hooked around her neck and drew her down and he kissed her mouth deeply.

"Let me go, foolish man. I'll have to find something for your wound."

Hastily she made a temporary bandage from her new blanket and then went hunting for what she would need. Tope-kia had taught her a little about medicine; now was the time to apply what she knew.

Kee-chi-he-ja-ka she found in abundance, and gathered some. One sap pine she found was literally girdled with the small protuberances that contained the resin which Tope-kia said reduced pain and inflammation. She also gathered Sin-des-nes-ni, the inner bark of the willow, useful for reducing fever, and Hon-kos-kao-ga-sha, the root of which halted the flowing of blood when applied promptly.

Later she would have time to concoct more herbal remedies, but these could be used right away and must be if Thunder Horse were to survive.

Returning to her man, she found him feverish and incoherent. Removing her first primitive bandage, Sachim set to work on the musket-ball wound.

Only once did he come alert—from the pain, Sachim

thought. As she plugged either side of the wound with clean bandages, he shouted out only a single word, "Sachim."

"Yes, hush," she said quietly as she worked at the wound, realizing that the flap of skin the musket ball had torn on its exit would have to be sewn up. "Hush, I am here, it is good." She babbled on, saying nothing, her voice soothing to Thunder Horse, who lay still and only from time to time twitched with pain.

When she had done all she could, she sat, her legs under her, and took his feverish head on her lap, stroking his forehead, watching as the sun again set, not knowing who was out there wanting to kill them.

They were three days in that place, Thunder Horse drinking only tea brewed from sycamore bark, eating only huckleberries and the stale corn bannock Sachim had packed for their journey.

Still he grew stronger and there seemed to be no infection in the shoulder. By the second day he had been able to sit up and talk to Sachim.

"They were Sauk," Thunder Horse told Sachim.

"You are sure?" she asked in surprise.

"Their hair was roached," he told her. Then he described their paint and Sachim knew.

"Skull Clan," she said.

"Who are they?" he asked, and Sachim told him as simply as possible. When she was finished he said, "Then they are violently opposed to the Sioux."

"Yes. Tomorrow Runner will never forgive them."

"Or you?" Thunder Horse asked.

"No. Skull, as he calls himself, hates everything Sioux. He knows you and I are married. Also, I think, he hates women with a relentless fury."

"He is mad."

"Yes, of course. He hates you, me, all of your people— and the Sauk themselves. The council delivered him up to the Sioux."

"How could he gather so many warriors around him?" Thunder Horse wondered.

"It is a time of change, of turmoil. Many Sauk wish to war with the Americans—Black Hawk included. The young men wish to win glory in battle. Yet the Sauk are at peace. Black Hawk is gone. He would have none of these outcasts in his band. Then they need a leader, these young men, and they have found one in Skull."

"He could mean trouble, this man. If they kill Sioux, then Sioux will kill Sauk—whether they are Skull Clan or not. The Sioux would not know."

"At least the Sauk council should know. Perhaps they could send a runner to the Sioux camp and explain that this is not the will of the Sauk people."

"Would my people believe that? Would it matter if they saw their own friends or family dead?"

"I don't know. Something must be done." Sachim looked eastward. "If only Back Hawk were here."

"He is that powerful?"

"He is the only one the warrior clans listen to."

"The whites," Thunder Horse said.

Sachim looked at him, waiting for a further explanation. Thunder Horse said, "Does Skull war on the whites?"

"No one knows. I think he would if he had the chance to strike against a small force, yes."

"Then that too would be blamed on the Sauk."

"Yes . . ." Sachim thought back to the strange incident on the trail north when a white had shot Ha-te-ka for what seemed to be no reason.

"What are you thinking?" Thunder Horse asked, putting his arm around her, studying her eyes.

"Skull. It may be that *he* is the enemy. Everyone's enemy. It may be that he is capable of destroying everything."

"I don't know how matters stand with the Americans— they will not cross the river, they will not anger the Sioux nation—but I know our council will not tolerate Sauk raiders," Thunder Horse said. "The man should be stopped. He must be stopped."

But who was there to stop him? With Black Hawk away making his own war against the Americans in the east, the council still satisfied with itself and its treaty, who was there to stop Skull from doing as he pleased—even if it plunged the entire Mississippi Valley into war?

She was dead.

The old woman had died in her sleep.

When Sachim and her Sioux husband returned to the camp along the great river it was to find that Grandmother had died before Sachim could be there to say good-bye, to send her along the Hanging Trail with a death song and a prayer for reunion with those she had loved: Sun Wolf, her husband, her sister, Crenna, all of those who had gone before.

Now the old woman lay still and silent, hands crossed on her blanket, and Sachim could only kneel beside her bed and weep while Thunder Horse, his chest and shoulder wound bandaged, watched.

Finally he moved forward and placed his hand on Sachim's shoulder. "What must be done? I do not know your ways."

"She must be placed in the earth," Sachim said. "I gave her my promise that she would be buried next to her husband and my mother. Across the river."

"Then we will do it."

"Tonight, we must do it tonight," Sachim said, briefly bowing her head to hide her tears.

"Then we will." He squeezed her shoulder again and then withdrew his hand not sure whether Sachim wanted to be alone in her grief or needed his support.

"Will you get a canoe?" Sachim asked. "Tope-kia will let us use his. His lodge is beside the broken oak."

"All right," Thunder Horse agreed. He ducked out to find the medicine man.

Sachim remained on her knees in the deepening shadows of the lodge, watching her grandmother's deeply placid, utterly still features. She was gone now and what she had done in her life would always remain a mystery except for the few tales she had chosen to tell. Eighty years on the earth—so many days, and each with a promise on awakening, a fear on going to sleep, a thousand memories, many blurred by time, many intentionally put aside in the mind. She had been young and never dreamed of growing old; then she had been old and at times had trouble remembering how it felt to be young. Men, love, war, hunger, dreams—a life locked into a single mind and never really shared. She would sleep now with her dreams locked away as the dreams of a thousand thousand Sauk were locked away in the earth's silent vault.

"It is time to go," Thunder Horse said, bringing Sachim forth from her reverie. "I have Tope-kia's canoe. He would like to go with us."

"Will you help me carry her, if you can?"

"Of course,"

Thunder Horse slipped his good arm under the old woman's legs, noticing that Sachim had washed Grandmother, had braided her hair and put on her best jewelry. Sachim struggled to lift Grandmother by her shoulders. She seemed to weigh nothing, yet lifting her was awkward.

Slowly they made their way outside, where Tope-kia waited, helping them along to the canoe as the stars twinkled overhead. Grandmother was placed in the bow of the birchbark and they shoved off from shore, paddling silently across the great river toward the burial ground.

The moon, rising earlier now, painted bands of gold on the face of the Mississippi. White fires glowed against the sky on the far side of the river. Sachim and Tope-kia paddled in silence. Thunder Horse sat in silence, cradling his injured arm.

They slipped into an inlet well-known to Tope-kia and Sachim. Here the Sauk had taken duck; here Grandmother had gathered pond lilies and delighted in the sight of fish breaking water to feed, of orange-and-blue dragonflies skimming over the water.

In the dead of night it was still and dark but for the gleam of the rising moon that shone through the trees, scattering golden highlights.

They took Grandmother from the canoe and built a litter. Carrying her over the wooded rise, they walked down across the dark land toward the great oak which stood alone in the center of the cornfield.

To their left was a white house. A dog came out and began yapping at them as they made their way to the burial site. They walked past the Sauk dead, some long gone to the Hanging Trail, others who had died too recently.

Beneath the oak, Tope-kia and Thunder Horse began to dig the grave while Sachim sang.

> Now you will go home
> Now you will go home
> To where the Great One waits for you
> To where your friends wait for you
> To where it all began
> Now you will go home
> And there will be a little sadness in our hearts.

Then Grandmother was placed into the earth and covered with her last blanket: the good soil from which corn sprang and new grass and everything which fed the Sauk and gave them life.

There was nothing left to do then, but for Sachim to wipe away her tears and take the comfort of Thunder Horse's arm wrapped around her. The moon broke free of the horizon and rose slowly, becoming smaller and silver. They walked back to the river and paddled home across the great river.

"Have we got title to that land or not!" Willie Havens was furious. "I've got a deed at home in my trunk. Given me by the government. I worked that land, built a house, plowed my fields—paid you, Mr. Surveyor."

"It's your land of course," Joshua Ferguson said. He smiled and flicked the ash from his cigar. The surveyor himself was a land owner, having appropriated six sections along the river where any port would have to be built if the city continued to grow. Josh Ferguson had grown a long mustache now and let his sideburns creep down his narrow jaw in the new fashion. An informal election the month before had chosen him as mayor, primarily because no farmer had the time to take on the duties and also because Ferguson was perceived as an educated man.

Hank Greeley cleared his throat and Ferguson glanced that way. "Seems the man's got a real complaint," the trading-post operator commented.

"You bet I do, and the army does nothing," Havens said. He was sweating profusely and took a moment to wipe at his broad face with a folded blue handkerchief.

The sodbuster went on. "Here I got title to a half section along the ridge and I can't keep the Indians out. Last night there was some up there, planting one of their dead. A woman howling some damn thing, sounded like a wolf baying at the moon. I can't plow that tract. Think I want to dig up a bunch of bodies? If it's my land, why don't they keep off? There's enough dirt on the other side of the Mississippi for their burying."

"It's really not a matter I can do anything about," Ferguson said, lifting his boots onto his desk. His office in the rear of the trading post was cluttered with trade goods and bales of furs. It wasn't much, but Ferguson figured things would improve. "It's a matter for the military or the governor's office."

"The governor! Listen, Harrison was all right, but this

clown down there now! St. Louis don't care what happens upriver anyway. As for the army—you ever try to get Davenport to make a decision?"

Ferguson smiled indulgently, sympathetically.

Havens rushed on with his argument. "Don't anyone realize that these Sauk that we're being so nice and friendly to are at war with the United States? I get a newspaper from Philadelphia. I can read. Black Hawk was with this Tecumseh at Frenchtown and at Fort Malden, fighting with the British! That's a fact. How do we know what in hell the Sauk, and the Fox for that matter, are going to do next? Massacre me and my family in our sleep, likely."

"Captain Davenport's doing his best to maintain the status quo," Ferguson said soothingly. At Havens' blank look he added, "To live up to the treaty."

Greeley spoke up again. "Treaty gives them the right to the burial grounds, Willie. That, and they got hunting rights on this side of the river."

"Damn foolish treaty, then. A man buys a piece of land, he expects the use of it. I'm not alone in my thinking, Greeley. Wally Short can't put his fence up because of the burial ground. Lewis Menken's got Indians walking through his cornfields on their way to gather rice at the slough. Scared his wife half to death. Had one painted Indian on his back doorstep one day last week."

Haven leaned across Ferguson's desk, bracing himself with clenched hands. "That's not the half of it and you know it. Don't think folks aren't aware of the McCutcheon family slaughter or the raid on the Stills place. Those were *Sauk*, Mr. Mayor."

"I wasn't aware of that," Ferguson lied. In fact he was well aware of it, and happy with the turn things were taking. There was land left on this side of the river which the Sauk held by treaty. And on the far side there were millions of acres. A man could grow rich. Very rich, and that was Joshua Ferguson's sole aim in life.

"What would you suggest, Willie?" Ferguson asked carefully.

"What we suggest—my neighbors, the people who elected you mayor, and myself—is that you hie yourself up to Chicago and talk to the governor of Illinois. John Reynolds is supposed to be a man who can get things done. You ask him, Mr. Ferguson, ask him why if we're at war with these

Sauk Indians they can walk around here like they own the world while Davenport sits there in his office afraid to move."

"If he wanted to he doesn't have the manpower," Ferguson said.

"There's plenty of militia in the Chicago barracks. I know. I did duty up there once."

"There's the treaty."

"I think killing settlers maybe breaks that treaty," Havens said. Then, satisfied that he had made his point, he snatched up his hat and stalked out of the trading post. Ferguson glanced at Greeley.

"What do we do?" Hank Greeley wanted to know.

"Talk to Keokuk."

"And what? Buy him off?"

"Naturally," Ferguson said, leaning back farther in his chair. "He'll sell anything for a price. Take the moccasins from his grandfather. We've got leverage. How much do you figure the Sauk have taken in credits?"

"Somewhere near ten thousand," Greeley grumbled. He wasn't happy about that situation. The Sauk, instead of trapping for furs, had discovered that they had to do nothing at all but walk into the trading post, make their mark, and leave with whatever took their fancy. As a result, Greeley was losing money.

"All right. It's time to put in a demand for that money. Think they'll bring in ten thousand dollars in furs by next week?"

"Sure. And I think the sun's going to start rising in the west," Greeley answered sourly.

"Then they'll have to make some sort of accommodation, won't they?"

"Land?"

"What else have they got, Hank?"

"A lot of my goods," Greeley growled.

Ferguson laughed. "Don't worry about ten thousand dollars, Hank," the new mayor said, rising to look out the filthy back window. "It'll look like nothing to you one day, I promise you. Out there's where the wealth is," he said, looking westward. "Land. If there are a thousand settlers here today, there will be five thousand in five years. Land is what it's all about." He turned to smile at Greeley. "And in the end even the Indian doesn't get hurt. The Sauk can always move west. Hell, there's half a continent out there empty still. There's no end to the land—and no end to the profit a man can make off it."

Greeley shrugged. You had to admire the man's thinking, no matter what you thought of his motives. But then Greeley was also in it for the money. He had come this far with Ferguson. There was no point in jumping off the wagon now.

"Think Keokuk will sell out?"

"I know he will. He'll have no choice anyway. And if he does . . ."

"Then what?"

"Just in case, Hank, I'm taking a little trip."

"A trip?"

"That's right. To Chicago. I think John Reynolds should be informed of the depredation and murders the Sauk have been engaged in, don't you?"

"That's not much to hang anything on," Greeley said dubiously. "Scattered incidents . . . no one even sure if Sauk did those killings."

"If we have to, we'll manufacture some evidence, Hank. This really isn't the time to let the truth stand in our way."

Greeley only shrugged. He had no love for the Sauk, not since the time that Ke-ke-tai had murdered three of his friends. Still, the way Ferguson went about things was enough to chill your blood. It didn't seem that life or death meant a thing to him. Only those gold dollars. Well, maybe Keokuk would pay up. He was easy to deal with. He had the old council members where he wanted them. A little rum, a little advice from his mustached *Prophet*, a few trade goods, and the old men were happy to go along with whatever he told them.

If only . . . Greeley went outside and watched the soldiers drill. If only Black Hawk didn't return. That would be a different story altogether. A man could get killed.

But Black Hawk was far away—Ontario, the last anyone heard—fighting for the British in a war no one thought they could win. Maybe Ferguson had this nailed down. He seemed to have no doubts.

The trouble was that no one on the frontier was going to challenge the Sauk and Fox. Not when things were generally peaceful. If Keokuk said no to their demands, John Reynolds wasn't going to do a thing. Not while the peace lasted. No one wanted a second front in this war.

And the Sauk were peaceful. Why wouldn't they be? They had all they needed, all they could want. Three Sauk braves walked through the gate and headed for his store as Greeley watched. He sighed and turned back into the trading post, seeing more profit slipping away.

Skull was flat on his belly. He paid no attention to the gnats that swarmed around his head as he lay in the long grass studying the farm below him.

He turned his painted face toward his warriors, his Skull Clan. Young, disaffected, they were ready to rebel against the old ones, the council, to retake what was theirs from the whites, from the Sioux.

Skull's mouth tightened. He was pleased. They followed him without question. They did as they were told, and did it savagely. Skull jabbed a finger toward the farmhouse where a woman with two yellow-haired girls had appeared, and they started downward, ready to do what must be done.

10

THE leaves began to turn and the Sauk looked southward. Winter was coming and the time had come to prepare for the long trek to their southern camp.

Ta-wa-shuk's belly was growing round. She laughed and said that the night Ha-te-ka had played his flute for her she had conceived his child. Sha-sak teased her unmercifully, but admitted that she was jealous. Cliff Arrow had never been able to give her a child.

Sachim was not jealous. She had no cause to be. Within her too was a small life, not yet showing itself to the world, but there all the same, nurtured and growing. Sachim had told no one but Thunder Horse. To him she had whispered the secret early one morning while the sun reddened the river and gilded the treetops.

And he had laughed. He had laughed and hugged her tighter, keeping her in his bed for another long joyful hour.

The Sauk had nearly accepted Thunder Horse, although he was a man living on the fringe of their society. He belonged to no clan and could take part in no ceremonies. He must have been lonely at times, but he told Sachim frequently that she was all the company he needed.

"Besides," he said, "when the child is born it will hunt with me. We will play games together."

"It will be a long time before the baby comes," Sachim answered, "and a long while after that before it can hunt or play."

"Time will pass. It passes quickly with you." He shrugged.

The tribe had begun to gather provisions for its winter trek. Rice and corn were harvested, meat hunted and dried, fish smoked. The hunters were gone long; the women worked nearly from sunup to sunset.

For Sachim the work was pleasant. She had much to be happy about and many friends to work with. She and Ta-wa-shuk laughed together and felt each other's bellies. Old Sha-sak teased them both and gave them hours of advice. Little Creek seemed happier now, as if time were wearing away the pain she felt over Ke-ke-tai's murder.

The work went easily, picking corn from the dry stalks, carrying it in the woven baskets they wore on their backs. When the day grew too long, too hot, they would swim in the river.

The water was cool and flowed slowly through the ox-bow which looped through the trees bordering the corn-field. Sachim had stepped from her dress and now she eased into the water, sucking in her breath as she reacted to the coldness.

"Go on, go on," Sha-sak said, bouncing toward Sachim. "It's good for the baby. It will be a good swimmer. If I had a young body like you two, nothing would bother me, not a little coldness."

"That's the reason you aren't cold," Ta-wa-shuk laughed.

Sha-sak rubbed her bare protruding belly and laughed as well. "That is so, that is so. I eat well and so I stay warm. I keep my man warm too."

Little Creek was the last to arrive. She placed her empty basket down on the ground and slipped her dress up over her head. And the man shot her.

Sachim saw it. The bullet pierced Little Creek's breast and exited through her back, breaking her spine. The woman crumpled up, dropping to the earth to lie near her basket.

Sachim couldn't move. She just stared in disbelief. Someone was screaming, but she didn't know who it was. Little Creek was dead. Someone had killed her.

"Run, Sachim. Run!" Sha-sak was shoving her from the water and Sachim only then realized that another shot had been fired. They scrambled from the water, clawing their way up the muddy bank. Sachim had time to snatch up her dress as they ran for the shelter of the trees. Another shot was fired, this one spraying them with bark as the bullet struck a pine tree beside them.

Sachim was still looking back, staring at Little Creek's body. Sha-sak, still naked, her heavy breasts heaving, grabbed Sachim's arm and turned her, pulling her on toward the safety of the deeper woods.

They ran on toward the village. If anyone had heard the shots, no one paid attention. No one came out to meet them. There was much hunting by the Sauk and the whites across the river and the sounds of guns went unremarked.

"Dead," Sachim panted. The word ran through her mind endlessly. Dead. Little Creek was dead. She could not accept it. If it weren't for the others being there, Sachim would have doubted her own eyes. Little Creek could not be dead.

But she was and Sachim knew it. She was lying on the bank of the oxbow with a hole through her body and her blood leaking out, shot by someone. Who?

"Who shot her?" Sachim asked as they slowed their pace. "Who shot Little Creek!" No one answered. Sha-sak was ready to fall down in exhaustion; her large body was not meant for running.

Ta-wa-shuk was giggling uncontrollably. Sachim stared at her. "Our babies will be good swimmers. And good runners too!" Then Ta-wa-shuk broke into tears and they halted, trying to catch their breath, Sachim hugging Ta-wa-shuk.

They staggered on into the village. A woman came running with blankets to cover Sha-sak and Ta-wa-shuk. "What happened? What are you three doing?"

"Little Creek . . ." Sachim, still gasping for breath, said, and she told the story. A crowd had gathered. Thunder Horse had appeared from somewhere and he put an arm around his wife's shoulder, bracing her.

"Who did it?" Pak-wa asked, but Sachim could only shake her head. The Sauk warrior started off toward the oxbow at a run. Thunder Horse ran with him.

Ta-wa-shuk was still crying hysterically and she was taken back to her lodge. Sha-sak, completely exhausted, sat on the ground, a blanket covering her. Sachim turned one way and then the other in confusion. What was there to do? The trembling in her legs annoyed her but couldn't be denied. She too sat on the ground while the crowd continued to gather, asking the same endless questions.

Thunder Horse and Pak-wa returned with the body of

Little Creek. That was all they had found. There was no sign of the murderer.

"He had to be white," someone said. That raised angry murmurings.

"Sachim?" Sha-sak said. "Remember the man who shot Ha-te-ka? On our northward march."

"I remember. But why would someone follow us this far to kill a woman?"

"I don't know, but I *feel* it was him. The same one."

Sachim dismissed the idea. It made no sense. But what sense did the murder of Little Creek make anyway?

"A white did this," someone said again.

"We don't know that."

"Who else would have?"

"Perhaps a Sioux."

"The Sioux don't kill women," Thunder Horse said.

"There are no Sioux near us," Pak-wa put in.

"Then a white."

Keokuk and Napope had arrived. Keokuk looked down at Little Creek's body as if it were that of a dog. Napope asked what had happened and again Sachim had to recount the attack.

"It was not a white man," Keokuk said.

"How can you know that?"

"Why would they shoot a woman? They are friends of ours."

Sachim snapped, "Of yours, Keokuk!"

Napope interrupted. "Arm yourselves and search again. Perhaps whoever did this is still out there, waiting to kill more of our people. Let us try to discover who did it."

"And if it is found to be a white?" Pak-wa asked.

Napope looked confused. He frowned and asked, "What do you mean?"

"What if it was a white settler? What then do we do?"

"It wasn't a white settler," Keokuk repeated firmly. "Arm yourselves, look for the one who did this. There is more corn to bring in."

Sachim stared at Keokuk in disbelief. He wasn't worried about finding Little Creek's killer. He was worried that the women wouldn't bring the corn in!

Thunder Horse stayed behind as the men went back toward the oxbow to search more thoroughly. He helped

Sachim up and slowly walked her back toward their lodge. Neither of them said anything. There was little to say. Little Creek was dead.

Nothing was found of the murderer. Sachim could only help Little Creek's mother prepare the body and travel with her across the river, where yet another grave had to be dug.

The day after the first snow, the Sauk started south again. There was no joy among them, no singing as they traveled. Little Creek's death seemed to be an omen. There was a dark cloud in the sky, a towering horse-head-like thing, and it followed them for many miles.

The camp was somber; even in the south the winter was leaving its mark—cold gray days with barren trees thick and lifeless along the river. A week of rain turned the camp to a bog, and the cold wind blew constantly.

It was raining the day Black Hawk returned from the east. A hum passed through the camp and then a shout. Sachim looked out from her lodge to see the horsemen riding slowly into the camp like ghostly warriors, the colors of their clothing washed out by the grayness of the day.

Their horses walked heavily; they had come a long way. Keokuk and the Prophet stood with blankets over their heads, watching the incoming riders.

They were fewer than when they had left, but Black Hawk was well and Sachim saw the unmistakable form of White Bear. Keokuk said something Sachim couldn't quite make out above the hiss of the rain, something about the council, and Black Hawk just nodded wearily.

"Come in!" Sachim said, waving her arm. "Come in and warm yourself."

Black Hawk turned his horse her way, and White Bear followed. They had no lodges here and would welcome a fire, protection from the rain. Black Hawk left his horse's reins trailing and came to Sachim. He looked very tired indeed, his strong face lined with worry.

"Hello, my little spirit woman," Black Hawk said. He glanced back to make sure White Bear was following and then ducked inside the tipi. Thunder Horse, shirtless, was sitting by the fire, wrapping sinew around the grip of his new bow, and Black Hawk smiled faintly.

"So you have come for our woman."

"I have come. She has accepted me," Thunder Horse said, rising. The Sauk war leader just nodded, seating himself. White Bear entered the lodge, dripping water. He too noticed Thunder Horse immediately and Sachim saw a look of pain flicker in his eyes.

"Thunder Horse," White Bear said.

"Do you know White Bear?" Sachim asked with a nervousness she couldn't conceal.

"How can I forget a man of that size?" Thunder Horse said. "One who came to our camp alone to reclaim his stolen horses."

"Sit down," Sachim urged. "I have corn soup and, if you like, dried fish."

"I will eat anything you have," White Bear said, sagging to the floor.

"And everything," Black Hawk added. He was still studying Thunder Horse. "You live among the Sauk now."

"I do."

"How do they treat you?"

"No one has tried to take my scalp."

Black Hawk grunted. Sachim gave him a wooden bowl filled with hot corn soup and a horn spoon. When she had also served White Bear she sat down near the fire to watch the men eat. White Bear, she noticed, had a fresh scar across his cheekbone. Steam rose from their clothing and after the first bowl of warm soup, Sachim convinced them both to remove their shirts and take blankets for their shoulders.

They ate silently while Thunder Horse worked on his bow. When they had finished eating, Thunder Horse filled a pipe for them. Only then did Sachim ask about the war.

"It went badly, very badly, Sachim. Many times we seemed on the verge of a great victory, but always there were more Americans, new cannon. The British wanted us to do the fighting while they hid in their forts."

"Tecumseh . . ."

"Tecumseh is dead. His dream is dead. We could have won, Sachim, if the tribes would have done as he asked—ally themselves into a single nation, an *Indian* nation, but there were too many who did not want to fight another's battle, too many who wanted to be leaders, too many who delayed their decisions endlessly in council.

"In the end," Black Hawk said, putting the pipe aside, "they were too many for us."

"What will the British do now?" Thunder Horse asked.

"Return to Canada. All of them."

"War will not come here then?" Sachim asked.

"No," Black Hawk said, "I do not think so now. Who is there to fight?"

They spoke no further of the war then, but of marriages and Skull and Keokuk's close ties with the whites and his wealth, of Grandmother and the rain which seemed endless.

They rose an hour later, thanking Sachim for the meal. "But you may stay here," Sachim said. "Where else can you go?"

"Many lodges," Black Hawk answered. He smiled and added, "Many where the warrior and his wife have been married longer." White Bear looked away as Black Hawk said that. Thunder Horse noticed.

When they were gone the Sioux asked his wife, "Does the big man love you?"

"He once thought he might," Sachim said with some embarrassment.

"I thought so," Thunder Horse said. "Well, why shouldn't you be loved by many?"

"I *give* my love only to you, Thunder Horse," Sachim responded, putting her arms around his waist, looking up at him, expecting his kiss, which came quickly, followed by many others before Thunder Horse stepped back and went to the tent flap, tying it down.

The rain, trial that it was, made pleasant sounds against the buffalo-hide lodge and Sachim lay contented by her husband, listening to the rain, to the slow steady beating of his heart beneath his strong chest. But if Thunder Horse could sleep, she could not. The ominous feeling with her since they had come south was still there. When she closed her eyes she could still see Little Creek crumpled against the dark earth. She did not dare to dream.

"There will be no war," Black Hawk had said. And if he did not wish to make war, then there would be none.

But the feeling was there, that terrible feeling that something beyond the comprehension of the Sauk, something beyond her dreams, hovered over them, shadowing the land.

She turned suddenly to Thunder Horse, teasing his ear

with her tongue, reaching for him with searching hands, awakening him, arousing him, needing to reenter the world of their lovemaking, where such thoughts could not trespass.

If the winter was long and the weather abominable, still it was a good time for Sachim and her husband. There was time for laughing, for discovering each other, there was time for long and lazy days spent only making love.

Thunder Horse could turn serious, of course. When he spoke of his father and Yellow Sky he became so.

"My brother hated me as a child. Perhaps it grew out of simple envy, I don't know. He was like a shadow at times, an unhappy shadow who tripped our snares and ruined our fish traps.

"I was shown no more favor than Yellow Sky; perhaps it was simply that I was older and able to do things before he could, and in consequence my father made much more of a fuss over my killing my first deer than he did when Yellow Sky repeated this small triumph."

"You were always a step ahead of him."

"Yes, and that must be frustrating, but in Yellow Sky it went beyond frustration. Things I cherished would disappear or be found broken. He sulked for months when I was finally made war leader, although the eldest son is expected to take his father's rank."

"Now he has his rank, now you are gone."

"Yes, but he will not cease to hate. He is that sort of man. That sort of child."

When the Sauk returned to their home camp, the trek northward seemed longer than ever to Sachim. Riding a horse was uncomfortable with her belly swelling larger each day, and so she walked. Thunder Horse sometimes rode his war pony but more often walked beside her among the Sauk and Fox, the constantly fighting children, the old gray-haired travelers who might even now be returning home for the last time, the proud warriors who had fought with Black Hawk, the younger braves who worshiped the older men and their leader, and the giggling young girls who now seemed far from Sachim's age and experience to her.

Black Hawk had scouts out on either side of the marchers. There would be no repeat of last year's sniping if he could help it.

Black Hawk himself was not a happy man. He was troubled and perplexed. "The council," he told Sachim, "treats me like a renegade. Keokuk trusts the Americans more than he trusts me. I cannot understand these times, what is happening. The whites have moved onto our land and it is allowed. In other days the Sauk would have risen up and done battle with them. I cannot understand these times."

"Don't judge the council too harshly, Black Hawk. They only want peace."

"And their new prosperity."

"And that as well, yes. Rather than see their young men die, they have made an accommodation."

"Yes, and the Cherokee made an accommodation, and the Shawnee and the Creek. I see this all. The whites are moving toward us. It is a great flood. Those who do not move are forced to. Those who do move lose their birthright, the land."

"Still, we have avoided conflict, avoided blood. We have our trading post and enough land."

"Yes, Sachim," the war leader said. "For now. For now."

She asked Thunder Horse, "Do you think Black Hawk is right?"

"I don't know. The Sioux think little about it. We are a strong nation. How can the Americans ever challenge a mounted Sioux army on the long plains? For now there is peace, Sachim, that is all I know, and that is good for the Sauk, for us, for our child."

Yes, Sachim thought, it was good that there was peace. Black Hawk was wrong about that. There must be no war.

The morning the Sauk reached their home camp was cool and bright. They could see smoke rising from many white fires. The frost was on the grass underfoot, crackling as they moved over it. Sachim had felt dizzy on rising, but now she was fine. She rested a hand on her abdomen as she walked.

The rider came in rapidly from the north. It was one of the scouts Black Hawk had sent out to watch for the white sniper. He rode recklessly toward them, and Sachim, startled, looked beyond the rider, thinking someone was pursuing him, but that wasn't the case.

"Black Hawk!" Sachim heard the warrior yell. Then, seeing the war leader, he veered toward him and dismounted before his horse had halted, leaping to the ground to rush up to Black Hawk, who led his own horse.

"What is it?" Thunder Horse asked. Sachim could only shake her head. She could see the scout gesturing, see Black Hawk stiffen with anger. Then the war leader swung aboard his own horse and raced out of the long line of Indians, the scout behind him, still gesturing.

It was another hour before Sachim and the people discovered what had caused the excitement. It took them that long to walk to where Black Hawk sat, his horse overlooking the long valley.

Sachim felt her heart drop. She clung to Thunder Horse's arm. More whites had come and they had built houses on land which was not theirs. Around the rice pond, across the hunting ground. They had done worse than that.

The sacred burial ground was no more. The great oak still stood there, but the graves of the Sauk had been plowed up and now corn had begun to grow there.

Black Hawk was outraged. "Our dead have been desecrated. They have stolen our land while we were gone. This is how they honor your treaty, Keokuk!"

"We will demand money," Keokuk said.

"Money! Our dead have been dug up, white corn will grow there, and there, where they have no right to be. And there!" He stabbed the air with his finger. "There are boats in the slough where our rice grows. Our hunting lands have white houses on them, and you speak of money!"

"The council will discuss it," Keokuk said calmly.

"Let them." Black Hawk's voice was unsteady. His hand was clenched involuntarily. "Let them discuss it until you are old and gray."

He turned to White Bear and the giant lieutenant turned his pony, knowing what to do.

"What is happening?" Thunder Horse asked.

"He will strike now," Sachim said. "He has endured enough."

She should have felt horror, fear, apprehension, but she felt strangely removed from events now. It had been inevitable; deep inside she had always known this would come. Black Hawk had been at war with the Americans for a year. He had many warriors, blooded in battle, men who would follow him, only him, who felt no allegiance to the political council.

It was time. Black Hawk took his paint from his war kit.

"What are you doing!" Keokuk was screaming. "I do not support this. Where is Quash-qua-me? Napope! This man is going mad. Are you outside of the law now, Black Hawk! I do not support this."

"Go to the whites, Keokuk," Black Hawk said quietly. "Collect your gold. Tell them that Black Hawk alone is responsible."

Behind Black Hawk his veteran soldiers had begun to mass, joined by as many youths as dared defy their parents and the council. The Sauk war leader said, "No one will be killed. We will shed no blood. But no house shall remain on our land, no living crop on sacred soil. That is my order. So it must be."

Keokuk still screamed, "You are destroying us. We have a peace treaty! Criminal! You are worse than Skull!"

Black Hawk ignored him. Looking at White Bear, he nodded and the Sauk rode down into the valley.

Willie Havens was drinking water from his new well. He held the wooden bucket in both hands, took a deep drink, and wiped his mouth with the back of his hand. He looked proudly at his miles-long new field and started to raise the bucket again.

The Indians rode over the rise and across his newly plowed field in a long picket line, their horses destroying his work. Havens dropped the bucket and sprinted for his house. Inside he locked the door, closed the shutters, and broke out his rifle. He peered out of the loophole in his wall, waiting for the Sauk to attack, but they didn't. They simply rode back and forth across his field—a month's plowing gone— whooping and waving guns in the air.

After half an hour or so they rode off toward the new Castle place by the rice pond.

Taking resolve, Havens went out his front door to stand watching as smoke began to billow up from the new house, a house Havens had helped build.

"Savages," he said bitterly, "savages."

There was his year's crop gone, and he had no seed corn left. The Castle house was burning. They were a nice young couple just up from Nashville, too.

Stunned and angry, Havens watched as the devastation

continued. Another house went up—whose, he couldn't tell—and then the Yount place. There was smoke in the slough, and that had to be Walter Simpson's flatboat.

"Savages." And where in hell was the army!

Savages.

Harold Parret was no greenhorn. He had been to Dakota to hunt buffalo, spent a winter up along the Milk River in Montana, and trapped with that crazy Frenchman LaCroix in Quebec, but the sight of a hundred painted Sauk bursting from the trees beyond his fields was enough to chill any man's blood.

Parret, encouraged by a new bride and a small bank account, had finally decided to give up his wandering ways and purchase a newly opened section along the Mississippi where the soil was rich and a man could build a house for the children he meant to have before he got too old.

All of that dream seemed to be wiped away as Parret stood blinking into the sunlight, trying to convince himself that he wasn't seeing what he was seeing.

The hell he wasn't. He raced for the house, yelling for his young wife to grab his rifle, though what good it was against a hundred armed Indians, he didn't know.

Rose Parret was small, blond, and flighty. She appeared in the doorway, drying her hands on a dish towel.

"Did you call me?" Her eyes opened wide as she too saw the onrushing Sauk, and she screamed, throwing her hands into the air.

Parret barely got inside before his wife slammed the door shut and barred it. By the time Parret had gotten his rifle from above the stone fireplace and returned to the front of the house, it was surrounded by Sauk warriors.

"You!" the one who seemed to be the leader called out.

Parret didn't answer. He loaded his rifle and wiped his hair out of his eyes as Rose clung to him.

"You, American!"

"What do you want?"

"Come out, go away. Your house will be burned. We do not wish to hurt you."

"You don't, do you! Sure looks like it!" Parret yelled defiantly.

"Come out," Black Hawk said again. "Go away. You will not be harmed. I, Black Hawk, give you my word."

"I'm not likely to take no Indian's word for nothing. Army'll be here soon, you better scoot."

"The army is not coming," Black Hawk said.

Rose touched Parret's arm. "Harold, maybe we'd better go out."

"No!"

"Your house will be burned," Black Hawk said as two warriors on horseback approached the cabin with burning brands. "Come out. If you do not trust me, think of this: any death is preferable to burning alive."

"Harold!" Rose Parret's eyes were horror-filled. The settler gave in.

"All right. I'm keeping my gun, Black Hawk. Anybody tries to hurt my wife, I'm killing you."

"No one will hurt your wife," the Sauk said.

The door opened and slowly the Parrets came out, walking through the circle of parting Sauk warriors. Parret held his wife's hand. His cocked rifle was in his other hand. He glowered at the Sauks, who looked straight ahead. He and Rose kept on walking for a quarter of a mile without stopping. When they turned to look back, their house was a mass of flames spewing dark smoke into the clear spring sky.

Parret stood with his arm around his wife, watching his investment and labor go up in smoke. Finally he grumbled, "Come on."

"Where are we going?"

"Where can we go? The fort. Captain Davenport's got some explaining to do."

Captain Davenport was trying very hard at that moment to explain things to the settlers who were crowded into the fort with wagons, children, livestock, and pets. All of them were armed, all of them angry.

"Just what *are* you going to do?" Willie Havens demanded angrily. "You haven't explained that yet, Davenport."

"I am going to give you all the best shelter we can and ask Hank Greeley to give you supplies temporarily," answered Davenport, who did not like being addressed by his last name alone.

"We're talking about the Indians, and you know it," shouted Walt Simpson, a curly-haired man with six children and a limited future now that his flatboat had been burned and sunk in the slough.

"They outnumber us five to one and you men know that," Davenport answered. "A counterattack might set off a mass slaughter. As it is, I haven't a report of the Sauk killing a single person."

"What about the McCutcheons? What about the Ibsen family?"

"That was another band of Indians, from what our scout tells me."

"What about it, Perkins?" Parret asked.

Bart Perkins spat tobacco and stepped forward. "Them was Skull Clan. Outlaws. Today's raid, from what I hear, was Black Hawk himself. Hell of a difference."

"What kind of difference?"

"Somethin' like eight hundred warriors' difference," Bartholomew Perkins answered, supporting Captain Davenport's position.

Havens said, "So if they outnumber us, we play dead, is that right?"

Captain Davenport had a piercing headache. He wished he were back in his office initialing reports, sipping occasionally at his bonded whiskey.

"Havens, you know the situation here. You didn't pull in yesterday. You know as well as I do that the treaty . . ."

"Signed way back in 1804," Havens interrupted.

"Signed in 1804," Davenport went on less patiently, "gave most of the original homesteaders their land legally. You also know that some of the land built on since wasn't deeded over. You also know that plowing up that burial ground is a part of what brought this about."

"So you stand with the Indians," Havens said, turning to the others for support. He spread his arms helplessly. "This is what our army does for us. No matter that the Sauk was on the British side of the war."

"If you don't like it, petition the governor," Davenport retorted, growing brittle.

"Well now, Captain, you know something—that's just what we've done. Where you think Joshua Ferguson is right now? At Chicago. And if you can't do a thing, won't do a thing, I expect the governor will!"

John Reynolds turned from the wall where he had been studying the rather remarkable portrait of his remarkable-

looking wife and put on his professional smile. The two men
who now entered his white-and-gold office were clean, newly
shaved, and dressed in new suits, yet both had the smell of
dust and the frontier about them. Reynolds, the governor of
Illinois, had occasion to meet such men every day. He greeted
them and was introduced.

"Name's Ferguson," the oily-looking, narrow man said.
"This is Ginger Sweet."

The second man was mentioned as if he were of no importance whatever, and Reynolds rightly took him for some sort
of bodyguard-factotum. Sweet's bulldog face was expressionless. His wrists were large enough to strain the seams of his
white shirt and blue coat at the cuffs.

"What can I do for you gentlemen?" Reynolds asked. He
remained standing, as he was to do throughout the interview. A minor medical problem made that advisable.

"Got a petition here," Ferguson said, "from the citizens
of southwest Illinois. We need some help down there."

Ferguson withdrew a petition from his inside pocket and
gave it to the governor, who was shrewd enough to see that
he was dealing with a man of some cunning. Ferguson spoke
with the drawl of the western states, cutting his sentences
short, swallowing consonants, but his eyes indicated a different sort of man entirely. He was no dirt farmer. Reynolds
studied the petition, taking in the gist of it.

"Indian raids."

"Yes, sir," Ferguson said, holding his hat in his hand.

"What is your position, sir?" Reynolds asked.

"Mayor of the community. River Fork we call it."

Reynolds nodded and walked to the opposite wall to study
his map. "Why, Fort Madison is located there."

"That's correct, sir."

"The commander—"

"Captain Harold Davenport. Says he can't do a thing.
Says he's outmanned."

Reynolds frowned. "Are these allegations true?"

"What, that the Sauk raiders have murdered fifteen settlers in the last six months, that Black Hawk has destroyed
our houses and crops? Damn right they're true," Ferguson
said with manufactured indignation.

"Can you tell me what the root cause is?" Reynolds
asked, placing the petition on his desk, weighting it with a
silver inkwell.

"Sure. They're Indians." Ferguson smirked.

"I see." Reynolds cleared his throat. He didn't like this man, not a bit. Whatever was happening down south, however, was affecting a lot of people; that was obvious from the number of signatures on the petition. "I'll see that this is looked into," the governor said.

"Looking into it won't do us any good," Ferguson said. "What we need is soldiers—with the will to fight."

"I'll want to examine the treaty," Reynolds said stiffly. "From what I recall, the problem with the Sauk and Fox is an involved one."

"Sure," Ferguson said, sneering, "investigate while people down south are getting murdered."

Reynolds swallowed his reply. He was, after all, a politician.

Ginger Sweet spoke for the first time. "The Sauk made war on the United States. Black Hawk was with Tecumseh at Fort Meigs and Frenchtown."

"I am aware of that," John Reynolds answered with the same stiffness. What *was* it these men wanted? Ferguson didn't impress him at all as an indignant homesteader.

"Been a lot of trouble," Sweet added. "You can see it writ down there."

Ferguson shot a sharp glance at Sweet and he fell silent.

"I certainly intend to look into this, gentlemen," Reynolds said, moving toward the door to his office suggestively.

Ferguson said, "We'll be at the Clayton House. Might let us know what you intend to do. Folks down home expect some kind of help."

"I will be in touch," Reynolds said, opening the door. He nodded faintly as the two exited his office, and after a moment's thought he called his secretary, "James, have Ed Gaines come around, will you?"

"Yes, sir."

Reynolds walked back to his desk and briefly reread the petition. He did not like something about this affair, but was unable to pin down what it was. His duty, however, was clear, and by the time General Edmund P. Gaines, the Western Department commander-in-chief, arrived, Reynolds—sitting uncomfortably at his desk—was ready to issue his order.

"There's something going on at Fort Madison, Ed. Davenport doesn't seem to be handling the situation to anyone's satisfaction. I'd like you to go on down and have a look. A show of force, maybe . . ."

"I have seven hundred militiamen ready now, sir," Gaines said. "And two steamboats standing by. One outfitted with cannon."

Reynolds was surprised but Gaines explained, "We were ready for the British to make a westward push, but it never came. If we need a show of force, we've got it."

"All right." Reynolds drummed his fingers in thought. "First, Ed, review the treaty with the Sauk, will you? Get legal advice if we need it. Something rings untrue here. We don't need a war in the south if we can avoid it, and damn me if it doesn't seem that someone wants just that."

11

IT had been decided. Black Hawk felt that he had given in enough and nothing good had come of it, nothing but broken promises, desecration, and difficulty for his people.

"We will not cross the river. We will stay here, on our home ground. The treaty gives us the right, Manitou gives us the right. Here we have always grown our corn, here he have always harvested rice, here we have always hunted. Build your lodges once more."

"The council does not agree," Quash-qua-me said.

"Keokuk does not agree, you mean. Keokuk, who wishes to sell all of our land. We have always lived here—who wishes to cross the great river so that the whites may live on our land and destroy what belongs to us, our canoes, our fields, our forests, our homes?"

It was decided in the end, not by the council, which continued to debate, but by Black Hawk's will. The Sauk went out again to collect bark and suitable lodgepoles; again they planted their corn in their own fields. Again they hunted their lands.

Black Hawk had further advice for his people. "Trade with the whites only when you must have goods. Pay with furs; do not use credits. You must understand that they are not giving you things without a price."

Thunder Horse was amazed at the influence Black Hawk had on his people. Perhaps they had put up with the council's indecision long enough, or maybe they could now see through Keokuk and his plans. They had heard that Keokuk was ready to sell even more land before Black Hawk's return, ready to guide the old council members into a betrayal of the people. If that was so, Thunder Horse did not know.

But he knew a leader when he saw one; he knew a warrior.

Spring passed as it had since Manitou brought the Indian to the land, blooming, greening, burgeoning. The river was a swath of quiet grace flowing placidly through their wide country.

Sachim watched the rebuilding of the village with satisfaction; there was a comfort in having things as they once were, as they should be. The whites still farmed their own land, land legally purchased, but the squatters came no more, and if each side gave the other wide berth, there was no trouble between them—but the whites now carried weapons as they worked. They strapped scabbards holding rifles to their plow handles and wore belt guns.

Sachim worried little about trouble now. Black Hawk was here; the Sauk were strong. He had achieved what he felt compelled to do and now wanted no more war. There would be none.

The fields sprouted the first tiny green plants. The fishing was good, game abundant. Sachim's belly was ripening rapidly and she and Thunder Horse laughed at the splayfooted walk she had adopted.

Fort Madison was still crowded with homeless settlers. Ferguson had promised to get their land back, with force if necessary, but he hadn't yet returned from Chicago. Some of the homesteaders, like Willie Havens, had discovered drink, with time on their hands, and sat soaking up whiskey at Hank Greeley's store, muttering under their breath at the army's cowardice, at Davenport's incompetence, cursing the damned Indians.

"Bastards fought against us in the war. Now the government protects them. What about our rights?"

"Every cent I had was in that land, in my house," Parret agreed. "Bought it legal. Now the government backs down."

Walt Simpson just growled. He had purchased his flatboat in St. Louis with borrowed money and come upriver hoping to transport goods for the army and the new town. The Indians had burned his boat, he was in debt up to his neck, and he had no plans for the future worth pursuing.

The door opened and they barely glanced that way as hot, humid air off the river blasted briefly into the dark sutler's store. Only Bart Perkins reacted, turning his head to spit on the floor as Thaddeus McCutcheon entered and asked Greeley's Delaware assistant for a drink of whiskey.

"Back, are you?" Perkins muttered.

McCutcheon slowly swiveled his head toward the buckskin-clad scout. Thad McCutcheon didn't smell any better than ever. He had a tangled beard to his waist now. His hair was nearly as long. The rifle he had placed on Greeley's scarred counter was scored with several dozen notches.

"All these civilians," McCutcheon said, drinking his whiskey in a gulp. "Davenport needed a meat hunter again."

"I didn't think they'd have you back," Perkins said casually. "I thought Davenport had more sense."

"What're you baiting me for, Perkins?" the big man asked. "You drunk?"

"I don't drink till the sun goes down. No, I'm not drunk, I just don't like you and never will. You're trouble."

"Why!" McCutcheon roared, turning toward the men at the long plank table, looking at them as he spoke to Perkins. "Because I hate Indians, 'cause I kill a few? That why, Perkins?"

Willie Havens muttered, "Only man with guts in the territory."

"Yeah, I killed a few Indians," McCutcheon said, taking another whiskey. "Why shouldn't we take some of our own back from the stinkin' Sauk?"

"The man's right," Harold Parret said.

"Damn right I'm right. Army won't do it. Who's gonna do it? You ever have family hacked up in front of you? Lousy Indians, lousy bastards."

"The man's right, Perkins," Willie Havens said.

"He is, is he?" The scout glanced at McCutcheon. "Show 'em your scalps, Thaddeus."

"Scalps?" Harold Parret repeated shakily.

"Sure," Perkins said. "McCutcheon's got such a grudge against these *savages* that he makes real civilized war. He takes scalps, don't you, Thaddeus?"

"Maybe," McCutcheon said cautiously as he finished another drink.

"Maybe, hell."

"All right, so I do. What of it!" He banged his glass down

on the counter. The impassive Delaware Indian filled it again.

"Some of them are women's scalps, aren't they, Thaddeus?" Perkins persisted. A low growl had begun to sound in McCutcheon's throat.

"What of it? Women give birth to more warriors, don't they? What do you think of this one, Perkins? Damn you!" And McCutcheon, in a frenzy of hatred, slapped a scalp on the counter. Perkins picked it up and examined it as the other men in the store leaned toward them, staring in disbelief.

"I think," Bart Perkins said, "that it came from a kid. A little girl."

"Little Indians get to be big Indians," McCutcheon ranted. "I had a kid too. Only the Indians killed him. So what if it was a kid?" Whiskey had begun to glaze his eyes. "I took her and held her head underwater. She thrashed about for a long time. When she was good and drownded I yanked her head up, cut her throat, and skinned her scalp. Then I tied her to a rock and dumped her in the river."

Perkins asked quietly; "How did that make you feel, McCutcheon?"

"It made me feel *good*!"

Bartholomew Perkins looked away briefly, and then he turned sharply, his fist driving into McCutcheon's face so hard his teeth cracked and blood from his nose sprayed the counter. McCutcheon staggered back and sat down hard on the floor. Bart Perkins picked up McCutcheon's musket-rifle and slammed it against the counter, splintering the musket's stock. He tossed what was left of the weapon to McCutcheon and then turned and strode from the store with McCutcheon's curses ringing in his ears.

Outside, Perkins stood taking deep breaths to calm himself. Soldiers drilled on the parade ground and settlers' kids raced around the fort playing tag. The sky was blue, with a few scudding high white clouds.

Perkins walked to the orderly room to find the one-eyed Sergeant Monk sitting, legs crossed, chair tilted back against the wall.

"What's up, Bart?"

"McCutcheon's back."

"Yeah."

"I'm leaving. The army owes me two weeks' pay."

Monk nodded, let his chair legs slap to the floor, rose, and filled out a pay voucher. "Sorry you're going, Bart. Where you headed?"

"Away. Dakota maybe. There's tragedy coming, Monk. You can feel it, can't you?"

"I feel it," Monk answered. "Wish I could leave myself. I happen to be a soldier, though."

"I know."

"Paymaster'll take care of you." The two men shook hands and then there was nothing to say but, "Good luck to you, Bart."

"Good luck to you," Perkins said, tucking the voucher away inside his shirt. "Good luck to all of you." Then the scout turned and strode out of the office, leaving the door open so that the warm air filled the orderly room. Monk walked to it with a sigh and kicked it shut.

The dream was of a child wandering free across the golden summer grass while larks dived and darted against a pale sky, of a child tumbling to the earth to lie there laughing, smelling the sweet scent of the grass, watching the bees hum among the crimson flowers. There was distant thunder, and before the child could sit up, scowling in a childish way, the sky had gone dark and lightning crackled against the backdrop of thunderclouds. The Thunderbird spoke endlessly, its great dark wings sending winds across the plains, battering the trees and tangling the girl-child's hair. When the rain began to fall it was silver and cool, but it changed to blood red and when it touched the flesh it was hot. Whatever it touched, it stained red, and the rain formed crimson rivulets which snaked away toward the foaming great river. They were there again, always there, the skulls floating on the river, skeletal arms reaching skyward toward clouds that had gone red. He came, the laughing youth with the powerful arms, walking on the dark, dark red water of the river, calling out to the woman who drifted away from him. When the current became too swift he sank beneath the river and she could see only his arm for a long while and then nothing at all as the river raced toward the sea. The sea was red beneath a lightning-scored black sky, and the waterspout rose, lifting the woman to the sky, toward the storm, beyond it, until she was flying once again through the white world beyond the angry, roiling elements below. When the eagle came, its feathers were white, softly glowing, and she rode it to the mountain peak. Below there was only white cloud, above white sky. They came walking, their eyes blank: all of the Sauk. They moved skyward in slow-paced strides, naked, pale as if they had no blood in their veins. The woman called out but they did not answer and no eyes turned her way. She named them one by one as they passed, but still they did not answer. Their mouths had been filled with salt and their eyes with oil. Time had found them. Time would devour them, and the woman wept, her tears washing away the white clouds, touching the earth with warmth. The child stood, looked skyward, and laughed aloud, prancing across the long-grass plains, lifting her skirt to kick her heels together. That was there, that moment, and then the world went dark again and Sachim knew that time had ended.

Sachim wept. Her husband lifted her and held her gently. Outside it was dark and warm. She was naked in their bed, as was Thunder Horse. His body was strong and warm next to hers, touching her. Her breasts pressed against his chest and she lifted a tear-streaked face to his kiss. He held her; he touched her full abdomen and asked; "Did you dream?"

"It was nothing at all."

"What *was* it, Sachim?"

"The child will be a girl," the far-dreamer said, and she could say no more as he cradled her body in his arms. She could not tell him that the Sauk would be no more, that the river would run with the blood of their people.

That was the morning the steamboats came down the river and runners from the Fox villages upstream woke Black Hawk from his sleep and led him from his lodge to watch the coming of the white army.

Sachim had been awake for hours, ever since her dream awakened her, and now she and Thunder Horse went to the river to watch the arrival of the steamboats.

Catch Fish was one of the Fox runners Two-Knives had sent to Black Hawk, and he spoke excitedly now. "You see, two boats. There are many men on board. Six . . . maybe seven hundred. The first boat has cannon, Black Hawk. Eight cannon."

"What do they want?" Thunder Horse wondered.

Black Hawk answered without turning. "Our blood."

"It can't be," Sachim exclaimed. "We have done nothing."

"So it seems to us. How does it seem to them?"

The boats dropped anchor at Fort Madison and Sauk

scouts reported that a man with white sideburns and much gold on his uniform went to the fort to talk to Davenport. Later Davenport, in his finest uniform, had come out and gone on board the lead steamboat.

That was at noon. By three in the afternoon nothing more had happened. Black Hawk had summoned his warriors and they were spread out along the riverbank, watching from the shelter of the trees, waiting.

Keokuk had appeared, in a towering rage. "You see! You see, Black Hawk, what you have done!"

"I have done nothing," the war leader said calmly, "except to reclaim what was ours all the time."

"There will be war. All of what we have gained will be lost," Keokuk shouted. "You are a traitor, a renegade."

Black Hawk answered with dignity. "*I* am not the traitor, Keokuk."

Black Hawk returned his eyes to the river. The first steamboat with many blue-uniformed men on its deck drew abreast of the Sauk village. The cannon were being loaded now, and Keokuk, in a shrieking rage, continued to yell at Black Hawk.

"We will all be killed!"

Black Hawk didn't respond. He only watched the riverboat, glancing at his warriors. A smaller craft was lowered from the stern of the steamboat and the Sauk saw two officers and half a dozen soldiers step into it. Davenport was one of the officers. The other they did not know except that he was a man of high rank.

The sailors began rowing toward the shore while one of them waved a white flag of truce. Black Hawk started toward the beach, behind him White Bear, Sachim, Thunder Horse, and Napope.

The boat was beached and the high-ranking officer stepped ashore, the sailors watching warily as the Sauk approached.

"Davenport," Black Hawk said tonelessly as the Americans approached.

"Black Hawk. Napope. Keokuk. This is General Gaines. He has come from Chicago." Davenport was very nervous. His face was red, his watery eyes unhappy.

Napope took charge. "What is it you want here with all these soldiers, with those cannon and boats?"

Gaines, who had been stroking his white muttonchop whiskers thoughtfully, replied, "You people must go back across the river. This land belongs to American settlers. If you do not go, we shall be forced to disperse you—with cannon if necessary."

Black Hawk leapt forward angrily. "This is our land, we will not leave!"

Gaines blinked. "I'm sorry, I didn't catch your name."

"My name is Black Hawk, General. I am a Sauk. I am a warrior, and so was my father. Ask those young men who have followed me to battle and they will tell you who Black Hawk is. Provoke our people to war and you will learn who Black Hawk is."

"The idea is not to provoke a war, but to prevent one," Gaines said. "We have received reports of Sauk raids, of the destruction of property, of murder."

"Skull . . ." Sachim whispered, but Gaines didn't hear her.

He asked Black Hawk, "May I take it that you are the chief of the Sauk?"

"I am the council chief," Napope said. "The council speaks for the Sauk, not Black Hawk."

"I don't understand," Davenport said to Napope. "What has caused your people to cross back to the eastern side of the river?"

"It is our land," Black Hawk said flatly.

"We were living together, trading together," Davenport continued. "There was no trouble."

"It is our land."

"Napope, Keokuk," Davenport pleaded, "why can you not cross the river again? Things will be as they were before."

"We have built our lodges and planted our corn," Black Hawk replied.

"Napope?"

"I do not know," Napope said in some confusion. "That was our desire. But the whites had dug up our burial grounds, they had cut timber in our hunting grounds."

Gaines asked, "Isn't it possible for us to compensate you for what has been done, to offer more trade credits?"

"It is our land," Black Hawk said again, and Gaines studied the man, seeing where the trouble lay.

"There are better solutions than war," Gaines suggested.

"The council must meet," Napope answered. "We do not want war either. We see your strength. There would be much destruction."

"Over what?" Keokuk demanded. "Davenport is right, there is land enough for everyone. If the river is on our right hand or on our left hand, what does it matter? We have a few troublemakers among us. Men who want power not theirs by law." He looked long and hard at Black Hawk. "Napope does not want war, Quash-qua-me does not want war, Pa-she-pa-ho does not want war, I do not want war. How can one man take us toward a war we do not want? It is outside the law of the Sauk. It is destructive for all of the Sauk. It is death for those who wish to live."

Black Hawk said, "I have seen broken promises. I have seen that the whites can do as they like, even to digging up the bones of our fathers. I do not want war, but I will fight for what is ours."

"And if you do, sir," Gaines said, "I promise you that we will meet again and the cannon on board that steamer will level your village and kill many of your people. Those of you who want peace, cross the river! Those who wish to die, stay here with Black Hawk."

Then Gaines nodded to Davenport and started back toward the boat. "That was strong enough," Davenport muttered.

"I don't think we'll get much out of Black Hawk by speaking softly."

"No, but I'm not sure we want to challenge him, sir."

"Apparently this council of chiefs sees things our way," Gaines said, stepping into the boat.

"Yes, if only Black Hawk did," Davenport said as the boat was pushed away from shore and the sailors began their rowing.

"Captain, let me ask you something frankly. You have been reluctant to enter into hostilities. Is that caution, because of your knowledge that you are numerically inferior, or is there something else involved?"

"There are other considerations," Davenport said, wiping the mist from his face.

"Such as?"

"Have you looked over the treaty we have with the Sauk?"

"Looked it over, yes. I haven't studied it in depth. Governor Reynolds arranged for a U.S. attorney to review the document, and in his opinion it was entirely valid *and* ethical. Apparently the tribe has been well-compensated and, outside of Black Hawk, was pleased with the terms."

"That's accurate as far as it goes," Davenport said, looking toward the steamboat. He hesitated. "Yet there have been certain infringements—not serious, but infringements all the same. If Black Hawk is now violating the spirit of the treaty, it is a fact that we have already violated the letter of it."

General Gaines looked thoughtful. He hadn't been sent here to begin a war, but to bargain from a position of strength. If there was something to what Davenport was saying, it needed looking into in more depth.

"You have rum, Captain? And coffee?"

Startled, Davenport stammered, "Of course."

"Then," the general said, "I suggest we retire to your office with treaty and map in hand and warm ourselves while we study this situation more thoroughly. No matter what I might have told the Indians, I have no intention of blasting their village to ruin unless that is the last option."

Davenport was relieved. He was a military man but he had no urge toward wanton destruction and unnecessary war. Once the general had time to understand the situation entirely and the council of the Sauk had met, surely some agreement could be worked out. It calmed his jangled nerves a little to know that Gaines wasn't one of those senior officers eager to advance his career through bloodshed. As for Davenport, he would much rather negotiate than fight. He looked forward to explaining matters in detail to Gaines. He was looking forward even more to coffee and rum.

The Sauk council had ignored formality and etiquette, and immediately and passionately begun their meeting—without Black Hawk.

Keokuk spoke for the majority when he said, "We have nothing to gain by being stubborn. We have everything to lose by remaining here. Brothers, let us return to the far side of the river. If we must leave our corn, then the whites will give us credits in the store. We will be comfortable. There is land there, as there is here. Who wants this war? Who wants to see the young men die, the women, the children, for one man's pride? Not I. I will tell you this as well: the Prophet has dreamed. He has dreamed of a land of plenty, of peace, of wealth. He has dreamed of a dark bird that wishes to scavenge that land like a carrion bird. A great bird. . . . Who can say if it is a black hawk or a vulture?"

* * *

"Well then?" Sachim asked. "What will we do?"

Thunder Horse looked at his wife. They walked together through the maple forest, arms around each other's waists. The Sioux brave stepped over a massive root and shrugged.

"How will you have it, Sachim?"

"Black Hawk will not leave. Most of the tribe will cross the river. Keokuk has convinced them. To stay here with the warriors would be dangerous. To stay here with our baby nearly ready to be born is unwise."

"Yes, Sachim." He knew his wife well by now and so he waited.

"Yet this is our land. Black Hawk is right," she concluded.

"If you wish to stay, we will."

Sachim finally managed to nod. They would stay. It was unwise, it was foolish perhaps, there was the baby to consider. Yet there was a principle involved—more than a principle, the life of the Sauk, their way, their existence perhaps. Who were these men who could come down the river and demand that a people leave their home? They were wrong and knew it. Sachim leaned her head against Thunder Horse's shoulder and they walked on.

At the river, the Sauk crossed in small groups, some in canoes, others on hastily built rafts. There was no anger, no sorrow, only a certain resignation on the faces Sachim saw there. Ta-wa-shuk, also full with child, was paddled away in Ha-te-ka's birchbark. Quash-qua-me sat on the edge of a raft looking old, far too old. Sha-sak, who was never unhappy, looked worn and weary. The bounce and verve was gone from her great body. The lodges of the Sauk again stood hollow and empty.

Black Hawk scowled. He was not angry but disappointed. "It is right," he said at last. "Let the old go, the women and the children. If there is to be a war, then they do not belong here. You, Sachim, do not belong here."

"But you know I do, Black Hawk," she said quietly. "This is my home."

Later in the day the word came from the Fox villages to the north: more American militia had come, marching down from Chicago. And in the night some of Black Hawk's warriors slipped across the river.

"Why?" Black Hawk asked, looking eastward. The sky was darkening with rainclouds, the wind shifting the trees,

drifting leaves through the air. "Why?" he asked again, but
he knew why his warriors had gone. They had spent a year
fighting a losing war to the Americans and come home to
search for peace, to sleep with their women and play with
their babies.

This was a fight Black Hawk could not win.

"Well?" Gaines rubbed his weary eyes. The meeting with
Davenport and his aides, Higgins and Monique, had lasted
all through the night. There was a point at which alcohol and
coffee could not sustain vigor and intelligence, and General
Gaines felt he had long since passed that point.

He pushed away the papers in front of him. The territorial
map curled itself on its own. Monique shrugged; Higgins
looked to his commanding officer.

"You know what I think, sir," Davenport said.

"Monique?"

"It's not the Sauk who have violated the treaty, sir," the
young lieutenant said.

"No." Gaines scratched his belly. "No, I don't think so
either. Just who sold that land to the newcomers? Captain?"

"Ferguson."

"The surveyor?"

"He's the one. Mayor of the community. But I saw the
deeds. Keokuk's mark was on them as well. Maybe Ferguson assumed he had the council's authority. Wish to hell we
would start to realize the complexity of tribal law. It's too
easy for someone to call himself chief of this tribe or another
and sign over anything. To the Indian's mind he *is* a chief
and no one takes the trouble to look any further into things."

Gaines was more concerned with, "What do we do now?"

"Make war," Lieutenant Higgins said, "*or* pacify Black
Hawk."

"And which would you choose, Lieutenant?" Gaines asked
sternly.

"No sane man chooses war, sir."

"No." Gaines rose, stretching his arms, yawning. "And so
we know what has to be done, but how?"

"And how," Davenport asked, "do we pacify both Black
Hawk and the settlers who've lost their land?"

"We've made our show of force," the general officer said.
"It didn't accomplish much. Our alternative now is to take
our hats in our hands and make concessions to Black Hawk."

"It grates," Monique said.

"It is," Gaines said, "what is right and proper. The governor sent me here with few instructions—I like to think he had confidence in my discretion—but of those few instructions the paramount one was to do 'what is right and proper.' "

Monique had formulated some very precise ideas on what an officer needed to do to get ahead in the army; precisely, fight and win battles. He had come west for that purpose, only to miss the fighting in the east during the last British war. Now he found himself sitting with two senior officers who had the enemy outnumbered, outgunned, outpositioned, and refused to attack. He glanced at Frank Higgins but there was no commiseration in Higgins' pale eyes and Monique returned his gaze to the window, where the gray light of predawn had begun to glimmer.

"I suggest, gentlemen, two hours' sleep and then a return visit to Black Hawk's village. I'm afraid we owe the man an apology." General Gaines buttoned up his tunic, yawned deeply, and then nodded a good morning to the other officers.

Davenport yawned in return, as if it were some sort of secret salute, and waited for the general to leave. He would not sleep himself; there was rum left.

Higgins and Monique put on their caps, adjusting their chin straps, and went out into the morning that was beginning to glow faintly red behind the gray of the clouds.

"We have the cannon," Monique said, looking southward.

Higgins was surprised. "You don't attack if you're in the wrong and know it."

"They were British allies, weren't they?" Monique asked without shifting his eyes.

"Yes."

"We have the cannon," Monique repeated. "We have the soldiers."

"I've got to get some sleep, Monique," Higgins said, looking worriedly at his fellow officer and friend. Monique seemed not to hear him. After Higgins was gone, he said it once again, to himself.

"We have the cannon. Finish them now before they finish us."

The steamboat came again the next day, moving like a white phantom through the gray mist of rain, and Black

Hawk watched it come. His remaining warriors were again dispersed along the river, ready for whatever was to come.

When the big boat dropped anchor, Sachim was with Black Hawk and she was the first to point out, "There are only a few soldiers on deck. No one is manning the cannon."

"What is it, then? The man came with his war talk and now he is back wanting—what?" He turned. "White Bear. Take three men and scout to the north, make sure the Americans are not sending their militia up behind us."

"Now the canoe again," Thunder Horse said, and it was true. Gaines and Davenport were climbing into the rowboat, being brought ashore. Again the white flag flew, but Black Hawk wasn't reassured by it.

"What is this? One last ultimatum?"

Gaines and Davenport made their way toward the war leader, the one-eyed sergeant carrying the flag of truce. Gaines saluted Black Hawk, but the Sauk leader made no response.

"We must talk," General Gaines said.

"Here we are. Let us talk."

"Out of the rain?" Gaines suggested.

"As you wish, but I must warn you. At any time, cannon-balls may strike the lodge we shelter in."

"I don't think so," Gaines said with the merest shadow of a smile.

"Then we shall talk. Follow." Black Hawk turned and walked through the rain toward his lodge, with Sachim and Thunder Horse following him. White Bear had returned quickly. He made a negative signal to Black Hawk. There was no militia marching on the village.

Inside the lodge it was dark, dry, and a little musty. Black Hawk lit no pipe, offered no presents. Protocol was ignored with the enemy.

"What have you come to say?" He glanced at Sachim, who seated herself awkwardly with Thunder Horse's help.

"Is the woman a general too?" Gaines asked.

"She is the one who knows the truth from a lie. She is a spirit woman, a far-dreamer, still immature, but seeing farther than we see with our poor eyes. She sees into the soul of a man and knows if what he speaks is false."

"Then she is welcome," Gaines answered. "For she can tell you that everything I am going to tell you is the truth."

No one responded to Gaines's remark. He plunged ahead.

"We *do* wish to be friends with the Sauk, Black Hawk. We do wish to work our problems out peacefully."

"Then admit that the whites are wrong."

"They *are* wrong," Gaines said slowly. Black Hawk's eyebrows lifted with surprise. "The treaty as it stands shows that."

"Then it is settled. Tell the whites to go away."

"They've gone," Gaines said. "You chased them away, Black Hawk." The general went on, "I want your people to have their own cornfields back—as it was to be. I want you to have your rice. I want you to have your hunting grounds. So does Governor Reynolds. So would President Madison."

"The soldiers you brought must go."

"They will go. Only Davenport's men will remain."

"All as it was before?" Black Hawk asked with some suspicion.

"All as the treaty dictates."

"Sachim?"

"I see no lie in his eyes, Black Hawk. I believe this man."

"Then," Black Hawk said, "we can be friends. Thunder Horse, hand me that pipe and kinnikinnick. We will smoke to peace, and hope the smoke rising toward Manitou pleases him."

Davenport couldn't stop grinning. Gaines himself sagged a little with relief. Black Hawk appeared greatly pleased. Yet Sachim watched and listened and wondered. It was true that Gaines was speaking the truth, and yet the awful premonition of blood to come remained in her heart. Outside, the wind blew. The rain fell down.

"What do you think of that, Monique?"

Lieutenant Monique glanced sideways at Hank Greeley, lifting his shoulder a fraction of an inch in a shrug. "I don't make policy."

"No, nor do I," Greeley said. "I asked you what you thought of General Gaines bringing more'n seven hundred militiamen all the way down here from Chicago, giving Black Hawk everything he wanted, then turning around and going back home. What? Hear that silence, men? Guess we know what the lieutenant thinks."

"Know what I think?" Thaddeus McCutcheon asked from the corner of the store.

"Hell, yes, everyone knows what you think, McCutcheon," Willie Havens said sharply. "Kill 'em all."

"Well? What's wrong with that?"

"What would you do if you were in charge, Monique?"

"Follow orders," the dark-haired young officer answered.

"Like 'em or not, huh?"

"Like 'em or not," Monique said, and it was obvious he didn't like the way things were being done at Fort Madison.

The door to the sutler's store opened and banged shut and a man in a dripping black coat walked in, whipping his hat to shake the water from it.

"Here he is," someone said sarcastically. "The man who was going to straighten everything out."

Joshua Ferguson looked up, eyes blazing. "Think I enjoyed it, going all the way up to Chicago, bringing militia back just to have Gaines back down?"

Hank Greeley emerged from behind the counter to take his boss's coat. A barely perceptible look passed between the two men.

"Monique? Believe you're wanted over at headquarters," Ferguson said, wiping back his hair.

"I'm not on duty," Monique grumbled. "What now?"

"You'd have to ask them."

Monique picked up his cap, finished his drink, and stumped toward the front door. When he opened it, a gust of wind drifted rain into the sutler's store.

"How about a whiskey, Hank?"

"Sure, mayor."

"*Mayor*," Havens said sourly. "What good's it do us to have a mayor when we got no town left? What have you done for us anyway, Ferguson?"

"Gaines is gone," Ferguson said, leaning on one elbow at the counter.

"So?"

"Davenport is going," Ferguson revealed.

"The hell he is! Who says so?"

"I do. I ought to know," Ferguson said smugly. "I'm the one who suggested it to the governor, told him that we really didn't see eye to eye with the captain down here. Said he wasn't getting along with the settlers. Davenport's been promoted—and he's getting out of Illinois."

"And who's taking his place?"

Ferguson nodded toward the closed door. "Just what do you think they want Monique at headquarters for?"

Harold Parret looked at Ferguson with awe. "You done all that?"

"Sure, why not? I'm the mayor. I'm the man who laid out these tracts—it's *my* town. I got no town if the Indians are allowed to move in and out as they please, buffalo the army, burn people's houses, murder."

"All right—Monique sees things more our way, but I don't see what we're gaining."

"You will. Monique will back us all the way. Starting tomorrow, you can move back onto your land."

"Sure," Parret said with mockery, "and what about the Sauk?"

"Most of 'em are across the river."

"Black Hawk isn't."

Ferguson finished his drink and pointed a finger at Parret. "Take my word for it, you can start moving back. When you go onto your land, soldiers from this fort will be going along. Then let's see what Black Hawk does."

"My old lady—"

"Leave your woman here. After things are settled, send for her. Get your crops down. Hank will let you have seed corn on credit, won't you, Hank? Sure, there's a risk, but if you don't want to take that risk, if you're not man enough to, you don't belong out here in the first place. I'll take a quitclaim on that property for what you owe me, Parret. And by God I'll sell it to a man with guts enough to work that land!"

"You saying I don't have the guts?" Parret asked, taking a step forward.

"I told you how things stand, that's all. I broke my back getting this worked out for you, for Havens, for Castle, for all of you. For what? I don't care if you stay or go—I just tried to do what's right." Even Hank Greeley almost took Ferguson seriously. The sincerity and righteous anger had been blended theatrically and convincingly.

McCutcheon said, "When the army goes down, I'm going along."

"Talk to Monique. Maybe the army needs a new scout. Bart Perkins has pulled out."

One by one the men finished their drinks and left, their faces thoughtful or flushed or expectant. When Greeley and

Ferguson were alone the sutler locked the door and took a bottle and two glasses to a table.

"You got this figured out, Joshua?" Greeley asked.

"Down to the last hair. The Sauk have only a third or so of their people on the east side of the river. That cuts 'em down to the garrison's size. Plus the garrison has more muskets, cannon. If Black Hawk raises a fuss, Monique won't hesitate to slap him down. If Monique can't handle it, why, we go back to Chicago and explain how Black Hawk tricked Gaines."

"You're talking a lot of blood if this gets out of hand, mayor," Greeley said.

"That's a risk we have to take," Ferguson said as if he were taking a risk on his own. The surveyor poured another drink. His eyes glowed softly in the low lamplight, shining with ambition.

"Greeley, you give those sodbusters all the seed corn they need."

"I'm so deep in the red right now—"

"Listen to me!" Ferguson hunched forward. "If Black Hawk drives those settlers off, Gaines or somebody will be back. If those sodbusters leave owing us money, that land is ours. When the militia kicks the Sauk back out, we own half the valley."

"Yea, but—"

"There isn't any *but* about it, Hank, trust me. We win no matter what happens."

"Suppose there's no war at all?"

"Then we call in Keokuk's credit. That gives us a foothold on the west side of the river. He'll have to give us more land to pay what he owes."

Hank Greeley shook his head in admiration. Ferguson was devious, crooked as a snake, but he had a brain. Greeley wasn't fool enough not to realize that he himself was being used, but he was in so deep now that he had little choice.

"I'll give 'em what seed I have. I'll have more shipped up from St. Louis," he agreed finally.

Both men turned toward the door as someone tapped on it. Greeley got up and let the man with the bulldog face in.

"He's here," Ginger Sweet mumbled.

"All right," Ferguson rose and told Greeley, "I've got to

go. You're making the right decision. Stick with me and you'll retire in two years."

Or be dead tomorrow, Greeley thought, but didn't say. Even this far out on the frontier there was only so much a man could get away with—but Greeley would be damned if he could see a flaw in Ferguson's work, find an illegality in the plan.

It didn't mean the man wouldn't fry in hell.

Outside, it was dark, raining very hard. The slanting rain struck the hard-packed earth of the parade ground and rebounded a foot. Ferguson, hat tugged low, followed Ginger Sweet to the storage room abutting the stockade.

Inside, the man waited in the darkness. "Hello, Keokuk," Ferguson said, closing the door. "Light a candle, Ginger. My friend and I have some talking to do."

"Thunder Horse," Sachim said very quietly. He was asleep but the sound of her voice woke him instantly. He rolled to her in the darkness, hearing the rain's constant drumming on the bark roof of the lodge.

"What is it?"

"A drop of water hit me. One little raindrop." She reached out and squeezed his hand. Thunder Horse held it, waiting. Sachim did not wake him to complain about a single raindrop.

When she said nothing more but he felt her quiver and place his hand on her distended belly, he asked, "Is it time, Sachim?"

"Yes, husband. Time."

"What shall I do?"

"It is raining so hard."

"Yes."

"I hate to ask you, but I would like it if you could find Sha-sak and bring her to me."

Thunder Horse sat up, kissed Sachim's forehead, and then quickly dressed, throwing a blanket over his head and shoulders. Sachim gave a single tiny cry, as if surprised, and Thunder Horse hurried out into the night and the rain. Lightning struck close by, and thunder rumbled constantly. The wind knocked a dead branch from a maple tree and it fell within a few feet of Thunder Horse's head. He practically had to swim to reach Sha-sak's lodge. The low ground was flooded and Thunder Horse could hear the river rumbling past beyond the trees.

Sha-sak was up and dressed. "I knew it would be tonight," she said.

"We have to hurry."

"We will hurry, warrior. Don't worry, there is time. The first ones are always slow."

The big woman had packed all she would need in a buckskin sack. She nodded to Thunder Horse and they started back toward the lodge where Sachim lay waiting.

It is time, Sachim thought with amazement more than fear. A time had come when she must do something she had never done before, something which seemed impossible although it was done every day. It was an incredible thing, this slow growing of her belly, the changing of her body, the development of a baby within her. Impossible. It could not be! She rubbed her hands over her naked belly. The baby was not moving now, but she had been told it was not supposed to. Her bed was soaked with her fluids now and the pains which came were very close together.

She became suddenly frightened, lying there alone in the darkness. Why she should be afraid, she did not know, but she was. Terribly afraid. She calmed herself deliberately and allowed her mind to wander to a far place, a soft white place where white flowers grew from soil like fleecy clouds. When she opened her eyes again the pain returned; but Sha-sak was there and it would be all right. Gentle, good-hearted Sha-sak.

Sachim closed her eyes and endured.

Thunder Horse paced back and forth in the rain like a madman as lightning struck across the tumbling skies. He was barefoot in the deep mud, his blanket and clothing soaked through with cold water. From within the lodge he heard Sachim yell. Once and loudly. Then she began to chant:

Manitou give this child life
Good life.
Manitou give this mother courage
Much courage.
Manitou bring this child forth
Quickly forth.

Thunder Horse stood transfixed, the rain washing over him. Sachim's voice repeated the chant endlessly, her words sometimes broken by a gasp, sometimes interrupted by thunder which shook the earth.

And then there was no more chanting, there was no sound but the storm and, distantly, the raging river. Thunder Horse waited, afraid to move, afraid to enter the lodge.

It seemed that an hour passed before Sha-sak's round face appeared, beckoning. "Now, you are a silly man," she scolded, "standing in the rain. Are you foolish? Do you want your daughter to have her father die of being cold?"

"There is a daughter?" Thunder Horse asked as if it were difficult for him to move his lips and form the words. Sha-sak nodded and he burst into a grin, rushing past her to where Sachim lay wrapped in blankets, a low fire burning.

Beside her was the baby. "You are all right?" Thunder Horse asked. "The baby is all right?"

Sachim yawned. "All right. Take off your clothes . . . all wet." Then her eyes closed. "Sleepy," she muttered.

"Did you name it?" Thunder Horse asked. He got to his knees and rested his hand on Sachim's damp, warm forehead. Opening the small bundle beside her, he saw the unformed face of his baby.

His.

"I called her Little Raindrop. Remember? One little raindrop."

"I remember," He sat quietly beside her.

"Take off your clothes," she said with another yawn, but he sat there still, his face glowing with firelight, his eyes fixed on the beautiful, amazing sight of his wife and their baby sleeping side by side.

When he finally rose, Sha-sak was still there. Thunder Horse nodded at the sack she held. "I don't know what the Sauk do," he said.

"It will be buried. There will be a little song."

"You will do it?"

"Yes," Sha-sak answered. "But not tonight! I will dig no hole tonight."

"Sleep here. Don't walk home."

"No," Sha-sak answered. "Not tonight. It would be like spending your wedding night with you." She touched Thunder Horse's arm. "You sleep, though. If you can."

"If I can," he agreed.

When Sha-sak had gone—humming as she walked through the rain—Thunder Horse returned to the fire. He stripped off his clothes and spread out a fresh blanket and then he lay there: watching.

A child had been born to them. A child whole and healthy. Sachim was well. At times a feeling welled up inside him so that he felt like shouting out loud, like running out into the rain again and waking the village.

They had a child.

"One Little Raindrop," he said thoughtfully, tilting his head to study her. Then he laughed and the baby stirred. He let the fire burn out and finally rolled up in his blankets. But he did not sleep.

They had a child.

12

SOMETHING had changed. A world had turned over; body, mind, soul, and heart had altered in a subtle and mysterious way. Sachim awakened thinking that. For a time she could not remember what had happened. All she knew was that she ached. Her abdomen felt oddly flat, but painfully so. Her breasts ached.

Sachim touched her belly and then her breasts. Milk leaked from them; a small creature stirred beside her, opened its mouth and cried out, and then it was all clear, joyous. She had done what was impossible, what no woman had ever done before, and brought forth this beautiful baby.

The hard pain of the night before was already a dream. Sachim shifted in her bed, uncovered her breast, and drew the eager baby to her nipple. That too hurt, but simultaneously gave great satisfaction. She lay back, her milk flowing, her baby beside her. Thunder Horse snored so that he made her laugh even then.

The world had turned.

Sachim patted the baby, feeling deep happiness, but beyond that there was concern. *Something* had gone wrong. She listened, her eyebrows drawing together. There was a murmuring from outside which she could not explain to herself, a murmuring which disturbed her to the depths of her heart.

"Thunder Horse." She stretched out a hand and shook him. His snoring stopped and he rolled toward her. Remembering, he too smiled.

"The baby."

"Yes. The baby is fine. Thunder Horse, go out and see what is happening. Something is wrong."

Thunder Horse didn't stop to question her feeling. He knew his wife well enough to know that what she sensed was more than a woman's whim.

He dressed quickly and went out into the gray of morning. The rain had stopped but clouds still clotted the sky and the wind still blew. Water lay everywhere in shallow ponds.

At first he saw nothing, heard nothing, but there was movement in the birch forest on the little rise to the north of camp. Movement and a little color. Thunder Horse started that way, jogging through the trees.

Black Hawk was the first man he saw.

"Where is your wife?" Black Hawk demanded in a tone totally unlike him.

"In our lodge. Our baby was born last night. What is happening, Ma-ka-tai-me-she-kia-kiak?"

"Look. Go up to the top of the hill and look." Then Black Hawk walked away, his face grim, his back rigid.

Thunder Horse went to the ridge and looked down into the valley, seeing immediately why Black Hawk was angry.

The whites had returned.

White Bear was there, standing motionless, the wind moving his roached hair and the feathers in it. Thunder Horse walked up beside the giant.

"What will happen now?" the Sioux asked.

Slowly White Bear turned toward him. "I do not know. There are soldiers down there. You can see them near the rice pond. They have cannon there. Perhaps one behind the white lodge."

"I thought the white leaders agreed that we have the right to this land."

White Bear only shrugged. He believed nothing the white leaders said. Thunder Horse watched the valley for a little while more. White Bear, his massive arms crossed, glowered at the scene below.

When there was nothing more to see, Thunder Horse started to go. Before he left he told White Bear, "Last night the baby came. It is a girl."

He walked away then, and had gone four strides before White Bear called out to him.

"Thunder Horse!"

"What is it?"

"I am glad." Then White Bear returned to his watching.

Sachim was waiting expectantly and she listened with a darkening mood as Thunder Horse told her what had happened.

"How can they do this!" she said so sharply that the baby cried out.

"I don't know. The important question now is what Black Hawk will do."

"What can he do?" Sachim shifted the baby to her other breast. "If he makes war now, the cannon will destroy our village."

Thunder Horse bit his lip. He had his wife and his baby and had believed that they had a secure home here. Now he was not so sure.

"This is bad, very bad," he said heavily.

"Go to him," Sachim said, touching his wrist. "Ask Black Hawk what he means to do. We must know."

"I don't think he knows yet himself. The soldiers are our equal. The cannon give them the advantage. He is furious and frustrated, but he is not a madman. He wants to attack, I think, yet knows he cannot."

"You will talk to him?"

"Yes. If you wish it."

"We must know. Now we must know," Sachim said and she lay back, stroking the downy head of her baby. Little Raindrop had fallen asleep, her belly filled, perfectly comfortable, warm and secure. She trusted in them; they must not fail her.

Black Hawk stood alone at the river, watching the rain-swollen red-brown behemoth flow past, carrying trees and tangles, growling as it rolled on.

He knew Thunder Horse was beside him, but he didn't turn his head. "What would you do, Sioux war leader?"

"I do not know, Black Hawk."

"The council does not support me. Many of my warriors have crossed the river. The soldiers have come into our cornfields."

"If the women and children were not here . . ."

"Then we would still be outnumbered. Then those women and children would lose their warriors. I have seen men recklessly enter battle, to win or to die. Dying gains nothing for the people we are fighting for."

"No. Nor does a bad peace."

"I will not cross the river! I will not surrender our land."

"You will fight then," Thunder Horse said. He too watched the broad muddy waters of the great river flow.

"No," Black Hawk said at last. "Not now. I will talk to the council, I will speak with my warriors. When I have strength, when I have strength . . . then we shall see."

The baby grew larger. Soon it rode on Sachim's back in a cradleboard or hung in it from a tree as her mother worked in the small garden she had dug. There was little enough to plant in the garden. Seed was scarce. The white trader would suddenly give them no credit, although Sachim had seen whites loading sacks of seed onto wagons.

Corn flourished in the valley and the Sauk went hungry. A young hunter went out one day with a bow, arrows, and salt and never returned. The Sauk could not reach their rice pond with the soldiers everywhere, nor could they use their hunting grounds. There would be no maple-syrup harvest that year.

For those families who had no hunter there was no choice—they crossed the river to live with Keokuk's band. Those few who crossed back and forth brought enticing tales.

"They have everything there. We have nothing. Are we mad? Keokuk still trades with the whites. He still gets credits. They have corn growing to a man's waist already. They have dried beans and salt and maple-sugar candy. They have new blankets and muskets with plenty of powder and balls. Why do we stay here? Are we mad? Or is it only Black Hawk that is mad?"

Black Hawk heard this talk, but he ignored it. Others couldn't—those who saw beyond the summer to a hungry winter without good blankets, those whose children cried because of empty bellies.

Many more left, including some of Black Hawk's most loyal warriors. "We stayed to fight beside you, Black Hawk, but we do not fight. I have a young wife across the river. She sleeps alone. Why should we stay here out of stubbornness?"

"Because," Black Hawk answered angrily, "it is *right*! This is our land."

"If it were all rocks and swamp, would we still stay here? This is our land, but what good is it to us? We cannot grow corn or hunt."

Black Hawk had no answer for those who spoke like that.

They were right. But he too was right. This was Sauk land and they had the right, perhaps the obligation, to stay.

It was an unhappy time for Sachim, but still there was much joy in her life. The baby grew and learned to know her and Thunder Horse. On the worst of days, they had their lodge and small family. Thunder Horse was a hunter and so they were never without meat.

Still they knew that life was better, safer on the far side of the river, and they were uncertain. "Can we remain here, Sachim?" Thunder Horse would ask.

"Can we leave Black Hawk?" Sachim would reply, and Thunder Horse could only shake his head. Which way was right?

The answer was provided for them, and for all of the remaining Sauk when the first frost had whitened the ground and they could feel coming winter in the air.

The girl was named Da-ka-ta and her brother Shetha. They were bored and hungry.

"I want to have corn to roast," Shetha said. He was fourteen, tall for his age, and narrowly built. He and his sister had done nothing all morning but search for turtle eggs, but found none.

"We have no corn," his sister snapped. Da-ka-ta was an imp and she could be very funny. Just now she was cranky and cold and unhappy.

"We have corn. We helped plant it. We worked all day, very hard, for a week."

Da-ka-ta looked northward, toward the cornfield. Just beyond it was a white house and a fence. "There are soldiers there."

"There are no soldiers." Shetha stood looking that way. "There is no one there, no whites at all."

"We can't go over there."

"For a few ears of corn? We would take it and be gone before anyone knew. Besides," he added sullenly, "whose corn is it? Ours, it is our corn, Da-ka-ta."

"I do not want to go," the girl said, "I am frightened."

"Frightened of what! There is no one there. Go home then, *girl*. Go home while I pick some corn to roast."

Hunger or pride caused Da-ka-ta to answer, "If you are going, I will go." But she was trembling as she said it.

"Come on then." He took her hand but Da-ka-ta yanked it away.

"Just a few ears, Shetha, just a few."

"That is all I want. Follow me."

They slipped through the trees, following a little game trail which dipped down into a fern-strewn gully and then ran along a little bench where exposed tree roots blocked the trail. They had played here often and could have come this way in the darkness.

At the head of the trail, through the columns of tree trunks, they could see the green-brown stalks of corn. Shetha glanced at his sister and grinned.

Creeping up out of the gully, he crawled on hands and knees into the corn. Rising to a crouch, he began to pluck ears from the stalks. Da-ka-ta nervously followed his lead. Moving down the row, his eyes searching for the largest ears, Shetha began to hum softly.

A crow swung by overhead and he watched it for a moment. When he looked down again he saw the flash of blue. A uniform. Shetha dropped his armload of corn and rose, his hands flying over his head.

"Just corn, see . . ."

Da-ka-ta, too stunned to move, remained in a crouch. She too saw the two men in uniform, saw them raise their muskets, saw the puffs of smoke.

Then the roar of sudden thunder filled her ears and she was spun around, knocked back to lie still against the dark earth, corn scattered around her body.

The bodies were not returned. Tonka-te was hunting and he saw the soldiers take the bodies away to bury them. Their mother was inconsolable. When she arrived at Black Hawk's lodge her skirt was torn, her hands dirty, her hair snarled.

"This is a place of dying! It is a place of sickness and hunger and abuse. You brought us here. You promised us our land, our corn! You gave us nothing, nothing but death!"

Then she fell sobbing to the ground at Black Hawk's feet and the Sauk leader looked at the people who had followed her there.

"She is right," Black Hawk finally said. "The woman is right. This is a place of dying. It is time to leave. I have failed you."

As the sun set they crossed the Mississippi, leaving the land to the Americans and the carrion birds. One of their lodges was burning. The whites had seen them prepare to go, loading their canoes with their few belongings. A lodge—whose lodge?—burned, and soon others would be burned. The flames lifted into the sky and merged with the red-orange of sunset above the dark river.

"We have burned their lodges; they have burned ours," Sachim said quietly. "Who has profited?"

On the far bank friends and relatives came down to meet the arriving Sauk. Ta-wa-shuk and Ha-te-ka were there with their new baby, born the same day as Sachim's. And there were others there, those who had not come to welcome their tribesmen, but to gloat over the failed rebellion.

Keokuk, wearing a white blanket and silver necklace, stood with his arms crossed, watching the canoes being dragged up onto shore, watching the solitary figure of Black Hawk walk toward the village.

The Prophet was there and he too enjoyed this failure. The return of the would-be leader of all the Sauk, the would-be conqueror. Sachim held her baby, rocking it as Thunder Horse recovered their goods from the last canoe. Then, with her husband at her side, she walked past these two self-satisfied Sauk leaders toward the village beyond the trees.

Sachim paused and watched the smoke rising from the lodges. There was something plaintive about it, something indescribably sad. These were the same lodges, the same people she had grown up loving. They were Sauk—so was she.

Yet something had changed irretrievably.

"Thunder Horse, do we have to be here?"

He looked at her oddly, tilting her chin up. Her eyes were mysteriously damp. "No, not if you do not wish it. But where shall we go?"

"Away. Away for just a little while. So much has happened. I want us to be together away from the river like we were at the wild-rose camp, remember?"

"Of course I remember. We can start that way in the morning," he answered.

"It doesn't have to be there, Thunder Horse." She took his arms and looked up into his eyes and then put her face against his chest. "Just somewhere away. For a little while."

With the sun on their backs they started out early the next

morning, Sachim with the baby on her back, Thunder Horse carrying a sack with a few supplies and his bow and arrows. Larks burst from the grass at their approach in a whirring storm of yellow and brown. The baby shrieked excitedly as they did so.

The day stayed clear and warmer than it had a right to be. On the second day they found the spot where Sachim wanted to camp.

"Here!" she said, suddenly halting.

"Not the wild-rose camp?"

"No, Thunder Horse. Here." She lifted her eyes to the towering pines, watching the woodpeckers flutter among them. The air was rich with the pine scent. They were on a narrow, half-mile-long ridge which Thunder Horse had meant to merely traverse. From there they could see far out onto the plains, toward the distant reddish hills.

It was a silent, cool island thrust up above the land, Sachim thought. If only they might stay there for a little while and be at peace with the baby and each other. In ancient times perhaps Manitou had pushed the hill from the flat plains and dotted it with trees, meaning for it to be used one day by Sachim.

The trees spoke to her. The silence of the day carried a humming, beyond the muted buzz of the insects and the bees, beyond the stirring of the pines in the wind. "All mad," she said to Thunder Horse as she swung the baby from her back. "Those people back there. Land everywhere. Yet they must fight and steal for a tiny piece of it."

"There is an end to land, Sachim," Thunder Horse said as he stood beside her, watching the empty plains.

"Is there? I can't imagine it now. People need so little. A place for their lodge, a place to hunt. A man to laugh with, a child to nurture. But we would rather contend, rather kill."

"I had better get to work," Thunder Horse said, "if we are to have boughs for a lean-to tonight." He took his hatchet from his belt and tossed his shirt aside. Sachim sat down and opened her blouse to nurse the eager baby.

She watched her man, watched the ripple of his muscles as he worked, cutting pine boughs, the concentration on his face. He spoke to himself and his eyes seemed amused at something.

How had he come into her life? A man who only gave but did not take, one who had given up all he might have had for her and never once spoke with regret over losing his position, his people. But he had come and Sachim loved him more than she ever had. The baby whimpered slightly and she shifted it to the other breast, feeling the milk flow out of her, give life to the baby.

The baby too he had given her and she knew that he would die to protect them. He would work and not complain, lay down his life and not hesitate in doing so.

In the pine-bough lean-to they lay watching night come as great silver stars began to pierce the orange veil of sunset. Sachim shifted the baby to one side and snuggled nearer her husband, resting her head on his arm. She took his strong hand and kissed his fingers.

He rolled his head to look at her and then smile as he saw Little Raindrop curled up asleep, warmed by her rabbit-fur blanket, loved and sheltered.

"Such a beautiful thing," he said.

Sachim too looked at the child. "Yes, a beautiful girl."

"I thought once that our love could be no more intense than when I first lay down with you, Sachim. Then the child came. She makes our love . . ." He hesitated. Thunder Horse was not a man of many words. ". . . greater, larger. . . ."

"Complete?"

"Complete, yes. When we made love together I felt as if I were taking such a great gift from the universe that I had no right to it. Who am I, after all, but another warrior? Now I see that I not only took from the universe, but gave back to it—and someone better, more to be loved. Fresh from Manitou's garden, she has no flaws, no bitterness nor anger nor selfishness—"

"Just a little at times. When she is hungry."

"Yes," Thunder Horse laughed, "when she is hungry. But then perhaps I see her as a father."

"A father who is in love not only with his wife, but his baby," Sachim said, slipping her arm across his bare chest, "and that is right, Thunder Horse."

Thunder Horse built a little sledge and on it they placed the baby, wrapped in blankets, towing Little Raindrop behind them as they walked the hills. The child delighted in everything she saw. The world was new and exciting and good. There was no evil and nothing to fear.

The baby slept and Thunder Horse and Sachim lay naked together on the hill rise, the light breeze washing over them, teasing their bare flesh. Thunder Horse lay on top of her, looking down with wonder as Sachim's eyes shone with the light of her love, with the fulfillment he had given her.

He wanted to say something. Twice Sachim saw him move his lips as if he would speak; but in the end he gave it up and lay pressed against her, his body moving rhythmically, gently, as she stroked his dark hair, his powerful back.

"I know," she whispered to him, "there are no words to tell it." Then, laughing, she hugged him tightly, knowing with joy that she too could give him pleasure, that she was needed if his world was to be right.

Thunder Horse lay naked, resting, and Sachim tickled his flat abdomen with a dandelion, smiling as he twitched.

"We could build our lodge here, Sachim."

"Yes," The smile was gone from her lips. Thunder Horse sat up and wrapped his arms around his knees.

"At the river things are bad. They will get no better."

"Do we have to speak of these things?" she asked, tying back her hair.

"Not now, not if you do not wish it."

"Not now then," she said, and she laid her cheek against his bare leg, watching the distant land. When the tear trickled down her cheek and touched his leg, she sat up, kissing the tear away. "Is it growing cold?"

"Maybe a little."

"Too cold for the baby, Thunder Horse," she said, rising, He rose to take her by the shoulders and draw her against him.

"What is it, Sachim? The people?"

"Soon they will be traveling to the winter camp in the south."

"You want to go with them?"

"It is right," she said. "They are my people."

She said no more as they dressed and walked back to their lodge, towing the baby behind them, but in the morning when she awoke Thunder Horse had already packed their belongings. He knew his wife well.

After the baby had nursed they started again toward the river. Sachim was looking forward to the long journey despite everything. The trek to the southern camp was like a cycle in her life, the changing of seasons. It was something that she longed for in a way she could not even define to herself. It was the way of the Sauk.

Yet when they finally reached the river two days later she could only stand and stare in puzzlement. No preparations had been made. No meat was being smoked, no one was putting away supplies for the long trip.

"What is happening?" Sachim asked, but Thunder Horse could only shake his head.

They found Ta-wa-shuk carrying a bundle of sticks for the fire. The woman dropped her burden, cried out with delight, and then hugged Sachim, making a fuss over the baby.

"Ta-wa-shuk, why isn't the camp making ready?"

"Making ready? Oh, did you think we were going to the southern camp? No! Come home with me right now, Sachim! What manners I have. Come and have something to eat. We will talk. You have no lodge! No matter, you will stay with us."

"But, Ta-wa-shuk . . ."

"Come, you are our guests. Come!" She tugged Sachim forward by the hand and Sachim could only look back at Thunder Horse in confusion.

"We travel south each year. It has always been that way."

"But why go when there is no need?"

"Who buys these blankets, who buys this food so that we must not hunt? Keokuk?"

"Yes, Keokuk."

"And what," Sachim wondered, "does he pay for these things with?"

Ha-te-ka said, "I know you are close to Black Hawk, Sachim, but do not believe that everything Keokuk does is wrong. He has helped the tribe more since he became council chief than Black Hawk ever could."

"He is council *chief*!" Sachim asked, startled.

"Yes, while you were gone this was done. You had not heard?"

"No . . . I didn't know," she said faintly.

"What happened to Napope?" Thunder Horse inquired.

"To Napope? Nothing. He claimed to be too old to act as chief. He is still on the council, but it is Keokuk alone who deals with the Americans."

Sachim said, "And would sign treaties."

Ha-te-ka pointed out, "We have a treaty, Sachim. We need no more."

"No," she answered, "we need no more."

"I'm afraid Black Hawk is beaten," Ha-te-ka said with

some compassion. "But then, perhaps Keokuk is right. After all, we have what we need. I have a new son. I do not want to go to war."

"But we are at war," Sachim said. "The war has already begun and we are losing it. Slowly, an inch of ground here, another there. Slowly it is all going. A little rice, a forest, some fish. Now others must feed us, now we are not free anymore. That is the war—a war for our freedom—and I tell you truly that we are losing it."

White Bear rapped on the lodge and entered, ducking low. He looked around and nodded. Behind him, outside, thousands of stars twinkled brightly in a deep sky.

"Sachim. Thunder Horse. Black Hawk would like to speak to you."

"To us?" Thunder Horse was puzzled. "If he wishes."

"You will watch Little Raindrop for me?" Sachim asked her friend.

"Of course. She will be asleep soon."

Sachim picked up her shawl and followed White Bear from the lodge. Thunder Horse was behind her, as perplexed as his wife was. What could Black Hawk want with them now, at this time of night? The air was cool, the sounds of frogs along the river raucous. Beyond the great pine stood the lodge where Black Hawk had made his bed. Inside, the war chief of the Sauk waited, standing, his eyes half-closed in thought.

As they entered, the eyes came alert. "I thank you for coming to my lodge," Black Hawk said. "I know it is late."

"There is something of importance you have to say, Black Hawk, or you would not have called us here."

"Yes." He looked around, lost in this borrowed lodge. "Sit by the fire. I don't know if there is anything to eat."

"We don't need to eat," Thunder Horse said. "What is it you wish to tell us?"

Black Hawk hesitated, glanced at White Bear, and then told them; "There will be war. There must be war."

"But you said . . ."

"I know that. On the far side of the river I said that. Now that I am back, I have had second thoughts. These are not decisions that I make now and then cast away like leaves blowing on the wind, as you know, Sachim.

"I wished to stay across the river even if I had to fight. That was right. But the people hadn't the *will* for it. Making them stay when they had not the will for it weakened me more. I wondered if I had the right to make war, to go against the council's wishes. Then I began to doubt my own will.

"Yet I see things in a different way now. It is as if crossing the river, leaving the land behind, caused a door to open in my mind. Before, I wanted to make war because I was angry. No one shared my anger.

"Now I do not want to make war but I know I must. This is because I know what the will of the white man is. It is his will to tear us from this land, and if his will is stronger than ours, then he shall do it. This I see now. Without anger." He looked to his lieutenant. "Tell them, White Bear."

"The council is going to sell more land. They cannot pay for what we have taken in credit."

"More land!" Sachim was astonished and angered. "The land we have across the river? Land they will not allow us to live on?"

"Some," White Bear said. The big man frowned. "And much on this side of the river, Sachim."

"Here? And what do we do then? Where do we live?"

"They will allow us to stay for a time."

"Until more settlers come and they decide to throw us off our land again!"

Thunder Horse spoke quietly. "This is Sioux land." His eyes met Black Hawk's and they were as hard as Sachim had ever seen them. The Sauk had always controlled this land, but the Sioux had claimed it for their summer camp. Whoever owned the land, Sachim considered, Keokuk had no right to sell it.

"Then will the Sioux fight for it?" Black Hawk finally asked.

"Fight for it? I do not think so. We have much more land. All of the plains to the mountains. All to the north until the Cheyenne country is reached."

"If they don't fight now, when will they fight?" Black Hawk demanded.

"Fight the Americans? I think never," Thunder Horse replied.

"Then I think you are wrong," Black Hawk said. "Every day there are more Americans, and still more. They flow into our land like a great river. One day they will be the neighbors of the Sioux."

"They will never live on Sioux land," Thunder Horse said very sharply. "And the Sioux councils will never sell themselves the way Keokuk has. We need no white goods. All we need comes from the buffalo, and so long as there are buffalo there will be a Sioux nation! This I know, this I tell you."

"You have not told us everything you are thinking, Black Hawk," Sachim said. She wove the unraveled fringe of the blanket they sat on as if all of her concentration were on the threads, yet Black Hawk knew she was listening intently, her mind not on the insignificant, but on the grave discussion at hand. The discussion which, she knew, involved the fate of an entire people.

"I have not told you everything, no. You know I have few loyal warriors, at least not enough to force the whites to withdraw from our lands, but, Sachim, this is more than a battle which the Sauk must wage. I have seen it in the east. In the north. Everywhere the Americans are encroaching. Everywhere they buy what they need or take what they want. It is the same for every tribe.

"They sit and wait, wanting peace, letting their neighbors pay the price. And then when it is too late for them they wish to take up the war ax.

"It is nearly too late for the Sauk," he told them with a heavy voice.

"What is it you are thinking of doing?" Sachim asked.

"All we can do. I want to stop the whites. I want them off Sauk land—if we cannot do that, then we will make a treaty they will understand, one they must honor, one we can defend.

"There must be no white man west of the great river. From here on the land must be Indian. From here on we must say: that is the Mississippi. Do what you will there, but do not cross or you will be killed," Black Hawk continued.

"And how," Thunder Hawk asked, "will the Sauk guard the great river from Dakota to Louisiana?"

"We cannot." Black Hawk lifted his eyes. He poked at the little fire with a stick and it flared up again briefly. "We must do this together if any of us are to survive. The treaty must be made with the Sauk and with the Fox, with the Mascouten and the Kickapoo, with the Winnebago and the Potawatomie, and with the Sioux, Thunder Horse."

"The Sioux will never agree to this. We do not make such alliances. We have no need of them."

"One day there will be a need," Black Hawk promised him.

"It is a great dream, Black Hawk," Sachim began hesitantly.

"It must be more than a dream! Can you not even see that, far-dreamer? Have you not in your dreams seen the white everywhere, like locusts in our fields? Tell me the truth now. Tell me what you have seen."

"What I have dreamed," Sachim said in a whisper, "is what you have spoken. It will be so. It will be so."

Thunder Horse looked at his wife with mystification. Her voice was very low and she swayed back and forth slightly, her half-open eyes looking at nothing, or perhaps beyond everything. It lasted only a moment or two and then she smiled.

"You know that what I say is true, Thunder Horse," Black Hawk insisted.

"I know nothing! I know what you say. You want many peoples to fight for you, including the Sioux. Tell me, then, how will you convince all of these people to fight for your cause when they see no threat to their homes."

"I will make sure that they see it. I shall beg and threaten. Remind them of old obligations. The Fox will fight with me; they always have. Two-Knives and I have seen many battles."

"And the Sioux?" Thunder Horse asked with a tinge of mockery.

"I leave the Sioux to you, Thunder Horse."

"To me!" It was the first time Sachim had seen a man literally struck dumb. He tried to speak for a minute but couldn't form his thoughts into words.

Black Hawk was unperturbed. "You are the son of Far Eagle. Your brother is war leader of the Sioux. Whom else would I send to speak with them, Thunder Horse?"

Thunder Horse's voice had returned. He shook his head and chanted, "No. No. No. Folly, Black Hawk."

"Folly? Why do you say that?"

"Listen, my friend," Thunder Horse implored. "My brother, Yellow Sky, despises me. My father has disowned me for leaving to marry a Sauk woman. The Sioux will never make this pact you wish for, and if they would, I am the last man you should send as an envoy."

"But you will do it?"

"No," Thunder Horse said adamantly. "I will *not*."

Black Hawk studied the young warrior's face for a long moment and then shrugged, turning his attention to White Bear. "You must begin immediately if you are going to travel north for me, White Bear. The Mascouten will be leaving for their summer camp and the snows may begin early. What of Fire Storm and Cliff Arrow?"

"They are ready, Black Hawk. Each has three horses. They are awaiting only your word."

"Then it will be done—except for the Sioux," Black Hawk said, glancing at Thunder Horse without rancor. "We will find a way. I may go myself. First I will speak to Two-Knives; then we shall see."

Black Hawk was busy with his plans so Sachim gestured to her husband and they rose, leaving the lodge to Black Hawk and White Bear.

Sachim and Thunder Horse stood alone in the night for a time.

A falling star streaked earthward and they watched it fall.

"Am I wrong?" Thunder Horse asked, turning his wife so that he could hold her against him.

"Only if you think you are," she replied, kissing his chest.

"His idea will never work. It is folly."

"Perhaps."

"The Sioux would never agree to such a treaty."

"You would know better than I," Sachim said, leaning her head against his shoulder, inhaling the manly scent of her warrior husband.

"But you believe there will be war, a great war, I know that. You know, Sachim, we could do what we once discussed—go into the far western lands and live alone, you and I with the child."

"Yes, we could," she agreed, and then was silent.

Thunder Horse held her close for a long time, then stood back, watching her placid face, her star-bright eyes. "I will tell Black Hawk that I will go to the Sioux camp," he said with a sigh.

"As you will have it, Thunder Horse," she said, but she was smiling now as she hugged him once more.

Before they could return and meet again with Black Hawk, he had another visitor. Without announcing himself, Keokuk stepped into the lodge of the war leader and stood watching Black Hawk pack his bag.

"We will not have this," Keokuk said at last.

"Have what?" Black Hawk slowly straightened and turned. The firelight carved deeply shadowed lines in his weathered face.

"War! There is no need for it. The council will not have it!"

"Does the council know you are selling more land?" Black Hawk asked without changing his expression.

Caught off guard, Keokuk visibly flinched. "It has been agreed," he said evasively.

"Do the people know?" Black Hawk took a sudden step toward Keokuk and the council chief flinched again.

"It is for their good as well. They have benefited. All of us owed money to the white traders. Now we will owe nothing."

"Now we will have nothing. Soon we shall all be crowded on a piece of land not large enough to graze a single horse, and you will tell us all that we are wealthy—thanks to the Americans and to Keokuk."

"And how wealthy will we be after you begin a bloody war!"

"We shall see."

Keokuk grabbed Black Hawk's arm as the war leader turned away. Black Hawk shook his hand off angrily. Keokuk leaned nearer, his teeth showing.

"Do you think you can defeat the whites? Do you think you and your few warriors can overwhelm their muskets and cannon?"

"I do not know," Black Hawk said seriously. "I only know I cannot defeat them by moving away, moving away—that can only defeat our people. Go now, Keokuk. We have nothing to discuss."

"Do not come back to this camp, Black Hawk! I warn you. Do not come back unless you wish to die at the hands of your own people!"

Black Hawk watched the empty doorway to his lodge until the blanket fluttered back over it, blocking out the stars and the river beyond.

It was cold that night. Breath rose from Tyler Gunn's nostrils as he tried to sleep. He had never thought he'd long for his bunk back at the Fort Madison barracks, but it beat sleeping out in a field in a tent with seven other men. Private Gunn rolled over and tugged his blanket over his face. It was no use. He wasn't going to sleep at all on this night. By starlight he squinted at his watch, noticing that the two hands were creeping together at twelve. Midnight. Joiner would be wanting his relief from guard duty.

He sat up, rubbing the back of his neck, and tugged his boots on over his hole-riddled socks. Hearing the soft footfall, he glanced up, expecting to see Joiner's stocky form, his beefy face.

Instead he saw the mask of death—a skull peering at him. Gunn tried to dive for his weapons. He was much too slow. An ear-splitting shriek rose from the throat of the specter and he rushed at Gunn, other skull-faced demons on his heels.

Gunn saw the war hatchet rise and fall but he could do nothing to fight it off as the skull-faced thing stood over him, hacking at his neck and head.

When it was over the eight soldiers lay naked and dismembered in the tent. Skull himself and six of his men were dressed in army uniforms. Gunn's had been too bloody to use.

"Which house?" Camp Dog asked.

"The nearest," Skull replied. "They will feel the safest."

They walked down the old trail leading to the broken pine, Skull watching his chosen men march with their muskets across their shoulders. Ahead the little house was dark. There would be no trouble, none at all. The sleepy-eyed settler would open the door to a party of soldiers, no matter if it was the middle of the night.

He would open the door and no one inside would have a chance of surviving.

Skull glanced at the starry sky and nodded with satisfaction. It would be a good night.

When the soldiers began to spill out of the barracks at four in the morning Joshua Ferguson cursed and rolled over. The bell not far from his window was clanging furiously and he could hear shouted orders. There was no choice but to rise, throw on his robe, and stagger out.

He met Hank Greeley. Greeley, his hair tousled and his eyes red, was carrying a smoking lantern. "What the hell's happening?" Greeley demanded.

"How should I know?" Ferguson walked to the front door

of the sutler's store, fumbled with the latch, and opened up, Greeley at his shoulder.

Sergeant Monk was rushing down the plankwalk tucking in his shirt, and Ferguson grabbed his shoulder as he passed.

"'What is it, Monk?"

"Looks like the Indians massacred some of our men. Then hit two farmhouses." Monk hurried on, yelling at his men.

"What the hell are they going to do in the dark?" Greeley wondered aloud.

"Nothing." Ferguson turned, a thin smile on his lips. "But Monique is ready for a fight and he can't wait to get to one."

"You act like you like this, Josh."

"That's right. Let's go back inside. I've seen soldiers before." They stepped in and closed the door. Ferguson crossed the room and took a cigar from the store's great humidor.

"If the Sauk are kicking up, Monique will want to hit back hard," Greeley said.

"He'll want to. After second thoughts he'll realize he hasn't got the men to do it." Ferguson lifted himself up to sit on the counter. "He'll want militia and he'll get them."

"And if the Sauk fight back, we lose all the credit we've given Keokuk."

"Don't be a fool, Greeley. We're not in this for furs and hides. For land! You forgetting that treaty with Keokuk? The way it's written, they can live on most of that land. But if there's a war? If the militia runs them off? Hell, Greeley, we can start moving people across the river by spring. We've got five million acres there, Hank." Ferguson blew out a stream of cigar smoke. "We've just had our fortune made for us. Black Hawk has started a war he can't win. But we win, my friend. We win big."

The morning was clear and cold, a northern wind scalloping the river. Black Hawk, mounted on his spotted pony, waited while Thunder Horse and Sachim said a last goodbye to the baby and kissed Sha-sak.

He was puzzled by what he saw across the river. Although he could barely make it out in the distance, he could see soldiers, many of them, shifting positions, walking through the woods in a picket line. There were many more soldiers than had been there before.

"What is it?" Thunder Horse asked when he rode up beside the Sauk leader.

"I can't tell. I don't like it, though."

Thunder Horse too looked across the great river, watching the tiny blue figures. Sachim finally was able to bring herself to leave the baby and she walked her pony to the two men, giving them an inquisitive look.

"What is it?" she asked.

"Nothing to do with us," Black Hawk said, but he wasn't so sure.

Sachim swung onto her pony's back, waved a last goodbye to Little Raindrop, and followed the men out along the northern trail toward the Fox Village. She had no doubt that they would be welcome in the Fox camp; little that they would agree to follow Black Hawk as they had in many other battles. It would be good to see old friends, cousins, among the Fox, Sachim thought. That part of their journey would be a pleasant one.

It was the second leg of their trek which concerned her. The long ride across the plains to the forked river where none of them would be welcome, to Thunder Horse's homecoming in the land of the Sioux.

13

T HE wind rustled through the long yellow grass. Here and there, buffalo wallows, vast, muddy hollows, had been scoured into the earth by the great beasts. But there were no buffalo in sight, for they had begun their southern migration and soon the Sioux would follow. Now and then Sachim, Black Hawk, and Thunder Horse saw pronghorn antelope bounding away at their approach and twice they saw large elk herds on the move. Thunder Horse spoke little now, and Black Hawk even less as they neared the Sioux camp.

A single tree stood against the land, weathered and gray, its great forked branches stark against the sky. It seemed an apparition, more a symbol than a living thing to Sachim. A knot of emotion began to form in her stomach and she felt her throat tighten.

"It is wrong," she whispered. Thunder Horse glanced at her curiously. "There is something wrong with the tree."

"Wrong? It is a tree, that is all."

"I see now," Black Hawk told them, laughing. "Look closer, Thunder Horse."

Nearing it, they could see that the great tree was filled nearly to the tips of every branch with perching crows. Sachim shook her head—that was not it. That was not what she felt.

At the approach of the horses the crows rose, raucous and milling, darkening the sky—a thousand black leaves blown free.

And they left *it* uncovered.

A litter had been placed in the branches of the tree and on

the litter was the body of a Sioux warrior dressed in white elkskin, wearing a streaming war bonnet. Beside him on the litter lay his weapons, his bow and arrows, his hatchet and musket.

"That . . ." Thunder Horse began. Then his face fell in dismay. "It is Far Eagle," he murmured. "It is my father."

He slipped from his horse's back and walked to the tree, looking at the war bonnet, the nearly mummified face, the beaded elkskin shirt.

"It is my father," he repeated, turning to Sachim. She could do nothing but walk to him and hug him tightly as the crows circled, complaining loudly, and the wind shifted the long grass.

Thunder Horse stood for a long while just looking at the litter. When he was finished he walked stiffly to his horse, mounted at a leap, and rode out without waiting for Sachim and Black Hawk.

"This will make things worse for us," Black Hawk said. He held Sachim's horse as she swung onto its back.

"Yes." She looked again at the litter and then at Thunder Horse's back as he rode on alone with his grief. It was another mile before Thunder Horse held his horse and they caught up with him. His eyes were expressionless, his mouth compressed into a straight line. He leaned over and kissed Sachim and they rode on as if they had seen nothing.

The Sioux camp, when they came upon it, was lost in smoky haze and river fog. It appeared mysteriously, and then just as mysteriously, parts of it would fade away. Many campfires burned, for the day was cold. The river ran but it was the color of ice. Bare-limbed willows stood against the sky.

The three approached the camp slowly, Thunder Horse leading the way. They would be expected by now—surely Sioux runners had reported their coming—but there would be no welcome for them.

Thunder Horse led them through the camp and was looked at like a phantom returning. No one spoke or lifted a hand. The smoke and river mist mingled and intertwined, moving wraithlike across the ground among the tipis, at times obscuring the legs of their horses.

The great yellow lodge was ahead of them and before it stood the man with the bear-claw necklace. The sun symbol dangled across his chest, and he had German silver and fox fur in his hair and two eagle feathers in a braided knot at the back of his skull.

Yellow Sky had come out to meet his brother.

"Ride on now," were the first words Yellow Sky spoke. "Ride on and live."

"I have not come to stay or to ask for anything, but only to guide my friend Black Hawk here, Yellow Sky."

Yellow Sky's eyes shifted to the Sauk, taking in the strong jaw, the paint, the roached hair, the quietly determined eyes. So that was Black Hawk, was it? The great warrior of the Sauk. Yellow Sky's mouth twisted in an expression of contempt.

"I do not wish to see this Black Hawk. Ride out and guide him back to the river."

"We need to council," Black Hawk said. "This is not a visit to a friend, nor to an enemy. It is simply a matter of need—for the Sauk and the Sioux. If either is to survive as a people, we must council, Yellow Sky."

"What is this man talking about?" Yellow Sky asked his brother as if Black Hawk were not there.

"Just what he has said, brother. There is a need to council. There is war working along the river and the Sioux will be caught up in it."

"What war?" Yellow Sky scoffed. "I have heard of no war."

"Please," Sachim said, speaking for the first time, "may we discuss it with you, Yellow Sky? You do not have to like us or smoke with us. When we are through talking we will go; you do not have to chase us away, but this is important. You know it is important to bring Thunder Horse back to the village where he is not wanted."

"I do not speak with women. Nor with Sauk. I do not speak with my brother, who has turned his back on his people."

"If you do not listen," Thunder Horse said, "you are turning your back on them as well. There is a war building along the river, Yellow Sky, it is true. Please, let us talk to you."

"It is cold," Yellow Sky said after a minute. "I am going into my lodge. Follow if you wish."

Then he deliberately turned his back on them and entered the great yellow buffalo-hide lodge.

"He has agreed," Thunder Horse said dryly.

"No matter how he has agreed," Black Hawk believed. "He has agreed to listen. That is all that is important."

Inside the tipi it was smoky and warm. As Thunder Horse ducked through the flap and looked around, he saw his sister, thin and unhappy as ever.

"Hello, Heart Song," he said, greeting her.

Heart Song took half a step toward him, then glanced at the scowling Yellow Sky and returned to her silent work, beading a man's shirt.

Yellow Sky did not seat himself, anticipating a short interview, and so the others stood as well. It was Black Hawk's duty to speak and so he began.

"Yellow Sky, as you know the whites are crowding to the river, flocking like pigeons in the trees. In consequence the Sauk have moved across the great stream."

"And onto Sioux land where they have no right to be," Thunder Horse's hotheaded brother answered.

Black Hawk gestured with one hand. "That is of no importance just now."

"To the Sauk. Perhaps it will be one day," Yellow Sky threatened.

"Yellow Sky, unless the whites are stopped now, they will certainly cross the river as well."

"They will not! We have sold them no land."

Black Hawk didn't mention Keokuk's deal; that would only bring more anger.

Instead he said, "There is only one certain way of keeping the Americans on the far side of the river and that is to form an alliance among all of the Indian people, to designate the Mississippi as the final boundary beyond which no white may live."

"*This* is what you have come to ask me for?"

"Yes. If you will let me go on—"

Yellow Sky just laughed, loudly, harshly. "You have come to ask the Sioux to fight for the Sauk because they haven't the heart to fight for themselves. The Sauk have allowed themselves to be pushed across the river—onto our land! —and now you ask the Sioux to help you return to the eastern bank?"

"I do not ask you only for the Sauk's sake, but for the sake of all of us."

"You wish us to fight if a white steps onto the land of the

Mascouten. If an American farms Fox soil. If a Kickapoo will not fight for himself! You are a fool, Black Hawk, if you think that we will do so. My brother is a bigger fool for bringing you here, believing that we would follow this scheme of yours.

"The Sioux land is inviolable. The Sioux cannot be defeated. You have run like dogs and now that you have let yourselves be driven to this side of the river you wish the Sioux to fight for you! I tell you this, Black Hawk, we would be as willing to war with the Sauk. *You* have taken our land, not the whites. What do we care for Winnebago or Potawatomie soil? Do we covet it? Should our blood flow into it?"

With a disgusted gesture Yellow Sky growled, "Be warriors—make your own battle. Do not come crawling here."

"I crawl to no man," Black Hawk said stonily.

"Then do not crawl for the whites. What is yours, keep. What you have lost, reclaim. This is what the Sioux will do, what we shall always do."

"Until they are too numerous to fight."

"That day will not come."

"Sachim knows—"

"My brother's wife, the far-dreamer, this woman who walks with spirits, *knows*," Yellow Sky mocked. "Then she knows this and knew it before: the Sioux will not fight for the Sauk who have let themselves be defeated without a single battle."

"Is that your final word? Will you not let us speak to the council?"

"No."

"Then I am sorry, Yellow Sky. I am sorry because you do not understand that this is the last day of our life, all of our lives, along the great river. The Americans will come. And the Sioux will be defeated. Perhaps not now, but in fifty years from now. And you, an old man, will look back and say, 'I surrendered the last chance we had out of anger, because rancor closed my ears and made of my heart a stone.'"

For a minute Yellow Sky stood before them, apparently considering Black Hawk's words, but then, with a venomous glance at Thunder Horse he snorted, "Go fight your own war. It is time for you to leave, and another hour may mean your lives."

He swept out of the tipi then, leaving the four of them in silence. Thunder Horse walked to his sister and kissed her. "Do you need anything, Heart Song?"

"Nothing," she said tremulously. "I am well and well-fed." She asked, "Was there a baby? Is there a baby, Thunder Horse?"

"A girl, yes."

"Take her then and flee. If Yellow Sky does not hear you, I do. If the Sauk do not war with the whites, then they must war with the Sioux. War haunts both banks of the river. Go"—she looked at Sachim—"take the young one and go."

"Thunder Horse?" Black Hawk said. "What can we do now?"

"Leave," the Sioux said grimly. "Leave before he has us killed."

He kissed his sister again and then led them out into the mist and smoke of morning, wondering if Black Hawk's words might have had more effect if he had not come with them—he, the hated one, the one who could do no right in Yellow Sky's eyes.

They rode slowly out of the village, slowly onto the long plains, and Thunder Horse's heart was heavy with the unhappy knowledge that what Black Hawk had said was true. If the whites were not stopped at the great river now, then there was no stopping them, not even by the powerful Sioux nation, nor by the Cheyenne, nor the Blackfoot.

They would come in endless numbers and they would win their victory and the great nations would be no more. Thunder Horse glanced back at his village only once and then turned sober eyes eastward, toward the great river where it would begin.

Black Hawk said, "Perhaps it does not matter. We have the word of Two-Knives that the Fox are with us. With the Mascouten and Potawatomie, with the Winnebago, we will have a large force, we will be united and strong."

Sachim didn't answer him. Thunder Horse was silent for mile upon mile, looking straight ahead until they again passed the crow tree, veering wide of it. Then Thunder Horse looked away, far away to the south, thinking who knew what about a father who had died without forgiving his son.

The sky darkened as they neared the river and it began to rain, a slow, soaking rain that turned the land to mud and began a hundred rivulets that ran away toward the Mississippi, swelling its mass, driving it southward.

They lifted their mounts into a trot and rode on swiftly through the gray of the storm and through the darkness of coming night. They could smell the river now, the life and corruption of it, the ruined soil and frothing freshness.

It was at flood tide, the oxbows becoming moving lakes, the tributaries backing up despite their frenzied motion. Beneath the moon the river was white and deep red, shimmering silver.

Following the river, they came to the Sauk camp, finding it silent and dark. A lone figure came forward to greet them, and there was no doubting who it was, even by the pool light of the rising quarter-moon.

White Bear walked toward them as they rode into the camp and there was something solemn about his movements.

"Black Hawk," he said.

"What is it? I know you, White Bear. What has happened?"

"The Sioux?" White Bear asked hopefully.

"We left with our scalps. Nothing better."

White Bear nodded. "Come into my lodge. I have mint tea. And rum."

"Do we need rum, White Bear?"

"Perhaps."

Weary and cold, they followed White Bear to his lodge. Sachim had tea, the men rum. "What is it, then?" Black Hawk asked. "More trouble with the council?"

"Very little. Keokuk still threatens to kill you, but he knows there are too many warriors who stand with Black Hawk to have that done. What has happened is graver, I fear. The Mascouten refuse to join you, Black Hawk."

"That is not possible! Red Blanket owes me many favors, war favors."

"I spoke to him for four hours. He refuses to engage the whites."

"Coward!" Black Hawk exploded.

"I am afraid," White Bear said after sipping his rum, "that this is not the worst of it. Fire Storm and Cliff Arrow have returned from the Winnebago and the Potawatomie camps." He raised his eyes. "They also refuse, Black Hawk."

Black Hawk rose angrily to his feet. "This is not possible!" He made a chopping gesture with his right hand. "Do they not understand what is happening along the great river?

Don't they know that their lands will go next if they do not stand with us now!"

"They know that you *believe* this is so, Black Hawk, but they do not want war. I think, frankly, they fear your hot blood, fear that you will attack and not defend. They know you still favor the British, but the Americans are here in force, not the British. To side with you is to side with an enemy of the Americans. They want only peace."

"Keokuk's peace?" Black Hawk asked bitterly. "Very well, I will travel to their camps myself. I will go and explain and remind them of past favors."

"It will do no good," White Bear said pessimistically.

"It must do some good!" Black Hawk responded. "It must, or we are all finished. This I believe, this I know. The only way to prevent war is to stand together. The surest way to bring it on is to isolate ourselves tribe by tribe."

He told them, "I will sleep and then travel at dawn. Have horses and provisions waiting for me, White Bear."

It was still raining when Thunder Horse and Sachim returned to their own lodge, joyously greeted the baby, thanked Sha-sak for watching her, and settled into a warm bed to sleep.

"He is right," Thunder Horse said in the darkness. "I was not convinced but now I am. I can feel it, feel war stealing up on us. And there is nothing we can do about it."

Sachim rolled to him, slid her leg up over his, and clung to him silently as the rain fell down. He was warm and strong and his lovemaking kept the beast away. The beast which waited just outside their lodge, lurking in the rain: war.

"A blatant act of war!" Joshua Ferguson said with fury. Reynolds stood leaning against the mantel of the fireplace in the governor's mansion's east room. Ferguson had done most of the talking, only occasionally yielding to the other settlers or to Captain George Monique, acting commander of Fort Madison.

"General Gaines reported that Black Hawk had been pacified."

"Oh, yes, pacified," Ferguson said sarcastically. "So that soldiers are slaughtered in their sleep, citizens in their homes, fields destroyed, houses set afire, livestock driven off. Some of our people can't take it any longer—they're removing themselves to Chicago, hopeful that the army can protect them *here* at least."

"Yes, Mr. Ferguson," the governor said, rubbing an eyebrow behind which a nagging ache flourished. "Captain Monique, I've not had time to read your full report. Is the situation in fact out of hand?"

"Very badly out of hand, sir. I've had to withdraw my soldiers to the fort along with most of the area settlers. We are in fact besieged by Black Hawk once more. Eight of my enlisted men butchered! We are safe nowhere outside the walls of Madison.

"Unfortunately, that isn't the worst of it. A Mascouten informant has advised me that Black Hawk is trying to gather all of the tribes for one great push against us, wanting to drive out every last white in the area."

"I had great hopes of avoiding trouble with Black Hawk," the governor said, "especially after Gaines's report. Yet, my first duty is to protect our citizens, and if Black Hawk is trying to mass the Indian nations there is only one way to proceed. We must answer force with force, with all the force we can possibly muster."

The man chosen to lead the army against Black Hawk was Brigadier General Henry Atkinson, experienced in the War of 1812. Shrewd and competent, he had bested Tecumseh's massed Indian forces on two occasions. His second in command was Colonel Zachary Taylor, originally of Virginia, now a Kentuckian. Taylor had a reputation of being tough as leather but willing to compromise if need be. Together they assembled the largest army ever seen in the Mississippi Valley. If Black Hawk meant to mass the Indians he would find the opposing force just as large and better equipped.

The rains had come to Chicago and the streets were muddy, crisscrossed with deep wagon ruts, and the ground, churned up and then refrozen overnight, treacherous to travel. Yet there were thousands of new people roaming the town or camped outside it in tent cities. Some of these were refugees from downcountry, those who had fled the area as the news of an Indian uprising spread. Many more were volunteers hoping for a multitude of reasons to attach themselves to the militia that was massing here.

"Rabble," Zachary Taylor said, turning from the window, his sharply defined features set in a frown. "Some of these men are nothing but cutthroats. I don't know if they're worse than the boys who just want to shoot off their guns at something—preferably an Indian—or not."

General Atkinson rocked back and forth slowly in his leather-covered chair. Edmund Gaines looked toward the rain-smeared window himself.

"Eighteen hundred men, Zack," Atkinson told his second in command. "We can't pretend we can't use them."

Taylor shot back, "And feed them and equip them and try to discipline them."

"Still, they'll fight. If Black Hawk has been successful in bringing the Mascouten and Winnebago into his army, he'll have close to two thousand warriors—skilled warriors—at his command."

Taylor sat down and rumpled his hair before looking up at his commander. "That's the problem," he believed. "His men will be experienced in woodland combat. Ours are rank amateurs, not counting the four hundred regulars from the First and Sixth infantry. Give me those men and a few cannon and I'll wager I could defeat the best Black Hawk can throw against us."

"Those aren't the governor's sentiments, Zack."

"No."

That effectively closed the discussion. The militia volunteers were here and they were to be utilized, undisciplined rabble or not.

"Ed," Atkinson said to Gaines, "I'll let you pick the best six hundred of the volunteers. You and Captain Monique can try whipping them into shape. Zack, you'll have to include some of these mounted volunteers in your group as well. The First Regiment seems to be well organized. That's Captain Abe Lincoln's group."

Taylor frowned. "Yes, sir, I know that regiment. Lincoln's second, Lieutenant Jefferson Davis, has been shining up to my daughter since they rode up here."

"That'll give you a chance to keep your eye on him then," Atkinson said, fighting back a smile. "The First and Sixth will be divided. I'll use Major Stillman as my aide-de-camp. We'll depart as soon as possible via steamboat. We can't leave Lieutenant Higgins cut off at Madison."

"Gentlemen." Atkinson rose. "Good luck. From what I hear of this scoundrel, the sooner we eliminate Black Hawk, the better off we will be. Everyone—Indian and white. Black Hawk is a renegade even among his own people. With luck we'll be able to rid the territory of this savage and get back to peaceful relations with the Sauk."

"That brings up a question, sir," Gaines said, "Keokuk and the majority of the Sauk want peace. Is their camp considered out of bounds as far as being a military target?"

"Keokuk is our best hope for peace, General. He is to be left alone. It is Black Hawk we want, only Black Hawk. This man must be crushed."

Black Hawk's second journey to enlist allies in his cause came to the same end. There were none who would fight, none who would stand up and say, "This far you have come; no farther will you go."

"There is a rumor," Black Hawk told Sachim and Thunder Horse, "that the Americans are assembling a greater army than has ever been seen. This I have from the Mascouten who have been to Chicago lately. A thousand, two thousand men and more have come there to fight. To fight me."

"I don't understand," Thunder Horse said. "Why have the Americans chosen you to attack? You have never yet killed a white man."

"Skull," Black Hawk said, and Sachim nodded agreement. She said, "There are many tales now about Sauk attacking white soldiers, farmers, murdering them. It is Skull's doing."

"Can't they be made to understand that?" Thunder Horse asked.

"Who will speak for the Sauk?" Black Hawk asked in return. "Me? Will they listen to me, Thunder Horse? Perhaps Keokuk? He who has already threatened me with death—he whom the whites look upon as a man of peace. There is no one to listen, no one to speak."

"What will we do?" Sachim asked.

"*We*?" Black Hawk offered her a poor smile. "This is not anything for you to be involved in, far-dreamer. I will do what I must. Keokuk has given his command. Those who wish to follow me will cross the river again. I have five hundred Sauk warriors who will come. One hundred Fox are pledged to follow. Some will bring their families."

"We shall go too," Thunder Horse said quietly.

"Why? There is no purpose to it, Thunder Horse."

"There is purpose. Sachim believes in your war. I am her husband, a warrior, a Sioux by birth, but one who has been fed and nourished by the Sauk. My daughter is Sauk."

"This is not your war."

"It is mine as much as yours. I understand now, finally, what you are trying to do. If Yellow Sky cannot see it through his anger, if the Mascouten cannot see it through their fear, if the Kickapoo cannot see it through their ignorance, *I see it*. And, Black Hawk," the young man said with dignity and determination, "I too am a war leader."

"You have discussed this between you?" Black Hawk asked, looking from one to the other.

"We have," Sachim answered. "The world works in many ways, Black Hawk, but always there is a right course and a wrong course for one to take. One day we must all walk the Hanging Trail, this we know—but I do not want to walk it with shame and meet again all of those who have gone before."

"There is the baby," Black Hawk said, looking at the sleeping Raindrop.

"The baby," Sachim said firmly, "is Sauk." She turned her eyes down then, ashamed of the tears in them.

"What world does the baby have if we pass without struggling to keep what was hers by birthright?" Thunder Horse asked. "Her land, the way of her people. Shall we simply sell her to the whites now?"

"As you will have it," Black Hawk said. "You are not children. I would be happy to have you with me, Thunder Horse. And do I not always need my dreamer!"

"When?" Sachim asked. "When do we leave?"

"As soon as the Fox arrive. With the morning mist, I think."

Thunder Horse asked soberly, "Can we win, Black Hawk?"

"We can win. Cannon do not move with our fleetness. The American generals do not know the land as we do, nor do their soldiers fight with their hearts as we must. We will win. We *must* win."

As Black Hawk had predicted, the Fox arrived with the morning mist. Two-Knives himself led them, and the scarred Fox war leader leaned down from his war pony's back to clench Black Hawk's hand. Behind him his men filtered through the damp gray of morning, their horses glossy with the mist, their hair limp and beaded with dew, their faces painted and grim. The great river flowed past and all eyes went at least once to the Mississippi, the Destroyer, the Provider, that was so indifferent in its majesty.

As the morning sun bored a tunnel through the river mist they crossed the river again, the warriors, swimming their horses in the lead, canoes and rafts behind. Ahead was their land, ahead the enemy who had taken it.

On the far bank they rested their horses and Two-Knives asked, "What are our targets, Black Hawk?"

"The soldiers, only the soldiers. Leave the few remaining white settlers alone. They will go when the soldiers go. We do not now wish to begin making war on women and children."

They rode and walked through the deep woods to a camp along Finger Creek. From there, they could survey the land for miles around, and surrounded by woods they could not be easily approached. Black Hawk felt himself invincible in the woodlands, for the whites still kept to their outdated tactics of massing men in formation. From here he would strike, here he would return to regroup and rest.

Scouts were out already, marking the location of the white forces, counting their numbers and their cannon.

Before they had placed their packs down or made preparations for the camp, the others came.

Black Hawk, standing beside the mounted Two-Knives and Thunder Horse, turned slowly at the sound of approaching horses, reaching for his musket.

They emerged from the woods, half a hundred of them, their faces painted white and black. Leading them was Skull, who had shaved his head and was wearing a white soldier's jacket.

Skull rode toward Black Hawk and spoke, though his eyes never met the war leader's, but shifted from uncertain point to uncertain point in the hazy distance.

"We have come, Black Hawk. We have come to help you. I know you need warriors. We have consented to fight with you."

Black Hawk's voice was taut. "We do not want you here, Skull. Take your renegades and ride away."

"Renegades? And you are not, Black Hawk?" Skull's shifting eyes came briefly to rest on Sachim and Thunder Horse and an expression of sheer hatred flickered across his face. "I am a renegade, but you are not. This is something I did not understand."

Skull laughed suddenly, running a hand across his shaven head. "You are alone, Black Hawk. Who will fight with you?" He leaned across the neck of his painted pony, still not looking at Black Hawk, although once he glanced at Two-Knives, the Fox leader. "A few Fox. A Sioux. A woman. Mighty allies! The Sauk will not fight for what is theirs. *We* will fight!"

"This is a war against soldiers," Black Hawk said, "not against women."

Skull sat straight up on his horse's back and with thumb and forefinger gripped the lapel of his bloodstained army tunic. "No woman gave me this, Black Hawk." He sneered.

"And no armed fighting man," Black Hawk answered. "I do not want you, Skull. You are a killer without a cause. You are a renegade, not just to the Sauk, but a renegade to all men."

Skull looked vaguely disappointed, but his shrug was insouciant. "So it will be. You may be sorry, Black Hawk. I think one day you will be very sorry that Skull does not ride with you." Then he spun his horse, letting it rear up on its hind legs, and with a shrill war cry rode from the camp, his Skull Clan thundering after him.

"What will he do now?" Thunder Horse wondered.

"Who knows what a madman will do. But I will not have him with us. Now we know who the enemy is, which direction to strike. Why have another enemy in our camp?"

By the time the sun was high above the river and the haze had burned away in the forest, Thunder Horse had finished building their lodge, which was nothing more than a pine-branch lean-to.

He sat then with his war bag, removing his paint, his arrowheads of honed steel, and his medicine bag, which would be knotted into the mane of his red war horse.

Sachim watched, cradling the baby in her arms, and for the first time Thunder Horse saw fear in his woman's eyes.

"There is still time," he told her, "time to ride away from the river, from the war, to the far mountains."

She shook her head. "I do not want to run. So long as you are sure that you wish to make this fight yours."

"It is," Thunder Horse answered as he streaked his face with yellow war paint, "my fight."

She had not seen her husband as a warrior before, had not seen him apply the yellow and blue paint to his face, his forehead disappearing in the deep indigo. She had not seen him place his war hatchet on his blanket and test its edge with a horsehair nor tuck his long war knife into his belt. He counted his musket balls and checked the powder in his powder flask, making sure it remained dry. His war bonnet with its many feathers was in his hands. He straightened a twisted feather and then placed his bonnet on his head.

"Is it to be today then?" she asked, holding Little Raindrop closer to her breast.

"It is today. At sunset." He rose, hovering over her as if wanting her kiss, and then turned away as if afraid that his warrior's powers might be weakened by that kiss. "I must paint my war pony," he said, snatching up his paint and musket, his war bag and medicine sack. Then he ducked out of the lean-to and Sachim bowed her head, a tear falling onto the round face of Little Raindrop. The baby stirred, wiping at her face with an ineffective fist, and then slept again, slept as Sachim watched the sky, waiting for sunset to come with its bloody flourish and following darkness.

14

CAPTAIN Lincoln rubbed his smooth-shaven lantern jaw and looked toward the river, watching the sun flatten and go red, dropping toward the dark horizon. The crickets made a racket which rang in his ears. He tugged at an earlobe and continued his rounds, greeting his sentries with a nod. The regulars from the Sixth Infantry paid little attention to the lanky commander of the volunteers, but Lincoln was untroubled by that.

Weatherly Johnston was standing watching the forest as the shadows began to deepen and make a mystery of movement and dimension. A cousin of Lincoln's stepmother and a worker in Lincoln's losing effort to be elected to the Illinois State Assembly, he was not really a military man and was unable to call Lincoln anything but "Abe."

"They're out there, Abe, I can feel 'em."

"Something you saw?" Captain Lincoln asked.

"No. I told you. I feel 'em."

The two men stood together, studying the deep maple and birch woods as the shadows beneath the trees pooled and spread like a dark inkstain flowing across the earth. Owls hooted deep in the trees and nighthawks darted after insects. Weatherly Johnston's musket went to his shoulder suddenly and he nodded. "Right there, Abe."

"Don't shoot," Lincoln said, touching the soldier's arm.

"By God . . ."

"He's got a flag of truce."

The Sauk was huge, the biggest Indian Lincoln had ever seen, with the shoulders and neck of an ox. He was painted but unarmed. Approaching their position, he waved the flag of truce back and forth until the captain called out, "Come in, we respect the flag."

The big man lumbered forward, moving like a grizzly bear, Lincoln thought, the flag now at his side.

"You are the white leader?" White Bear asked.

"No. Major Stillman is the senior officer just now," Lincoln answered. Atkinson and Taylor were upriver, Gaines still marching from Chicago with his militia volunteers, though he was expected at any time.

"Then he is the one I would see," White Bear replied.

"Who are you?" the captain asked. Johnston stood warily watching the big Sauk, ready to use his musket if need be, although the Indian seemed unarmed.

"My name does not matter," White Bear said. "Black Hawk has sent me. He wishes one more attempt at understanding before the war bows speak."

Lincoln nodded slowly. He looked beyond White Bear, half-suspecting a trick, but he saw no movement in the dark woods. "Come along, then. I'll show you Stillman's tent."

White Bear ambled along behind the white officer who was as tall as he was but weighed less than half of what the Sauk weighed.

Stillman was at his portable desk studying maps of the area when Lincoln led his charge in. The major leapt to his feet, nearly knocking the table over. His hand went to his sidearm but White Bear, white flag still in hand, was obviously not a threat.

"Good God, Lincoln . . . what is this?"

"He says he's come from Black Hawk, sir," the captain answered.

"From Black Hawk, has he? Can the savage speak English, then?" Stillman said.

"Yes," Lincoln answered quietly, "he can."

"From Black Hawk, eh?" Stillman walked toward White Bear, measuring him as he approached. His hand was still near his holstered pistol. "Does your chief now wish to sue for peace? Now that he sees we mean business, that we have many soldiers, many big guns?"

"Black Hawk wishes once more to try to speak calmly to you, to explain what has happened to us, how things have come to this."

"Then where is he?" Stillman asked with a laugh, looking to Lincoln for encouragement.

"He has sent me," White Bear said. "He has sent me to say we do not want this fight. It profits no one, but we have been bullied and pushed and injured. We want only our land, our corn. We want only what was ours before and should be ours now. This is Black Hawk's message. Now I have said it."

"Arrest this man," Stillman said, turning away.

"Arrest him?"

"You heard me. He's an enemy soldier, isn't he? Black Hawk's lieutenant."

White Bear stiffened and glanced toward the tent flap where two white soldiers had appeared. Lincoln protested, "Sir, this man came in under a flag of truce. I think—"

"What you think is irrelevant, isn't it, Captain? You have an order, I expect to have it carried out—*if* you irregular officers know how to carry out orders."

"Sir . . ." Frustrated, the captain took one step forward and then spun away. "Soldiers! This man is under arrest."

"This," White Bear said as the soldiers came in, muskets leveled, "is how you honor a flag of truce? You will regret this. Believe me. It would have been better for you to talk than to raise Black Hawk's wrath."

Lincoln nodded and the soldiers took the unresisting White Bear away. The captain saluted the unresponsive Major Stillman and exited, going out into the evening, where the first stars blinked on through the orange blur of sunset above the river.

The Sauk had been taken to a tent guarded front and rear by soldiers. Lincoln shook his head and walked away, thinking that the big Indian's words rang true: it would have been better, far better to talk.

Black Hawk looked up at the sound of approaching feet. "Is it him?" he asked Thunder Horse.

"It's Ha-te-ka," the Sioux answered.

Black Hawk kicked at a pebble and waited for Ha-te-ka to report. "Well?" he demanded.

"White Bear is still in the camp. He went to one tent and then was taken to another by armed soldiers."

"What does that mean? Can they have taken him prisoner?"

"He was under a flag of truce," Ha-te-ka said.

"He has had time to say what we wished to say." Black Hawk looked to the western skies. There was only a memory of color there. The stars crowded together in the deep sky.

"They would not have arrested him," Ha-te-ka believed.

"What other explanation is there?"

Thunder Horse said, "Perhaps they wanted to talk further. Perhaps they wanted to wait for some chief to arrive. Gaines is twenty miles away."

"Perhaps," Black Hawk said, rubbing his wrist with his hand. "Perhaps not. Someone should go down and see. I will take Nikia and—"

"You cannot go, Black Hawk," Thunder Horse said quickly. "If White Bear has been arrested, then surely they will arrest you."

"I can't desert White Bear."

"I will go down and see," Thunder Horse replied. "Give me Ha-te-ka and Nikia. We will ask what has happened to White Bear." Black Hawk hesitated, but as Thunder Horse handed the Sauk war leader his musket, he capitulated.

"All right. Someone must go. Thunder Horse, if something befalls you, the whites will pay. Ask in peace, leave in peace if you can. If not, I tell you this: we will be ready to strike."

"As it must be," Thunder Horse answered. He took Black Hawk's hand briefly, strongly, and looked to his lean-to.

"Do you wish to tell the far-dreamer?"

Thunder Horse hesitated. "No. Why cause the woman worry?"

"Then go along. Nikia! Go with the Sioux. White Bear has not returned. Ha-te-ka. Go too, if you will, and call Pak-wa to me. I swear, if there is treachery below, then the Americans will pay a great price."

Thunder Horse looked to Ha-te-ka and the grinning, toothless, Nikia. "Shall we go down now?"

Ha-te-ka tossed his bow aside and with a white blanket made a flag of truce. "I am ready," he said.

"Will you go, Ha-te-ka?" Thunder Horse asked. "Ta-wa-shuk has a new baby."

"Has not Sachim? Forgive me, Thunder Horse, but you are Sioux. I am Sauk. Have I not a duty to go?"

Thunder Horse rested his hand briefly on Ha-te-ka's shoulder and gestured to Nikia. Together the three warriors started off through the dark forest toward the American camp below while Black Hawk began to gather his men.

Sachim had been dozing. A white bird came and touched her eyelids with its feathers and she sat up, pawing at them. There had been something . . . the bird. Its wings had been stained with vermilion, and its eyes golden, and reflected in them were the skull-men.

She looked at the sleeping Raindrop and with a sudden rush of anxiety uncovered her daughter, feeling her body, looking intently at the smooth, coppery flesh. All right. She was sound, whole, beautiful. Sachim kissed the unformed face of the infant and tried to lie down again to sleep, but still a fragment of the dream bothered her.

What?

What was it that hung on the very edge of her consciousness, a tantalizing yet fearful image? Sachim's eyes opened wide suddenly, and she reached for her shawl, already knowing. She looked again at her sleeping baby, ducked outside, and rushed to where Black Hawk stood giving orders to his lieutenants.

She started to ask him but did not. She knew. And so there was nothing to do but stand looking down into the valley, toward the ancient burial grounds, to where the whites had pitched their tents and built their campfires.

Weatherly Johnston blinked twice and then wrapped his thumb over the curved hammer of his .50-caliber musket, drawing it back. "Hennesey?" he hissed.

"What?"

"We've got some Indians coming in. Is that a flag of truce?"

Corporal Hennesey spat out a stream of tobacco juice, cocked his own musket, and peered into the shadows of the forest. "Looks like a flag, all right," he said.

"Let 'em come in, then."

"What happened to the last one?" Hennesey asked.

His sergeant shrugged. "Don't know. Abe took him off. All I know is we don't fire on a truce flag . . . but keep your eyes open, Maynard."

From the woods they came silently, carefully. The man with the flag didn't appear to be a Sauk. Johnston's forehead furrowed briefly and then he knew—he had seen Sioux before. "That's right," he told himself, "I heard Black Hawk was massing the western tribes."

So that wasn't just some general officer's pipe dream. The Sauk really did have allies, and plenty of them. But who would've thought the Sioux would involve themselves in this war?

The Sioux was followed by two Sauk. All three of the men were wearing war paint. Johnston spoke to the Sioux. "What do you want?"

"A warrior has come down here to speak to your chief. His name is White Bear. Black Hawk is his friend. Black Hawk has sent us to ask what has happened to his friend White Bear."

Johnston looked around at the sound of footsteps. Four soldiers with muskets had appeared at the sight of the Indians. "Far as I know," Johnston said honestly, "nothing's happened to this White Bear."

"Then where is he?" the Sioux asked.

"Don't rightly know." Johnston looked toward the major's tent and then asked one of the soldiers, "Seen Captain Lincoln around, Smitty?"

"No, not for some time. Want me to hie off and find him?"

"You'd better," Johnston said. The three Indians stood uneasily before him. Johnston looked from them to the armed soldiers. "I think you'd better do just that."

Holding his cap, the soldier took off across the camp, weaving among the fires and tents. Johnston turned toward the Indians, crossed his arms and waited.

Major Isaiah Stillman emerged from his tent, adjusting the chin strap of his cap. The night had gone cool and river haze drifted through the trees, lighted weirdly by the campfires.

A young soldier the major didn't know by name ran to him, halted abruptly, and saluted raggedly. "Sir, we got some Indians over here . . ."

"Indians?"

"Yes, sir. Two of 'em Sauk, the third one—"

"Arrest them," Stillman ordered brusquely.

"Sir, they came to see—"

"Arrest them, soldier! Are you all idiots? Can't you see what they're doing here? They're spies, dammit all! Counting men and guns. Arrest them."

"Yes, sir," the soldier said numbly. He forgot to salute until the captain had walked past him. The soldier looked around the camp for help. He and Johnston weren't going to arrest three Indians alone. Near the huge broken oak a fire burned brightly enough for the soldier to see three men he knew from Kentucky, and the Indian scout. He started that way.

"Captain says for us to arrest three Indians over on the other side of camp. Put 'em in with the big one."

"Indians? In our camp! What're they doing here?" one of the Kentuckians asked, reaching for his rifle.

"Spying, the captain says."

The Indian scout lifted pouched eyes to the young soldier and seemed to smile. "I guess I'll go along."

"If you please, Mr. McCutcheon. Maybe you can speak their lingo."

"I can speak it," Thaddeus McCutcheon said, lifting his musket. "Watch yourselves, men," McCutcheon warned the young soldiers. "They might look unarmed but an Indian's got his ways. Don't let 'em close to you. And don't hesitate if they make any move. This is a war, soldiers—they're the enemy."

The young soldiers, none of whom had ever shot at a man, took this dutifully to heart. McCutcheon knew. He had been in this country a long time. His own family had been massacred by Sauk, they said.

Johnston was still standing in front of the Indians when the group of soldiers arrived with McCutcheon in the lead. "Took your time, Smitty," Johnston said. He was obviously nervous.

"Couldn't find Lincoln. Major Stillman says to arrest 'em."

"Arrest 'em? They come in for a powwow."

"You go argue with the major then," the soldier answered.

"What did he say?" Nikia asked Thunder Horse.

The Sioux answered quietly, "He says they are going to arrest us."

Nikia grew indignant. "They will not arrest me! Are they mad? We came to council with the white leaders."

He-te-ka said, "Be calm, Nikia. They have many guns."

McCutcheon muttered, "Be careful, men, they're cooking something up."

In Sauk Nikia repeated vehemently, "I will not be locked

up. Think of Ke-ke-tai! Remember there is no way out of a white jail."

"Be calm," Thunder Horse cautioned. "They are ready to shoot, I think." Thunder Horse took one step toward Johnston. McCutcheon's musket cocked as he did so. "Listen, soldiers, we have come to find our friend, to talk with your leaders. We do not intend to be taken away and locked up. Do you not honor a flag of truce—"

Nikia turned and ran. Thunder Horse reached out to grab him, to stop him, but the man tore free of his grip. Thunder Horse whirled around to see Ha-te-ka, panicked himself now, sprint off in the opposite direction. A gun spoke, light and heat stabbing out, so close to Thunder Horse's face that he felt the unburned grains of powder pepper his flesh, burning it. He saw Nikia stumble but run on. McCutcheon shouldered his musket and aimed at Ha-te-ka and Thunder Horse leapt for the man's throat, a savage cry rising from deep in his throat.

Still McCutcheon got his shot off and Ha-te-ka buckled at the knees and folded up, pitching face first onto the ground.

Thunder Horse slammed McCutcheon to the ground and wrapped his strong hands around the scout's throat, strangling him with all of the fury that was in his heart. Close thunder filled the Sioux's ears and he felt boring, fiery pain in his side. Still he would not release his grip. His own blood spilled out onto McCutcheon's body.

Thunder Horse's head spun crazily; hands clutched at him from behind and a rifle butt was driven against his skull. He could no longer fight. The strength was gone from his hands, but the man beneath him would do no more harm on this earth.

Thunder Horse was rolled aside. He heard someone say, "McCutcheon's dead. I guess he was right—can't trust no Indian."

The Sioux warrior lay staring up at the stars, which swirled slowly and then blinked out one by one. "Sachim," he said, and then the last star was gone and Thunder Horse lay still.

White Bear stood in the darkness of the tent, listening to the spate of gunfire and the sudden following silence. Outside, his guards spoke hurriedly.

"What the hell was that?"

"They attacking?"

Both men were at the front of the tent then. Instantly White Bear smashed the unlighted lantern which hung from the tent pole, snatched up a shard of glass, cutting his hand, and sliced a rent in the canvas. He gripped the opening he had cut and tore it wide with powerful shoulders. Ducking through, he dashed for the woods, musket fire following him. The Sauk ducked low reflexively and zigzagged his way through the forest, his heart beating steadily, rapidly, as soldiers took up the pursuit.

They had no chance at all of catching up with the giant in the darkness of the forest, a forest White Bear knew from childhood, and soon he was free, pausing for breath in the star-cast shadows of the trees, the only sound around him the constant chirping of crickets.

Below he could see the white camp, men scrambling this direction and then that, some of them trying to put out their campfires. They thought themselves besieged, and White Bear shook his head—this was no army, but a group of children with weapons.

He started on toward the camp of the Sauk, wondering what had begun the shooting he had heard. Probably, he guessed, the white soldiers had seen shadows in the woods and begun firing in panic. It was certain that Black Hawk hadn't attacked. If he had, there would be many dead soldiers in that war camp by now.

White Bear stopped running and plodded on. He could not see the Sauk camp, but he knew where it was, knew every dip and rise of the land, each tree.

The man came staggering toward him out of the deep shadows, arm across his belly, and White Bear hesitated until the man called his name.

"White Bear." The voice was low, tortured.

"Nikia, is it you?"

White Bear rushed to the man, catching him just as he collapsed. There was blood smeared across Nikia's shoulder and arm.

"What are you doing out here, Nikia? What has happened?"

The man in his arms answered painfully. "We were sent to look for you. The whites opened fire. Ha-te-ka. Dead. Thunder Horse dead."

"Dead! Why would they . . . ?" Then he was no longer thinking of either warrior, but of Sachim. Her grief was something the big Sauk could not stand to witness. Nikia, clutching at White Bear's shoulder, echoed his thoughts.

"How can we tell their women? How can we tell Ta-wa-shuk?" he asked. "How can we tell Sachim?"

White Bear didn't respond immediately. A strange sound was on the wind and he lifted his head. Eerie, penetrating, it was the sound of pain, the sound of death, rising and falling chantlike. White Bear looked toward the Sauk camp and said, "There is no need to tell her. She knows."

White Bear got Nikia to his feet and they struggled on toward the home camp. In the end, White Bear had to shoulder the Sauk warrior and carry him, as the loss of blood caused Nikia to faint.

The first man they saw in the camp was Black Hawk. Beside him was the medicine man Tope-kia.

"Gunshot," White Bear said. Then, "Thunder Horse . . ."

"We know." Black Hawk looked toward the lean-to where Sachim lay, her stifled cries rising and falling. "What of Ha-te-ka?"

"Dead, Nikia told me. How is he, Tope-kia?"

The medicine man looked up, shaking his head. "Help me take him to my lodge. Send for his woman. Perhaps he will live, perhaps not."

"Black Hawk," White Bear asked, "what do we do?"

"Do what we should have done before, White Bear. Do what we must. Make war. Are you willing now?"

"I am willing. I am eager," White Bear answered. "First. . ." He nodded toward Sachim's lean-to.

"Yes. I will gather the warriors." He turned. "Send for Two-Knives! It is time."

White Bear wiped at his face, finding blood there. Then he walked heavily to Sachim's lodge. He crouched low and peered into the lean-to, seeing her on her belly, child beneath one arm, sobbing so that her body shook. It was not the time. He could not speak without his voice breaking, he knew, and he did not know what to say.

He rose to leave and Sachim turned her tear-streaked face toward him. "Kill them, White Bear! Kill them all." And then she again turned her face away and continued her uncontrollable sobbing.

White Bear made a meaningless gesture with his hand, a gesture of sympathy. Then White Bear's hand clenched into a fist and he walked away, calling for his war horse.

White Bear prepared his war horse and gathered his arrows. A musket was a white weapon, useful for certain things, but an experienced archer could fire a dozen times while a man with a musket reloaded his more sophisticated weapon. White Bear would carry his musket as well, but it was his bow and goose-feathered arrows that he trusted.

Black Hawk was with Two-Knives when White Bear arrived. The war leader of the Sauk and the leader of the Fox conferred in quiet voices. Between them, etched into the earth, was a plan of the American camp.

"We ride through the camp once," Black Hawk was saying. "I will lead the charge . . ."

"No."

All heads turned. The woman was small, her voice clear but soft. Her face was painted black; her hair hung loose to her hips. She seemed to glide across the earth as she came, as if she had no weight except that which was in her heart, making of it a stone. Black was the color for mourning, black the color of death.

Sachim came forward, her face black and eerie, turning from Two-Knives to Black Hawk.

"You must rest, Sachim," Black Hawk said.

"Now no one can rest. Now death has come. Whose death must it be, the Sauk's or the whites'! It must be theirs if we are to survive."

"I was explaining the plan of attack," Black Hawk said.

"No!" Sachim weaved a little on her feet and White Bear stepped forward to catch her, but she waved him away. "This plan is the one they will expect, Black Hawk—a night charge directly at their camp."

"It has served us well in the past," the war leader objected.

"Everything in the past is of no consequence now. I *saw* our battle just now."

"Dreamed it?" Two-Knives asked.

"*Saw* it. This is how it must be. This is how it *will* be." And she told them what she had seen.

Major Stillman was enraged. He couldn't have said exactly what had angered him to such an extent. If he had paused and logically examined his situation, he would have recognized that he had boxed himself in with his capricious decisions. Stillman wasn't inclined to pause and logically study the situation. He was more immediately concerned with staying alive.

"What do we hear from Gaines?" he demanded as he paced his tent floor.

Captain Lincoln answered, "No word yet, sir."

"General Atkinson?"

"He hasn't yet reached Fort Madison," Jefferson Davis answered.

"Then we're effectively cut off."

The two junior officers exchanged a glance. It was obvious that they were cut off, obvious that no military commander of judgment would have provoked the Sauk under those circumstances.

"Our position then is a defensive one," Stillman said. "I want the camp fortified against an Indian raid, barricades erected—"

The first shot from without interrupted the American military commander. Davis leapt from his canvas camp chair and went to the tent flap.

"What is it?" he asked the sentry on duty, but before the man could respond, staccato firing intensified from the west, near the river.

Stillman was buckling his saber as he ran out, calling for his orderly and his horse. Lincoln followed after his commander. "What is it?" Stillman kept calling. "An attack?"

It took a full minute before they could find anyone who knew. Then Johnston, rushing out of the darkness, a hole in his cap, reported.

"Sir we've got a force of fifty Indians trying to breach our western line. Cannon?"

"Yes, dammit! Shake Artillery awake. Where is Lieutenant Dobbs?" Forgetting his horse, Stillman ran toward the western perimeter, still calling for caissons. "Grapeshot will back the beggars off," he panted.

Reaching the hastily constructed breastworks to the west side of the camp, Stillman wriggled up beside a smoke-blackened sergeant. "Where are they? What's going on?" the officer demanded. The sergeant, busy reloading his musket, could only shake his head.

All Stillman could see was the winking of muzzle flashes in the forest, the whine of musket balls whipping past above their heads. The roar of his own undisciplined muskets was loud in his ears.

"Hold your fire, damn all!" Stillman bellowed. "What are you shooting at?"

Stillman's orderly arrived leading the major's leggy bay horse. Behind him the caissons rattled toward the breastworks, cannon rolling behind them, and rushing gunners, half-dressed, running after.

"Here they come!" Davis shouted, drawing his own saber.

"Now, you fools! Fire!" Stillman hollered, placing one foot on the breastworks, raising his saber overhead. "Get those cannon into position! Grapeshot, gunners!"

The Sauk stormed out of the forest, firing as they ran, and Stillman saw one warrior go down. The sergeant next to him spasmed and came erect and Stillman saw the black hole bored through his forehead. His hand flapped in an odd gesture like an incompleted salute and the soldier pitched forward, dead.

"Cannoneers!"

Three men wheeled the first of the cannon into position, but before it was fully set a Sauk musket ball struck one of the soldiers in the thigh and he fell to the ground, dragging himself away.

"Fire!" Stillman commanded, and a ragged volley followed. Another Sauk was seen to go down but the remaining Indians answered with their own volley. "Reload!"

Stillman's men were fighting desperately. The Indians were shadows, here and then gone. A second, more-organized volley fired as the major dropped his saber in signal and the Sauk began to retreat, firing as they went.

"By God, we'll finish them now," Stillman vowed. He mounted the breastworks and cut the air with his sword. "Charge. Charge! Run the bastards down."

The blue-jacketed soldiers swarmed over the breastworks and pursued the Sauk toward the river, muskets firing at random, some shots dangerously close to their own comrades. Lincoln leapt the breastworks and charged on on long legs, Davis beside him.

"No good," Jefferson Davis managed to pant.

"No," Lincoln agreed, but there was no stopping the charge now. Stillman's five hundred men roared through the woods, filling the night with savage yells and gunfire. The volunteer army was like a beast without a head suddenly. Davis flung himself to the ground as a burst of grapeshot from behind sprayed the trees around him with lead balls. It could have done very little injury to the fleeing Indians. Davis picked himself up and rushed on.

The counterattack had grown to a mass charge through the forest as five hundred soldiers pursued the fleeing Sauk toward the river.

And when they reached the Mississippi—the Sauk were gone.

They had simply disappeared, as if they had all submerged themselves in the wide river. Stillman looked around, growing suddenly uneasy. In a moment he had the right to feel more than unease.

The Sauk charged out of the forest and the muskets opened up. Arrows punctured flesh and soldiers fell. Stillman saw a man, arrow in his eye, stagger past, and he went to the ground. The soldiers turned one way and then the other, seeking targets, but each time they saw a Sauk, the warrior seemed to vanish back into the woods. They were nothing but shadows.

Stillman formed his men up, shouting, gesturing wildly. There was no retreat. The river blocked off any movement. There was nothing to do but form ranks and fight back against the unseen enemy. And the soldiers dropped with savage regularity to lie sprawled against the beach as Stillman bawled out unheeded orders.

At Fort Madison the rider arrived a little after midnight, swung down from a sweaty horse, and knocked at the commandant's quarters.

General Henry Atkinson had arrived only an hour earlier on the steamboat *Fisher* and was exhausted. He sat up angrily and stumped to the door, flinging it wide to reveal a soldier with a torn tunic standing before a backdrop of starry sky.

"What in hell . . . ?"

"Stillman, sir. Cut off. Two hundred and seventy men dead."

"What! Find Captain Monique. We'll reinforce."

"Too late sir. It's over, all over."

The soldier stood there like a mannequin, face waxen. There was blood on his sleeve, the general noticed.

"All right, soldier. Report to the surgeon."

"Yes, sir."

Atkinson stood staring at the stars for a long minute as the soldier left, leading his bedraggled horse. Then sharply he turned away, banging his door shut.

* * *

On the hillrise the woman with the blackened face pointed down into the long valley. "Now is the time. Burn the houses while the soldiers are is disarray. Now is the time, Black Hawk, burn them all. Let not one remain to mar our land. No single relic of the white man's presence must be left standing. Burn them to the ground!"

Black Hawk and White Bear glanced at each other. This was not the woman they knew. A spirit seemed to have taken over her body, a war spirit, a spirit of grief. She stood, pointing still toward the valley, her face invisible in the darkness except for those eyes. Those glowing eyes. White Bear looked to Black Hawk again and at a nod from his leader the giant warrior moved out to lead his men on this mission of vengeance. Black Hawk rested a hand briefly on Sachim's shoulder. She seemed not to notice it. Then Black Hawk too was gone, trotting toward his war horse.

Only Sachim remained, her face blackened, her arm still extended, until the first house began to catch fire and the screaming whites ran from it. Soon the world was nothing but dark trees, vengeful bonfires, and destruction. Smoke rose to the skies, a prayer to the memory of Thunder Horse, and Sachim slowly lowered her arm as the world crumbled and fell to ruin.

15

THERE'S the authorization." John Reynolds threw the paper on his desk, stared unhappily at Gaines, and said, "Black Hawk will be crushed, believe me."

Gaines hadn't much spirit left after being forced to withdraw before the onslaught of Black Hawk's army. They had fought like madmen, the Indians. Attacking from the trees, at any time of day or night, pushing Gaines and his force back, decimating the American contingent. On top of the slaughter Major Stillman had suffered it was enough to force Atkinson to withdraw to Chicago, which was itself in chaos. Reports carried from the south, horror stories told by panicked immigrants, had people in the streets armed and wary. There was even talk of abandoning the city before Black Hawk could strike.

Atkinson still believed Black Hawk had formed a western alliance of tribes. "If he only has five hundred men, I'm Pontius Pilate," the general said. He lit a cigar, crossed his legs again, and looked at Major Stillman and Gaines, both of whom agreed hastily. They preferred believing Black Hawk had thousands of warriors to thinking they had been outgeneraled to such an extent.

"That," the governor of Illinois answered, "no longer matters. He will be defeated, he will be outnumbered. The pressure's on from all quarters now. The Senate passed a motion to allow Winfield Scott to transfer some of his Great Lakes forces down here. It's become a political issue, gentlemen," Reynolds said in a way which indicated political is-

sues were far more important than mere military matters.
"You ought to see the Philadelphia and Washington papers."

"I have," Zachary Taylor grumbled. "They can't decide if
Black Hawk is the reincarnation of Genghis Khan or a red
Napoleon."

"Developers from down along the river have been lobbying like crazy—this Joshua Ferguson, remember him? What's
in it for him anyway?"

"Land," Taylor said sourly.

"I remember him well enough. I just didn't think he had
that sort of political clout."

"He's got a hot issue," Gaines said. "Are Americans to
be safe in Louisiana Territory or not?"

"Reviewing all the reports I've seen," Reynolds confessed,
"I still for the life of me can't discover what triggered Black
Hawk's war. Apparently his own chiefs, like this Keokuk,
wanted peace."

"The spirit woman," Gaines said. At their looks of incom-
prehension the general explained. "It is said that Black
Hawk has a magic woman, some sort of shaman, who tells
him every move to make. That if she says the spirits want
war then there must be war."

"Damned superstitious savages," Atkinson muttered.

"Quite right," Reynolds said, clearing his throat. "The
point is that we do *not* apparently have all of the Sauk and
the Fox against us. This Keokuk and others like him must be
rewarded. I've authorized an annuity directly from the trea-
sury to be paid to the man and those who stand with him.
The peacemakers among the Indians, gentlemen, must always be rewarded and honored. Men like Black Hawk . . .
must be broken."

Atkinson was concerned with his own brand of politics,
military politics. "If Winfield Scott is coming down, does
that mean he will be in overall command?"

"He will."

Atkinson fell silent, feeling he had never gotten a chance
to show what he could do. Gaines's operation was a farce,
Stillman's suicidal. So Scott could come in and pick up
another star for his epaulets.

"All present forces will remain intact—as much as volunteer militia can be kept intact—what with leaving to harvest
crops and see to women in childbirth, what-have-you. To

these forces Scott will add the Second Infantry—fifteen hundred men—and the Fourth Artillery. Believe me, with these combined forces, it won't matter if Black Hawk has recruited the entire armies of the Sioux, Shawnee, and Cherokee nations." Reynolds wiped at a bead of perspiration on his eyebrow. "He will lose. He cannot help but lose. We shall, gentlemen, reclaim our lands legally given by treaty, legally paid for in gold."

With their numbers in a six-to-one ratio against Black Hawk's, there could be no other outcome.

Or could there?

No one had any hope that Black Hawk would surrender peacefully. Not now. His spirit woman had told him to fight; he fought. What would the woman tell him when she witnessed Winfield Scott's massed army moving into the area?

"He'll fight on," Gaines said quietly. "I'm coming to know something about the man. He'll fight on. There will be a lot of casualties. I hope that along with the other supplies, Scott brings bandages. We'll need them. In numbers."

She waited and watched the sunset sky spread color against the clouds floating high across the Mississippi. She could watch the drifting clouds and send up a prayer, or speak to the endless river for hours. But there was no answer. Thunder Horse would not be back.

He was dead. He was gone. He walked a distant trail. Fury had been born in Sachim's heart, a fiery wish to strike back against the *thing*. That had faded to sadness and then become simply emptiness.

She could only be grateful that she had Little Raindrop to give love, to accept love, to sleep next to her, hugging her in the empty nights.

But what sort of life would her daughter have before her now? Black Hawk had gone again to plead for allies, but even he seemed to have little hope that he would succeed. Time and guns were changing the land, changing the world so that one day Sachim saw there would only be the dead Sauk and those who lived as satellites of the Americans, having little land of their own, dependent on white handouts.

She did not want her daughter to live either way, but to roam free, to swim and fish in the great river, to walk the long land, gather rice and tap the maple trees and one night to have a warrior play his flute for her following the crane dance.

She looked westward now, wondering if she and Thunder Horse had made the right choice. Maybe they should have packed a few possessions and tracked toward the far mountains to live alone. But neither was that a proper life for a young girl like Little Raindrop. A child needs family and roots, the tribe, other children to be with.

Sachim clutched her breasts suddenly—the pain was terrible. She closed her eyes tightly as they filled with tears. There was a rumble in her ears, a trembling in her legs so that she had to sit down or fall.

The sudden pain in her heart pushed all previous thoughts aside. She could only sit panting, her eyes still tightly shut, still streaming tears.

Somehow she knew what the rumbling was now. And slowly from out of the darkness in her mind's eye she saw them coming. A thousand, another thousand, yet another thousand marching soldiers, their feet causing the earth to shake. They were coming and there was no stopping them. Human locusts swept toward the river, their clothes bright, their faces lost in shadow, their guns long and fixed with knives, and the people fled before them, rushing toward the river which ran red.

In fright, Sachim opened her eyes and she turned her blurry vision northward. Was it true? Could there be that many soldiers? Were they coming?

She knew that it was true. Her dreams always were. When they would come, where they would strike, she did not know, but they would come and Black Hawk could not stop them—not now, not without allies.

Sachim had intended to return to the village, but now she turned the other way. Along the river, ancient layered gray rocks projected out of the water. They were moss-covered, but denuded they were used by the young men as diving platforms. Now at the hour of sunset it was a cold, tedious climb up the face of the rocks, but as the sunset faded to a last thin band of color above the trees, Sachim achieved the top of the ledge. There she removed her clothing, and standing, arms spread, began to chant:

We are the children of
Manitou

Our enemies are strong
We are the children of the great Manitou
Strike our enemies, strike them!

The sun sank with a last flourish of faint scarlet rays and the land went dark. There was only the river muttering past, carrying vague threats and promises. Sachim stooped and picked up a jagged shard of stone and with it she cut her thigh. Blood trickled hotly from the wound. Again she cut her own flesh, the other thigh. Then she raked the jagged stone across her breast. And again she began to chant.

Hours passed slowly, the stars growing bright. Voices rose from the river. The spirits of the Sauk moved on the wind-blown shadows of the clouds. Sachim stood and sang, growing weak. Her long hair drifted free. Blood smeared her body. She was there but not there; she grew lighter and drifted away on the wind herself, carrying her song to the tormented skies.

"Dammit all to hell!" General Winfield Scott entered Reynolds' office and threw his gauntlets down on the governor's desk. His boots were muddy, his tunic unbuttoned at the top. The general was furious. "Have you heard?"

"I have," Reynolds said.

"Asiatic cholera, the surgeon calls it. The Fourth Artillery has lost thirty percent of its force. Most of the rest are scarcely on their feet. The Second in Detroit already has two hundred dead out of fifteen hundred. Then this rain!"

"What about the militia?" Reynolds asked.

"Gaines reports a third of his people are down with cholera, a third have hied themselves home for the winter. I'm going to have to disband them, you know," Scott said abrasively.

"Once they're disbanded, we're done for the year."

"I know that. We won't be able to regroup until summer. That gives Black Hawk plenty of time to build his own forces. There will also be a lot of volunteers who won't come back in June or July to wait around again—these men came to fight, not to suffer a cholera plague and sit waiting in the rain!"

"This won't set too well in Washington," Reynolds said.

"It doesn't set too well here, Governor. But there's no

choice. I'm going to have to disband the militia." He looked pained and disgusted as he said, *"Asiatic cholera."*

The winter was long and cold but peaceful. Ice clung to the birch trees, shimmering in the sunlight. Sachim walked the snowy trail to the great oak and stood beneath it for a long while, looking at Grandmother's grave.

"What can we do, Grandmother?" she whispered. "Whatever can we do now?"

Black Hawk returned, rebuffed again by the neighboring tribes. The rumors of the great American army had reached the plains. For some reason they had not attacked, but they would.

"Can we run?" Black Hawk had asked. "Can we surrender? Can we throw away our heritage? Tell me, Sachim."

Now, quietly, Sachim asked Grandmother the same questions. She got on hands and knees and dusted the snow from her grandmother's grave, and kneeling there, she knew the answer to her questions, the tragic, debilitating answer: they could do nothing. Black Hawk could fight, but that would accomplish nothing; she could pray again for just a little time, but in the end the inevitable time would arrive.

The time of the whites, for the time of the Sauk was fading.

Sachim rose, slapping at the mud on her knees, and she walked to the other grave where Thunder Horse's bones rested. They had buried him in the Sauk fashion, not in the Sioux manner. He had said himself, "I am Sauk now," and so it had been done.

She stood looking down at the grave as the wind shifted the light new snow. Her eyes flooded with hot tears suddenly and she collapsed to lie against the grave, digging her fingers into the dark, half-frozen earth.

That day White Bear came to her lodge. Little Raindrop was playing at sticks and pebbles and she turned briefly, lifting a chubby hand in greeting before returning to her play.

The massive warrior stood uneasily in the middle of the lodge. Sachim had to ask him, "What is it?"

His eyes turned down. "Winter will be hard here."

"Yes."

"You will need meat."

"Yes, White Bear."

"You need a husband, Sachim. The child needs a hunter for a father. We should wed."

He had spent two hours rehearsing his speech, a grand speech in which he truly professed his love, in which he would explain that he understood about Thunder Horse, that he would do his best always to care for Sachim and the child. With variations it was a speech White Bear had practiced for years. Yet now the time had come and all he could say was, "We should wed." Embarrassed, he continued to look away.

Sachim touched his powerful arm and answered. "Perhaps we should wed," she said softly.

He had already begun to turn away and now his eyes, stunned and unbelieving, locked with hers.

"Did I hear you?" he asked.

"We shall wed." She smiled and if it wasn't a whole-hearted smile, White Bear understood that as well. She lifted herself on her toes and kissed his cheek. White Bear murmured something that made little sense and then turned away, ducking out the blanket covering the lodge's door and into the cold night.

He wiped at his cheek and then, his mind a turmoil of emotions, walked away very rapidly. It was unseemly for a warrior to cry.

Time was short. It wasn't only Sachim who knew that. The people as a whole sensed it. Snowfall, as inconvenient and even dangerous as it was, was welcomed. Winter would last one more day, one more week.

Individuals reacted differently to the knowledge that time was closing in on them. Some sat and brooded; others laughed and pranced around like maddened things. Sachim spent the time in the only way she could. She loved the baby and played with it, taught it what she could; and she did her best to make White Bear happy. Vast, shy, stolid White Bear, who took his own duties as a husband seriously and plodded off through the deepest snow on the worst of days to hunt and fish, to trap so that Little Raindrop could have a blanket of fur and a little fur cap.

When he slept, she did not know. It seemed there was no time of the night when Sachim could not open her eyes and find him just looking at her with a love so deep it was nearly embarrassing.

Then she would roll to him and comfort him and keep him warm. At times she would withdraw, just a little, pull away in her sleep as if startled, but he understood that—he knew the man she expected to find beside her was Thunder Horse. She would awake with a twitch, her eyes searching, and she would look at White Bear with puzzlement. Then Sachim would try to give her love, try to reassure him, but it was difficult. He knew that. He had seen her often enough at Thunder Horse's grave.

But he was with the woman he had always loved and if there were unconscious moments when she betrayed herself, she gave all she could to White Bear, and that was enough.

The sound was small and yet very disturbing. Sachim sat up in the night and looked carefully around the lodge. Her husband slept, snoring softly. The baby was curled against his huge arm. All was as it should have been, but for that tiny sound.

Sachim rose from her bed, putting a blanket around her. She walked to the entranceway and studied the stars. The wind was surprisingly warm on her cheek and as she stood there a drop of water melted from an icicle on the lodge's roof and fell onto her hand. Another drop fell free and splashed into the puddle beside her, making only a small sound—a terrible sound. She returned to her bed and crawled in beside White Bear, snuggling up to him, needing to make their winter last just a little while longer.

When the snow was gone and the ground unfrozen, they started out to plant their fields once more. This year was different—there was no singing, no joy in the cornfields as the women moved along the rows.

"Who knows if we will ever eat this corn," Sha-sak said, straightening up to wipe her forehead with her hand.

"We will, " Sachim said. Her voice wasn't as cheerful as she tried to make it. "We must *believe* we will. We would be a sorry lot next winter if we had no corn because we were too lazy to plant it now."

"Yes, I suppose," Sha-sak admitted with a shrug. Little Raindrop was running toward her mother. She stumbled over a row of earth, fell, looked up in surprise, and then began crying, looking at her skinned hand.

Sachim laughed and scooped the child up, letting her ride

on her back. The day grew hot and the women withdrew to the trees to eat their lunches in the shade. Sachim sat Little Raindrop on her lap and fed her bites.

"Who is that!" someone shouted, and Sachim turned to look. A runner was coming in from the north, running through the trees toward the camp.

"What is happening!" a second woman called. The runner didn't even slow to answer them. Without realizing it, Sachim was on her feet now, staring after the messenger.

"Oh, no!" Sha-sak said. "It has started."

"Come, Little Raindrop," Sachim said, picking up the child, who was disappointed at not finishing her meal. Sachim started toward the camp with the other women. At first they moved slowly, trying to put off the moment of knowing, but by the time they reached the camp they were nearly running themselves.

They needed to ask no questions. The warriors were preparing their war kits. War ponies were being brought into the camp. Sachim looked around in anguish.

Little Raindrop was at her side now and she tugged the girl along by the hand. "Come on, come on, come on!"

The girl, understanding none of it, looked up with astonished eyes. Her mother was never so brusque. Fear transmitted itself to the child and she began to cry. Sachim stopped, picked her up, and continued on.

White Bear was just emerging from the lodge and she rushed up to him, hugging him briefly before she stepped back to look into those kind, resolute eyes.

"It is true then? They are coming?"

"Yes. A great army. There are boats on the river too," White Bear answered, bending over to gather up Little Raindrop. She pulled at his ear and stuck a finger to his nose.

"What about the women and children?" Sachim asked. "Will we be traveling as well?"

"You must," her husband answered. "There may be a second white army, perhaps traveling up from St. Louis. It will not do to leave you unprotected."

"Then I will be quick. Help me pack, Little Raindrop. White Bear must ride with the men now."

The child looked in question at her mother and then just nodded, accustomed to a way of life steeped in turmoil, uncertainty, and fear.

The warriors left first, riding ahead to intercept the white army. The women, following, would make a camp at the Bad Ax River. They would have no fires there, no lodges, only provisions in sacks. How long it would last, they did not know. How far would they have to travel, how many more sorry camps would they be forced to stay in?

Black Hawk rode out nearly last, and his eyes, going over the refugees, the women and children, were cold. His face was drawn, and he could only have been thinking that he had failed his people miserably. In a moment that look was gone and he heeled his war pony, racing it toward the head of his cavalry column of Fox and Sauk braves.

The rest of the tribe was left to start on through the dust, traipsing northward toward a wretched future. As they passed the cornfields their eyes turned that way and then returned to the long trail ahead.

They trudged on for hour after hour. Sachim found herself watching the pebbles she passed, counting steps; and then their approach would startle a covey of quail in the underbrush and the whirring of their stubby wings as they burst from the trees would cause her heart to race madly.

The children grew weary and the old straggled behind. No one spoke and yet all of their thoughts were the same. The war had come again. How could they survive it? What would be left if they did? Their thoughts were on the war, on their lost home—and with the men who rode ahead, preparing to meet the war as it approached.

The column extended for miles. Black Hawk crouched in the trees looking down at the mixed infantry and cavalry units moving southward in a long line, following the trail through the forest. Many of the men wore no uniforms. Perhaps they were settlers coming back to try to recapture the land.

"Cavalry?" Black Hawk asked.

"Five hundred?" White Bear guessed.

"Where is the artillery?"

"They will be brought up last," White Bear said, wiping at a gnat which clung to his eyelash.

"They mean to trap us between the old camp and the river."

"We can't attack now," White Bear said.

"No. Let them bunch in their night camp. While they are weary and thinking of meat for their stomachs is the time, not while they are strung out like this."

"After dark?" White Bear suggested. "Cannon are virtually useless after dark."

Black Hawk turned away from the sight and reminded White Bear, "So is cavalry. I want to attack mounted. So then the time is just at sunset."

"They will march another ten miles," White Bear thought. "They will be near the Bad Ax. Very near."

Black Hawk looked back again at the long column and nodded. "I know this, White Bear. We have no choice. We chose the wrong camp for the women and children but now it is too late to change anything."

Winfield Scott had formulated the plan of attack. Captain Monique, still attached to Gaines, thought little of it. "Black Hawk won't be at that camp," Monique decided.

Lieutenant Jefferson Davis glanced at the regular-army officer and asked, "Why not?"

"I know the Sauk," Monique said confidently. In fact he probably did understand Black Hawk better than most of the senior officers, but the way he spoke made his understanding sound all-encompassing. "He has eyes everywhere. When we do reach the camp we'll find it empty—and likely find Black Hawk at our rear."

"Have you discussed this with Gaines?" the Mississippian asked.

"No point in it. Gaines doesn't seem to have any more faith in me than Atkinson has in Gaines, or Scott in Atkinson."

Davis laughed.

"You could approach Colonel Taylor about this matter," Monique, unsmiling, suggested.

"I'm not high on Taylor's list right now," Davis admitted. "He knows darn well I mean to marry his daughter—and will—but he's not sure he likes the idea that much."

"It seems," Monique said, "that someone had better begin communicating with someone here. Gaines doesn't have much control over his volunteers—and some of them are just adventurers, a few common criminals."

"You know some of them?" Davis asked.

"Many of them. Men who lived down here before Black Hawk ran them off, like Willie Havens there, or Harold Parret. I should have stayed at Madison. Frank Higgins has been on a holiday down there. Except . . ." Monique looked with pleasure at his captain's insignia. For a moment he was lost in contented reverie. Volunteering for this had brought him a second bar.

He smiled for a moment and then remembered where he was and who was out there, likely watching every movement the column of soldiers made.

"We've got him seven to one," Jefferson Davis reminded Monique, but that did little to cheer up the captain. He had seen Black Hawk's warriors before.

Watching the American army from a distance, his men keeping to the hickory and birch forest, Black Hawk was ahead of the whites when they began to set up their camp-site. He glanced at the sun and nodded to White Bear. Let the warriors put on their paint.

If that very morning things had seemed impossible, they now seemed manageable with skill and luck. A first strike at the encamped army might eliminate as much as a quarter of the enemy force.

If it could be done with utter surprise. Time and again Black Hawk warned his men of the need for caution. There must be no movement, not the slightest sound to warn the Americans, who seemed to have no idea they might be attacked—they were too confident in their numbers.

There was still no sign of cannon-armed steamboats on the river, and that too was good.

"With luck," Black Hawk said under his breath. He wished that the far-dreamer were there. Perhaps she would know the outcome of this crucial battle. But Sachim was at the Bad Ax camp downriver and Black Hawk could only wait and worry, running over his plan endlessly.

The sun began to fall, changing colors, which spread out across the land and the shimmering river beyond the trees. The Sauk moved out through the forest, a rising wind help-ing to cover the sound of their horses.

Long, mingled shadows moved before the horses of the painted Sauk. The trees were deep and dark, holding golden fire at their tips. The warriors spoke not at all now. With hand gestures Black Hawk deployed his men left and right.

The whites had made their camp on open ground along the river for the convenience of the large body. It was not a good defensive position at all, Black Hawk noted with deepening pleasure.

He could see far up the valley to his right and all the way to the river on his left. In a few minutes all of his force would be in position. The sun would be in the right place, the land not quite dark. Black Hawk would charge out of the sun. He could see the wheeled cannon now, in a row, tarpaulins tied over them. They would be useless, too slow to bring to bear. By the time they could be loaded it would be over, one way or the other.

Black Hawk stiffened. He saw movement in the poplar wood beyond the white camp. There should have been no one there, but someone was. Two-Knives pointed. The Fox leader too had seen it—but what was it?

In a minute the answer was in full view. Muskets roared and horses thundered toward the American camp as Skull made his charge from the poplars.

"Fool!" Black Hawk groaned. The renegade Sauk was attacking with fewer than forty horsemen, intent on raiding, inflicting casualties quickly, and then withdrawing—perhaps riding right through the camp, a tactic he had learned from Black Hawk himself.

"Are we ready!" Black Hawk shouted.

"I don't see White Bear yet. No, not yet, Black Hawk."

The whites ran for their muskets. Soldiers whipped the tarpaulins from the cannon and began preparing them. Skull was already nearly through the camp. Two Sauk were down, perhaps a dozen whites.

"Ruined," Black Hawk said violently. "Completely ruined. Now they are in ranks, now they are ready for us, now they have the cannon. Ruined!"

Through the trees rode the skull-faced Sauk, coming directly toward Black Hawk. Skull himself was in the lead, grinning victoriously. He had struck. He had made his raid. He had lost the battle Black Hawk might have won.

Settling darkness couldn't mask the fury on Black Hawk's face. The great veins in his throat stood out. His hand clenched around the handle of his war ax.

Skull arrived on a black horse whose head was painted white, its mane and tail braided. Behind him came his riders, making their way upslope after the brief, unexpected raid.

"So now, Black Hawk!" Skull shouted triumphantly as he drew his horse up beside Black Hawk's. "So now do you not think you should have accepted my help?"

Black Hawk's hand moved, the war ax flashed through the air. The head of the ax buried itself in the flesh of Skull's arm and the Sauk renegade howled with pain as his horse reared up and spun away on hind legs. The horse raced downslope as Skull continued to scream, and Skull's astonished riders stared at Black Hawk with dark fury.

A few of them had started forward menacingly, but from the woods to their left and from their right, Sauk and Fox warriors appeared and Skull's riders turned, heeling their horses, whooping as they rode away, following their badly wounded leader.

Black Hawk himself slid from his horse's back, turned away from his warriors, and walked away alone silently into the trees. There was nothing to say.

"Bad Ax?" Two-Knives asked White Bear.

"I don't know. I think he'll want to withdraw. We'll wait—in a little while he will be himself."

The shots had been heard far away at the Bad Ax camp, but no one could make sense out of the brief flurry of reports. There should have been more shots, very many more.

Sachim could do no more to solve the puzzle than anyone else. The women she sat with had found shelter behind some tall rocks overgrown with vines, cleft by the gnarled roots of an oak tree. The children were cold because they could build no fires. Fires might bring the Americans to their camp. The old people shivered in the darkness. Sachim felt stiff and weary although she knew it would be impossible to sleep on this night. Across the countryside other groups of Sauk sat huddled together, barely speaking, fearful of making noise. They were like wild hunted things.

Across the river in the peacemaker Keokuk's camp, people had fires and warm corn soup and they sat smoking, talking, and laughing as loudly as they liked. But they too were wretched, broken, Sachim considered—it was only that they did not know it yet.

The baby slept and Sachim pulled her blanket higher, under her chin. Then, after kissing the baby, she rose and moved away from the camp, trying to walk off the stiffness the damp of night had brought.

She wished the men would return, although that was not their plan, wished to see White Bear on this night, to cling to the comforting strength of him.

The moon was rising behind the trees now, a great flattened eye following Sachim as she walked the river trail. She was not the only one who couldn't sleep, who felt the need to move around that night. Someone was sitting beside the trail, watching the river. Sachim lifted a hand.

It hung there in horror as she took three more steps and drew near enough to see *it*. The thing wore a skull's head and it was caked with blood. In its hand was a bloodstained war hatchet. The moonlight glinted evilly on the steel head of the hatchet.

"Skull . . ." she said, and then she didn't have the breath to say another word, nor the breath to call for help, to scream, although she wanted to. Her diaphragm seemed to knot up and clog her throat. She turned stumbling and started to run, hearing the footsteps behind her. The thing, moon-streaked, bloody, was chasing her and it held the hatchet raised.

"Sioux slut," Skull said. "Sioux woman. Sioux bitch."

Sachim looked back again and then her foot hit the tree root and she fell sprawling. She dragged herself upright and started on, her legs feeling leaden, her heart racing madly in her breast.

He was close, very close. She did not want to look back, she could not!

A hand caught her arm and Sachim was spun around, thrown to one side roughly.

She tried to rise but couldn't. Peering through her tangled hair she saw whose hand it had been—not the killer's, but White Bear's. He had thrown her aside to get her out of the way and now as Skull lunged at the giant, White Bear's hand caught his wrist. White Bear's knife was a silver flash in the night. It buried itself in Skull's belly as the renegade thrashed and cursed and spat, still trying to kill, to destroy.

Slowly he sank to the ground, White Bear over him. The warrior stood over the dead brave for a long minute and then turned toward Sachim, picked her up as if she were a child, carrying her back to the camp as she clung to his neck and buried her face in the hollow of his shoulder, sobbing.

During the night it rained; a storm drifted in from the north, smothering the river and the forest with clouds. Sachim lay wet and miserable beside White Bear. No one slept. They all watched the sky as if by doing so they could hold back the dawn and the war.

The sun, when it rose, was a dimly seen gray ball behind the massed clouds. The rain continued to fall as the warriors rose and prepared their weapons.

Beneath a pile of furs and blankets, Little Raindrop slept. Sachim drew back the covers and looked once at her sleeping child, stroking the girl's head, feeling the ache begin in her heart. She had already decided, and when Black Hawk walked through the camp, appearing haggard and worried, Sachim caught up with him.

"I spoke to White Bear," Sachim said.

"Yes?" Black Hawk moved on toward his horse, only glancing at his spirit woman.

"Is it true that we may be cut off, pushed up against the river?" She drew her beaded shawl tighter as the rain drove down, pushed by a hard wind. Black Hawk stopped.

"He told you that? Yes, it is possible. Very possible. The Americans have been reinforced during the night."

"Then we must cross the river," Sachim said, looking toward the Mississippi through the swaying, rain-glossed trees.

"It can't be done. Yellow Sky forbids it. We war here—against the whites; or there—against the Sioux."

"White Bear said someone could speak to Yellow Sky. Plead with him to let us cross the river."

"Yes. It is a chance. A humiliation for the Sauk, but if Yellow Sky could be convinced to relent, we could at least move the women and children to the far side. The Americans would have much trouble crossing with their force. Only a few at a time could come. But"—he shrugged—"with the Americans here and the Sioux at our backs we have no chance at all."

"I will go," Sachim volunteered. Black Hawk's eyebrows drew together. "I have already decided, Black Hawk."

"The Sioux have no liking for you."

"They have a liking for none of us. Yet Little Raindrop is Yellow Sky's niece, his brother's flesh and blood. Perhaps for her sake, for the sake of his brother's memory, he will allow us at least a little time on the eastern bank."

"Do you think so?"

"I am not Yellow Sky; I do not know. I can only ask— who else can go? Who else speaks their tongue so well as the woman who lived with Thunder Horse, who else is related by blood to Yellow Sky's band?"

"It may be dangerous."

"We wade in danger, Black Hawk. I will go if you allow it."

Black Hawk studied the eyes of the slender young woman for a moment and then nodded his assent. "As it must be. Walk with Manitou, spirit woman," he said, placing his war-hardened hand on her shoulder. "Have you told your husband what you wish to do?"

"I will not tell him. Let him go into battle without this added concern."

"As you will have it. I must go. I plan a rear attack today. The whites must be led away from this camp. They must chase me far. I will taunt them and lay ambushes, one after the other. If they are so foolish as to pursue, then I will whittle them down soldier by soldier. Such is my plan." He looked to the cold skies. "May Manitou grant me success."

Then Black Hawk walked to his war pony and swung aboad, taking his bow and quiver from his war sack. Sachim watched him for a minute. Would she see him again? Of course—Black Hawk could not be defeated. He was the heart of the Sauk, their soul and conscience and defender.

"Sachim?"

She turned to find White Bear there and she hugged her husband tightly. He stroked her damp hair and lifted her chin. "Will you miss me so much, fear for me so much?" he asked.

"Yes," she murmured. "Yes, I will miss you, White Bear. Fight well, but be careful."

"Yes. A warrior's commandment. Sachim . . ." He kissed her and stammered, "I do love you. With a love like the great river—unending, enduring, powerful."

"I know that, White Bear," she replied with a soft smile. She touched his huge arm. "Go now, and be victorious."

He kissed her again, quickly, and then walked away through the rain and the mud. Sachim whirled away and walked back to where her baby still slept. Sha-sak was squatting nearby, looking through her provision sack, muttering about the ruined corn cakes. Sachim touched her friend's hand.

"I need your help, Sha-sak."

Sha-sak turned and rose. "My help?"

"I need to build a raft. You will help me, won't you?"

"A raft! Sachim, what are you thinking?" the heavy woman asked.

"I am crossing the river."

"In this rain? Alone?"

"In the rain." Sachim glanced at her baby again. "But not alone."

"Not the child as well, Sachim!"

"I must. I'm going to Yellow Sky's camp."

"You think you will be welcome there?" Sha-sak asked with shocked confusion.

"It is for the tribe, the people, Sha-sak. Please do not ask me more questions. Will you help me?" Sachim gripped her friend's arms and looked into her eyes until with a lip-fluttering exasperated sigh Sha-sak nodded.

"I will help you, but I am afraid for you, afraid for the child."

"Even Yellow Sky would not harm his own kin," Sachim believed.

"And the river? Are you kin to the river as well, Sachim?"

Sachim looked away and smiled. "Perhaps," she answered.

For she had been born by the river, nurtured by it, fed by it. It had cooled her when she was hot, given her water to drink, fed her corn crops, produced their rice, ducks, and fish. And when she dreamed, did she not dream of the Life-giver, the terrible, beautiful, living thing?

"Perhaps."

With the help of three other women the raft was built in a few short hours. The rain had abated, but the river, swollen by the storm, frothed past red and gray, angry. Sha-sak looked worriedly at it, but said nothing more. The child, well-bundled, eyes fearful yet trusting, was placed on the raft and tethered to it with a length of rawhide running from a log end to her wrist. Sachim similarly tied a tether to her own wrist. A sack of provisions was lashed to the raft as well.

Sha-sak watched it all with silent suffering. Sachim had lost her mind. What did she hope to accomplish? Yet there was no sense arguing with her. That was as futile as arguing with the river or asking it to slow its rampaging course.

Sha-sak could only stand on the empty gray-pebbled beach and watch as the spirit woman pushed off into the turbulent current and paddled toward the far-distant shore through the rain.

Perhaps Sachim had been right, Sha-sak thought. Perhaps she *was* one with the river. Sha-sak watched until the current had taken Sachim far downstream, and the raft and her figure became only indistinct tiny forms like leaves upon a stream. Then, with another exasperated sigh, Sha-sak returned to see if there weren't some dry corn cakes somewhere in the camp.

16

THE Sioux camp was a day's walk from the river. The rain had stopped, but there was a fresh storm on the horizon. The grass Sachim walked through was calf-high, heavy with moisture. There were many oaks here, a few poplars, and now and then a solitary pine. The deer had come out of their thickets to graze and they only lifted their heads at Sachim's approach. Animals had never been frightened of her, nor had she ever killed one.

Mushrooms grew in profusion—red, white, and purple, their heads lifted on bent stalks. The rain had brought them up with a flourish. Little Raindrop was heavy on Sachim's shoulders and from time to time the child had to be put down to walk, which she did in a child's manner—kicking at mushrooms, discovering flowers hidden in the grass, picking up sticks and throwing them away, shrieking with glee when a rabbit bounded away at their approach, running after a wandering blue-and-red dragonfly.

Sachim watched the girl and felt her heart swell. She took a proffered dandelion and tucked it into her jacket. Then as Little Raindrop ran away again on her chubby legs, Sachim wiped her tears away.

She had already decided.

The Sioux camp was vast, scattered among the rolling hills. No one came out to investigate Sachim's approach although she had no doubt she had been seen. There were only a few people out and about—the new storm was moving rapidly toward them and most of the Sioux preferred to sit inside their warm tipis around a glowing fire, talking, story-telling, preparing their meals . . . Such simple things, Sachim thought. Things denied the Sauk by war.

Yellow Sky's familiar yellow lodge was situated on a low grassy knoll. Three horses were picketed outside and they turned incurious heads toward Sachim as she walked to the lodge and called out.

"Yellow Sky. Heart Song?"

It was Heart Song who peered out. The tragically sad young woman looked surprised and then concerned, then delighted as she saw Little Raindrop peeking shyly through her fingers at her.

"It is Thunder Horse's baby!"

"Yes, Heart Song." Sachim handed the reluctant Little Raindrop to her aunt. Heart Song's bleak face lighted with a smile and a warmth came into her eyes as she held each little finger and petted the child's dark hair.

"You have come to see Yellow Sky?" Heart Song asked, her anxiety returning.

"Yes."

"He is here, but . . . I do not know, Sachim. Is this wise? Where is Thunder Horse?"

"Dead. The war took him."

"The war?"

"With the Americans. He is dead . . ." Momentarily Sachim's voice broke, but she caught herself. "And the child is all that is left of him on this earth."

Yellow Sky appeared suddenly, bare-chested, more scarred than Sachim remembered him, lean and hard and dark. "What is this? Why are you here, woman! Get inside, Heart Song . . . Wait!" He frowned as he spied Little Raindrop, who was reaching frantically for her mother. "What is this?"

"Thunder Horse's baby," Heart Song said fearfully.

"Where is my traitorous brother?" Yellow Sky lifted his gaze.

"He has been killed," Sachim answered.

"So?" Yellow Sky pursed his lips thoughtfully and then shrugged. "Whites?" he asked.

"Yes."

"So? Why did my brother involve himself in that war? He was stupid. Why does Black Hawk fight when there is no need? He is stupid. The Sioux do not fight—is that why you are here, to ask us again to save you?"

"No, Yellow Sky." Sachim took the baby as the Sioux war leader watched.

"A girl-child?" he asked.

"Yes."

"So," he said, as if he would have expected nothing else of his wandering brother than that he would have the temerity to produce not a warrior, but a girl-child.

"Black Hawk does not ask for warriors," Sachim said, putting the baby on her hip, where it sucked at a finger and stared at Yellow Sky.

"Then what?" Yellow Sky demanded. "Why are you here in my camp where you were forbidden to come?"

"The Sauk wish to cross the river, to escape the white army."

"And hide in our land, and bring war to us? No!" Yellow Sky said with a definite gesture.

"It is little enough to ask, Yellow Sky. Simply that you do not war on the Sauk as well."

"I have answered. Cross the river where Keokuk is camped. Ask Keokuk for shelter, ask Keokuk for warriors. I will not have the Sauk and their war here."

Sachim had expected no other response, but that did not make it easier to accept Yellow Sky's dictum. He waved a hand and then turned back toward his tipi. Sachim grabbed his arm and he spun back, his face dark with anger.

"Woman, you try my patience! I have told you how it will be. Go back to Black Hawk. Tell him to stand on his own, to be victorious or fail on his own—tell him that the Sauk may not cross the river. They are not welcome on my land and you are unwelcome in my camp."

"And the child," Sachim asked.

Yellow Sky's expression stiffened. "What do you mean? What are you speaking of now, woman?"

"The child," Sachim said, swallowing a word, "is Sioux. She is of your blood."

"My brother's daughter? Yes. What are you asking?"

"Keep . . . her," Sachim said. For a minute she and the war leader simply stared at each other. "Keep her with you. Let her be raised as a Sioux. I do not want to see her suffer what will befall her, what I have dreamed will happen to the Sauk."

"Please!" Heart Song said passionately, gripping her broth-

er's arm. Yellow Sky stared down at her. He looked at the
baby and snapped out an answer.

"As you will have it, woman. What does it matter to me?"
Then he ducked inside his tipi and left the two women and
the frightened child alone.

"Sachim . . ."

"Take her."

"You cannot mean it! Are you sure?"

"Take her." The baby had begun to cry, and Sachim had
to pry her fingers free of her hair, to force her into Heart
Song's arms. Then she had to turn hastily and walk away
with the child's cries ringing in her ears, with her heart
thumping and her stomach knotted with anguish. She walked
long, and the rain that had begun to fall drove down against
her back and uncovered head. She walked on and did not
think, refused to think, and as night gathered she still walked,
her clothing soaked through, her legs weary, her mind empty
but for the steady guilty hammering, the pain and sorrow.

Sachim fell to her knees and then lay sprawled against the
grass, her face against her arm. The sobbing racked her
body and her stomach heaved until she had to turn her head
and be sick upon the grass. She tried to rise but her trembling
limbs wouldn't support her. She lay there as darkness fell
across the empty land. The world was cold and bitter but for
the heat of the endless tears streaming across her face. She
tore the grass from the earth and beat her fists against the
ground and then lay still.

The rain fell down.

The Sauk came out of the rain like demons rising from the
ground—painted, shrieking demons with deadly talons. The
soldier beside Lincoln fell to the ground clutching his belly,
and Lincoln from one knee fired back with his revolver,
seeing an Indian sag to the side of his pony and veer away.
A second shot missed a wildly painted onrushing Sauk who
leapt his horse over a hastily constructed barricade and
placed a well-aimed flaming arrow into the supply wagon.
Flames curled skyward as the canvas top of the wagon went
despite the drizzle and the efforts of Captain Lincoln's men.

The gunfire continued long after there were any visible
targets. The volunteers were frankly panicked, shooting at
ghosts, at cloud shadows and mist-veiled trees.

"Hold your fire! Hold your fire!" Lincoln bellowed, waving his pistol-clenching hand back and forth. The shooting sputtered away to silence and the world went gray, silent. Lincoln looked around carefully. It was eerie and unsettling. The Sauk struck and then were gone again, like the mist which covered their attacks and retreats.

Jefferson Davis rode up and swung down beside Lincoln, his cap lost, hair washed down across his forehead.

"Casualties?" Captain Lincoln asked.

"No estimate. Thirty dead maybe. Half that mortally wounded."

"This is no good, Jeff. We'll never run them down tugging caissons and cannon after us."

"Then what?" Davis asked. "We go into the woods after them and we've had it." The Mississippian wiped back his hair. A futile saber hung from his hand. "You'd think the *American* army would know something about these tactics after the Revolution."

"I thought they taught you all about it at West Point."

Lieutenant Davis grinned. "Not *all*, apparently. The fact is, Abe, we've got an enemy superior in this sort of fighting. They strike and vanish. No standing army can combat guerrilla tactics. And we're not willing to adopt them ourselves."

"So then," Lincoln asked, "what do we do?"

Davis spat. "Wait for the generals to decide," he answered.

That was exactly what the generals were trying to do. Gaines and Atkinson, along with Colonel Zachary Taylor, were conferring in a flimsy canvas tent three miles away from Black Hawk's latest, still-unreported raid on the forward phalanx. Taylor was the most animated of the officers, furiously diagraming his thoughts on a large sheet of yellow paper as the general officers smoked.

"Broken Saber?" He gestured with his fingers without looking at the Indian scout. The Delaware came forward and stared at the paper. "Here? Here is Black Hawk's base camp?"

"Just there," the Delaware Indian answered. "Bad Ax River."

"For God's sake, Taylor," Atkinson said testily. "What does that gain us? Black Hawk obviously isn't there, is he?"

"No," Taylor said, "but his women and children are."

"So what?" Gaines grumbled. "Are we to attack *them*?"

Colonel Taylor's mouth twitched into a near-smile. "No, sir. But what if Black Hawk thinks we are going to?"

"I don't . . ." Atkinson came to his feet, cigar in hand. He walked to the table and stared at the diagram. "He would fall back, wouldn't he? To protect his tribe."

"Broken Saber?"

The Delaware shrugged. The scout was an enigma to Taylor. He seemed neither pro-American nor anti-Sauk, neither a warrior nor a man of peace. He apparently worked for his wages and nothing more. Yet he had found the Sauk village, if the sorry camp could be called that, and done many more hazardous jobs for the Americans, some beyond the call of duty and beyond the obligations a man had to assume to collect his pay.

"Black Hawk," the Delaware judged, "will fall back to the camp. Black Hawk, he is for his people, for his women and old. Black Hawk if he thinks the camp is under attack, he will retreat there."

Taylor lifted his eyes to Atkinson. "I think so too, General."

"Why should he?" Atkinson asked. "He has us and he knows it. Why retreat to an indefensible position to protect a few squaws and babies?"

"Because," Taylor answered, "he is that sort of man. Would we do anything less if it were our families, our noncombatants?"

"But the man is a savage. They don't think the same way we do," Atkinson contended.

Broken Saber spoke without being spoken to—the only time any of them had heard him do so. "Black Hawk, he will fight. He will go to the camp. He is a man."

"Well?" Taylor asked.

"If it can be a coordinated strike," Gaines said with growing excitement. "What is Scott's position?"

"Ten miles upriver. Moored. If the rain hadn't delayed him, he would be here now."

"But this is fortuitous! If he were already downriver, Black Hawk would be alerted. As it is . . ." Gaines was deeply pleased. "We have him, sir, that is my considered opinion. We finally have the man where we want him. Black Hawk is done."

Atkinson would hold his forces in reserve in case the pincer was evaded by Black Hawk and he took some unpredicted course such as striking out for Chicago. Gaines would march directly toward the newly located Sauk village with his army and militia volunteers, approaching in a long

picket line meant to contain all Sauk attempting to escape.
An ultimatum would then be issued to Black Hawk, who
was expected to draw back to his camp or be cut off from his
noncombatants. Once he was in the camp, Winfield Scott
would close the trap from the river, sealing off the Sauk and
Fox.

Gaines's excitement had faded by the time the meeting was
completed, but not his conviction. "We have him."

Sachim sat with her head down, her eyes closed. Sha-sak
urged her to eat, but it was no use. Nor would the spirit
woman talk. Her grief was deep.

The rain swept in and then blew away again. The camp
remained cold and damp and sorry. When Black Hawk
returned in the late afternoon, they saw how it had gone.
Dozens of warriors were injured, many struck by canister
loads from the American cannon. In the woods, canisters
loaded with shot were much more effective than balls or
even grapeshot. Lead fragments flew in all directions, cutting a bloody swath. Most of the damage had been suffered
during Black Hawk's last raid when one of the American
lieutenants had camouflaged a circle of cannon behind infantry ranks. The infantry had quickly retreated inside the circle
and the gunners had touched off withering fire that crippled
and killed horses and men.

There were cries of sorrow as women searched for their
husbands and sons, and Sachim, shaking herself from her
lethargy, staggered to the war horses, looking for White
Bear, only half-believing that he had survived, that he could
survive. The war was all—it demanded all.

But she saw him and rushed to him, clinging to his neck as
the great Sauk warrior lifted her from the ground and hugged
her as tightly as his massive arms allowed.

"And the child? Where is my baby girl?" White Bear
asked, searching the camp. There was an emptiness in
Sachim's eyes he could not understand at first. She could not
answer him just then, and so she took the giant warrior by
the hand and walked with him deep into the rain-damp
woods, where, nearly an hour later, she told the man what
she had done and again wept deeply as he held her and the
rain began once more.

They came in the morning as Black Hawk had known they

would. Withdrawing from his field position, he had swept back to protect the camp. Gaines's column was advancing with precise menace. It was obvious to the Sauk and Fox leaders that the camp had been discovered.

Pulling back, Black Hawk had fought a trio of sorties intended to discourage Gaines and then attempted to distract the American general with various diversions. Gaines had fallen for none of these tactics, but had continued to march implacably toward the river.

Gaines had flanking forces out to prevent the Sauk from retreating to the north or south, and the pincer was slowly closing, pressing the Indians against the river, which was an effective American ally now.

There was no choice. The Americans were half a day's march away. They had cannon and superior manpower. Black Hawk's decision was the only possible one.

"We will cross the river," he announced.

"The Sioux . . ."

"The Sioux we know. They may war, they may not. The Americans we also know. *They* will war. We cross the river. We cannot fight here, cannot win here, and so we must move on. It must be, it *will* be."

The camp, which had been a morass of inactivity moments before, now became a frenzied anthill of motion, with men and women moving out to cut logs for rafts and packing their few remaining provisions. Sachim worked frantically, lashing logs together, the feeling gnawing at her that this was not enough, that there was no time left for the Sauk.

Distantly they heard gunfire and their heads automatically lifted and turned. "Perhaps the Skull Clan," someone muttered.

It could have been. The Skull Clan wasn't going to stop the march of the Americans either. Nothing was. The river was the Sauk's only hope.

"Oh, no!" Sha-sak cried out, and rose, pointing upriver. The steamboat was no more than half a mile above their position, so near that they could see it was bristling with cannon, the decks crowded with soldiers.

Some of the women began screaming, moaning. Warriors rushed to the beach. Sachim stood staring, looking across the river toward their last chance, the chance now yanked out of their hands by the American gunship.

As the steamship, the *Warrior*, came nearer, Black Hawk

came up beside Sachim. Suddenly he looked terribly old. The war had done this to him, she thought.

"What can we do?" she asked.

"There's nothing."

"The army behind us . . . ?"

"Much too close. They have us circled."

"Then you will fight?" she asked anxiously.

Black Hawk looked around at the old, the very young, the unarmed women. "No," he said. "I will surrender, Sachim."

"Black Hawk!"

"Is there another choice? I have already sent for a flag of truce. We are through—let them be our masters. We can fight no more against this force."

On the riverboat Captain Throckmorton, commander of the *Warrior*, turned at the sound of slowly approaching steps. General Winfield Scott in his full dress uniform acted not only as if he were commander of the boat but undisputed master of all he surveyed. In fact, Throckmorton decided, the tall aristocratic man was exactly that.

"Can you see the camp?" Scott asked.

Throckmorton handed over his brass telescope and pointed. "Beside that inlet."

"Women and children?" Scott asked, turning the lens to focus the telescope better.

"Yes."

"Too bad. I'd like to shell the bastard. I've had the cannon loaded with canisters. Wonder how Black Hawk would like a little of that down his throat."

He lowered the glass and then quickly raised it to his eye again. Something was happening on the shore—exactly what, he couldn't be sure. "Seems to be a group of warriors . . . wait . . . a hundred or more. Detaching themselves from the others."

"Armed?"

"Can't tell. Better signal your helmsman to take us in a little closer . . . waving a white flag."

"A flag of truce?" Throckmorton asked.

"I really can't tell, Captain," Winfield Scott said, closing the brass telescope before handing it back to Throckmorton. "Can you?"

With that, Scott turned his back and walked slowly away up the wide planking of the *Warrior*'s deck. Throckmorton watched the general's back, glanced toward the shore again, and then hastened to the wheelhouse to instruct his pilot.

"The general wants to get in closer. Opposite that group of warriors."

"Ones with the flag of truce?" the helmsman asked. The captain didn't answer. If General Scott couldn't tell what that flag was, Throckmorton had decided to be equally blind. The helmsman said, "We're low on fuel, sir. Steam gauge is way down. Scott was in such an infernal hurry to get downriver. . ."

"Worry about that later!"

"Yes, sir," the boat's pilot said with a shrug. He began turning the polished spoke wheel before him and the *Warrior* paddled its way toward the shore where Black Hawk stood with his unarmed warriors.

"They are coming," White Bear said. "What terms will they demand, Black Hawk?"

"All we have or hope to have," Black Hawk said grimly. "Perhaps my head as well."

"They are slowing in the water. They'll have to put a smaller boat ashore."

Black Hawk nodded again. He was ready. He had accepted defeat, as bitter as it would be. He felt strangely calm, studying the boat, the actions of the men on its deck. Suddenly he stiffened. He reached out and gripped White Bear's arm.

"They're going to fire on us!"

Before the words were out of his mouth the cannon were touched off, six of them at once, and the air was filled with flying lead pellets, with fire and smoke and death. White Bear turned to Black Hawk and then collapsed. His face was half eaten away. Black Hawk felt hot blood streaming down his own chest and when he tried to turn, his right leg gave. Around him his men were dying, writhing on the ground, some horribly mutilated. Other warriors ran for the trees as the cannon spoke again. Black Hawk crouched, trying to drag White Bear to safety, but it was no use. He didn't have the strength to do it.

And it would have been of no help to White Bear. The giant Sauk was dead.

Black Hawk turned once to look at the white boat; then he staggered toward the trees. Someone took his arm and helped him along. Cannon shot pierced the forest, ripping the limbs from the trees, inflicting more injuries as the warriors raced toward the camp.

The camp was vast confusion, with everyone asking questions no one had time to answer. Weapons and war sacks were snatched up, children shouldered, the wounded and halt half-carried as the Sauk ran toward safety deeper in the woods.

Sachim looked around her in panic as she ran. She could not see White Bear anywhere, but in the confusion it would have been remarkable if she had. Still, he would have come to her if he were able.

"Black Hawk!" she shouted. "Black Hawk."

Black Hawk looked toward Sachim and sorrowfully, wearily shook his head. Sachim stumbled, forced herself upright, and ran on. While she was running there was no time to think. While she was running there was no need to mourn.

They halted in a thick grove of vine-wound maple trees. It was dark there, cool. The wounded lay everywhere. Sachim flopped to the ground for two long minutes and then rose to help with the bandaging.

Black Hawk was in a rage. She had never seen him that way before. He was painting his face, filling his quiver with arrows.

"Black Hawk?"

"I have no time to talk—not even to you, little one."

"What are you doing?" she demanded.

"What I must. If I cannot make peace then I will make war." He looked toward the river. "I will make war. Shall I let my people be slaughtered? Shall we go meekly to our graves?"

He turned abruptly and swung aboard his war pony. Followed by his able-bodied warriors, he rode out of the casualty-filled camp at a gallop, his war cry echoing through the trees. Sachim watched until the last warrior was out of sight and then she did all she could do, returned to tending the injured, the dying.

Captain Throckmorton stood at the rail of the *Warrior* watching the burned and battered woods. He could see many bodies on the beach, but not a living Indian anywhere.

Throckmorton glanced away for a moment and when he returned his attention to the beach he saw live Indians, hundreds of them. They broke from the forest like a living storm, their war cries sending a chill up Throckmorton's

back. He heard a small thump and looked to his right to see
a soldier, the top of his head blown away by a musket ball,
topple over the rail and into the river.

Throckmorton ducked and ran toward the wheelhouse,
keeping low. On deck the cannon opened up again, the roar
filling the captain's ears. From the comparative safety of the
wheelhouse Throckmorton watched the battle develop.

Sauk snipers fired on the boat from the woods, their
locations, constantly changing, given away only by puffs of
smoke. Meanwhile a large force of Sauk, swimming their
horses toward the *Warrior*, fired with bows and arrows at
the soldiers on deck, striking their targets with amazingly
deadly frequency.

The cannon, mounted not on swivels, but on plates, couldn't
be brought to bear easily. Gunner after gunner was shot by
Indian marksmen as they tried to reload the six-pounders.
Winfield Scott was in a fury, though what he expected his
men to do that they weren't already doing was beyond
Throckmorton. The general, futile saber in hand, stalked the
deck shouting unheard commands.

"Captain!" the pilot shouted, ducking reflexively as a
musket ball slammed into brightwork behind him. "Captain,
fuel! We're down to the red line on steam, sir."

"Do your best."

"Chief engineer has done his best. We're just plain out of
fuel." Another musket ball sang through the wheelhouse,
tearing splinters from the mahogany wall behind the pilot.
"If we can't backwater, sir, we'll start drifting—and likely
drift right to shore."

Throckmorton looked toward the shore—the last place on
earth he wanted to be. He himself looked at the steam
gauges and watched the dropping needles.

"Dammit all," he snarled. And Throckmorton had to be
the one to tell Scott. The deck of the *Warrior* was a scene of
carnage. In the water a dead pinto pony floated past, followed by its former rider. Throckmorton stepped over the
body of an American soldier and found Scott.

A volley of cannon fire drowned out the general's violent
response and Throckmorton ducked, putting his hands over
his ears.

"No choice, sir," Throckmorton said. "We'll drift to shore
if we lose our head of steam."

"I can see that," Scott said angrily. "Dammit all! Retreat?

Retreat from these savages?" An arrow from nowhere embedded itself in the planking next to Throckmorton's leg
and he was inclined to think that retreat wasn't at all a bad
idea, steam or no steam. Scott half-turned away, his order
not an order at all but the comment, "Do what you have to
do, then."

Throckmorton made his way back to the wheelhouse and
told the worried pilot. Sauk along the shore followed the
Warrior for a mile downstream, sniping, reloading, running
after them again. Those in the water had long ago given up
the attack, and after another mile the snipers on shore too
were gone. Throckmorton took out his stubby pipe and lit it
with trembling hands.

"I'll be in my cabin," he said to the pilot.

"Have one for me too," the man answered. Throckmorton
grinned and started below, trying not to look too closely at
the dead and wounded. When he reached his cabin he shut
the door behind him, closing out the worst of the screams
and tortured moans. Then he opened his brandy and took a
deep drink to calm his nerves. Remembering, he took one
for the pilot as well and then sank into his padded chair to
stare at his river charts without really seeing them.

"Cannon fire. Scott's opened up on Black Hawk," the
sergeant reported to General Atkinson.

Atkinson had ears as well and he answered impatiently,
"Yes, dammit!" Scott had attacked without informing him in
advance. Gaines was there at the river, and he himself was
left in the rear as a reserve. The hell with that! "Forced
march, sergeant. Leave the cannon, leave all supplies but
ammunition. I'm not going to be left out of this now."

It was a ten-mile march to the river, but Atkinson wasn't
to be deterred. Under his encouragement his men broke
from their walk and into a jogging run, muskets in hand,
stripped of packs and nonessential gear. With any luck . . .

Black Hawk's warriors, weary and wounded, sagged to the
earth in the cold forest. Bow and arrows, muskets, were
simply cast aside. The exhaustion for many was total. Still,
they had won a victory, a great victory. Black Hawk drew
Sachim aside.

"I am sorry . . . White Bear was a great warrior. Now,

Sachim, we must solidify our gains—before the whites return. Are the women capable of making rafts again?"

"If it must be done."

"The river must be crossed, and it must be done now," Black Hawk answered. "Who knows when that boat may return, or other boats arrive. Who knows when the American army may find us? It must be done." His voice was hoarse with weariness and emotion. "The river must be crossed, no matter what awaits us on the far side."

"I will see what can be done."

"Sachim?" He touched her shoulder lightly. "Have you dreamed of this time? What will happen?"

The far-dreamer could only turn away. She couldn't bear to answer him. The dream must be a lie! This one time it must be wrong. With effort, with courage, they could overcome that terrible dream. She needed to believe it.

But again the image came, a fleeting image. A river of blood.

With Sha-sak she started toward the river. Neither woman spoke. Both were too tired, drained by the events of the day. Sachim had a sudden vivid memory of White Bear, of his good, boyish ways, belied by his massive warrior's exterior, of the way he had so gratefully slept with her, watching her as if it were not every man's right to have a woman to comfort him, but a gift from Manitou; and she cried.

She lifted her eyes to the far shore again, seeing in her mind the far Sioux village—*that* she had done right. It had been necessary, however painful. This night Little Raindrop would sleep warm and well-fed, and if she was suffering in her heart, that would pass. Heart Song was a good woman, and Yellow Sky, despite his many faults and wooden manner, was a man of position, a good hunter and strong protector.

But still the tears came, and bitterly Sachim wiped them away. The women had good steel trade axes to work with and they carried these along. Sachim glanced at her ax, turning the hickory handle, thinking she would have preferred the old way to having white steel. Once they had girdled their trees with mud and then set fire to them, chipping away the burned wood before burning them again. It was a slow process, yet it had been their way, and when the tree fell it brought a small thrill to the heart. Once they had gathered rice and the men had separated it, singing as they worked; once there had been crane dances and the moccasin game with the children searching for the pebble hidden in one of the shoes. Once there had been maple-sugar candy . . . and a future, and promise, and love. Once there had been good and glorious dreams.

"This one, this dead one," Sha-sak said, tapping on the trunk of the birch. "We—"

The shot interrupted Sha-sak. The women stood immobile for a long minute. Then a second shot followed on the heels of the first. A third, a dozen, a hundred following shots rang in Sachim's ears. The women dropped their axes and raced back toward the camp.

Before they could reach it, they were met by fleeing Sauk running toward the river. People shouted, "Swim! Reach the far shore!"

Sachim halted, turned in bewilderment, and then started after the others, Sha-sak gripping her hand as they ran. Looking across her shoulders, Sachim saw the first of the American soldiers emerge from the woods.

They were young—that was what astonished her—very young, beardless men, some of them appearing very frightened. But they knelt and fired and the Sauk fell. Sachim picked up a rock and hurled it at a soldier.

"Run, run . . ." Sha-sak shouted, yanking Sachim around. And then the musket ball entered Sha-sak's back and emerged below her breast. The stout woman fell, her mouth filling with blood as she tried to speak. Sachim ran on, toward the river, the Life-giver, the Protector.

Atkinson came onto the beach, still mounted on his gray horse. Victory elated him. He had the bastard Black Hawk. *He*, not Gaines, not Winfield Scott.

"Fire at will, fire at will!" Atkinson yelled nearly continuously.

His soldiers complied.

Women and children fleeing into the river were shot down, some on the beach, others in the water itself as they tried to swim to the distant far shore. Children bobbed facedown in the water and the river swirled with red.

Atkinson charged on, his gray horse rearing as he waved his saber overhead. Gunsmoke drifted through the air, acrid and dark as the muzzle flashes of his soldiers' muskets winked brightly.

The river raged past; the Sauk continued to try to escape

into it—their only avenue of escape, but an impossible one. General Atkinson continued to shout the order, "Fire at will!"

The battle was brief, half an hour at the most. When it ended two hundred dead Sauk, men, women, and children were counted. Only twenty American soldiers had died, Atkinson was satisfied to note. Ten-to-one casualties. His career was made.

"Do we bury them, sir?" one powder-blackened, grizzled soldier with an Alabama accent asked.

"What for?" Atkinson asked with genuine surprise.

"They're people, sir."

Atkinson didn't bother to answer. They weren't people. They were Indians.

Black Hawk's body wasn't among the dead. The devil had escaped again. *That* was the sole thorn in the crown of achievement Atkinson had assumed.

"He *has* to be here. The bastard has to be here," Atkinson said as he turned over Sauk and Fox bodies with his foot.

But the Sauk war chief was not there, and Atkinson could only fume that the capping touch on his victory had somehow been lost. Later in the evening as he waited for Winfield Scott's return, he reversed his own order.

"They're starting to stink," the general said. "Plant them."

17

SLEET fell through the darkness, spiraling down from the lost and angry sky. Sachim supported Black Hawk as they walked onward toward a last sanctuary, the Winnebago village at Prairie La Crosse, Wisconsin. "There," Black Hawk said, "Blue Ears will see that he must give me soldiers. We shall rest for a while, Sachim, and then we shall attack again. We shall avenge ourselves. We shall attack and reclaim our lands—and this time I will not deal so lightly with Keokuk, believe me." But even Black Hawk did not seem to believe this would or could happen. The world had become a place without promise, with only defeat and darkness.

Sachim helped the limping war leader along toward the distant Winnebago village, her ears open, her mind shut. She had managed to keep herself from thinking—about Little Raindrop, White Bear, Thunder Horse, Sha-sak, the Sauk homeland. She did not want to think, did not want to dream, did not want to remember or project her hopes.

She walked as they had walked for a week; she felt the sleet. She breathed in and out. That was all there was to do, and it was of as much use as screaming, crying, dreaming, loving, or making war. Useless. All of it, useless.

The man on her arm twitched, with pain presumably, and Sachim studied his face in the darkness. Could he really be well past sixty? Not Black Hawk! Could time move on like this, indifferent to the wishes it left behind, to the times and places, the people abandoned to its whims?

Sachim did not regret the way time seemed to swirl away—it was the dreams it had left behind. Hope and passion and youth and love all seemed gone and there was nothing left at all; not even the people had survived. The *people*.

Well, then, had Keokuk been proven right?

No, she decided firmly. It was his own personal dream that had destroyed Black Hawk and in the end destroyed the lifetime of the Sauk.

Keokuk was wealthy. He would live comfortably to the end of his days, but there would be no future generations. None with the freedom to plot their own course, to live as they wished. Time and Keokuk had conspired against them, and the evil that had been done in the name of comfort ensured that never again would a proud, free Sauk walk the long land.

Night deepened and the sleet turned to snow. They came upon the Winnebago village and smelled the meat roasting over smoky fires, the fish and corn soup. Black Hawk slipped his arm from Sachim's and straightened himself with difficulty.

"It is not seemly," he said; and they walked on toward the lodge of Blue Ears.

The Winnebago was an old friend of Black Hawk's. Many years they had hunted together, and frequently they had picked up the war hatchet against a common enemy. But those times were gone and if Blue Ears accorded Black Hawk every courtesy, he was restrained, nervous in fact.

The tale of the war to the south did nothing to ease Blue Ears's anxiety. "I will return, or course," Black Hawk said. "I will punish the invaders. With the help of the Winnebago and the—"

"My friend, my friend, my good and very old friend, Ma-ka-tai-me-she-kia-kiak," Blue Ears said heavily. "Do you not see now that it is over? Do you not see that there will be no new allies for you? Not among the Fox, not among the Kickapoo."

"Among the Winnebago—"

"No," Blue Ears said, shaking his head, "not among the Winnebago. You walk an ancient dream, Black Hawk. The time you wish for is gone; the dream is dead."

"I see. I am then a fool," Black Hawk said.

"Not a fool. A man out of time. A man walking alone. The Americans are here. We will deal with them as we dealt with the Spanish, the French, the British."

"Then you are all fools!" Black Hawk said hotly. "The Americans are not here for a day. They have not come to trade or trap and then pass away. They have come to stay—to build, to populate the land. And so we, all of us—Sauk, Winnebago, Sioux—must go. For all time."

Blue Ears was offended and he couldn't hide it. He rose and paced the lodge for a minute angrily. "Then we are fools," he said at last. "But we survive. Where is the Sauk nation? Dead. War was made, foolish war. I must ask you to leave now, Black Hawk. Leave or be arrested."

"Arrested?" Black Hawk half-laughed, but Blue Ears was utterly serious.

"You bring trouble to my people. If you are found here, then we are the guilty ones in the eyes of the Americans. *We will not fight them.* Nor will any people, not after your lesson to us. Can you not see, Black Hawk, you have destroyed yourself, your people. We cannot have you destroy us! You are a renegade upon the earth. You have no people, no friends."

"I see," Black Hawk said, his lips barely moving.

"You do not see! Old debts, old promises, old oaths—all are gone or going. You wish to remain here, to raise an army. But you cannot win. It is foolishness, Black Hawk! You are growing old and foolish at once. You have fought for your people, to protect them all these years. Well, now to fight is to condemn them to death, to slavery at least. It is Keokuk in the end who knew which way the river ran.

"You have done what you could for your people. Very well, now I must do what I can for mine. Go, for you are a criminal. Go, or I myself will send for the Americans. It must be so, it must be so."

The snow had stopped. Black Hawk went out into the night and stood there shivering. He knew without looking that Sachim was there beside him, as she had always been.

"I must give myself up," Black Hawk said, still refusing to look at Sachim.

"You must not!"

"Yes. Where can I go? I have no friends on this earth. The Sauk may be treated better if I surrender, if I take sole responsibility for what happened."

Sachim had no answer for Black Hawk. In her heart she felt that he was right. She wanted nothing less than for Black Hawk to be imprisoned—or executed—but perhaps it was the only way left. One man's life for the welfare of a people.

"You will go, Sachim," Black Hawk said. "Go to Prairie

du Chien, there are soldiers there. Ask them what guarantees they will give for the people if I surrender."

Still he did not look at her. His face, sharply silhouetted against the starry sky, still handsome, was determined.

"I will go if you wish it," Sachim said.

"It must be," he said, and then he walked slowly away, his head held high, his shoulders back, and she knew what he was thinking. He was looking back, back to the river, back to earlier times, seeing his life flow past, wishing now only to assure the Sauk of future times a good life; as he had always wished for it, fought for it.

The fort was loosely constructed. Unbarked log buildings rambled across the interior yard. Soldiers lazed around, their heads turning as the young woman in buckskins walked past them toward the headquarters building.

Sachim walked up the steps and entered. Three soldiers were inside. She spoke to the one behind the desk.

"I wish to see whoever is in charge."

"Look, lady," the sergeant said, "the Indian-affairs officer—"

"I come from Black Hawk," Sachim interrupted.

"You what!"

"May I see the soldier in charge?"

The sergeant hesitated, glanced at his commanding officer's door, and then nodded. "Just a minute."

General Street was tugging on a boot when the sergeant rapped at his door. Muttering a curse, he stamped his foot down into his boot and shouted, "Enter!"

"Sorry, sir. There's a squaw out here says she's from Black Hawk."

"Black Hawk?" The most wanted man in the territory had generated a search involving a thousand soldiers for the last month and now a woman simply appeared at Prairie du Chien and announced that she had seen the man. "Don't let her leave!"

The sergeant waited while the general tucked his shirt in and put his tunic on; then he showed Sachim into the general's office.

She entered, tossed her head, and stood staring at General Street. Somehow he had expected this slender woman to be cowed by him, to turn her eyes down, wring her hands, but she was not what he had expected. She was strong, this one. The woman had no doubt seen and endured much. Black Hawk would send no puppet to do his talking. Street offered a courtesy nod and stepped nearer.

"The sergeant says Black Hawk sent you."

"He wishes to surrender," Sachim said.

"He . . . wishes to surrender. To me. Here?"

"Yes. It is that simple. Yet he wants assurances."

"What sort of assurances?" Street asked warily.

"That his people will no longer be tormented. That the surrender of Black Hawk will end hostilities. That they will be resettled on their land, on any land that they may hold without interference, where the hunting is good, where the water is good."

"I can't make those assurances." Street, biting at his upper lip, retreated to his desk and sat down, playing with his paper knife, a tiny ebony dirk. "Not on my own. I'll have to talk to the governor. General Scott will be involved, I'm sure. Have him come in . . ."

"He must have these assurances," Sachim insisted.

Street was thoughtful, silent. "Very well, I agree. Tell Black Hawk I will see to it. Tell him if he surrenders and agrees never to raise a weapon against the United States of America again, he may return home with his people and live in peace."

"So it will be?" Sachim asked cautiously.

"So it will be." Street managed a smile. He had the authority to promise nothing, but he was damned if he was going to let Black Hawk get away. There would certainly be another star in his future if he could pull this off. "Tell Black Hawk to surrender himself in three days. In this office." Street tapped the desk with his letter opener and rose. "You can trust me," he said gratuitously, but Sachim just shook her head sadly and turned away.

She nearly walked into Lieutenant Jefferson Davis arriving with a report from regimental headquarters. He stepped aside and turned his head curiously to watch her exit.

"Sauk, isn't she?" Davis asked.

Street, beaming, indicated that the door should be closed. Then he proceeded to tell Davis about the coup he had pulled off.

Black Hawk listened to Sachim's report without expression. "I will go then," he said.

"You trust this man's word, Black Hawk? For myself, I did not believe him."

"I shall go. It must be done."

Blue Ears was relieved if uneasy. "I am sorry, my friend. Truly sorry."

"You did not make this come to pass, Blue Ears."

"If I could . . . The women have made you a gift. A white deerskin robe with much beadwork. It is a sign of the friendship in our hearts. It would be an honor to the Winnebago if you would wear it when you council with the whites."

"Very well," Black Hawk said. His attention, Blue Ears noticed, wandered, as if Black Hawk were indifferent to all of this, as if he had seen his life's purpose flutter away and with it his great heart. There had to be something left to say, but what it was, Blue Ears did not know. He touched Black Hawk's shoulder briefly and went away, wondering for a single moment if the Sauk leader had not been right, if even as Black Hawk's way had gone, the time might not soon come when the Winnebago, the Sioux, the Kickapoo way might vanish. But Blue Ears did not wish to dwell on that, to admit that he might have abandoned not only his friend but also his own people.

General Street, Jefferson Davis thought, was going to burst the copper buttons off his uniform if he inflated any more. Well, why not? Gaines, Atkinson, Scott had all tried for weeks to track the Sauk leader down and had failed. Now Black Hawk had simply fallen into Street's lap. Davis, after his service with Atkinson, knew that the brigadier general would be fuming, cursing his luck. His pursuit of a second star was obsessive; even his successful strike against the Sauk forces hadn't assured his promotion.

There was a murmuring along the stockade wall and then a shout from a soldier. "Here he comes!"

Davis turned toward the gate, standing beside and a pace behind General Street. Now Davis too could see the man. He walked like a prince, a long white deerskin robe over his shoulders, roached hair colored with ocher, a necklace of silver around his neck. Beside him walked the woman Davis had seen in Street's office.

Black Hawk entered the fort with dignity, perhaps with disdain. He crossed to where Street waited. Soldiers moved nearer, silently, drawn by the impact of the moment, the historical weight of it, or perhaps by the magnetism of the man himself.

"I am Black Hawk," the Sauk war leader said to General Street.

Street's answer was brief. "Lieutenant Davis. Have the prisoner placed in irons."

"Sir?" Davis was stunned.

"Irons, sir. You do hear me?"

"Yes, sir. Sergeant?"

Sachim stood staring at the general, who was self-satisfied, smug. Black Hawk was expressionless. Perhaps he had expected nothing else.

"I have surrendered myself," the Sauk war leader said. "Do you think I will now run away?"

Street replied loudly, for the benefit of his gathered soldiers, "I do not know, sir, what you might wish to do—but by God, I promise you you will not flee."

The sergeant, running toward Black Hawk, held a set of irons aloft. He placed them on Black Hawk's wrists and ankles as the Sauk stood docilely before the general.

"Where are my chains?" Sachim asked. "Will you not chain me too, you deceitful warrior?"

"Of course not." Street seemed genuinely shocked. "You may go on your way, woman."

"My way," Sachim answered, "is the way of Black Hawk."

"As you will have it," Street said airily. "See that the woman too is given a cell, Lieutenant Davis." Street saluted the company in general, and then, well-pleased with himself, retreated to his office to prepare self-congratulatory reports of his capture of the West's most wanted renegade.

The soldier was gentle as he guided Sachim into her cell and closed the oaken door, but still she hated him. She hated them all, these invaders, conquerors, liars, killers. She stood still for a long while staring at the walls of her cell and then she sat on the bed provided, a bunk supported by two iron chains embedded in the wall. From time to time she could hear Black Hawk moving around in his adjoining cell, his leg irons clanking against the stone floor.

In the morning Sachim heard the whistle from the river and an hour later the soldiers came to take her to the boat. "Black Hawk . . . ?" she asked.

"Don't worry about that, lady. He's going along for sure."

"The boat will take us home?" Sachim asked, looking from one guard to the other. "As the general promised."

"Don't know, lady," the mustached man answered. "Our job's to take you to the boat. What the general promised, I got no idea."

Each man took an arm, and Sachim was led out into the brilliant sunlight. Lieutenant Davis stood waiting, his shoulders slightly hunched. The wind was cold. It would snow again, the winter storms coming across Lake Superior to invade the Sauk land with cold.

"Sir." The mustached soldier saluted. Davis glanced at the woman prisoner and nodded.

"We'll go on down."

"Black Hawk?" Sachim asked again.

"He's coming," Davis answered, and then Sachim saw him. Led by three men, still wearing his chains, Black Hawk was being brought onto the parade ground from his cell. On the plankwalk in front of the military headquarters building General Street stood watching, rocking on his heels.

"We are going home?" Sachim asked the lieutenant, but he did not answer.

"Let's go," he said to his soldiers instead. "The *Winnebago* will have her fuel on by now."

"Winnebago?" Sachim said.

"Yes, miss. That's the steamer's name," the lieutenant answered. An unexpected, ironic smile touched Sachim's lips and she shook her head, walking forward to follow Black Hawk to the dock.

On board they were locked up again and placed under guard. Through a small round porthole Sachim could look out at the river, which glittered in the sunlight. It flowed away southward; it flowed away.

They steamed southward all day and into the night and Sachim's hopes began to rise. Perhaps they were going home after all. The country grew more familiar. There was the Maquoketa with its many caves and spirits, there the Long Plain. Just at sundown they passed the mouth of the Wapsipinicon. On the opposite shore, though she could not see it, was the Crow Meadow. The land was Sauk, and distantly she saw smoke which could have been from Keokuk's camp.

The whites had not lied then. They had not lied. . . . If they were released, a peace signed, then she could journey

to the Sioux camp, perhaps within the week. She could find
Little Raindrop and bring her home.

The steamer continued on, its paddles slapping insultingly
against the face of the Mississippi as the sky darkened and
the river went black.

An hour later the boat stopped. Sachim felt it butt up
against something and she rushed back to the porthole,
peering out, seeing nothing. She thought they must be at
Rock Island, but why? Perhaps here Black Hawk must sign
his surrender papers. Her mind whirled with fears, hopes,
expectations, doubts, with joy and anger, each emotion tangled with the next as they passed in hasty procession.

It seemed forever before the soldiers came. Sachim eagerly followed them out on deck. She felt deep relief; the
night air was cold, but it smelled of the river, of times past,
of the empty land and woodsmoke.

Her guess had been correct—they had put in at Rock
Island, where a fort, Fort Armstrong, had been constructed.
By torchlight she and Black Hawk, still in chains, were
taken toward a low structure which was well-lighted, well-
guarded. Inside, General Winfield Scott and his adjutants
waited.

"So," Scott greeted his old adversary, "it appears your
time has come, Black Hawk."

"My time," Black Hawk responded, "has gone."

Scott frowned and then chuckled. "Quite right, old man.
Come and gone. You took on someone too big for you,
didn't you?"

"I made war on time," Black Hawk said, but Scott didn't
understand or take the time to try to. He looked at Sachim
and then demanded of Jefferson Davis, "What is the woman
doing here?"

"I understand she is his adviser, sir."

"Damn right." The speaker was Captain Monique. "And
the cause of all of this, sir. That is his so-called spirit woman,
the one who communes with the spirits, the one who advised
him to make his great war."

"Is this true?" General Scott asked Sachim.

"I dream," she said quietly.

"And you advised Black Hawk to make war?"

"I dreamed and the dream was of war," she answered,
knowing there was no point in trying to explain further.

"Very well, no matter," Scott said. "Why you could not

have followed Keokuk down a peaceful road, I don't pretend to understand," Winfield Scott said. "He too, they tell me, has a prophet. But his prophet must be a true dreamer, for he dreamed of peace and Keokuk made peace. Now he is well, now he is our friend. Now his people live without fear or want."

Scott lit a cigar on a candle. Then he turned and said, "Reparations are in order, Black Hawk." He showed the Sauk a rolled sheet of parchment. "These are the demands of the United States of America: 'To the United States the Sauk nation and the nation of the Fox as well as the Winnebago who demonstrated their hostility by sheltering the criminal, Black Hawk, these mentioned tribes agree to cede the territory below described, totaling ten million, six hundred thousand acres of land. For this the above-mentioned tribes will receive from the government of the United States twenty thousand dollars a year for thirty years in addition to a forty-square-mile permanent reservation on the Iowa River—hereinafter described . . .'"

Scott paused. "Shall I review these terms?"

Black Hawk shook his head. "What have we to bargain with? As it is, it is."

"You should know that Keokuk has agreed readily to these terms already. He is a forward-looking man, Black Hawk. He knows that the time is gone when the Indian needs vast empty tracts of land to live comfortably."

"Yes," Black Hawk said carefully.

"A further stipulation is explained in this paragraph: 'It is decreed by the Congress of the United States that the Sauk shall henceforth be construed and administered as a single tribe without separate bands and subchiefs. All of the Sauk nation shall be under the leadership and administration of a single chief, the man known as Keokuk.' Do you understand this paragraph, Black Hawk?"

"Yes. I understand it," the war leader answered.

"And you agree?"

"How can I not?"

"Very well. You will then sign this document?"

"Yes." Black Hawk made his sign on the parchment—a small sparrow hawk winging away across the yellow treaty.

Scott appeared relieved. "Fine. Then it is done. You will serve your term here and be treated well, I assure you."

"My *term*? Imprisonment? I was told I could go home."

Scott laughed. "Not just yet. It's taken us this long to capture you; I don't think anyone is quite ready to turn you loose to see what sort of hell you can raise."

"I have given my word. You have given yours," Black Hawk said.

"Sorry," Scott responded, slipping the ribbon back onto the rolled parchment. "You made a mistake, old man. You should never have lifted your war ax against the United States. You were bound to lose, you know. Bound to lose all along. Your spirit woman here should have told you that, Black Hawk."

"But you see," Black Hawk answered, "she did."

Sachim and Black Hawk were led from the room, leaving Winfield Scott to stare after them, wondering. He shook off his speculative mood in moments, turned and opened his brandy decanter, and drank a toast to victory.

18

THE days, the weeks, the months passed with intolerable sameness. There was cornmeal mush for breakfast and weak tea, an exercise period in the yard when all the bored and curious soldiers stood watching Sachim make as many rounds of the fort as time allowed, sometimes calling out things she pretended not to hear. Lunch was invariably beef and potatoes followed by three dark hours until the next exercise period, then a supper of rice and cheese.

The days then were not cruelly unbearable—it was the nights, those long seemingly endless nights when she could not sleep and did not dare to dream but stood at her barred window craning her neck to see the river, trying to see beyond it to the far plains where her baby girl grew and learned and perhaps began to forget.

Newspapermen came to see Black Hawk, one of them bringing a copy of a Chicago issue with a print of Black Hawk in full regalia riding a prancing, wide-nostriled war pony.

Black Hawk was exciting to Easterners—a cunning war leader, demagogue, hero, feathered knight, or bloody savage, depending on which writer had been at work.

Black Hawk was bewildered by the attention the press gave him, but he spoke with dignity to them, his voice quieter now, sometimes cracked. He was nearly seventy years old, Sachim realized, and she who had always been a child beside him was no longer so young herself.

"They say," Black Hawk told her derisively during one of their visits, "that I am a *hero*. I ask you—how can I now be a

hero? They say that I am one of the most famous men in
their country. I cannot understand this." He shook his head.
"They have not even told the truth about me. How can I be
famous because of false legends."

He could not understand it, nor could Sachim, but it was
true. The newsmen continued to come, from Philadelphia
and Chicago, from St. Louis and Washington, from New York
and Baltimore. It was inexplicable to Sachim, until one day,
thinking it over carefully, she realized the truth.

Black Hawk was a great foe, a powerful warrior, a leader
of men, and yet the young country to the east had defeated
him. The young country, flexing its muscles, was marching
westward, and no opposition, no matter how strong, could
deny it its destiny. Black Hawk was a symbol of that senti-
ment, a symbol—through his defeat—of the strength of America and its leaders. His prowess was publicized so that the
Americans could brag that their prowess was greater; his
sagacity and strength, the size of his army, were all embellished
so that the Americans could proudly declare that they had
beaten this giant.

She understood that; yet even Sachim was astonished when
the young yellow-haired captain opened her door one day
and announced:

"You're going on a long trip, lady. If you need anything,
tell me. We'll bring a dressmaker in and you'll want some
new boots."

"I am going . . . home?"

"No. From what they tell me, lady, you're going to Washington, D.C. President Jackson wants to meet you."

"The white leader! Why?"

"You're have to ask Old Hickory. Me, I can't figure it and
don't try to."

Jackson wasn't unknown to Sachim—she too read the
white papers. He was an Indian fighter. He had fought the
Creek in the South and the Seminole in distant Florida. In
between he had won a battle against the British at New
Orleans. He was hardly the man to admire Black Hawk.

Or maybe just the sort of man.

The journey was long; by wagon and steamboat and at
times by railroad they traveled east, and Black Hawk watched
with awe as they traveled deeper into white territory. There
were many people. Thousands upon thousands, great cities
and factories, endless fields, and everywhere soldiers.

"We could never have won. Never, even with the Sioux," he said. "This is the future; we are there."

In a room in a big white house, one called the Blue Room, Sachim and Black Hawk sat and waited for the great leader of the Americans.

When he came he was shorter than Sachim had imagined, but his face was craggy. He had squinted into many suns, this one, seen pain, and taken blood.

He too was a warrior.

Andrew Jackson approached Black Hawk, looked measuringly at him for a long while, and then asked him to rise. The two men shook hands. The handshake lasted a long while. Perhaps they knew each other, these two warriors, both scarred, both nearly seventy years old, both tried in combat.

"I know your name, Black Hawk," Jackson said. "Now I know your face."

"I know your face from medallions," Black Hawk answered. "Now I know the man. I am a man," the Sauk war leader said, "you are another. We did not expect to conquer the whites. They had too many houses, too many men. I took up the hatchet for my part, to revenge injuries which my people could no longer endure. I say no more of it; it is known to you. I have heard that Keokuk was once here; you took him by the hand and allowed him to return home. You were willing. Black Hawk expects that like Keokuk we shall be permitted to return to our home.

"I have grown old; I do no wish to die in a far land. This woman has done no wrong; she wishes only for her home and her child."

"Well?" The attorney general was Benjamin Butler of New York. He looked to the president, who was peering at a glass of Kentucky bourbon held to the light in the Oval Office.

"What's your thinking, Ben?" Jackson asked in response.

"The man's still dangerous."

"You think so? He's getting on, Ben."

"Not much older than you, sir," Butler said, and the president winced.

Lewis Cass of Ohio was secretary of war. He agreed with Butler. "Suppose the man still has the legendary powers some of our lurid tabloids pretend he has, sir. It is still an unsettled situation out west. If Black Hawk *could* raise a multitribal army now, what then? Politically it is very unwise. Settlers in the new territories would be hard put to understand why this firebrand was returned to his old region just as they begin sinking plows into virgin soil."

Jackson was thoughtful and silent, standing before the snapping fireplace. "I believe the man," he said at last. "I believe him when he says he only wants to return home to live out his last years. Perhaps," the president said quietly, "it is because that is what *this* old war horse has begun to look forward to." He watched the fire again until an ember popped against the brass screen. "Still, I suppose you are both right. Much of the public wants nothing less than Black Hawk's head. Relatives of those lost in the war have difficulty understanding why the Sauk lives.

"We will see . . . we will see."

"Temporarily?"

"Fort Monroe, I think," Jackson said, finishing his drink. "Now, then, what did the Dutch ambassador have to complain about during special session?"

They returned then to prison, Sachim and Black Hawk. Black Hawk could not understand why he had been freed in the first place, and now could not understand why he had been placed back in jail. He grew silent and accepting of everything that was done to him; he communicated little even with Sachim, and she watched as that brightly burning fire began to go out in his dark eyes.

Sachim endured. She had to endure. Her daughter was out there somewhere and she needed Little Raindrop, perhaps needed her more than the growing girl now needed a mother. What else had she left? No father or mother, grandmother or husband—perhaps not even a people. But she had Thunder Horse's daughter. The girl was safe. She would endure until they could meet again.

It was almost a year to the day later when Sachim's cell was opened and a familiar man stood with two jailers peering into the darkness out of the sunlight.

"Yes, that's right," the soldier said. It was General Atkinson who spoke. "Pack her in with Black Hawk—see that she's cleaned up first, of course."

Sachim glowered. The general, spinning on a heel, strode away and she asked the young sergeant with the freckles,

"What is this now? Now are we going to return home, Black Hawk and I?"

"Got me," the young man answered. "Far's I know, the general's taking you on a tour."

"A tour?"

"That's all I know. Miss . . . ma'am . . . shall I bring you some fresh water?"

"Yes," Sachim said with resignation. Wherever they were going, she would need to be clean; wherever they went, it would be better than this tiny cell where a year of Sachim's life had been wasted. "Please bring water."

They left Fort Monroe in a coach guarded by six cavalry soldiers. General Atkinson rode inside with them, wrinkling his nose frequently.

"There's a great public interest in you, Black Hawk," Atkinson told him, "and in this spirit woman of yours. We're going to show you off. Partly as an example to other wild Indians, you understand? It won't hurt a bit in recruiting militia for the western states either, take it from me."

"As you will have it," Black Hawk said, lifting a hand which Sachim noticed trembled a bit.

"New York—you've heard of it?" At Black Hawk's nod Atkinson went on enthusiastically. "We're having a reception for you at the Exchange Hotel. Formal affair. Almost as if you were the head of a foreign nation," the general added with an irony Sachim didn't bother to point out.

They became curiosities again. Black Hawk and Sachim were taken to banquets and press meetings, fed and pampered. Wild things brought back from the West to surprise and delight Eastern audiences.

If it was better than prison, it was still no real life at all— being a museum piece. Again and again Black Hawk would tell his host, "I only want to go home, to walk the river valley, and be in peace." Yet it seemed they would never be allowed that simple wish. The tour continued.

It was five months later before Atkinson, sporting a new beard, approached them and announced, "You've got your wish, Black Hawk. We're sending you west."

"Home?" Black Hawk asked with dim hope.

"Perhaps after a while. Meantime you'll make a tour of the old battlefields—the reporters will be along—you can describe just how you were defeated. We've scheduled a banquet in Detroit, another in Chicago. You won't go hungry, I assure you."

The return to the West was as much a disaster as the Eastern tour had been a triumph. In the West the war was still too near and Black Hawk was not so much a heroic figure as a pagan enemy.

One night in Detroit Sachim watched out her hotel window as Black Hawk was burned in effigy in the center of the main street, sparks flying high into the dark sky, bright but quickly fading. The army guarded Black Hawk with twenty soldiers on that night and the banquet planned for the next day was forgotten.

At Green Bay it was worse. White troops had to protect their route to Chicago by force of arms as rioting Americans screamed for Black Hawk's blood.

Atkinson gave in. "It's ended, Black Hawk. I've gotten a dispatch from the War Department. The tour's canceled."

"Yes?" Black Hawk responded tonelessly. His gnarled hands were wrapped around the mahogany armrests of the green leather chair in his Chicago hotel room.

"You're going to go home," the general said, "and I can't say I'm sorry the spectacle has ended. For myself, I have had enough."

Black Hawk didn't hear the second half of the short speech. He was going home! That was enough. That was all.

"It is true?" Sachim asked the general with rising hope, with concomitant fear. "We are going home to the river?"

Atkinson answered impatiently, "Yes. That's right. There's nothing more useful you two can accomplish. The army has other priorities now. With the Sioux war heating up—"

"The Sioux?" Sachim asked anxiously.

"That's right. Recalcitrant people. By God, we will push them north and west. They stand in our way, woman. And they will be moved if it takes ten years or fifty. It will be done."

19

THE river was cool and dark and constant, an unending dream, a constant warrior. It was there that all life began, there that life ended.

In the camp of Keokuk, the old warrior Black Hawk was an embarrassment, a scarcely remembered legend among the young, a symbol of a futile past to the old.

The Sauk were well and growing wealthier. The year before, yet more land, twenty-six million acres, had been sold for three cents an acre. There was nothing left now to sell; there was only the reservation where Black Hawk wandered in dreams as the summer days grew shorter.

The white town had grown. Barns, stores, a blacksmith's shop, a school, all had been built along the river. All of that was of no interest to Black Hawk. He seemed content just to be among his people again.

Sachim had one obsession—her daughter. Out there in the Sioux lands Little Raindrop lived and played and dreamed. They heard tales of whites warring with the Sioux. They never came to the river anymore. Sachim had been told that Yellow Sky's band was far north, in Dakota.

Major Monique was in charge of the reservation. He was the same slightly cruel man he had always been. When Sachim went to visit him at the fort he was in his office, boots on his desk, tunic unbuttoned. He didn't rise and only managed to look disgusted that Sachim should interrupt him.

"What is it, woman?" Monique asked sourly.

"I have come to ask you again if I may go look for my child," Sachim said.

"You know you and Black Hawk are confined to the reservation. Why can't you get that through your head? Do you think the army can have you wandering around the country doing God knows what?"

"I only want to look for my child."

"No. I can't have it. You and Black Hawk ought to consider yourselves lucky to be alive." His feet went to the floor and he rubbed his forehead. "All in all, the government's been lenient with you, woman."

"Still, my baby—"

"If that baby meant so much to you, you should damn well have kept it with you instead of making war with Black Hawk!" Monique shouted. "You know the rules. Quit coming over here and bothering me."

Sachim had known what Monique's answer would be; still she had to try. She could have slipped off the reservation any night, she knew, but what would that mean for Black Hawk? Would they suspect some new conspiracy and lock him away? At his age he couldn't endure that.

Nor did she know with certainty where Little Raindrop was. Just out there somewhere on the plains. And if she found her daughter, what then? She could never bring her back to the reservation; they could not live with the Sioux. Sachim could only wait and hope and watch the river flow.

Black Hawk died the following month in his sleep.

Only then did Sachim really believe it was over, all hope for the future of the Sauk, the war, and her own time. Sachim washed his body herself and dressed him in white elkskins. He wore his bear-claw necklace and his silver bracelet when they buried him.

Long after everyone had gone, Sachim stood at the grave beneath the old oak and stared at nothing, her thoughts, her heart returning to other times and places, to the deaths of other men, the good and evil men she had known, to the old who had passed away and the too-young, friends, enemies, those she had never known by face or name. They now walked different trails beyond the sky.

She shook her head and whispered, "Greet Thunder Horse for me. Greet White Bear and Grandmother."

She turned then and walked away from the deep shadows of the great oak and with the cold wind at her back traveled along the river toward the reservation. A man had gone; a time had passed away.

As the world had altered, so had her dreams. She dreamed not of the river now but of Thunder Horse calling to her from the lodge in the skies, and of the little one. Beyond the river of her dreams were the long plains—and the tiny one, laughing, dancing, growing stronger beneath the good sun. When the dream was good, Sachim's daughter ran to her, her chubby arms outstretched, her voice filled with glee as Sachim waited to sweep her up into her arms and hold her before the golden sunset, and the thunder which boomed across the land was the approval of Thunder Horse, who loved them still.

There was little work to keep Sachim occupied. They grew a little corn, but most of it was purchased from the white farmers. From time to time an army wagon would come to the camp and crates of goods would be unloaded. No one moved, no one hunted. The people were well-fed, but their eyes were empty.

Keokuk was still there; he wore much silver now, and at times sported a white hat. He was arrogant and proud. Keokuk had nothing to say to Sachim.

The grave was empty.

Sachim stood and stared at the pit in the ground, Black Hawk's resting place. The wild rose she held dropped to the ground. She stood stunned, looking one way and then the other. It wasn't possible, but his body was gone. Had he risen up to take up the hatchet again, clawed his way from the cold dark earth to strike out once more at his people's enemies?

It was an insane thought and Sachim forced it aside. Pulling herself together, she tried to organize her thoughts, to make sense out of the senseless. *Keokuk*. She thought first of the Sauk chief. He had taken the body and desecrated it; but even for Keokuk that was unthinkable, an insult to the spirits of the dead.

It was then that she found the grooves carved into the earth, parallel ruts which could only have been cut by the wheels of a white wagon.

In a white-hot fury Sachim began to follow the tracks, half-running. The sky had begun to drop a light mist earthward, the day growing dark. Sachim hurried on, her fists clenched so that her nails bit into the palms of her hands. She must have run for an hour but she felt no weariness; she was hardly aware of her body as she continued on. She was emotion, pure and focused emotion.

Ahead was the fort, and that was where she expected the wagon tracks to lead, but they veered away toward the dark river, and as Sachim reached the bank of the river, she could see where a raft had been drawn up to shore and pushed off again.

She turned helplessly, taking deep breaths now. Then she spun and marched toward the fort, her eyes unfocused, her mind whirling. She wished for a war ax, for an army of warriors. They had done all they could imagine to Black Hawk while he lived, but even now that he was dead they could not leave him in peace.

She marched into the fort, seeing soldiers' faces only as pale blurs, hearing their voices only as distant, meaningless chatter.

Sachim stormed into the commander's office and was blocked by the one-eyed sergeant.

"Where you going, lady?"

"To see Monique." She tried to push past him but firmly he drew her back.

"No, you're not. I've orders, lady. You aren't to come to his office anymore. All complaints have to go through Keokuk."

"*Keokuk*," she spat. "As if he would care. I *will* see the major," she insisted. Just as resolutely the sergeant repeated: "I've got orders. You'll have to leave."

She spun away and marched out the door. The mist had turned to a drizzle and the wind was colder. Sachim ran her fingers through her hair and started toward the main gate. She nearly walked into the tall man in buckskins. Angrily she pushed at his chest and stumbled on.

"Spirit woman?"

Sachim hesitated, then stopped. She turned back, peering at the tall man. She had seen him before, long ago. Somewhere . . .

"I know what they did. I know where he is," Bartholomew Perkins said.

"Who was it!"

"I'll show you."

Sachim studied him skeptically. "Why should you help me? Why should I believe you?"

"No reason, miss," Bart Perkins answered. "It's just that

some things aren't right. Don't matter who you are, where you are. Some things aren't right."

They crossed the river on the new ferry, Sachim silent as she leaned on the rail, Perkins exchanging a word or two with the ferryman.

It was dark when they reached the white town and the scout led Sachim up a muddy road toward a brightly lighted circus tent. "There," Perkins said with a nod, and then he was gone, vanishing into the night.

Sachim could hear music, a fiddle and a concertina, their sounds strident and grating. People brushed past her and entered the tent. A sudden storm of laughter overwhelmed the music temporarily.

Sachim walked to the entrance to the tent and peered in past a ticket taker who was busy watching a dance team himself. A trained bear turned in a circle to the music. A huge snake coiled itself around a painted post. Two men juggling clubs performed in the center of the tent.

Sachim had to push her way forward to see what the crowd of people to her left were looking at. Music rang in her ears; her heart hammered.

Black Hawk's severed head rested on a green table, around it weapons and his necklace, his white elkskin burial costume. Sachim felt bile rise in her throat. She backed away quickly, forcing her way through the mob, pushing people. She thought she screamed but couldn't be sure. She saw nothing but the severed head, heard nothing but the pounding of blood in her ears.

She fought her way into the open air and stood in the drizzle of the night, doubled up at the waist, fighting for breath, struggling to clear her head.

She straightened up, holding her abdomen. Throwing back her head, she screamed her outrage to the rainy sky and then staggered away as white faces turned toward her and people shouted.

Behind the tent there was a corral where men were selling horses and mules. The auction was being held by torchlight, and without thinking Sachim took a torch from the corner post of the corral. It was not a considered act; but it was inevitable, as inevitable and necessary as the falling rain.

When she touched flame to the corner of the circus tent it caught swiftly despite the dampness.

Sachim threw the torch down and withdrew to the trees to

stand watching. A shout went up and people flooded out into the night from the burning tent. Men grabbed buckets of sand, buckets of water, and tried to put out the conflagration, but it was already too late.

Flames leapt high into the dark and rainy night and the circus tent with its grisly sideshow vanished behind a veil of smoke. Bits of canvas floated high and drifted away. The sky was alive with fire and light. People rushed in all directions, calling out futile instructions to the firefighters.

Sachim waited another half-hour and then turned away, away from the fire, the white town, the bitter memories. She would cross the great river for the last time that night and go out onto the long, empty plains. She might not find her daughter, she knew. She might find nothing but a lonely, barren world. There might be no happiness ever for her in life, but only more sorrow and bloodshed, more fire and rain.

Yet she could dream, and so long as she could dream, there was a purpose to life.

AUTHOR'S NOTE

From Black Hawk's last public speech at Madison, Wisconsin, July 4, 1838:

It has pleased the Great Spirit that I am here today. The earth is our mother and we are permitted now to look upon it. A few snows ago, I was fighting against the white people; perhaps I was wrong; let it be forgotten. I love my village and the cornfields on the Rock River; it was a beautiful country. I fought for it, but now it is yours. Keep it as the Sauks did. I was once a warrior, but now I am poor. Keokuk has been the cause of what I am, but I do not blame him. I love to look upon the Mississippi. I have looked upon it from a child. I love that beautiful river. My home has always been upon its banks. Now I will say no more; there is no more to say.

UNTAMED ACTION ON THE WESTERN FRONTIER

☐ **THE TERREL BRAND by E.Z. Woods.** Owen Terrel came back from the Civil War looking for peace. He and his brother carved out a cattle kingdom in West Texas, but then a beautiful woman in danger arrived, thrusting Owen into a war against an army of bloodthirsty outlaws. He would need every bullet he had to cut them down.... (158113—$3.50)

☐ **FORTUNES WEST #2: CHEYENNE by A.R. Riefe.** A spellbinding series! As the Civil War ended, cattlemen, sheepherders and farmers in Wyoming vied for the land against the fierce Cheyenne and Sioux. Dedicated officer Lincoln Rhilander had to defy his superiors to rout the redskins ... and had to choose between duty and desire in the arms of a beautiful woman. Stunning adventure! (157516—$4.50)

☐ **THE SAVAGE LAND by Matt Braun.** Courage, passion, violence—in a surging novel of a Texas dynasty. The Olivers. Together they carved out an empire of wealth and power with sweat, blood, bravery and bullets.... (157214—$4.50)

☐ **THE BRANNOCKS by Matt Braun.** They are three brothers and their women—in a passionate, action-filled saga that sweeps over the vastness of the American West and shines with the spirit of the men and women who had the daring and heart to risk all to conquer a wild frontier land. (143442—$3.50)

☐ **A LAND REMEMBERED by Patrick D. Smith.** Tobias MacIvey started with a gun, a whip, a horse and a dream of taming a wilderness that gave no quarter to the weak. He was the first of an unforgettable family who rose to fortune from the blazing guns of the Civil War, to the glitter and greed of the Florida Gold Coast today. (158970—$4.95)

Prices slightly higher in Canada

Buy them at your local

bookstore or use coupon

on next page for ordering.